T0304921

One Perfect Stranger

Dubliner R.B. Egan started out as an actor, working in London and performing alongside household names like Sinead O'Connor, Kevin Spacey and Celine Dion. Later he moved to Tanzania where he project managed the design and construction of a safari lodge outside the Ngorongoro Conservation Area with his wife. Together they operated a hotel and safari business for some years before settling back in Ireland. R.B. Egan now lives in Dublin with his young family and writes.

One Perfect Stranger

R.B. Egan

**HODDER &
STOUGHTON**

First published in Great Britain in 2024 by Hodder & Stoughton Limited
An Hachette UK company

A CIP catalogue record for this title is available from the British Library

Hardback ISBN 978 1 399 73218 5
Trade Paperback ISBN 978 1 399 73219 2
eBook ISBN 978 1 399 73220 8

Typeset in Sabon MT by Manipal Technologies Limited

Printed and bound by in Great Britain by Clays Ltd, Elcograf S.p.A.

Hodder & Stoughton policy is to use papers that are natural, renewable and recyclable products and made from wood grown in sustainable forests. The logging and manufacturing processes are expected to conform to the environmental regulations of the country of origin.

Hodder & Stoughton Ltd
Carmelite House
50 Victoria Embankment
London EC4Y 0DZ

www.hodder.co.uk

For Pam

'Drowning men, it is said, cling to wisps of straw.'
Fyodor Dostoyevsky

'Even the darkest night will end and the sun will rise.'
Victor Hugo

'Don't think,' Nicole whispers the words over and over like a mantra, her hands gripping the steering wheel tight, every muscle in her body stiff.

The big car coasts through the darkness but the minutes crawl and she grits her teeth. Forcing herself to concentrate, she starts to dream of home, deliberately picturing it in her mind, pushing her thoughts from the here and now.

It's the weekend and she's rising from a warm bed on a Saturday morning. Mark is coming up the stairs and she can smell the fresh coffee he carries in his hand. He's already been to the bakery to buy a sourdough loaf and there are two slices freshly toasted on a plate. From the living room comes the sound of laughter as the girls huddle together on the sofa watching cartoons on TV. The comfortable pillows Mark bought for her, the ones she covered with Egyptian cotton cases, are plumped just right and she sits up, stretching out her arms.

It's going to be a special day. A family day.

But then she hears a noise.

It's behind her.

It's inside the car.

I

THREE DAYS EARLIER

Tuesday, November 14,
Morning

'My sister says Rocky gave me asthma,' Holly says, her small legs swinging up and down at the edge of the examination bench in their GP's office. Her heels clip its underside with the rhythm of a metronome.

Facing the street high up on the third floor, tucked discreetly off Rathmines Road, the doctor's office is bright and clean in a functional kind of way. Grey carpet, white walls, black PVC covered furniture and three generous windows which let in lots of natural light. Nicole squints as the winter sun catches her eyes before hiding behind a dark cloud.

'She did?' Dr Fenton gasps, his disbelief deliberate and playful. 'And what's your sister's name?'

'Chloe.'

'So is Chloe older or younger than you?'

'Older. She's nearly twelve.'

'But are you not nearly twelve?'

'No!' Holly laughs. 'I'm seven.'

'Oh? I'm sorry, I stand corrected.' Grinning, the doctor makes a tiny apologetic bow as Holly tilts her head to the side. 'Chloe likes swimming, basketball and turtles.'

'Wow!' Dr Fenton marvels, carefully adjusting the stethoscope across Holly's shirt as he listens to her breathing. 'And what are your favourite things, Holly?'

3

'Sweets, lizards and Rocky the cat,' Holly informs him.

Nicole sways as she looks on. She's wearing a cream one button blazer suit and a striped cotton shirt. The slim fit jacket was a birthday present from Alva and she chose it deliberately this morning to look smart. But the eye drops have done nothing to conceal the web of red threads which now frequently mar her once bright green eyes. As she blinks they sting and she has to resist the urge to close them. It's a good thing Mark reminded her to make the appointment this morning because their health insurance runs out next week and the new GP isn't on the free childcare scheme.

'That's a great selection. I bet a lot of people would love to have sweets, lizards and cats too.' Dr Fenton takes a second to adjust his earpiece.

Curling a lock of chestnut hair behind her ear, Nicole glances around the room restlessly. There's a picture of the doctor on the wall. He looks exactly the same; trim black beard, neatly turned out in a navy suit and nodding. He looks bashful as he accepts some award. 'I wonder if you could do me a big favour now Holly and take two deep breaths for me.'

Holly beams, breathing in noisily, then blowing it out and popping her cheeks like a balloon. Nicole takes a deep breath too, holding it for a second before it escapes through the taut circle her mouth has made.

Dr Fenton removes the stethoscope and smiles.

'Am I going to get an injection?' Holly asks, bright blue eyes widening.

Dr Fenton shakes his head. 'You're very brave to ask Holly, but no, there's absolutely no need for any injections today.'

'Oh.' Holly holds a scrunchie in her hand and plucks a tangle of blond hair from it looking relieved and disappointed at the same time.

'And thank you so much for being a terrific patient. I believe that's all the checks I need to do.' He glances over to reassure

Nicole. 'Would you like me to help you down so you can join Mummy, or are you happy sitting there?'

'I can stay here.' Holly shakes her head, tapping the bench. 'Thank you.'

'Good, then you do that, and I'll chat with Mum.' Nodding his approval the doctor takes his place behind the desk and switches his attention to Nicole. 'The good news is that Holly has nothing to worry about in regard to cats because they are definitely not causing her any trouble. In fact her asthma is much better now so she's obviously been doing everything I asked.'

Holly's grin spreads ear to ear. 'Does that mean we can adopt Rocky now, Mummy?'

'What?' Nicole looks up slowly. This is good news, exactly what she wanted to hear. Normally she would be delighted that Holly's condition has come on in leaps and bounds in the space of two months, but this morning all she can think about is Mark. She cups the back of her neck with her hand, letting the weight of her head rest against it as she stares at her daughter.

Dr Fenton waits for her to say something. 'No sweetie. Remember we said that if we adopted Rocky it would make Mrs Lyubevsky sad. And until your dad and I discuss it, we can't have a cat.' When Nicole gets to her feet blood rushes to her head and she pauses, waiting for it to calm before walking over to Holly. Unexpectedly Holly jumps into her arms and Nicole rocks backwards before letting her down again.

'Oh look, Mummy, kittens.' Holly points to the doctor's desk and Nicole sees the picture of two kittens, with tiger striped eyes and cute pink noses playing in the sunlight outside a country barn. It's the cover image of a calendar. 'Oh, I love them Mummy.'

With a cheerful nod, Dr Fenton explains. 'Those belong to an old friend of mine who moved to the countryside. It's a calendar she made entirely from photos of her beautiful cats.' He glances at Nicole. 'And if your mum says it's OK, I'd love you to have it.'

Holly tips her head back and leans into her mother. Standing on her toes she presses her chin against Nicole's stomach. 'Please, Mum?'

'What, love?' Nicole's gaze has drifted to the window where she watches the grey clouds float across the sky like dark winged birds. She hopes the wind will blow them south, out of the city and over the Dublin mountains, where the rain can scatter in the pine forests. The shortening days are too wet already. Too damp. Holly taps her hands against her ribs and it brings her back. 'No, I don't think it would be fair to take the doctor's calendar, Holly.'

'It's OK,' Dr Fenton says, his face earnest, 'I'd be delighted for her to have it.'

Normally Nicole wouldn't accept but she can see the doctor's generosity is genuine, and as Mark pointed out, he's infinitely more helpful than their previous GP. 'OK then. Well, just this time. And what do you say?'

'Thank you.' Holly's eyes shine as she takes the calendar in her hands.

Dr Fenton returns his attention to Nicole. 'Maybe Holly might like to wait in the reception while we talk? It might give her a chance to look at all the pictures while we finish.' Nicole doesn't reply. She tries to guess what they might need to talk about privately. 'Rose, our receptionist has lollipops if Mum says it's OK?'

'Of course,' Nicole waves Holly off. 'Go on love and I'll be out in a minute.'

Dr Fenton guides Holly over to the reception area and returns instantly. When he walks in he closes the door behind him and sits at his desk.

Nicole sits also. 'Is everything alright Doctor Fenton? With Holly?'

'Holly is doing fine.' A smile lights up his face. 'The new medication seems to have cleared up a lot of her issues. I don't want to say anything yet as we are still waiting on the full test results but I'm hopeful that in a couple of weeks you could take her off it

6

and see how she gets on.' The tension in Nicole's shoulders eases a fraction. 'It's not unusual for kids of this age to develop asthma but also for it to clear without intervention.' Nicole thinks he is finished explaining but instead the doctor places his pen on the desk, sits back in his chair and frowns.

'Nicole, is everything alright?' His voice is soft when he speaks. 'I mean with you?' Stiffening, Nicole looks away. Out of the blue everything cascades through her mind at once. Their beautiful new house and how they can barely manage its upkeep anymore, how remote Mark has become, how badly her world has shrunk – she can't think of another person besides Alva and Eve who she sees now; the constant worry which closes in on her every night when she goes to bed, robbing her of sleep. 'You mentioned having trouble sleeping before. Is it any better now?'

Her eyes water. 'Not really. Our last GP gave me something to help but it didn't work, so I haven't used it much.'

The frown lines deepen on the doctor's brow. 'Do you remember what he gave you?' Nicole shakes her head. 'If you'd like me to suggest something I could always write you a prescription. I'd be happy to.'

Clutching her bag Nicole stands. 'I think I'm fine for now but if it gets worse, I'll let you know.'

'Of course.' The doctor's face softens as he gets up to open the door. 'Well if you have concerns about Holly don't hesitate to call.'

Outside in the street Holly stands holding Nicole's hand, the calendar clutched to her chest. Nicole is thinking about Mark, about the conversation she must have with him tonight. She knows avoiding it any longer will only make things worse. Cars snake in front of them, grinding up and down the two lanes, as dark clouds spread like bruises across the grey sky. A group of uniformed high school students march past plucking hot chips from a steaming box, scenting the air with vinegar and cooking oil.

There's a new message on Nicole's phone and she opens it. Two minutes remain on her parking, they'll have to hurry.

'Mummy?' Holly's grip tightens. 'Who's that man?' The calendar hangs down as she points across the road.

Nicole flinches. Standing on the busy pavement is a man in a high-vis jacket. There is a mobile phone pressed to his ear and he is staring at them. 'Do you know him, Mummy?'

The traffic shifts, obscuring him from view behind a truck.

With a sharp intake of breath she draws Holly closer. 'I don't think so.'

When the lights change the truck moves. Only now the man has vanished.

2

'Nina?' Their elderly neighbour stands patiently on the cheq-uered path, one step back from the arched porch to Nicole's house. Marwood Road in Rathgar is one of the quiet streets in the sought-after suburb and even in the winter gloom the terrace of Victorian red bricks looks pretty.

Nicole drops two heavy rucksacks in front of the door, slips the key into the lock, opening it and making way for Chloe and Holly to get past, only now noticing the white cake box in her neighbour's hands. 'I'm sorry, were you waiting out here for me?'

'Don't worry.' The skin crinkles around Mrs Lyubevsky's eyes as her cat Rocky slinks through the rail which divides their houses. Chloe scoops him up, big brown eyes wide with delight. 'Only for a minute, Nicole.' She smiles at Chloe while Nicole drops the bags into the house where they clunk on the wooden floor. Holly strokes Rocky's ginger head as her older sister rocks him like a baby, snuggling him into her chest and nestling her nose into his striped coat. 'I brought this for you.' Mrs Lyubevsky gives Nicole the box.

'That's a nice surprise.'

'Oh, it's nothing. You know how I love to bake, but since Leon departed I find I never finish what I make. He always used to take a half and then give a slice to any of his staff who were doing their night patrols. His way of keeping his security team sweet he used to joke.'

'I'll promise to share it.'

Chloe passes her the cat and Mrs Lyubevsky bows her head. 'I can see Rocky is very fond of you Chloe, and you too Holly.' Chloe removes the tie from her plait of thick dark hair and Holly pats Rocky's back.

Nicole wants to take her leave, but Mrs Lyubevsky is hovering. 'Chloe love,' Nicole says, 'take Holly inside and get changed into your pyjamas. I'll be in shortly, OK?'

Obediently the girls disappear and Mrs Lyubevsky waves them goodbye. Once they are out of earshot she places a hand on Nicole's wrist. 'How are you both getting on?' Her hushed voice drops to a whisper.

Nicole's shoulders sag. 'We're alright.' Usually she likes to chat with their neighbour. The elderly woman is sweet and agreeable, and even babysat for them once or twice, but tonight she needs time alone, to gather her thoughts before meeting Mark.

Mrs Lyubevsky knits her brows into a sharp crease. 'Two jobs isn't easy. I hope you're getting your rest.'

'When I can.'

A soft drizzle has started to fall, making tiny drops on the tips of Rocky's fur. Nicole glances at the sky, trying to guess if the rain is coming. Her sister Alva always said she was a hopeless actress.

'Well,' Mrs Lyubevsky whispers again, pressing Nicole's forearm gently, 'I've been meaning to get you.' She glances warily at the street behind her. 'You know how I like to be vigilant; "always be prepared so you're not caught unawares," as my Leon used to say, god rest him, so I thought I should tell you.'

She stops when she hears footsteps behind her. Mark has appeared.

'Hi.' He walks down the diamond patterned path, offering Mrs Lyubevsky a relaxed smile as Nicole's fingers tighten around the box. As always now, he is dressed casually: soft soled shoes, light grey jeans, a colourful scarf, with a black raincoat; for a second Nicole sees the easy going man she married fourteen years ago. His black hair is swept back and the porch light bounces off his eyes when he strokes Rocky. 'Cake?' He glances at the box.

'A gift from Nina.' Nicole lifts it up. 'Will you come in and join us, Nina?'

'No. You're very kind to offer,' Mrs Lyubevsky pats her elbow, 'but I'll have a word with Mark now that I've caught him. And I'm sure your girls are waiting for you.'

'Alright,' Nicole turns, tapping the box. 'Next time so.' Edging away she watches Mark. The skin on his face tightens as he smiles but his eyes look sombre, almost like the light has disappeared from them. The expression on his face is unfamiliar and almost cold when he steps across and pulls the door shut behind him.

Click. 'What is up with this machine?' With a pained expression Nicole stares at the laptop. The strange sound has just happened again, almost like a gentle cracking noise. It's the third time she's heard it today, and always when she writes in the journal she keeps. Her most recent entry is still on the screen and she whispers to herself silently – *dreaming of dad once more, why?* The cursor disappears so she taps the trackpad but nothing happens. Lifting her hands away she waits, surprised to see the cursor reappear and highlight the text. Without moving she keeps watching as the cursor then drifts to the bottom corner of the screen.

The laptop is old and she suspects it's got a virus. Shaking her head she tries not to panic. There's a copy-edit job on it she has to finish tonight and she hasn't backed it up. One of the mums, Jennifer, from Holly's school group had texted her out of the blue with it the previous week. At first Nicole was confused because she never confided to anybody from the group about how tight things were for her and Mark financially. She only had a vague memory of saying to Jennifer months ago that the office work Alva had got her was not paid very well so she was looking at finding something additional. She flattens her hands on the kitchen island, waiting as it hums, before starting to whir noisily. A new message box has appeared on the screen out of nowhere. It says 'Read Me'. It's not something she's ever seen before. Rubbing a hand over her face she snaps the screen shut.

There's a photograph upside down on the kitchen floor and she bends to pick it up. When she turns it over she sees it's the one she keeps on the fridge door. It's from the summer before last, a snapshot taken by a friend when the family went for a picnic to Phoenix Park on one of the hottest days of the year. Mark is shirtless, tanned and grinning behind oversized sunglasses; leaning into him is Chloe, her nose sprinkled with sun freckles, brown eyes beaming, beside her little Holly holding her doll out to Nicole like an offering; lastly Nicole bending down next to her and pointing to the camera. The colour of her cheeks is pink and she remembers how tipsy both her and Mark were from the prosecco and the heat. Earlier in the day things had almost fallen apart when Chloe lost her scrunchie and got into a state; only thanks to Mark spending half an hour helping her to find it did it eventually reappear. Then Holly dropped her ice cream into the cut grass and Mark had to walk all the way back to the car park with her so she could buy another.

Gently Nicole wipes it against her jeans, wishing the tension in her stomach to go away. Carefully she takes the cracked magnet from their last foreign holiday to Spain two years before and places it back.

Turning away she scans the open plan kitchen living room. The house interior is so pretty, exactly as they had always wanted it to be, with its reclaimed wooden dining table looking out through glass sliding doors to the back garden, two striped cotton couches in the adjoining front room, and the modern kitchen with its sleek island-cum-breakfast bar, all complemented by spotless grey walls.

It could be a show house, a picture of domestic bliss worthy of a magazine; and not long ago it was. Yet her only thought now when she looks at it is why they thought it was a good idea to spend their savings doing it up. She shuts her eyes, waiting for the familiar unwanted thoughts to invade her mind. And instantly they come. Why did she agree to Mark giving up his job as the chief cardiologist in one of Dublin's best hospitals? Why did she have to stop working in a job she loved all those years ago after Holly was born?

Why can't she find a proper job that can help the family financially? And why won't Mark talk about returning to his career? He knows the volunteer work he's doing won't pay their bills.

Gritting her teeth she listens as the answers volley back. Mark only ever agreed to take a break from his career. It was his choice to make, especially after the death of his only brother. And she knows she never meant to stop working, but the difficulties she had after Holly's birth made it almost impossible to return, so that by the time she thought she could, it no longer seemed to matter, especially when Mark's career was flying. But she doesn't have an answer for why Mark won't talk about getting back to his career. Yet she must get one. It's gone on too long and the family can't hold out financially forever.

The whining burr of the electric shower drifts down from upstairs. Nicole's hands flick to her temples and she rubs either side, her fingertips stiff and sore. Fifteen minutes, she calculates. Mark will be finished by then and it gives her enough time to put the girls to bed and read each of them a very quick story. Gathering herself, she raises a nervous smile, then goes to look for the girls.

With the girls tucked in and sleeping, Nicole returns downstairs. Mark slouches on a dining chair pushed away from the big kitchen table, his legs stretched out and his arms crossed.

'Tired?' Nicole keeps her voice light.

'Wrecked. The crisis centre was hectic today. Then Olly asked me for a game of squash after work and I foolishly agreed. Forty's too old for squash.' Yawning he sits back up and pulls the chair closer to the table where Mrs Lyubevsky's cake sits on a plate. 'Do you want me to make some tea?'

'No, I'm bringing it.' Nicole hurries to the almost empty fridge and grabs the milk carton, hastily putting the mugs out while silently steeling herself. She can't hesitate now. 'What did Mrs Lyubevsky want to talk about?'

'Oh,' Mark cuts the cake, plating a slice and handing it to her with a fork, 'you know how she is.' He takes his piece then, his movements slow, almost exhausted. 'She's very sweet but her imagination's a bit . . . ' He stops, his shoulders lifting into a shrug. 'She thinks she saw a man scoping out the road and is worried he might be a burglar.'

'A burglar?' The image of the man Holly pointed out across the street earlier flashes through her head. She won't mention it. It's not the time.

'Yeah, I know.' Mark swallows a mouthful of cake, smiling sheepishly. It's the smile that melted her heart all those years ago. The one with the kind eyes she sees so rarely now.

She tries some cake. 'Mark! This is stale.'

'Sorry, I should have warned you,' he says and for a second Nicole wants to forget all about her plan to confront him with the cold reality of their existence, with the questions he's been evading for so many months. Then she notices a shopping bag by his feet.

'Did you buy something?'

'Just a few bits for the girls.' Brightening, Mark pulls out some stationery and spreads it on the table. 'They had been asking me for art paper and colouring pens. I wanted to give them a treat. It's Smiggles.'

Nicole knows. It's the shop the girls love, the expensive one. Her fingers slide to her head then, and she presses against where the vein throbs. 'Mark, we need to talk.' A blush of red flares across her cheek.

The cheer leaches from Mark's eyes. 'Sorry Nic. It was an impulse thing.'

Nicole waits for him to look at her, but his gaze remains down. 'What's going on Mark?' Mark's brow furrows but he doesn't reply. Like a reflex his shoulders shrug. 'When are you going back to your career, love? This situation has been going on for months. You won't talk about it but we both know we're broke.'

Eyes downcast, Mark leans forward, inhaling deeply. Nicole waits for him to look at her but instead he sweeps his arm across the table dragging the stationery and dropping it into the bag. 'I'll take them all back. My mistake.'

'Mark, wait.' Nicole reaches for his wrist but Mark is on his feet and steps away.

'I'm sorry, just give me a few more days, alright?' His eyes glisten when he finally looks at her. 'Then we'll talk.'

Before Nicole can reply he edges past her, eyes fixed and staring, his expression so dark that for a fleeting moment Nicole doesn't recognise him. Then the door clicks softly and he's gone.

Rising from the seat, she trudges to the bin where she dumps the cake. Tears track her cheeks, but she doesn't notice as they dot the front of her shirt. Alva has always said that Mark changed because his youngest brother Luke died in Australia earlier in the year, but Nicole can't believe it could be so simple. Alva never got to see all the cards from the grateful parents thanking Mark for saving their children's lives; she didn't know how Mark kept them all in a locker by the bed, often with a picture of the same child now smiling and healthy.

The ache in her chest returns as she walks to the home office tucked away at the side of the living room. When she sits down she rests her elbows on the desk. The copy-editing job still needs to be finished and she can't allow it to be late, because it has to be finished by the morning. Jennifer said getting it done on time was the most crucial thing if she wanted another contract.

Gripping her head in her hands she runs her fingers through her tangled hair. Then something flickers in the dark, distracting her for a moment.

Click.

Hum.

Whir.

The laptop has turned itself on even though she knows she hasn't touched it.

3

Wednesday, November 15,
Very Early Morning

Though the laptop had surprised her earlier by coming on by itself it hasn't malfunctioned until now. The big wall clock in the living room ticks so loudly that Nicole can hear it in the office but because she cannot see its face she glances to the bottom corner of the screen and sees the time has passed 3 a.m. The copy-edit job is finished and Nicole is relieved, but the blank screen won't respond when she touches the trackpad. As she waits her mind drifts to the girls upstairs. Should she check to see if the second duvet has fallen off Holly again? Yawning, she decides against it in case her daughter wakes.

A book drops off the edge of the desk and she slides a foot out to retrieve it. It's *The Catcher in the Rye*, a present Mark gave her when they first met. Gently, she presses a hand to her eye and listens as the wind whistles through the cypress trees at the end of the garden.

Then a loud clicking noise interrupts the silence. It's the sound she recognises from before. Instantly she looks to see if her journal is open but doesn't see it. Instead she sees the floating dialog box again with the same two words. 'Read Me'. Annoyed, she leans forward, carefully positioning the mouse on the x in the corner of the box, but before she can click it the cursor moves of its own accord, drifting to the bottom corner of the screen before disappearing. In the same second three words appear in bold white letters against the black background.

Are you there?

Motionless, Nicole stares at the words. She remains that way, eyes locked on the screen, fingers suspended above the keyboard, her mind racing. What had seemed like an ordinary virus has changed into a real time conversation but she cannot understand how?

Warily she rises from her seat, her eyes wide with fear. It's so late and she craves sleep but her mind won't leave her alone, and she can't stop trying to figure out who it could be or what they might want. The pounding inside her chest grows when she sits back down.

With three taps she writes her reply.

Yes.

The response is instant. *There is a million euros in your bank account. All you need to do is drive a car. Yes, or no?*

Quickly she reads it a second time, pressing her fingers to her mouth as she whispers the hushed words in the dark. Then her disbelief turns to annoyance and she replies.

Who are you?

Nicole, this isn't a joke. Drawing back, the air sucks inside her lungs. It has to be a joke. What else could it be? And yet she's no longer sure and more text is already appearing. *Answer the question.*

There's a second of delay before she slams the screen shut. With the laptop closed the room becomes instantly dark and she sits still, listening to the house, but the only sound is the soft drone of the fridge and the ticking of the kitchen clock. She tries to make sense of the message. What had seemed like a routine prank had changed so suddenly to something serious; something almost believable. But how could anybody offer so much money to do something so simple? Then she remembers – the message said it had already been given to her.

Immediately she flicks the screen back up but finds it blank again.

'What?' Rising to her feet she grabs her phone. With one hand gripping the desk she keeps her balance and opens up her AIB banking app. Seconds slip by as her phone loads the image. The tightness around her ribcage ratchets higher, like some invisible belt clicking and shortening with each breath. She cannot understand the tension inside her body. It's clearly a scam; a late night deception. And yet somehow it feels too real.

Eventually the screen becomes clear. Her savings account, the one she had almost forgotten about entirely, has changed.

Just like the message said, the money is there. It now displays exactly one million euros one hundred and fifty three euros.

Her heart thumps so hard she feels the blood pulse inside her ears. Thoughts are already flitting through her mind; all the things the money could do for their family; how she wouldn't have to worry about their girls anymore, how their security would instantly be restored; all the breathing space that Mark would immediately have so he could return to his career when he's properly ready, how their whole lives, which have fallen asunder in the past year, could finally get back on track.

But then she stops, suddenly remembering that there was a condition: drive a car. Her first thought is drugs, and yet it makes no sense, because she knows criminals have their own people for that and would never pay that kind of money for something so simple. The request doesn't add up, there's no thread in it she can tie to anything tangible. But she's not stupid; this kind of money can only be dirty and what they're asking her to do could never be so easy.

The laptop hums behind her and she turns. A new message has appeared on the screen. *Keep the laptop with you. Wait for contact. If you value your family don't tell a living soul.*

Nicole rushes across to type a reply but the clicking noise sounds again. This time the screen goes blank and immediately the machine powers off.

4

Wednesday, November 15,
Very Early Morning

Breathless, Nicole darts from the office to the sliding door at the back of the house, double checks it's locked, before doing the same with the front door. Only when she's made sure all the windows are also secure does she rush upstairs to check on the girls. But Chloe and Holly are in their beds sleeping soundly.

Gripping the banister she waits at the top of the landing, eyes fixed on the ceiling, but all she can hear is the familiar sound of rain tapping gently on the roof. Swiftly then, she moves to the front room window where she draws back the curtain. Peering out, she searches the empty street. She doesn't want to see anything, but she has to look. Beyond the front hedge the street lights throw a watery glow into the darkness, but nothing stirs.

Pressing the palms of her hands over her face she pauses to think. A hacker has made contact with her at three in the morning and put a million euros into her bank account. That much is real. She saw it with her own eyes. But why? It's the question she can't answer.

The throbbing at the front of her head grows stronger as she moves to the kitchen. She stops, holding the island with her outstretched hands. If she can slow down for a moment she can figure out what to do next. Her phone is on the counter and she picks it up, realising suddenly that she already knows what to do: she must call the police. Immediately she pulls up Alva's number on her mobile and presses the call button. Yes, her sister will be annoyed, but when she hears the explanation Alva will definitely understand. Her sister is a senior ranking officer in the force. Handling these situations is what she does on a daily basis, serious crimes like burglary, murder, fraud. Is this fraud? She shakes her head. It can't be. She hasn't done anything.

Pushing the hair from her forehead she mops the hot slick of sweat with the back of her arm. The smell of her own body fills her nostrils and she tugs the front of her shirt, unsticking it from her chest. The line is already ringing and the noisy churring of the dial tone feels too loud in the empty living room where she paces back and forth. 'Come on Alva, please pick up.' After three rings her sister's voicemail message comes back down the line. '*Sorry I'm busy. Leave a short message and I'll be right back as soon as I can.*' The casual rhythm of Alva's voice finishes with a friendly '*Thanks*'.

Nicole jabs the end call button with her thumb. How will she explain to Alva what's just happened in a voice message? For a second she pictures her sister listening in surprise to her frightened whispers that someone has messaged her on her laptop, and within minutes given her a sum of money so vast it is insane. The kind of money that people only dream of; the kind that, she knows deep down, gives her a chance to make things right for the people she cares about most.

Images keep flitting through her mind; all their worries solved; Mark happy; the girls' future secure; her own stress lifted; breathing space; the golden chance to make things right again for all of them. The thoughts spin and spin, like she can't seem to stop them.

She tries her sister again but the call once more goes to voicemail. This time Nicole hangs up and runs upstairs. It's Mark she needs to tell. Now.

In the bedroom Mark is sleeping on his side facing the wall, his ribcage rising and falling with his breath. 'Mark? Hey?' She taps his arm but he doesn't budge. 'Mark come on.' She runs her fingers through his hair, 'Please wake up love.' This time he lets out a sleep filled groan but again shows no sign of waking.

Nicole draws back, remembering their earlier argument. Standing silently in the darkness she recalls the broken look on Mark's face as he swept the girls' presents back inside his shopping bag, the sinking feeling in the pit of her stomach as he walked up the stairs, leaving her alone at the dining table. How will he respond when she tells him this? Surely he'll agree that the idea is crazy and that Nicole doesn't get involved. But what if he didn't? What if he felt, like she does right now, that she could do the thing they've asked for, because driving a car couldn't be so hard. The idea sprouts like a weed inside her mind but she can't rid herself of it, not yet.

Hurrying, Nicole places the duvet back over him, slipping out of the bedroom to check on the girls a second time. Once again she finds them as she left them, Chloe lying on her side, her long plait of black hair draped over the shoulder and one arm wrapped around her Squishmallow, the poster of J-Hope, her favourite K-pop star, in its usual place on the opposite wall; little Holly wedged between her orange octopus, Bradley, and Mr Cuddles, the cat-scratched bear, all snug beneath a quilt of unicorns, little mouth open, fair hair stuck to her head.

When she returns to the kitchen she paces from the island to the sliding doors. The disbelief which has crowded every other thought out of her head has passed, but only to be replaced by suspicion. The whole thing happened too fast, and she knows, just like everybody else, this is how scams work. At 3 a.m. anybody is vulnerable because they're not even awake. 'OK,' she whispers, hurrying back to the office and opening the laptop once more. The thing to do is to check it again. It's the only way to be sure that she hasn't got it wrong.

The air pulls deep inside her lungs as she drops her hands to the keyboard, this time hovering above the keys as if the machine is a dangerous animal that could attack at any second.

Click. Hum. Whir. The background reboots with a picture of the family on holiday. A lump catches in her throat. Could it be just some simple trick with her phone? Will the laptop show something different?

She waits.

Once more it appears, just like before, her usually threadbare savings account with only a few euros remaining, now showing the unrecognisable figure of more than a million euros. She clicks into it for more information but there's nothing, no clue as to who or where it came from, just the numbers shining brightly like a ticking bomb of anxiety waiting to explode.

Logging out instantly, she snaps the screen shut but her gut twists so violently it makes her wince. In her panic she's forgotten what they said. *If you value your family don't tell another living soul.* She *can't* tell anybody. Not Alva. Not Mark. Not anybody who could help and tell her what to do because if she does, and their threat is real . . . ?

Shivering she waits for the thought to trail away but it won't. It lingers, festering inside her, twisting her gut tighter still. When she passes the hall mirror she sees her reflection which is ghostly pale and she recoils, fumbling in the half-light for the handrail to the stairs. The need to be with her children is like an itch on her skin. Leaving the lights burning she trudges up the stairs and into Holly's room. Careful not to make a noise, she eases in beside her, folding her gently in her arms. Her daughter's sleeping body is light and warm and Nicole draws her closer, nestling her nose into her hair and breathing in the smell of saliva on her pillow. No longer does she feel the urge to sleep. The only thing she wants is to keep her eyes and ears open till the morning comes.

5

Wednesday, November 15,
Morning

Nicole splashes her face with cold water. There is no time to put on make-up. She's already an hour late for work. She presses the towel to two puffy, swollen eyes, waiting for her heartbeat to steady. It was such a shock waking up to find Mark and the girls gone. Alone in Holly's bed she found the note, scribbled in Mark's handwriting. *I'll take the girls to school. Get some rest love. Mark.*

Her phone buzzes behind her on the shelf and she jumps. Mark's just declined two of her calls. But what is she going to say to him now anyway? She's already resolved not to say a word. It's the only way. She's clear on that.

There's a new message then and she sees it's from him. *Sorry in a meeting. Didn't want to wake you from your beauty sleep. Girls all fine. Chat later.*

She places the phone back and finishes drying her face. The towel drops down on the bed and she breathes out heavily, for the first time realising that it was lucky that Mark had left early. If he had been there what might she have said? Might she have accidentally blurted something out?

The doorbell chimes and a shadow flickers against the window beside the door. Quickly Nicole rushes to collect her bag and keys from the bedroom before hurrying down the stairs. Scooping two handfuls of chestnut hair, she scrapes it into a bun, checking the whites of her eyes in the hallway mirror. The now familiar spider web of red lines radiate from the green pupils like plaster cracks. Pausing to take a breath, she unlocks the door.

Exhaust fumes hang in the damp November air and the blue lights of an ambulance flicker as it wails past the tree-lined avenue of terraced red bricks. The man outside her front door has his back turned, displaying a yellow high-vis jacket. Slowly his big shoulders twist and he faces her, piercing blue eyes glinting from under a plastic helmet. Beyond him his bicycle rests against the hedge by the front wall.

Nicole flinches, suddenly recalling the man who was staring at her across the road from Dr Fenton's surgery.

'I'm sorry,' he holds up a cat in his hand, running a bloodied thumb across the dimple in his chin, 'but I found this fellow out on the road looking worse for the wear and thought I'd see if anyone knows who he belongs to?'

The orange tabby scrabbles its legs through the air and Nicole tries to regain her calm.

'Rocky!' she says, her voice almost tearful.

The man strokes him and Nicole notices a dark stain on the cat's ear. 'Is he yours?' Nicole shakes her head. 'Oh,' he shifts his weight from one foot to the other, sighing as he glances up the street. 'My apologies, guess I shouldn't be bothering you so.'

'He belongs to my neighbour.' Nicole points next door. 'I can give him to her if you like.'

He leans closer. 'You sure? I don't want to trouble you.'

Nicole extends her hands, 'It's no trouble.'

'My name's Chris by the way,' quickly he hands her the cat, wiping a red smear off his knuckles.

'You're bleeding,' Nicole says pointing at where she can see the red line of a deep scratch. The sight of blood doesn't normally bother her but this morning it makes her queasy and she swallows uneasily. The man looks at his hand for a second before plunging it inside his jacket. His eyes flit to the cat, then back out to the dark road beyond the hedge.

Rocky extends his claws, the muscles along his spine clenching.

'Poor fellow probably isn't used to strangers,' he says then, quickly adjusting his helmet, his gaze drifting over her head and

24

inside the house fleetingly. 'Well I won't delay you, and I've still a couple more drops to do before I finish.' There's a click as the chin strap clasps and he shoots her a thin smile. His movements are stiff and awkward as he gets onto the bike which looks small beneath his body. Nicole starts to close the front door when he turns once more. 'Hope the cat gets better and your girls enjoy him.'

Quickly Nicole shuts the front door and Rocky springs from her hands, scurrying down the corridor and into the kitchen. The dark blood has somehow got all over her fingers so she goes to the kitchen sink and opens the tap to wash them, staring down as the white porcelain reddens in a swirling pool. It only occurs to her now that she is holding her breath and she lets it out with a shake of her dripping hands.

Though she thinks the courier might have delivered to them once before she is certain she does not know him, so she can't understand how he knows they have girls.

Her heartbeat suddenly spikes then as she remembers about the money. The thoughts come flooding back; the surprise contact on the laptop last night, the sight of all those zeros in her normally empty bank account. The opportunity of wiping out all her families' problems in one fell swoop. She leans with her back against the door, feeling the coldness of the glass panel through her clothes. Then she recalls the demands. *Drive a car. If you value your family don't tell a living soul.*

She closes her eyes, letting her cheek rest against the icy glass. She has no idea how she can keep it a secret. No idea if it even makes sense.

The one thing she does know is that nobody knows anything about this.

It's only them.

And her.

Turning round, she opens the door and walks through it. She's already late for work. Maybe when she gets there she can figure things out.

6

'How long have you had the bike?' The sales rep in Halfords is young and clearly keen to help.

'It's old,' Chris Ashton says, stuffing the high-vis jacket into a plastic bag and feeling a lot more comfortable now he's back in his usual clothes.

The man taps a finger on his chin and runs a trained eye over the frame, rubbing the bristles of his short goatee beard. Next he takes the saddle in one hand and the handlebars in the other as he wheels it back and forth. 'Do you know what height you are?'

'Six two. Why?'

'This bike's probably two frame sizes too small. I think it's going to give you problems. Do you use it to commute?'

'Not really. I've just started using it.' Chris looks at the crooked rim of the wheel and runs his options. Ditching it and throwing it away right now to buy something new would be easiest. It's what he'd like to do. But he knows couriers seldom ride new bikes and it could look unusual. 'Can you fix it?' He hears the impatience in his voice. It's not deliberate but he needs to get moving.

'Certainly. We can fix pretty much anything. It just looks like a bent rim. The tyre looks pretty worn too. I'd suggest we give you a new wheel, with tyre and tube if you're happy with that?'

Chris takes out his phone. 'Whatever you say.' A message beeps on Chris's mobile. He reads it.

We could make enquiries for a fee. It would be discreet. Just let us know.

26

Quickly he replies. *No. Not necessary yet.* He hits send instantly.

'Would you like it serviced as well?' the sales rep asks.

What? Chris looks back at him, distracted. 'No, I just need it back quick. Can you have it ready in an hour?'

'Give me two. I've got your number. I can ring you as soon as it's done.'

Hastily Chris leaves the shop, scrunching the rolled high-vis jacket beneath his arm, silently mapping his next move.

7

Nicole opens the thick brown folder of customer names and addresses, sighs and closes it again, dropping it onto the desk next to her laptop. The back office of The Hartland Gallery is hotter than usual today and Nicole thinks about getting up to open the sole window behind her head but changes her mind.

Instead she opens a button on her shirt and blows a strand of hair from her forehead. The gallery is on Dawson Street, one of the busiest streets in the heart of Dublin and outside, beyond the walls of the office, the city buzzes and beats to the sound of grinding buses, the electric Luas railway, and the bustle of people on the move.

It's her third month in the office management job which she got through a friend of Alva's because the woman was going on maternity leave and needed some cover. When it's busy she usually finds time passes swiftly but on slow days her mind drifts off, remembering the job she had before Holly was born, working with the Irish Guide Dogs charity. It had meant so much to her, finding homes for companion dog puppies, making sure they were cared for, trained and developed until they could be taken back for their final journey to the lucky children that needed them most. Within a few years they had even promoted her to a management position for the greater Dublin area.

Nicole takes out the laptop she has brought from home and waits for the gallery stock file to load so she can update it. She doesn't want to think about her old job because it makes her sad

28

and she is grateful to both Alva and her boss Jemma for helping her out with a position she has no real qualifications for, except for some temping work she did during her year travelling after university. Gently she massages each side of her forehead with the tips of her fingers hoping it will ease the headache which has taken hold when suddenly there's a knock on the door and it opens inwards.

'Hey sis.' Alva folds her arms and leans against the door-frame, crossing one leg over the other. 'Thought I'd surprise you.' Alva is dressed casually in black slacks, a crisp white shirt underneath a navy overcoat, her work rucksack thrown over one shoulder. The highlights in her blond hair are brighter than before and she has a light tan. Nicole startles and springs to her feet. 'Why've you got that face on you?' Alva's grin breaks into laughter.

'What?' Nicole replies, her voice high.

'*That* face, Nicole. The one you always had when Mum would bust you nicking biscuits and you'd tell one of your hopeless porkers and do your face. Dad used to call it your hand in the jar face.' She steps into the office.

Nicole rubs her knee where it has banged against the desk as a jolt of nervous energy shoots through her. Suddenly aware of the laptop open on her desk, she snaps it shut and steps out to greet her sister. 'You're tanned?'

Alva tilts her head. 'Why are you so surprised? We've been in Greece. Remember?'

Nicole runs a hand through her hair. 'Yeah, I know. Sorry I'm chasing my tail today. When'd you get back?'

'Late last night. This morning I saw your missed calls so I thought I'd drop in before work and say hi.' Nicole nods, worry lines creasing her brow. Is Alva's appearance a coincidence? Of course it could make sense, since Alva's station over on Pearse Street is literally a five-minute walk from the gallery. Nicole presses her fingers to her chin as Alva checks her phone and puts it back in her pocket. 'You want to grab a quick coffee? If Jemma doesn't mind?'

'Sure.' Nicole gives her sister a hug then guides her out through the office door. In the same instant she turns to snatch the laptop off the desk and tuck it under her arm. Finally she exhales and hurries after Alva.

Alva squeezes the teabag with her spoon, lifts it from the mug and drops it onto the napkin where it makes a dark purple stain. The Brewbaker café is busier than usual today and the service staff bustle up and down the aisle past their table carrying away used cups and plates. Not long ago it was a place where Nicole would come to make notes in her journal on her laptop, oblivious to the thrumming of activity all around her, but today the espresso machine hisses and spits when it steams, cups smack rudely against saucers, spoons clink and double doors whoosh and slap as they open and close to the back kitchen.

'Well go on then,' Alva prompts.

'What?'

'The emergency, what was it?' Nicole stares at her blankly before reaching for her coffee which spills onto the tablecloth. The hot latte burns her tongue as she gulps it down. When she blows out her face is pained. 'You alright?'

'Fine.' Nicole fans her mouth trying to control the butterflies which are blooming inside her stomach. Could she still tell Alva? It was the first thing she wanted to do when they made contact. She remembers the final message and places her mug down heavily on the table. 'My fault. I had the phone under my pillow and must have pressed call by accident.' Snatching a napkin she mops where the coffee has spilled and then wraps the palm of her hand around her little finger and squeezes. It's an old habit she picked up when she changed primary school after their first house move. Their mother was always at her to stop, thinking it was a kind of tic, and she did. Only recently has she noticed she's started doing it again. And Nicole knows why, because she never lies to Alva. 'Hope I didn't wake you?'

Alva stirs her tea and the sound of metal scraping the rim of the mug feels like cold fingers on Nicole's skin. 'I was in transit. Didn't even see it till this morning.'

Nicole clears her throat, sensing a chance to switch the conversation. 'Tell us about your holiday then. We've never been to Greece.'

Alva beams as she picks up a sachet of sugar. 'Oh Nicole, it was fucking gorgeous, I'm telling you. You've got to go.' For a fleeting second the muscles in Nicole's stomach untangle and she tries to imagine what her sister would say if she told her everything. Surely she'd tell her she's done the right thing. But it's not Alva's family that they've threatened. Her sister's family don't need the lifeline that a million euros could offer. She tries to switch off the voice inside her head. It feels so long since she's enjoyed Alva's cheerful sweary voice and she just wants to enjoy the short catch up and hear her news. It dawned on her the previous week how many friends she's dropped in the last six months and how little joy is left in her life, bit by bit shedding each like a piece of old clothing. None of them could understand why because she knew they were too polite to probe. But Nicole knew. It was clear she had spent so much time trying to get Mark to open up that she forgot to open up herself. 'Aoife and Ben were in heaven.'

Nicole raises a smile imagining her niece and nephew hurtling down the beach and crashing into the sea. 'Those two are adorable. I bet they swam every day?'

Alva laughs. 'They did. They're like your Chloe, half fish the two of them.'

'I'm dying to see all your pictures.'

'Oh trust me, I have plenty. Turtle pictures taken by Ben for Chloe and lizards of all shapes and sizes snapped by Aoife for Holly.' Alva's laughter fills the space and for a fleeting second Nicole feels lighter than she can remember in a very long time. Alva then opens her rucksack and takes out a brown box. 'But my holiday isn't why I came to surprise you. Look what I have!'

Nicole puts down her coffee and watches as Alva opens the box and takes out a white dress.

'Alva? My god, is that . . . ?'

Alva laughs. 'Yes! Your communion dress.' She holds it up, letting it hang down so Nicole can see it. 'Do you remember?'

Nicole nods, a tearful gasp escaping. 'God, I could never forget it. It's beautiful.' She reaches out, touching the fabric.

'Look at all that gorgeous lace,' Alva twists it round, 'and that bow, do you remember how much you talked about that bow? And those flower patterns across the back with the tiny circles going over the shoulder.'

'But how come you have it?'

'Nic, have you forgotten?' Alva rolls her eyes. 'It got passed down to me, but then do you remember the following year I was the same size as you and could barely squeeze into it. Mum wanted to cry but dad thought it was hysterical.'

'Oh god Alva, I remember now. But where'd you find it?'

Alva folds it carefully back into the box. 'I didn't. Shaun found it.' Alva laughs. 'I finally pushed him into sorting out the attic and this morning he pulled out this box. I couldn't fucking believe it. I thought I had lost it years ago. Amazing isn't it?'

Nicole stares at the dress, remembering the day. How she rode around the estate on her new bicycle the whole day long, her white dress billowing behind her, Alva chasing her and laughing while catching up to ring the bell. Their mum and dad watching them both. So proud, so happy.

'It's beautiful.'

'Isn't it? It made me remember all Mum's old flowery summer dresses and the green where we always kicked a ball that was burst.'

Nicole nods, trying hard not to well up as her fingers wrap around the coffee cup. Her first instinct had been so clear: to call up her sister and let her take over, and even now it feels like she still could. But the threat keeps playing at the back of her head. She knows what's at stake and she simply can't risk it. A tear pushes from the corner of her eye and she wipes it away.

'Hey,' Alva taps the knuckles of Nicole's hand which has curled into a fist on the table. 'I'm sorry. I just wanted to give you a little surprise and I thought it might cheer you up. You seem a little down at the moment. Is everything alright?'

Nicole shrugs. 'I don't know Alva, I was just thinking of something Dad used to say to me sometimes and I could never understand it.'

'What was that?'

'He said I was always so kind to animals it made him worry.'

Nicole slides her hand away as Alva leans back in her chair. 'Did he used to say that? Fuck knows. He was a philosopher Dad, wasn't he, when he got going? Maybe it was after that thing with the swan.'

Nicole looks at her sister across the table. 'The swan?'

Alva shakes her head, her grin spreading. 'You must remember that time, I think you were around eight and you went over to the baby swan? The mother was chasing people around the park, hissing and flapping its wings, snapping its beak at everyone, but you walked right over to the little baby one with the broken wing.' Nicole listens, starting to remember. 'Mum was yelling at you to get away from it, but you just picked it up and the mother let you take it, didn't even flap her wings at you. Mum had to take it to the vet and get it fixed up. And she was giving out yards about it for months after, but secretly we all knew she was proud as hell and couldn't believe the guts you showed.' Alva grins. 'So I think that's what Dad might have meant. You have to try not to worry Nicole, everything's going to work out.' Alva places the lid back on the box. 'So, how are you and Mark?'

'Oh, fine.' She shrugs. 'Sorry Alva, I'm a bit spaced if I'm honest. I didn't get much sleep last night.'

'Shit, not the insomnia back again is it?'

Nicole nods. 'Not sure it ever went away.'

Alva frowns, she knows all about Nicole's insomnia. It was Alva who recommended she get some treatment for it.

33

Nicole picks up her coffee. 'Some days I just wish I had my old job back. I really liked working with the guide dogs. It was a good charity, one that meant something.'

Alva reaches across and grips her sister's hand. 'That's normal Nicky but don't blame yourself. You only stopped because you had postnatal depression; and then you couldn't go back because you had a job on your hands minding the girls. Have you forgotten how Holly didn't start speaking until she was three?'

Nicole shakes her head, the memories resurfacing, catching her by surprise at how raw they still feel: her confusion after Holly's birth at how she could be so overjoyed and yet so miserable at the same time; then her guilt that Holly's refusal to speak was somehow her fault. 'I don't think I'll ever forget that.'

'And then little Hol' eventually got past it and they discovered she was fine.' Alva sits back. 'And it made sense at the time for you not to go back because Mark's career was so demanding.' Nicole glances away unsure what to say next, worried that she might actually start crying. 'I know you're still worried about Mark, Nick,' Alva leans forward and drops her voice as Nicole places her cup back down. 'But Mark will come round, alright? Don't forget he lost Luke this year. He was his only brother and it just came out of nowhere. I mean anybody's head would be fried.'

'You're right.' Nicole rests her chin on her hand and stirs the coffee inside the mug, 'One day everything's normal and the next Mark hears his brother Luke's gone.'

The day they got told is forever etched into her memory. The short phone call from Mark's mother, 'an overdose' she explained, her voice cracking, not able to make sense of it. Mark's face had gone still, like it wasn't even registering, and all Nicole could do was put her arms around him so she could hold him. Because Mark was never somebody that ever tried to hide his emotions and suddenly they were all bottled up, like they were blocked by an invisible dam. Soon after he had resigned from his job in cardiology to volunteer with the crisis centre.

34

Alva's eyes soften. 'Sometimes men just need a bit of space to get their heads sorted out. He's a great father. When I see him with the girls they're always so happy. And the pair of you are good for each other.' She taps the box with her finger. 'The pair of you have juggled so much with the girls and the house move, Nicole. And don't forget, he's always had to be the man of the house after his dad pissed off.' Alva finishes the last of her tea. 'Hey, don't be fazed. It's just a bit of burnout. It'll pass.'

'Yeah.' Nicole nods, wondering now if she should mention another thing that's been bothering her. It feels silly, trivial almost, and yet for some reason she cannot put her finger on, she knows it's not trivial at all. 'I've been thinking of Dad a lot recently. I don't know why.'

Alva cocks her head, a confused frown ridging her brow. 'That's odd. I've been thinking about him too.'

'You two are so alike.'

Alva lifts the box off the table and places it on her lap. 'You mean mad to be spending our lives chasing shadows for not enough pay?' Alva smiles and Nicole senses her time running out. She leans forward, gripped by the urgent need to explain; about the computer hack; how these people knew her name; about how badly her and Mark have been struggling for money; and how they now have a million euros if Nicole can simply drive a car.

'Alva?' Nicole puts her coffee down but her sister is no longer listening. Alva stares at her phone, her face turning serious. A second later it rings and Alva picks up, squeezing the palm of her hand over the receiver.

'Sorry Nic, I'm going to have to take this one.' Rising to her feet Alva steps out from the table. 'Finlay speaking. Go ahead.' It's her cop voice; the one she learnt from their father, always listening keenly when he'd take an off duty call about a serious crime. The suffer no fools, pull no punches one. She snaps a sharp 'OK' and spins. 'Afraid I have to head off. It's a big case I've got on, one I've been meaning to tell you about. It involves a criminal called Doherty.' Nicole startles. The name is familiar but she can't place it. 'Coffee's on me.' Alva drops a note on the table and quickly kisses Nicole on the cheek.

Nicole keeps a stretched smile in place and watches Alva leave. As soon as her sister is out of sight she puts her laptop on the table and opens it up. Words appear one by one on the blank screen. Nicole goes very still, the pressure growing inside her chest as she reads them.

We're watching you.

Then instantly the screen fades to black.

8

Wednesday, November 15,
Afternoon

Nicole pushes back from the office desk, kneading her eyes with the heels of her hands. There's a ping and her heart thumps.

Girls having a ball. The breath releases from her lungs when she sees it's a selfie of her friend Eve. She's at the kids play centre Jumpzone and in the background her daughter Lily is playing with Chloe. It finishes with a big love heart emoji. Nicole checks the time on her phone. If she leaves now she'll have enough time to bus home, collect her car and go pick up her girls.

'OK.' She tries to relax her shoulders. She must stay calm and act like nothing's happened. The girls mustn't get any idea something's off and neither must Eve. It's important to continue as normal until she's figured out a way to solve this. Eve's been so good about collecting them and dropping them off, organising play dates and taking them out for treats. If Nicole doesn't turn up to make the collection she knows Eve will be curious why.

Looking at the picture she thinks about her friend. Perhaps it is true what Mark says, that Eve can be a little pushy but he doesn't know her as well as Nicole does, and even though the friendship has only been for eighteen months it really feels like so much longer. The truth is that Eve has been like a rock for her recently, especially as she lost more and more connection with her other friends when things started getting bad at home.

Nicole rises to her feet, tensing as she presses the phone keys and starts to text.

C u at six.

37

9

Wednesday, November 15,
Evening

'Mummy!' Little Holly's shriek is high and clear as she bounds into the air, her wheaten hair a circle of gold around her head. All around her young boys and girls bounce and squeal excitedly, their limbs flailing as they jump up and down on their personal trampolines inside Jumpzone. Right beside her Chloe dips down to the ground and springs sharply, hazel eyes shining as she kicks her legs wide while holding her long dark plait. Lily bounces close by, waving as she twirls.

For a second Nicole just watches, forgetting everything. She waves back and gives an encouraging smile. 'Look at you girls!'

On the drive over, grinding through the Dublin traffic, splashing through rain soaked streets, all she could think about was last night. But she won't think about it now. She has to remain calm, like nothing has happened.

Her phone rings. It's Mrs Lyubevsky.

'Nina, I'm so sorry,' she says, picking up, 'I saw your reply to my text when I was driving. I was just about to call you! I have Rocky and I'm going to be home shortly so I can drop him back to you.'

'Rocky?' Eve cranes down, planting a feather light kiss on Nicole's cheek as she slips past with two coffees. Nicole's breath catches as Eve sits on one of the plastic chairs beside the table, grinning and gesturing for Nicole to join her. Eve sweeps a strand of silky blond hair from her carefully made up eyes.

38

As usual she is dressed stylishly, today in a flowing navy dress matched with shining leather boots that climb halfway up two slim, tapered legs.

Nicole covers the mouthpiece, whispering. 'Our neighbour's cat. Poor thing got injured.' Eve makes a crestfallen face. 'I'll see you shortly, Nina.' Nicole hangs up as Eve draws out a chair. But she doesn't sit. Instead she stands rigidly, both hands gripping the back of the chair, eyes fixed on the coffee. She doesn't want coffee. How does she do this? She can't just leave. 'Sorry I'm late.' Reaching into her bag she pulls out the last remaining note. 'Here, that's payment for my two.'

'Nicky?' Eve picks up the twenty euros and slips it back inside the bag. 'Don't be silly. You know I'm always happy to treat them. Did you get your work finished?'

Nicole blows hair from her eyes and it sticks to her damp forehead. She's never liked relying on people's generosity. 'Some of it.'

Eve offers her a cup. 'Everything OK?'

'I really have to fly, Eve. I'm so sorry.'

Eve pouts playfully, throwing her best puppy dog face. 'I can't take it back – and they still have five minutes to go. Go on, stay for the coffee?'

Giving in Nicole sinks into the chair. 'Sorry.' She takes the cup. 'That's bad of me I know. But I'm really rushing today.'

Eve nods. 'I hate those days.'

'I'll be fine. Thanks for doing this by the way. And for the drink.' She smiles at Eve weakly, her fingers gripping the cup too tight.

'Hey!' Eve sits up, 'when I heard you mention Rocky just now it reminded me of something. You remember our animal sanctuary idea?' Nicole stares back, silently trying to recall the conversation but only retrieving the faintest recollection. 'We should chat about that again some time. You know, see if there might be something in it. I really liked the idea. I think it could be wonderful.' Eve makes big eyes and Nicole nods, straining to mirror her. When was it they spoke about it last? Weeks ago? Months?

She didn't know if Eve was serious. Her friend does so much free work for different charities. Perhaps she was trying to offer her something? Nicole's never opened up fully about what they are going through but Eve must have an idea. She knows Mark's real job isn't volunteering.

'Definitely,' Nicole says flatly, unsure what else to add.

'How's Mark doing?' Eve asks then.

Tensing, Nicole puts her cup down and looks away. There's a woman by the toilets in a grey suit talking sternly to one of the cleaners. She hands the cleaner a mop and marches away. For a second the memory of Nicole's mother comes back to her in a flash. It's been so long since she thought about her and she misses her too much. Shaking her head she banishes it. 'Oh, you know.' Her shoulders shrug when she exhales. 'Busy. Always busy.'

'I can imagine.'

Nicole's phone rings then but when she checks the display it isn't a number she recognises. 'Sorry, Eve. One sec.'

'Not at all.' Eve waves across to the girls. 'Take it.'

'I think it's my neighbour calling me back.' Nicole hurries away. Once she's out of earshot she answers.

'Nicole?'

'Yes.'

'Hi. Is everything OK?'

'Mark?' Her voice is almost a gasp.

'Yeah, who did you think it was?'

'Sorry. I wasn't expecting your call. Your number's not coming up.'

'I know. I'm calling on the office line,' he says quietly.

'Mark, there's something . . . ' A loud warning buzzer interrupts them. It's the notice coming over the speakers to let her know there's five minutes remaining on the trampolines before the session ends.

Mark's voice is once again audible at the other end of the line. 'I was just calling to say I'm off early so I'll be back in an hour. I was thinking of cooking a carbonara. Were you saying something?'

Nicole presses the palm of her hand against her forehead, the shock of almost blurting everything to Mark catching her off guard. How could she do that? She knows it's just the stress but still can't believe it. 'No. That's brilliant Mark. I'm at Jumpzone. I'll drop the kids home shortly and I'll call in on Mrs Lyubevsky and ask her to watch them till you get back. There's a backlog of work Jemma asked me to finish so I'm going to nip back to the office and get it done. I'll probably be a little late home tonight. Is that alright with you?'

'Take all the time you need.'

The second buzzer sounds signalling the end of the session and Eve strides off to help Lily down. Chloe and Holly clamber off the edge of the jump square, faces flushed and smiling. Nicole gathers her phone and bag but gets distracted by the beeping of Eve's phone which she has left behind on the table.

There's a new message. Nicole can't see who it's from but she can make out the end of the text. *Thank you for last night. XX.* She tries to guess who it might be. Eve had always been very firm that she would never date until her divorce with David had finalised. Nicole closes her mouth, realising she is staring, but Eve has already returned.

Swooping across Eve plucks up the phone. 'We've got to dash, Nic. Lily's got a violin lesson and the teacher does not do late.' Eve wraps her arms around her, kissing her quickly on either cheek. 'Listen to me, I know you're stressed out. I'll make a plan and we'll get out sometime soon. It's what you need. Alright?'

Chloe and Holly wave goodbye to Lily as Nicole inhales her friend's expensive perfume. Then Eve skips towards the exit, blowing kisses as she hurries into the darkness.

In the car park Chris Ashton clutches the plastic bag containing his high-vis jacket close to his chest, watching Nicole as she gets into the car with her two young children. When she starts the engine he walks away in the darkness, rubbing the deep scratch on his hand where the cat clawed him.

10

Wednesday, November 15,
Evening

The palms of her hands are cold as they press against her face and Nicole rests her elbows on the office desk. On the road outside a bus passes by, its diesel engine grunting and coughing smoke into the winter clouds above Dublin's city centre. Her eyes glance down at the thick, unfinished folder which is full of personal Christmas cards which Jemma's partner Andrew always gets ready each year before December even begins. The cards are made from Andrew's own photographs, always handwritten with a customised greeting and, in a few weeks' time, will be posted to his top one hundred customers home and abroad. Pushing them away she sits up and pulls the laptop towards her.

'Heya.' Nicole jumps at the sound of her boss's voice. When she looks up Jemma's head is around the door and she is smiling. Letting go of the laptop she flattens her hands on the desk. 'Sorry, didn't mean to interrupt you but I'm going to head off so you'll be all by yourself soon.'

'That's fine.'

Jemma points to the folder. 'If you want, I can take some of those home and do them. Andrew asked me to get them all out of the way tonight if we can.'

'Don't worry. I'll get them done.' Nicole places her hand on the folder.

'Alright then. But don't kill yourself. Just do what you can, alright? I still don't even understand why he always insists on getting them done so early. One of his quirks I suppose.' Jemma waves goodbye, disappearing behind the door once more. 'See you tomorrow.'

Darkness descends, and the room goes cold as the heating switches off. The city outside has quietened as rush hour comes and goes. The footsteps on the pavement scurrying to and fro lessen, the sound of the buses spluttering and groaning through the rain becomes more intermittent.

Nicole works steadily through the evening, handwriting addresses on the envelopes and filling in cards, as the rain patters against the window, but her eyes constantly flit across the desk to scan the laptop screen for any sign of the hacker's return. Yet there is no click to make her snap to attention, and as the hours pass she starts to doubt if her plan has any chance of succeeding.

Earlier it had seemed simple. She would work alone, undisturbed in the office, and simply bide her time. The hackers would most likely make contact and once they did she could tell them to take the money back. That way the whole nightmare could end instantly. She would give them reassurances that the police would not be contacted.

She takes a biro off the desk and rolls it between her fingers, running her other hand through her hair. The skin pulls tight across her face as she opens the browser on the laptop and goes online to check her bank balance. The pressure inside her chest returns as she waits, but it's the same as before. The money is there. All of it.

'Christ,' the word hisses from her lips as the tension she thought she had under control rushes back, pulsing through her body with every strained heartbeat. Does she really intend to give the money back? Why couldn't she simply do the thing they ask because anybody could drive a car? The money is hers now and she knows all the good things she can do with it to help her family. It could be the very solution she's been dreaming about for months.

The laptop screen has gone blank and switched into power saving mode. The thoughts are swirling like smoke around her, choking her ability to focus. All she can think about is the money and driving the car. For the first time it dawns on her that she hasn't ever stopped to properly consider the proposition. Who are these people? Why could they possibly want her to drive a car for so much money? Why her?

And why have they disappeared?

Opening the Chrome browser she goes online. There's a question that's been at the back of her mind since the first day she heard the laptop making those strange noises. She goes to the website Mark told her about. It's called Geeks Love Tech and the forum always answers tech trivia questions almost instantly. She types in her question. *Is it really possible to access an unattended laptop remotely?*

The wind blows outside making the glass in the windows shake. Instantly somebody called Technutter replies.

You want the long answer or the short one?

Nicole types back, her shoulders tensing. *Either.*

Your answer is yes.

The wind gusts again. 'Shit.' Quickly she types back. *Do you know how?*

But Technutter has gone offline.

The door to the front of the gallery strains against its hinge. It's an old building and this often happens, which is why she must not pay it any heed, but as the seconds slip by, and it happens a second time, her stomach tightens. Could it be the man Holly saw out on the street? Could he be the one who contacted her online? The man whose face she can't remember now. Nobody else on the forum replies to her question and she shuts the laptop down.

Rising to her feet she walks around to the side of the desk.

There's a letter opener on it and she picks it up, careful not to make a sound. Gripping the handle hard she holds it out in front of her and waits, trying to get her breathing under control. Have they come to find her in person here at the office? Is that the

44

reason they didn't make contact online? She knows it's possible. They've already told her they're watching her.

Sweat beads across the top of her lip. She pats her pocket for her phone but it's not there. When she looks across she sees it but it's on the other side of the room on the windowsill. She doesn't remember putting it there, her mind is so scattered.

There's another tapping noise outside the door. She's certain somebody's outside but she can't let them in. Surprise is her only advantage.

With one sharp lunge, she darts to the door and yanks it open.

It swings inwards with a gust of freezing cold air but there is nobody in sight. The gallery looks empty, unchanged from when she went into the office hours before. The black and white prints hang on the walls, the two new paintings she noticed this morning lie against Jemma's desk next to the till, still waiting to be hung or stored out the back. There is nothing to see but the lonely shadows thrown from the streetlamps outside, nothing but the chill of the cold, still air.

I I

Thursday, November 16,
Mid-Morning

In an almost empty car park outside her kids school Nicole sits inside her car. Drained from last night's lack of sleep she had closed her eyes after doing the drop off only to wake two hours later still in the driver's seat. The banking app is open on the phone screen. It's the joint account she shares with Mark. 'Seven fucking euros?' the words hiss from her mouth as she stares at it in disbelief. Slowly she slumps into the seat and the back of her head presses into the headrest. She can't believe her last pay cheque has evaporated so quickly. Then she remembers. The weekly shop, a full tank of diesel, Holly's visit to the dentist, the tax for Mark's car – the car she didn't have the heart to tell him to sell. She closes her eyes and drops the phone into the space underneath the car radio.

As the rain patters above her head on the roof, the bad thoughts return; how the hackers never made contact last night in the office as she had hoped, even though she stayed past midnight, barely leaving her enough time to catch the last bus home; how Mark was fast asleep holding Holly in his arms when she got back, still fully dressed and lying beside her on the duvet, clinging to her almost as if he was stopping her drifting out to sea. She couldn't wake him, couldn't explain all the things she so desperately wanted to share even if she knew she couldn't. And then the morning, waking late, not in her own bed but on the sofa in the front room downstairs where she had fallen asleep in a sitting position sometime after three.

The rush of the morning was a mess. Why was Mark gone? Leaving only a note to say: *Out for a morning jog with Ken. Talk later.*

Mark didn't like to exercise in the mornings. It didn't make sense.

Reaching across the steering wheel she rubs the windscreen with the back of her hand and makes a small circle in the steam which covers the glass. The muscles in her back twist and strain as she sits back and exhales.

There's a torn white envelope on the passenger seat and she picks it up. Had Mark deliberately hidden it? She knows he must have. Only that Chloe had said she needed money to go on her school trip today to the museum and Nicole had to search every last drawer and shelf in the house did she manage to find it by accident. Because Mark kept it amongst old surgery notes they agreed she would never touch.

She pulls the official looking paper out and reads it again. 'Three months,' her head shakes as the red letters stare back at her. 'Our mortgage repayments are three months in arrears but you never mentioned it, Mark? You told me the whole time that you had it covered from your own account.' Suddenly aware that she is talking to herself out loud she stuffs the letter back inside the envelope, forcing it inside the glove compartment.

The clock inside the car has just gone past eleven. A yawn squeezes past the back of her hand as she tries to wake up. The thought of home and having to sit by her laptop is too suffocating. What she really wants is to talk to Mark. Even if she can't tell him what's happened perhaps she could simply tell him that she's struggling and he might hear her.

Opening the car window to let in some air, she presses the phone keypad and calls Mark but it goes to message so she writes a text.

Call me.

Instantly his reply comes back.

Sorry love. Work gone mad. Chat soon.

Dropping the phone in her lap, Nicole presses her knuckles against her lips and fights the urge to bite. The stone in her wedding ring scrapes her tooth and she pulls her hand away, swallowing as tears cloud her eyes.

Then the passenger door opens and Eve appears.

12

Nicole notices the healthy glow of Eve's skin and the light gold shadow on her eyelids as she slips quietly into the passenger seat beside her.

'My god, it's wet,' Eve says, her voice cheerful but breathless. Rain drips from the sleeves of her waxed Barbour jacket as she lifts her boots inside and pulls the door closed. 'I just nipped into the chemist to get some lip balm and then spotted your car when I came out. This is a nice surprise, but what are you doing here?' Only now does she turn to glance at Nicole who mops her eyes with the back of her fingers. 'Nicole?'

Nicole raises a weak smile. How will she explain why she is sitting in her car, barely awake, crying when she should be at work? Could she really tell Eve? A surge of fear washes over her and she sits up.

'I'm fine, sorry. I had to rush in with Chloe's sports gear. She forgot her gum shield and hockey stick.'

'Oh?'

Nicole glances back at her friend, marvelling at how every strand of hair in Eve's tightly woven bun is in place and at the smoothness of her make-up for such a dank, drizzly day. 'You look well.' She tries to laugh.

'Nicole what's wrong?'

'Nothing. I just took a ten minute nap and haven't woken up properly.' Eve frowns as Nicole rubs her eyes. 'Last night I worked late at the office but then fell asleep on the couch.'

49

'You're working too hard. Remember what I said, you need to get out a little. Otherwise you'll run yourself into the ground.'

Nicole nods. She's too fragile right now and if Eve probes she doesn't know what she might reveal. 'I know. But shouldn't you be at work?'

Plucking a strand of hair from where it clings to her jacket sleeve, Eve laughs. 'I worked from home this morning. But guess what?'

'What?'

'I'm actually on my way to a social with a work group for early lunch.' Her white teeth flash a playful smile. 'And you've just given me an idea! You should come. My treat!'

'What?'

'You're coming with me. We're going to The Ivy in the city. You can have a few hours off, can't you? I'm worried about you, alright? And I'm sure Jemma'll understand if you were in until late last night.'

There's a lump in Nicole's throat and she swallows. 'Thanks. But I can't.'

Eve sighs, one hand resting on Nicole's arm as she searches her face. 'You would tell me if something was wrong, wouldn't you?'

Nicole doesn't reply. The tightness inside her chest is back. She doesn't trust herself to speak. Nodding she turns the key in the ignition.

The cabin lights up as Eve opens the door. 'I'm always here for you, you know that, right? And remember you're doing brilliantly, OK? I know it's difficult with Mark right now and you've got a lot on your plate but you deserve a little time to yourself once in a while. We all do.' Eve slips her hands into her pockets and pulls on black leather gloves. Pausing then, she turns back, but Nicole is staring out the window at the girls' school.

'You have to mind yourself, Nicole.' In a second Eve is gone, skipping over puddles in her heeled boots and disappearing into the rain. Nicole glances at the wet empty passenger seat. Beneath it, down in the footwell, is a padded envelope.

13

Thursday, November 16,
Mid-Morning

'Crisis centre, how can I help you?' the receptionist's voice is upbeat and friendly.

'Mark Reid, please.'

'Putting you through now.'

Chris Ashton paces to the glass door of his fifth floor apartment and looks out at the courtyard below. A pair of magpies jump about beneath the tree, searching for food in the small triangle of grass. The line rings but nobody picks up. 'Shit,' he mumbles, turning to walk back to the kitchen when he hears the receptionist's voice again.

'I'm sorry, there's no answer from that extension. Would you like to leave a voicemail?'

'No. It's fine.'

'Or I could take a message. What did you say your name was?'

'Peters,' Chris clears his throat, stalling. 'John Peters, but I won't leave a message. I'll try him again.'

'OK, bye now.'

'Can I ask, did you see him today?' he replies, his voice urgent. He cannot let the call end just yet. Not until he knows more. 'Did he come to work?'

There's a pause on the end of the line. After a second the receptionist comes back, her voice more wary now. 'I can't say but I haven't seen him personally. Is it something important?'

'No, I'll keep trying.' Quickly he hangs up and checks to see if there are any more messages from Ed Wiley but finds there's none. He'd like to go down and wait outside Mark's workplace but he won't. It's important he doesn't make any mistakes.

14

Thursday, November 16,
Lunchtime

'Nicole! You're here.' Eve springs from her seat to rush over. 'You came!' The buzz of conversation around the table stops for a moment as four women look up to inspect her. 'I'm so pleased.' Nicole nods, one hand in her pocket clutching the envelope. 'Girls,' Eve places a hand on her shoulder, 'meet Nicole.'

'Hi Nicole,' two of the women chorus her name, as another pair tilt their heads over shining wine glasses. They are all immaculately dressed with smooth skin and glossy hair.

'Lily goes to the same school as Nicole's eldest, Chloe. They're best friends. But . . . ' Eve pauses, her grin widening, ' . . . we actually met through her husband, Mark, after I bumped into him at the squash club.'

'Ah yes, Mark!' a woman with a black roll neck and big gold earrings says.

Nicole clears her throat but Eve starts to laugh and nudges her towards a spare seat at the far side of the long table.

'I'm not staying,' Nicole whispers.

'Don't be silly, sure you've only just arrived?'

Nicole turns so her back is to the table and pulls out the envelope. 'You left this in my car.'

Eve laughs nervously, waving a hand in the air. 'Oh that? Don't worry about it.'

'It's a thousand euros Eve?'

'Let's eat and we'll chat about it later.' Eve glances back at her friends, smiling.

'I don't want it!' The words hiss from Nicole's mouth and the table hushes. Eve's cheer withers under the watchful gaze of the entire table and her face falls. A second passes before she regains her composure. 'Just a moment ladies, please. We'll be right back.' Gripping Nicole's hand she stands up and leads them away. When she's walked out of earshot she stops. 'Nicky? What's up with you? I said it's fine. We don't have to talk about it now. Let's enjoy this meal. It's my treat.' For a second Nicole thinks Eve might be about to cry.

'I'm not being rude Eve, but I can't take this. I don't want to be a joke, to you or anyone else.'

Eve's eyes flash. 'This is not a joke Nicole.'

Cold air filters through the AC in the restaurant bathroom where soft music pipes through the speakers. It's a break from the stuffy air in the dining area and the loud voices around the table.

Nicole ducks her face, splashing freezing water against her cheeks. *This is not a joke Nicole.* Why did Eve say that? It's exactly what the hackers said to her when they made contact. Of course it has to be a coincidence. It couldn't be possible that Eve would contact her online. And even though Nicole knows her friend's well off she couldn't put that amount of money in her account. Or could she?

Retreating inside a cubicle, she locks it, pressing the phone hard against her flushed face, while Mark's number rings a third time. Her cheeks burn as it keeps ringing. 'You've contacted Mark Reid,' Mark's message plays and she pulls the phone away. She's about to open the lock when the front door to the restroom opens and she hears two female voices.

Immediately she cancels the call.

'Oh my god. Did you see that?'

'I know.'

'Eve's face!'

'Shit that was bad.'

'But who's the friend?'

Nicole clutches the phone to her chest, lifting her knees up so her feet rest on the toilet seat's edge. Beyond the locked cubicle door she hears the sound of running water in the sink. Another cubicle door opens and closes. It's followed by the sound of water dropping into the toilet bowl.

'One of Eve's lost causes clearly.' There's a snigger. 'Apparently it's all gone to shit between her and the husband and is heading towards divorce.'

'That's sad.' The cubicle door opens.

'It is. Though Eve says he's well hot. You'd fuck him in a heartbeat!'

'What? Stop!' Laughter mixes with the sound of a toilet flushing. Somebody opens a sink tap and it splashes noisily, followed immediately by the sharp whine of the electric hand dryer.

'Come on,' one of them says. 'Let's go find out more!' The dryer cuts out. There's a burst of noise from outside, an intake of hot air, and the soft thud of the door closing on its hinge.

Ashen faced, Nicole stumbles from the cubicle. Stooping down, she leans over the sink, her stomach knotting. Guttural noises heave from her throat but it passes. *Eve says you'd fuck him in a heartbeat.* Her eyes pull tight as the words burn through her head. Did her friend really say that? About Mark? Did she really tell her friends Mark was getting divorced? Gripping her fingers around the edge of the sink, her knuckles pushing against the stretched skin, she forces herself to stand.

Clearly Eve knows more than she ever let on about their circumstances; and she likes to discuss Mark when Nicole is not around.

What else does Eve know?

15

Nicole is woken up by her phone vibrating on the coffee table. She's curled up on the sofa in the foetal position, her hair smothering her face.

The pulsing at the front of her head makes her wince and she moves to a sitting position. How long has she been asleep? The last memory she has is putting their girls to bed, making a big effort not to slur her words as she read Holly her bedtime story. She'd drunk half a bottle of red wine when she'd got home to try and chase away the awful words still spinning in her head.

Her phone vibrates again and she sees his name appear. There are three missed calls on her phone from Mark.

She stumbles for the phone, her heart breaking a little bit at the thought of everything she so desperately wants to tell him but fears she simply can't. 'Mark?'

'Nicole? Is everything OK?' His voice is gentle.

'I . . . I miss you. Where are you?'

He pauses. 'Wicklow, at my friend Ken Byrne's place. Ken's off from work for a few days, and he invited me down to Round-wood. You know the place he inherited last year from his uncle?'

'Wicklow?' The sharpness in her voice catches her by surprise. 'You were supposed to be here. You've got work tomorrow. What are you doing?'

'I know.' His voice sounds tired. 'Look, it wasn't planned. There's just a few of us staying over. One of them is going into Dublin early in the morning so I'm going to catch a lift with him.

I'm sorry, Nic. It won't happen again. It was a spur of the moment thing Ken suggested after our run this morning. I'm just . . . '

'Mark, something's happened.' She cuts him off. 'Something really serious. We need to talk.'

The line goes quiet. 'OK?'

A burst of pain spreads across her forehead. She can't tell him about the hacker. She won't risk testing their threat against her family but she knows Mark isn't being totally honest with her. 'I know about the mortgage repayments now. I now you've been hiding things.'

There's an intake of breath. 'I'm sorry Nic. I want to explain.' He hesitates.

'What's stopping you?'

'Are you sure it's a good idea to talk about this on the phone?' Mark's voice is wary, but strangely hard also.

A shudder passes through her body. What if somebody has hacked their phone line? What risk might she be taking if she explains everything now?

'Tomorrow. Soon as you get back from work. We both sit down. This has been going on too long.'

16

'Is everything OK, Mum?' Chloe looks across from the passenger seat of their noisy Renault, a worried look in her round eyes.

Nicole finishes reading the note which Mrs Lyubevsky dropped through the letter box.

Nicole, something I forgot to mention to you yesterday. Just to say that burglars may be operating in our area so keep your eyes open.

Nina.

She folds the paper, peering out at the grey sky beyond the windscreen.

'What happened to Dad last night?' Chloe watches her mother tuck the note into her pocket.

'Nothing, and nothing's wrong Chlo.' Nicole pushes the hair out of her eyes. 'Your dad was out for the night with some friends and stayed over, that's all.' The blue digits of the car clock show it's quarter to nine and they are going to be late for school. Hurrying then, Nicole reverses out sharply into the road and stops. After quickly double checking her mirror she puts the car into first gear and starts to drive.

The wiper on the back windscreen judders as it sweeps the glass, squeaking harshly. In the distance behind them something has caught her eye. It's the courier. The one who introduced himself as Chris and brought Mrs Lyubevsky's cat to their door.

He moves along the wet pavement, stealing a glance over his shoulder. Nicole's fingers tighten on the steering wheel as she watches him pushing his bike slowly past their neighbour's house while staring into theirs.

17

Through the window glass of The Bite café on Duke Street, Nicole watches the pedestrians shuffle past. The image of the bicycle courier comes back to her and the intense look on his face as he stared at their house this morning. Perhaps he was simply doing his deliveries and she was being paranoid? The espresso machine hisses, emitting steam, as the girl behind the counter preps it and begins frothing the milk inside the steel jug. Taking her eyes off the laptop for a second, Nicole looks around. There are two empty tables behind her and after that the toilets. When a young couple get up to leave she counts only three people remaining. It's as private as she could hope for; she is satisfied it will do.

The Wi-Fi signal still hasn't returned on the bar at the bottom of her screen yet and her eyes flick back to the passers-by who stream past the window glass. The frothing machine bubbles loudly when her mobile rings. Though she can't recall who it is she recognises the number and answers.

'Mrs Reid?' a woman asks in a polite voice.

'Yes?'

'This is Rose from Dr Fenton's surgery. I'm putting him through to you now.' Nicole thinks about cutting the call but at the last moment changes her mind. Holly, she remembers. It must be about Holly's asthma. 'Dr Fenton?'

'Nicole, hi, have I caught you at a bad time? It's just about Holly.'

Nicole dusts the last of the sugar against her leg. In their consultation the doctor said Holly was fine. There was nothing more to discuss. She presses the phone closer to her ear. Then she remembers the tests hadn't finalised the day they went in. It feels so long ago now with everything that's happened. 'Yes?'

'It's good news so there's nothing to worry about. The tests came back and it's exactly what we were anticipating so I wanted to put your mind at ease by letting you know it's official. That's all.'

The chair squeaks as Nicole rests her shoulder against the window glass, stunned at how even a doctor's phone call has pushed her into full panic mode. 'I appreciate you telling me Doctor Fenton. Thank you.'

'You're welcome.'

The line cuts. The girl at the espresso machine signals to Nicole to come to the collection counter, grinning cheerfully as she puts the finishing touches to the froth on top of her waiting latte. Nicole withdraws the last few coins from her pocket and makes her way over, keeping one eye firmly on her laptop.

'Hope you enjoy it now,' the waitress says warmly. Nicole returns an exhausted smile, taking the drink in her hand as the butterflies kick off deep inside her stomach. Why did she order coffee when she meant to ask for tea? She doesn't drink coffee after lunch but somehow now it hardly feels it matters.

When she sits back down at the table the laptop screen is still blank. Gently she presses her fingers into her eyes and rubs slowly. Last night her mind wouldn't switch off but just kept running and running, endlessly rehashing everything that had happened. The last memory she has is lying on her back, staring at the ceiling, wanting to scream, only to find herself waking up like she hadn't slept at all.

Her fingernails drum against the tabletop. The whole day she has shut out the world; Mark and his decision to go to Ken's place in Wicklow on a whim; the burglar who Mrs Lyubevsky thinks is planning to rob the road; what Eve said about Mark; the one million euros sitting in her private bank account, which nobody knows about.

Except them.

And her.

'Them and me,' she blows the froth off her latte and checks the time on her phone once more. It's just gone half past four. The laptop screen lights up as the Wi-Fi signal reconnects. The whole day long, she has waited patiently for this moment, ploughing through her work at the gallery so she could get away a little earlier than usual. But now that's she's here she wants to leave, to flick off the computer and get home to her kids.

The questions which wouldn't leave her alone last night have restarted, fizzing back and forth, screaming for answers she doesn't have. Why have these people targeted her? Why did they put this money in her account only to vanish? Why pay up front if they don't know if she's agreeing to do what they ask? To draw you in, the silent voice inside her head replies. And deep down she knows that's exactly what's happened, because since it appeared, since the hacker made contact, she hasn't stopped thinking about it.

The back of her hand blocks a yawn as she stirs the foam, watching the chocolate powder swirl. Then she takes out an unpaid electricity bill from her bag and gazes at the laptop.

Something dawned on her last night as she lay awake in bed waiting for the morning to come. She has seen a million euros in her own private account. However, so far, all she has seen is numbers on a screen. Whoever approached her managed to hack in and speak with her directly online. Surely it means they could do something to her laptop to present images of her bank files which might not be genuine? She can't say how they would do it but it's not impossible. Which means the money wouldn't really exist, but just look like it does.

That's why she's come here to this quiet café, where no one will interrupt her. The bill trembles in her hand so she places it on the table and flattens it out. She needs to devise a test. The plan is simple. She will go online and pay their electricity bill – it will either succeed and debit the account, or fail and be rejected.

Drawing her seat closer to the table, she looks up and scans the café quickly, but finds nobody is paying her any attention. Behind the counter one girl stacks cups on the tray above the coffee machine as the second girl mops around her feet singing softly. The scent of freshly ground beans still permeates the air and there is the faintest sound of background music, some type of jazz, droning quietly. The other diners drink and chat. With a careful tap of the keys she inputs the Wi-Fi password and waits. She knows it's not a good idea to access sensitive information on public networks but she's here now and she's not changing her mind. The browser launches and she takes a breath. Hopefully the test will literally take seconds.

Gleeful laughter erupts from the nearby table then and Nicole lifts her fingers off the keypad. When she looks up she sees two middle aged women throw their heads back, mugs in hand, their faces creased and giggling. Nicole waits for the noise to die down before drawing the laptop closer. The only other customer is an elderly man who finishes a scone, sitting quietly by the window alone.

To pay the bill she must go to their electricity provider's web-site, so she keys in their customer information and number, as well as the amount due, and follows it up with the debit authorisation. At the end of the transaction she hits the 'Confirm Payment' button and waits. Seconds later the screen displays 'Payment Confirmed'.

The last remaining task is to open her bank account to cross check the new balance.

Squeezing her hands together she closes her eyes and tries to calm, then slowly she goes to the relevant web page and opens it up. The thumping inside her chest begins as she waits. But the wait isn't long. The page now shows nine hundred and ninety nine thousand eight hundred and seventy two euros.

There's no more doubt. Every cent of it is real.

The waitress brushes past her, smoothing her hands on her apron, beaming a big smile. Nicole hunches over. It dawns on her suddenly that she's done something else now, something she hadn't really intended. She's used the money for the first time.

A sharp sound interrupts her thoughts.

Click.

When she glances at the screen it has faded to black.

Hum.

Holding her breath she waits.

Whir.

One word now appears in bold letters in the middle of the screen.

Well?

18

'Can I get you anything else?' The waitress is back. 'We're going to be closing soon.'

For a second Nicole stares. 'Sorry, no – I'm fine.' The words tumble from her mouth in nervous gasps. 'When are you closing exactly?'

'Maybe twenty minutes. You can take your time.'

'Thank you.' Her eyes flick back to the screen, fingers typing furtively as the waitress returns behind the counter.

I'm here.

You took the money.

Her cheeks redden.

I was testing to make sure it's real.

It is.

There's a screech of wood on tile as the two women get up from their seats, their chairs scraping against the flooring as they push themselves away from the table. One of them glances over, then shifts her gaze to the toilet behind Nicole. 'Do you need to go or are you alright?' she asks her friend.

Nicole holds her breath, her fingers curling around the edges of the screen.

'Nah, I'm good.' There's more clunking and banging as they rearrange the chairs, pick up their purses and put on scarves and coats.

New words have appeared on the screen.

You must drive the car now.

Nicole waits as the women file out. When the door shuts behind them she types. *I haven't agreed.*

You took the money. One million euros is now yours. You've agreed.

That's not true.

Drive the car or face the consequences.

What are you saying?

A picture appears on the screen. Nicole recognises it instantly. It's the family picture of Mark with her and their two girls, the one from the summer's day in Phoenix Park when they were all so relaxed and happy. A red veil descends on the image, mimicking blood. Then it disappears.

Wide eyed, she looks to the staff working behind the counter, but they won't stay in focus. The pounding in her ears grows stronger, turning their chatter to indistinct noise. The text keeps appearing. *Don't push us.*

Who the fuck are you people? Her fingers smack the keys. *What do you want?*

For you to see sense. Don't make us hurt you. This money is yours. Help your family and drive the car. Tears well in her eyes. She takes a second to breathe before typing again.

When?

Tonight. Meet us outside Massey's funeral home in Inchicore 9 p.m. Park up and wait for a black jeep to collect you.

Instinctively she casts a glance towards the door. What if she got up and ran? Could she do that? It seems so simple. Swallowing noisily, she tries to think clearly but images of these people arriving at her house flash through her mind. She sees them vividly, masked and unidentifiable, breaking through a back window late at night, armed and moving at speed towards Holly's bedroom. Could she live with it if they harmed her children? Dropping her face in her hands she shuts her eyes. How can she possibly do this tonight? She thinks of Alva. She could pick up her phone and call her now but as she's thinking this another thought occurs to her. If Alva doesn't find them will the threat always hang over her head? Like an axe waiting to fall at any moment.

For a second she imagines having one million euros. Would it finally put everything right again? Isn't that what she's always wanted?

I can't decide. I need to know more.

No.

She hunkers down, closer to the screen. Suddenly she's so drained, like she simply wants to shut her eyes and drop her head on the table. She hasn't slept. She can't think properly but all she can do is type back. *When?*

Now.

Her fingers touch her neck but feel cold against her skin. A tear trickles down her cheek when she moves to shut the screen down. But at the last second she stops.

Inhaling slowly, the air fills her lungs and she holds it until it won't stay in any longer.

As she shakes her head it bursts out of her all at once.

And she types one word: *Yes.*

19

The car pulls over onto Grosvenor Road and stops. Outside the light has faded and a chill has entered the air as the early evening sets in. In a few minutes' time the after-school club will end and Chloe and Holly will come out. Nicole lets the engine idle as she tries to think.

She knows Mark won't be back till late. He already texted her about a suicide prevention workshop which is running into the evening. Picking up her phone she writes him a text.

What time are you home?

Instantly his reply pings back. *Workshop ends at 9. So 10 latest.*

Pushing herself upright, she sifts through the options as her pulse spikes. Then she gets an idea and writes Mark another text.

OK.

The last thing remaining is to organise a babysitter.

Nicole stands outside the front door to Mrs Lyubevsky's house, her hands stuffed deep inside her coat pockets, squeezing her car keys and working hard to keep her voice light. 'I'm sorry it's such short notice, Nina, and I know it's really bad of me to be imposing like this.' She almost adds 'if you can't, don't worry' but catches it just in time. Even the suggestion that saying no is an option could complicate things disastrously.

'Nicole, are you sure you're alright?' Mrs Lyubevsky tilts her head to the side, frowning slightly.

'I'm fine, honestly. Just a bit tired.'

'You have to be careful with your health. I mean you could be anaemic. Have you checked with your doctor? Some of these conditions we can know nothing about until one day?' She raises her eyebrows and two small shoulders shrug inside her grey cardigan. 'We keel over and it's too late.'

'You're right. I'll do that.'

'It's always best to know, isn't it?'

'It is.' Nicole waits for her neighbour to elaborate but she doesn't. 'So about tonight?'

'Oh yes, don't worry about that, I'm happy to oblige.' Rocky appears at her feet and the old woman groans softly when she bends to pick him up.

'I was hoping to get out around eight if that would work?'

The cat purrs as Mrs Lyubevsky runs a veined hand through his striped coat. 'That's fine Nicole.'

Anxious to make time, Nicole rushes back to the house and lets Holly and Chloe know that Mrs Lyubevsky is dropping over to mind them. Their elderly neighbour babysat a couple of times before when they first moved in and the girls like her so they're pleased. Chloe asks if they can watch a documentary on Netflix about a K-pop band she likes and Nicole agrees. Holly asks if they can have chicken nuggets and chips and if Mrs Lyubevsky will let them stay up until half nine and Nicole agrees to that too. In a hurry she gets them into the bathroom where she showers them hastily before helping them into their pyjamas. Once they are settled on the couch downstairs, she slips back upstairs to her bedroom.

There is no new message from Mark and she lets out a sigh of relief. Scrolling with her thumb then she checks the route on Google Maps to the meet point in Inchicore. It's not too far from their house and there are no traffic alerts so she guesses it should be alright. In silence she takes off her work clothes and puts on a pair of jeans, white trainers and a plain black wool sweater. The laptop is down in the office and she makes a mental note to double check it before she leaves, but she won't take it with her because she knows what she has to do.

Cold air blows through the bedroom window. She notices it hasn't been shut properly and walks over to pull it tight, cross-checking it a second time to be certain it's locked firm. Then she folds her arms across her chest, shivering as she stares into the darkness outside. Her leg is starting to shake and she tries to still it.

By midnight tonight she reminds herself, all this will be over.

20

Friday, November 17,
Evening

Chris Ashton quickens his pace, lengthening his stride to catch up with the man walking in front of him. From behind, he can see he wears a black knee-length overcoat. The cut tells him it's expensive and the man carries an umbrella in his hand which clicks against the bricked pavement as he walks. Chris does not want to surprise him, but guesses he might be the right person to ask.

Approaching carefully, he manoeuvres so he's alongside him. 'I'm sorry,' he turns casually, giving the stranger one of his friendliest smiles. 'I was wondering if you might be able to help me?' The man pauses, clearly a little surprised. He sports a beard and wears a red scarf. Chris has seen him around a few times coming in and out of the apartment block. He looks Chris up and down rubbing the sides of his greying beard with his thumb and finger. He's not unfriendly but looks like he might be in a hurry.

'Yes?' He presses the tip of the umbrella into the pavement as he grips the end of the scarf and tosses it over his shoulder.

Chris points to the pedestrian gate a short distance ahead. It's the one they all use to get in and out of the block. 'Sorry, the access code to the gate. I'm afraid I've forgotten it.'

The man moves the umbrella to his other hand and Chris thinks he's going to ask him a question. 'How come he doesn't know it? What apartment does he live in?' Or perhaps advise him to contact the management company. As they are walking out of the block, he might query how he managed to get in?

71

The man lifts his umbrella and points at the gate with the steel tip. 'The code to this one or the one at the back?' Chris thinks it could be a trick question. He isn't aware of a gate at the back, although it's certainly possible.

'This one,' he replies.

The man nods, his dark eyes blinking slowly. 'Come, we'll walk together and I can show you. It's true they can be easy to forget.'

2 1

*Friday, November 17,
Night*

Cars putter and cough in the congested darkness as Nicole makes her way through traffic towards Massey's funeral home in Inchicore. The heavy rain and biting cold are working in tandem to blot out any hint of joy in the world. All she can see beyond her windscreen is a blur of light and colour, the cars a swish of red and white each time the wiper blades lift the water off the glass. She listens as the phone tells her the journey has ended and pulls in. The funeral home is a low roofed building with a black front and the lights are out. The double yellow lines come to an end just beyond it and she eases the car forward to park up. Then she turns the engine off and waits, blowing on her hands to try and get rid of the chill which has seeped inside her bones.

The car clock tells her it's 8.47 p.m. It's a main street but nobody is around, probably because of the weather. Shivering, she grips the steering wheel and waits. Very soon the black jeep appears, pulling in just ahead of her and parking with the lights on and engine running. Steadying her hands which have now started to tremble, Nicole steps out and locks the car.

Wrapping her jacket tighter she walks quickly towards the jeep and the passenger door opens. A man in a long coat gets out and stands beside it. The cabin light shines on his pale skin and dark stubble as he towers above her. Nicole sees the lower part of one of his ears is missing and looks away.

'Inside.' His long arm whips the back door further open and he points a finger towards the inside. Nicole stares, her body

73

rigid. 'Hurry up,' the man says, gripping the door in his huge hand. Finally she climbs inside and the door slams with a loud clunk, making her jump. The driver revs the engine as the second man gets into the passenger seat and the jeep screeches away from the kerb.

The heating is on high and a smell of tobacco fills the space. The driver chews something, and his jaw moves back and forth, grinding noisily. Nausea rises and Nicole tries to swallow, shifting her body and fixing her seat belt. The leather seats squeak as the belt clicks, locking her tight. Staring straight ahead, she slides her hand inside her pocket, finds her mobile phone and wraps her fingers around it.

Street lights flicker an orange glow into the car and she glances at the driver. His hair is cut short and his dark eyes stare blankly from his fleshy face. Like the second man, he is dressed in an overcoat. It's only as he turns the steering wheel that Nicole realises they are both wearing black gloves. Closing her eyes, she draws in deep breaths. For a second, she thinks of the girls at home, trying to imagine their faces, trying to guess what they've eaten and if they're still awake watching the TV. Then the thought fades, instantly replaced by the memory of a dark night many years ago when she saw a young sex worker get into an oversized four wheel drive which pulled up beside her on the street. What became of her and did she ever come home? Is this what she's voluntarily given herself up for? Has she really been that naïve? Her stomach clenches as if to crush the thought.

The man in the passenger seat turns, his face a rough wall of bone and skin. 'You have your phone?'

Nicole nods, a sick feeling clawing at her insides as she grips the phone tighter in her hand. In an instant the man's hand flicks out and he holds it in front of her face. Nicole flinches. The edges of his mouth lift into a cruel sneer but it evaporates with the cracking sound of his fingers clicking.

'Hurry up. Don't make me ask you twice.' Nicole lifts it from her pocket, trying to stop her wrist from shaking as she places it in the man's oversized palm. He drops it in his lap as the driver taps the steering wheel and takes the jeep through a green light. 'Got another or only one?' The accent isn't local, but sounds American, possibly east coast. It makes Nicole think of her childhood friend Alex, the blond haired boy who moved to Dublin from the Bronx when he was seven years old. Within days Alva, Nicole and Alex had become inseparable and Alva spent the whole summer trying to imitate his New York twang.

'Only one,' she says her voice hoarse, as the memory scatters.

'You sure?'

'Yes.' She drops her gaze to the floor and hears the sound of the phone powering down. Then the man puts it in his pocket.

'You get this back when you finish the job. No communications with anybody until we're done. Understood?'

Nodding but not looking at him, Nicole agrees, then she closes her eyes once more, not wanting to see any more than she has to, while silently pushing the sharpest key inside her coat pocket between her knuckles, the way her dad showed them when they were teenagers. She wants to believe it gives her something, anything to fight with if she had to; but as she grips it tighter and swallows, the knot in her stomach twists. It's a delusion.

The cold truth is she is utterly defenceless. No phone, no explanation to anybody of where she has gone, no way out if things go horribly wrong. It's the kind of mistake that leads to innocent girls getting sex trafficked all over the world she guesses, only realising they have given up their freedom when it's way too late.

She covers her mouth, not sure if she's going to throw up, her eyes flicking to the door handle as she considers grabbing it and pulling it open. In the same moment the driver clears his throat, his pinched eyes tracking her every movement in the front mirror and she knows there is no point. The car is moving too quickly to jump out and she can guess they've child-locked the doors before she even got inside.

The car keeps moving forward and as the engine rumbles Nicole sways with the movement of the jeep, picturing her dad, remembering the stories he used to love to tell, especially when there were friends over or there was a celebration; always holding an audience with such ease, because whenever he spoke everybody in the room knew that nothing was made up and that his work gave him insights into a dark world few would have the stomach for; and he usually had a tale of warning for the children who got to stay up beyond their bedtime, a little keepsake of wisdom. 'Life is like a game of chess,' he'd told them once, 'one false move and the queen dies.' Would he have understood what she's doing now? She desperately wants to believe so, because she knows her father would have done anything for the family. And yet she knows, in truth, her father could never have understood at all. He was a decorated police officer who spent his life fighting crime; catching people who make regrettable mistakes and end up spending years behind bars.

The kind Nicole knows she may have accidentally become.

22

Friday, November 17,
Night

Nicole cannot say how long they have been driving. Nor does she know where they are. She isn't familiar with the area of Inchicore or what lies around it and can't ever remember being there before. Maybe it's Crumlin, or possibly Drimnagh? Neighbourhoods she's heard about in the news, many times for the wrong reasons – like the sex assault on the young woman by three men when she was walking home from the bus stop last month.

The driver speaks for the first time. 'Get yourself ready.' His voice is hostile. Opening her eyes Nicole looks out through the jeep's tinted windows catching a glimmer of a street sign but it disappears instantly. In its place she sees a derelict building with boarded windows and a crumbling brick façade covered in flaking, blistered paint.

The jeep turns through an open gate between two abandoned buildings onto a wider street with no lighting where a handful of run down warehouses loom on either side of the litter strewn pavement. In the darkness the buildings look like they've been kicked, punched and finally abandoned. As they meander further inside what seems like an industrial estate Nicole peers out at the offices, some of which have discoloured newspapers covering the window glass. Slowly they round a bend passing an empty white van in front of a sign which says 'Building Supplies' before heading towards one of the units. A shuttered door begins to roll up and the driver takes them inside.

There are no lights and the air is cold when the jeep doors open. 'Shut your eyes and get out,' the driver orders. Keeping the keys tight in her right hand, Nicole fumbles with the seat belt clasp as big-boned fingers dig into her arm, dragging her from the car.

When she stands, her breathing is shallow. The air smells damp, laced with mould and she tries not to breathe it in as a smoky cloth brushes over her lips. 'Stay still,' somebody says, pulling it tight across her eyes and knotting it at the back of her head. The material snags her earlobe, squeezing the earring into the flesh of her neck and she grits her teeth. They march her then, the hold on her arm like a vice as she is led over concrete sounding flooring and hurried through twists and turns within the warehouse. Any control she once mistakenly imagined she had is now long gone.

'Please,' her voice is barely more than a rasp. 'This is a mistake.'

Nobody replies but a hand lands on her shoulder forcing her down onto a hard seat. She loses her balance and another hand shoves her back straight. The cloth has covered her nose and she opens her mouth to get some air. The knot inside her stomach twists so deep she wants to cry out but she doesn't make a sound. Instead she clenches her teeth and tries to imagine their girls, Chloe holding hands with Holly and doing a countdown before they jump from a pier into the sea, Mark watching them from the beach, his smile beaming as he rolls his head in her lap. Was that day the last time they were truly happy?

There's a scrape of a chair, bringing her back, followed by footsteps. They stop then and the noise is replaced by the sound of her own breathing. Buried deep inside the pocket of her coat, between her knuckles, she grips the key, pressing the metal point hard against her leg.

'You've met my driver and his assistant?' a computerised voice asks, its robotic tone reverberating across the damp space between them.

'Yes.'

'Good. Your car is waiting. Follow the written instructions on the driver's seat.' Nicole nods back through the half-light. 'Use the in-car satnav and don't deviate from the course.'

'OK.'

'Leave the car at the location with the keys inside. Return to collect your vehicle and go home. Do not speak to anybody about this again, ever. If you do we'll take your children.'

Nicole sways, a dry heave pushing up from deep in her stomach. The fabric moves around her eyes, thinning to show the faintest outline of a person. Immediately she clamps her eyes shut. *No.* She must not see anything. She needs to leave.

'Ready?'

'Yes.' Squeezing her knees together, she tries to stop shaking.

'Any questions?'

'Once I do this, you'll leave us alone?'

There is no reply. Her heart begins to thump and somebody makes a noise, like they are rising to their feet. Instinctively her body braces.

There's a sharp sting across the side of her cheek as something collides with the side of her face, knocking her off balance to the ground. Inside her ear she can only hear a high pitched noise. When she puts the palms of her hands to the ground to push herself up the dirt clings to her skin.

Then the mechanical voice replies. 'Guess you'll have to wait and see.'

23

Friday, November 17,
Night

The fresh air is like a release and Nicole gasps, sucking it deep inside her lungs. Rain is falling and she stands with her face tilted to the sky. A shove in the back propels her forward and she cries out when her shin smacks metal. Another push and she's inside the car, the door slamming so violently the vibrations drum through her back. Wincing, she tugs the blindfold down and grips her leg.

The car lights are on and the seat belt reminder chimes. The men have already disappeared back inside and a clatter of rolling steel follows as the hatch shuts. The engine idles and the satnav shines from the centre of the dashboard, waiting for her to begin.

'Christ!' she throws her head back, the ache on the side of her jaw hot and stinging, the buzz inside her ear refusing to quiet. The seat belt reminder chimes louder and she snatches it from its holder. Even now she can't stop dreaming of sprinting back, begging that they call it all off but the wipers judder across the windscreen pulling her back to reality and she clips the seat belt. It's futile. These people are ruthless. They won't listen to her pleas.

The destination is already keyed into the satnav; the drive time says thirty-six minutes. Her hand stops shaking as she grips her fingers round the huge automatic gear lever, squeezing it with her thumb to switch it into drive mode. The written instructions on the passenger seat are one line long but nothing more.

Drop the car at Woodtown Cemetery. Return home. Do not speak of this again.

'Woodtown Cemetery?' she whispers, tapping the screen to begin the journey while pushing down on the accelerator. It isn't somewhere she's ever been, but she has heard of it; it's on the way to the ancient Hellfire Club, a place you only went to if you sold your soul to the devil.

The engine of the BMW is far more powerful than her own car and it moves quickly. Windscreen wipers automatically start, beating rhythmically back and forth across the glass, and she leans forward trying to steady her breathing. The map tells her what to do and she looks straight ahead at the dark road, turning and following each monotonous command.

Very soon she finds herself on the M50 travelling south but she doesn't have to go far because the drive time says twenty minutes and a distance of eleven kilometres. After a short stretch she is guided off the motorway and onto a minor two lane road with no lighting.

'Don't think.' Nicole whispers the words over and over like a mantra, her hands gripping the steering wheel tight, every muscle in her body stiff.

The big car coasts through the darkness but the minutes crawl and she grits her teeth. Forcing herself to concentrate, she starts to dream of home, deliberately picturing it in her mind, pushing her thoughts from the here and now.

It's the weekend and she's rising from a warm bed on a Saturday morning. Mark is coming up the stairs and she can smell the fresh coffee he carries in his hand. He's already been to the bakery to buy a sourdough loaf and there are two slices of it freshly toasted on a plate. From the living room comes the sound of laughter as the girls huddle together on the sofa watching cartoons on TV. The comfortable pillows Mark bought for her, the ones she covered with Egyptian cotton cases, are plumped just right and she sits up, stretching out her arms.

It's going to be a special day. A family day.

But then she hears a noise.

It's behind her.

It's inside the car.

24

Friday, November 17,
Night

Thump! It comes from the boot. Sharp and loud.

Nicole twists around to scan the back seats, which reveal nothing, and immediately the car loses control. It veers across the centre line into the oncoming lane. The rooftop lights from another vehicle flash twice and the powerful beams dazzle her eyes.

She ducks her head and swerves as the loud truck horn flares, its huge rig thundering past, splashing her window with a spray of water, a thump of air pushing and dragging against the car. The car pulls sideways and with both hands she clutches the steering wheel, holding it firm as the tyres screech on the wet tarmac.

There is another loud *thump*. The air squeezes from Nicole's lungs and her eyes widen. There is someone in the boot of the car. There is someone trying to escape.

Her eyes flick to the satnav screen which tells her there are seven minutes remaining to the destination. Sweat trickles between her shoulder blades and she buzzes the window down, her face suddenly too hot, the air inside the cabin too stuffy. Rain spatters her face, the heavy drops clouding her eyes and she shuts it immediately. With her sleeve she wipes the water off and presses her foot to the accelerator, feeling an instant tug underneath the seat as the big engine rumbles, surging forward.

A minute passes and the screen shows the destination time drop to six minutes, just as the voice directs her off onto what looks like a narrow country road. Nicole listens to the wipers as they beat across the windscreen, the sound a welcome distraction from the noise of her own breathing.

Thump. The sound comes again, louder this time, and somebody shouts muffled words she can't understand.

When her foot jabs the brake pedal it hits the floor of the footwell so hard that the car swerves, sending the tyres into a skid. The wheels screech and the stench of burning rubber seeps inside the cabin. There's a sharp jolt through her body as it surges forward before the belt catches across her chest, snapping her back in the seat.

Through the blur of the windscreen she can see only darkness and the beams of her own car illuminating the empty road. Rain patters on the roof and the engine idles as she takes a second to catch her breath.

Her arm is stiff as she elbows the door open to step out. The rain pelts hard on her face when she runs to the edge of the road, frantically searching for anything she could use to defend herself. But she knows she has to do this now. She can't go on pretending she doesn't know about the person in the boot; the person is clearly desperate to break free.

Spotting a piece of branch she bends down and tugs it loose from the grass.

Steam rises from her shoulders as she approaches the back of the car, gripping the branch tighter while pressing the fob to release the boot lid. There's a gentle pop and the lid slowly rises to reveal a large black plastic bag, its thick coils of masking tape lit faintly by the side light.

With her stick raised high, she reaches in to touch it but instantly pulls back. There is something warm and sticky on her fingers and when she looks closer she sees blood.

Frantically she rubs it on her sleeve, but a rustling noise interrupts her. The bag is now upright and moving towards her.

'No!' Gasping, she lunges with the stick but the body in the bag groans and pushes forwards, straining against the masking tape which binds its sides.

Snap. The branch disintegrates and her hand punches into the plastic folds. There is a grunt as it stops moving but then instantly recovers and leans further out. The person is escaping.

Panicking she grabs the boot in her hands to slam it, but it slips from her fingers. 'Shit.' The bag slaps against her chest and she jumps back. For a second she is frozen, torn between setting the victim free, because she knows that's what they are no matter what they've done; but her hands tremble by her sides as she stares at the trapped prisoner who struggles blindly, grunting with distress. If she does that the people she has only just got away from will come not only for her but for the very people she has been trying to help all along: her family. Turning her face to the sky she screams as the raindrops cloud her eyes, stinging as they stream down her face. 'I'm sorry,' she then whispers, both hands shoving the prisoner hard. *Thump*. Bone collides with steel and the bag collapses. Quickly she reaches in, gripping the plastic between her fingers, tearing a hole in the middle of it. Now they can breathe, she hopes. They must be able to breathe.

The boot lid whines and closes with a soft click. Shielding her face from the rain she runs to the driver's seat and gets in. A sob pushes up from deep inside as she wipes her face, her stomach clenching when the sleeve of her coat catches the wiper stick. They jerk frantically across the windscreen and the car lurches forward onto the road.

The satnav has started again and her eyes fill with tears as it drones robotically, directing her further into the murky darkness.

25

Friday, November 17,
Late Night

In ten minutes time it will be midnight. After she dropped off the BMW Nicole ran from the car and didn't look back. The cemetery was a distance from the village, down an almost deserted track, so only when she had run fifteen minutes in the heavy rain did she reach it and find an unregistered taxi for hire. Shivering and wild eyed, she managed to give the location of her parked car to the driver but offered nothing more.

Now back home in Rathgar, she pushes the gate inwards and halts her stride, pulling away strands of hair which hang limply in front of her eyes. Trying to steady her breathing, she wraps them behind her ear and starts to walk, but before she can get to the front door Mrs Lyubevsky draws it back and steps out.

'Nicole, is everything alright?' Their elderly neighbour wraps her cardigan around her wizened body, a frightened look in her eyes. Her grey hair is pulled into a tight bun and she stares at Nicole's saturated clothes. 'My god, you are soaked to the skin. What on earth happened to you?'

Nicole places a hand on the porch wall, fighting to keep her body upright. She needs to focus, to thank her quickly and let her go. 'Our car broke down. It's . . . ' the words dry up. What could explain her appearance? Her eyes drop to her grey coat where she has rubbed the blood from the body bag on her sleeve. The dark smear has been blotted out by rain but she folds her hand beneath the other arm to hide it. 'Let's not get into that now when it's so late and you need to get to bed, Nina.'

Mrs Lyubevsky frowns and holds out a phone.

Immediately Nicole recognises it. 'How do you have my phone?'

'It was dropped through the letterbox about an hour ago. I heard a noise and when I went to the hallway, it was lying on the floor.' Nicole takes it from her, swallowing as the elderly woman draws her cardigan tighter. 'Where's Mark? Wasn't he with you?'

Nicole stares at the phone, trying to understand how Mark cannot be back yet. There are no missed calls but the workshop must have ended hours ago. Mrs Lyubevsky tilts her head.

'Mark is coming.' Nicole hooks her arm over the elderly woman's shoulder. 'Let's get you home, Nina.'

They walk through the rain up to the front door of Mrs Lyubevsky's house, Nicole easing her constantly forward, pushing against the resistance she can feel coiled inside her tiny, hunched body.

'Nicole, your hands are shaking. If there's something wrong you should tell me, please.' At last Mrs Lyubevsky opens her door but doesn't go inside.

'I'm fine, Nina. Really.' Mrs Lyubevsky grips the door and shakes her head. With a resigned shrug, she gives in and steps into her house.

When the latch to the front door clicks Nicole runs. Seconds later she is upstairs inside her house but finds Chloe and Holly asleep in their beds. Holding her head in her hands, she hurries to the kitchen.

'Mark, where the fuck are you?' she seethes through clenched teeth, thumb scrolling her phone. Still there are no messages from him or missed calls. Pulling up his number then, she rings it but the line is dead; when she checks his WhatsApp she sees he hasn't been active since yesterday. A tear trips down her cheek as she paces from the living room to the office.

Then she hears the noise. Jolting she turns her head round to see the laptop open and shining in the darkness inside the side office.

Click. Her heart thumps and she moves across to it, her fingers gripping the back of the chair behind the desk. *Hum.* The screen illuminates blue before immediately fading to black and she holds her breath. *Whir.* The fan begins to whine as the white words cast their pale light across her face.

You know what you've done. Don't you?

Swallowing she types. *What have I done?*

Come on Nicole, you know.

Collapsing into the seat, she stares at the screen, the exhaustion in every muscle too much. There is a strange taste in her mouth and when she touches her tongue it leaves blood on her finger. The image of the body inside the bag returns, the way the person's head thumped off the lid of the boot, the sound of the gag in their mouth as they cried out, the heavy thud of their body as it fell back inside the hold. When she turns her hands she sees they are stained red. In a second her stomach twists and she bends down, lunging for the steel bin by her feet. The vomit spews from her mouth and lands inside it.

Immediately she types.

Tell me you fucker.

You know who was in the bag?

Who?

Your dearest husband, Mark.

26

Friday, November 17,
Late Night

Her hand clamps her mouth just in time to muffle the scream. Squeezing it harder she shuts her eyes. It seems impossible that this can actually be happening. She rocks back and forth, the struggle not to make a sound almost too much.

Again she types.

You're lying.

Where is he then? You think he's just late?

Nicole stares into the darkness. *What are you saying?*

There is no workshop.

She slides her elbows on to the desk, sinking forward, clutching her head between her hands. She must not give up. That's the only thought she has now. If Mark really is gone, then she's the only one who knows. She's the only one who can bring him back.

What do you want?

You have just kidnapped your own husband. The car you used has cameras inside and out with logged footage of you committing this act. We have bank records of you accepting one million euros, establishing motive for you to eliminate your husband who is not in agreement with your plans to launder the stolen funds. We have transcripts of your communications accepting your role in the operation. But . . .

The stench of vomit rises.

. . . more importantly we have your husband. And if you want him back you won't go to the police. Going to the police will be disastrous for you. But for Mark it will be fatal.

What do you want me to do?

Wait and see.

'Wait and see?' Nicole repeats the words, her body becoming still. The smell of the abandoned warehouse comes back to her. Squeezing her eyes shut, she waits, hoping the thumping inside her chest will slow. But it doesn't; her heart cannot slow. To get Mark back she must agree to their terms.

Sitting up, she jabs at the keys. *Who are you?*

The Paymaster.

Just tell me what you want. Her fingers flick to her temples and she keeps them there, pressing hard. The air in the office is cold and she shivers.

Tell a soul or go to the police you never see Mark again. Raise no alarms, arouse no suspicion. We'll be in touch.

27

Instantly Nicole rises to her feet and runs to the bathroom, the bin in her hands, her face twisted with pain. At the toilet bowl, she sinks to her knees, stomach churning, but nothing more comes up.

With a heave she gets to her feet, drops the bin and sits on the flattened toilet seat. Who is the Paymaster? Where is Mark now?

The pounding in her head grows as she runs up the stairs to their bedroom, her feet moving lightly so as not to wake the girls. Pulling open the wardrobe doors she plucks each hanger from the rack, patting down Mark's clothes, her phone pressed flat against her ear as she calls his number again and again. 'The number you have dialled is not in service.'

She flings the phone on the bed, instantly busying herself with his jackets and trousers, patting down his shirts, shaking out every last one of his shoes, but all she finds is a half-finished tissue packet, a few coins, a solitary used bus ticket dated Monday, and a Tesco receipt from two weeks ago.

The lids of her eyes are pressing down like weights and she gives in, collapsing on the bed. The energy she had seconds ago is fading. Face down, she breathes in, the smell of Mark still fresh on the sheets as her fingers reach out and grip the duvet. The image of the bag in the boot returns; once again it lurches towards her, groaning. Could it really have been Mark? How can she know? Outside the rain drips in blurry lines down the window glass.

Her eyes open then as a new idea forms. She could get into her car and drive to where she did the drop off. But as soon as she thinks this she realises it can't work; she can't leave her girls and if she took them with her and met the same people there when she arrived, what then? It's not an option; and she knows most likely the people have already come and taken Mark and the car away. She'd only be attempting something doomed to fail which would alert her kids to what's happened. The threat replays inside her head. *Tell a soul and you'll never see Mark again*. She won't risk it.

She keeps thinking until something else occurs to her then. Social media. It's exactly where to begin. Sitting back up she takes her phone and opens her apps: Facebook, WhatsApp, Instagram, but immediately they reveal that Mark hasn't used any of them in days.

Glancing around the room she sees the iPad on the bedside table and goes to pick it up. Maybe the search history will yield something? But seconds later her heart sinks – it has all been deleted, even the cookies too. Why? The only person who could have done this is Mark. She remembers the Find My app then and opens it. *No location found.*

She pauses, placing the iPad back down on the bed and her head dips as the tears well in her eyes. The last of her energy is dwindling but she mustn't give up.

Seconds later she is back downstairs, throwing on her shoes, grabbing keys and running out to check her car. Sweat drips from her forehead as she jerks the glove compartment open, rummages through old service bills, a de-icer, a hairbrush. Nothing. She keeps going, running her hand along the side pockets of the doors, the centre section, even under the seats and the pockets behind – a green sports sock, a dropped lolly covered in hair and grit, a crushed Coke can and an empty crisp packet, a doll missing her head and arm – nothing. Slamming the door shut, she looks for Mark's car, only now seeing that it isn't there. When did he take it and how long has it been gone?

The rain is falling again, flattening her hair and dripping off her face. Wide eyed, she stares down the road as her body begins to shake. Something stirs in front of her and when she looks up a fox slips between two parked cars, eyeing her warily before jumping a wall and disappearing. Why can't she find a single trace of Mark? She turns to go back inside when she sees a face at the window next door. Mrs Lyubevsky is staring at her, peering down from the upstairs bedroom window, her gaze stern, her brow furrowed.

The curtain moves, shielding her from view. Instantly the light in her neighbour's house turns off. But Nicole has already remembered something else now. Mark's laptop.

Mopping her face with her sleeve, she runs back upstairs to their bedroom and drops to her knees, shoving Mark's shoes out from under the bed while trying not to breathe the dust that kicks up from the carpet. Moments later her fingers tap the plastic top and she drags it out.

Carefully she places it on the chest of drawers, surprised to hear the hard drive still humming and awake. Eventually the screen flickers and Nicole's heart races, but seconds later it blanks again, leaving a white cursor blinking in the corner.

Tears brim in her eyes as she storms from the room to rush back down the stairs. In the hallway she fails to see Holly's welly as it catches the ball of her foot.

It squeaks when it slides across the floor, knocking her off balance. Her hands clutch at the air but already she is falling. A dull thumping noise follows.

Blood smudges the sharp edge of the radiator cover and she stops struggling.

28

Saturday, November 18,
Morning

'Mum?' Chloe's fingers touch her cheek gently. 'Oh god, Mum, come on, wake up.' She places both hands on Nicole's shoulders and shakes them now. The bloodstain on the white radiator panel in the hallway has caught her eye. It snakes in an arc to the corner of Nicole's head. Chloe traces a finger across it before jerking it away. 'Mum!?'

With a groan Nicole opens her eyes. 'Chloe sweetheart, what's wrong?' Her mouth is dry, the words little more than a rasp. As her eyelids adjust to the light they flicker and she takes in Chloe's worried face. Both her legs are sprawled at an odd angle to her body and cold to the touch. Gritting her teeth, she sits up.

'Jesus, Mum!' Chloe throws her arms around her mother and Nicole clings to her. 'What are you doing down here in the hall?' When Chloe's gaze switches to the dried blood on the radiator panel Nicole sees it for the first time.

'Chloe love, listen to me please.' There are tears in her daughter's eyes. She knows she must calm her down gently. If she doesn't the situation will get worse. The events tumble back into her mind in a rush: the stairs, the fall, the blinding stab of pain.

Chloe's fingers have moved to Nicole's head. When she lifts them away tiny flecks of dried blood fall from their tips. 'Mum what happened?'

'What time is it, love?' Nicole's voice is hoarse and faint.

'It's ten past nine.' Chloe grabs Nicole's phone from where it has fallen on the floor.

'Is Holly still in bed?'

Chloe nods. 'Mum, we have to call the ambulance.'

'Wait.' *Arouse no suspicion, raise no alarms.* She remembers the Paymaster's order. She must make sure she follows it at all costs. But her mind is groggy and when she looks again Chloe has run to the kitchen. 'Chloe what are you doing? I want to try our doctor first.'

Chloe returns, her face on the verge of tears, the phone pressed to her ear and ringing.

'Who are you calling?' Nicole asks.

'The doctor. His card was on our fridge. Look,' she holds out the phone and Nicole recognises the name of their GP.

'Hello?' They both hear the doctor's voice.

'Dr Fenton, my mum needs to see you now.'

'Who is this?'

Chloe hastily places the phone in Nicole's hand.

'Doctor Fenton?'

'Yes?'

'It's Nicole Reid.' Pressing down into the floor Nicole tries to sit up and a stab of pain shoots through the back of her head. Her mouth opens wide and she winces. She needs to keep it simple. To make him help her. 'I'm sorry,' she stops to take a breath, waiting for the pain to ease. 'I know this is out of hours, but I've had an accident at my home. I've banged my head.'

'Did you call an ambulance?'

'I don't think . . . ' She pauses, searching for the right words, then clears her throat. 'I'm sorry but I'd prefer to be checked privately. Please.'

The line goes quiet and Chloe stares at her anxiously.

'Well, I did have paperwork to catch up on this morning, so I'm happy to come in and treat you. But if it's bad I will need to recommend a trip to A&E. Is that OK?'

'I understand.' Nicole leans back, closes her eyes and cuts the line. There's a soft thud as her head rolls against the hallway wall. Her face creases and she bites down hard.

Chloe has wrapped her arms around her again and is starting to sob. 'It's going to be OK, Mum.'

Nicole strokes her hair, using her other hand to scroll through her contacts. When she finds Alva, she presses call.

29

'Any concussion?' Dr Fenton, teases the hair away from Nicole's scalp, dabbing lightly with cotton wool. The colour of the wool changes from white to deep red. His rubber gloves squeak and a smell of disinfectant lingers in the air inside his surgery. Nicole squints as the glare from the white walls assaults her eyes.

How long was she concussed? Minutes? Hours? She has no clue. What she can say for certain is that the radiator panel knocked her out cold when it cracked against the back of her head, but she knows if she tells the doctor this he could insist on her going into hospital for tests. What if they keep her in? It means she can't look for Mark. Tracing Mark is the only thing that matters now.

'No,' she replies. 'I don't think so.'

'Can you describe what happened?' The doctor places a soaked cotton ball on a steel tray.

'I was coming down the stairs to get breakfast ready when I slipped on one of the girl's wellies and that was it.'

'And then your daughter Chloe found you?'

'Yes. She came out of the living room when she heard the noise.' Nicole goes quiet but the doctor doesn't reply. 'I think I was dazed, just for a minute or two, and I strained my back, so Chloe found my phone and helped me make the call.'

The doctor takes another cotton ball and applies it to the cut. 'It must have given you a terrible fright. Any vomiting or acute headache?'

'No.'

'Good.' He rearranges her hair, doing his best to make it tidy. 'How's the pain now?'

Nicole lets her breath out slowly. 'Manageable, I think.'

Dr Fenton slips back to his desk, peeling the gloves from his hands. 'I've used glue stitches on it to try and make it less painful for you. They normally heal over in about five to ten days but you need to keep it dry and avoid stretching the skin.'

'I'm OK then?'

Dr Fenton's eyes soften. 'I hope so, Nicole. The cut's not too deep and the key indicators of trauma are absent. I expect it will hurt like hell for a week or so, but it should heal.' He takes a pad from his desk and begins to write. 'I'm giving you a prescription for painkillers so if you feel the need you can take them but use them as sparingly as you can.' He puts his reading glasses back on, finishes writing and signs. Then he passes it across the desk.

Nicole stands up. The doctor rises too.

'Nicole,' he hesitates, the smallest trace of a frown taking shape on his brow, 'is everything alright?' Nicole's heart thumps and she looks at him blankly. 'I mean, with you, at home?'

'Yes.'

'You did tell Mark obviously?'

Nicole signals a 'yes' by nodding her head but she doesn't look at him. Instead she lets her eyes fall to the floor and keeps them there.

'Good,' he then says a little uncertainly. 'Well, I trust he'll look after you for the next two weeks.' When Nicole glances up she sees the doctor is smiling but there are worry lines in his brow. 'You're going to need to rest and take it easy.' Holding the door open, he waits patiently and Nicole steps forward. 'Sorry, Nicole. Just one last thing.' Taking off his reading glasses, he slots them into the chest pocket of his sports jacket. 'Was there a particular reason you came here rather than A&E?'

'Yes.' Nicole takes a deep breath and clears her throat. 'I wanted an expert assessment and I guessed this would be the best place to get it.'

Dr Fenton bows. 'Of course. Well, if you have any problems with the stitches don't hesitate to call. And please pass Mark my regards.'

30

Eve yawns and stretches out, rolling over the white sheets of the queen size cherrywood bed. It's way too big for one person. She's felt that ever since David moved out. It's the last thing she ever imagined she'd admit but it needs a man, to make it less vast, less surplus.

Snatching one of the oversized pillows from the other side of the bed she props herself up to a half sitting position and spreads her arms out wide. Lily's on a sleepover so there's no need for her to make breakfast. It's Lily's first since Eve began the divorce proceedings and a huge relief when she finally agreed to stay over at her friend Clodagh Hopkins' house. For a while Eve feared the whole thing had got too much for her daughter and that she no longer wanted to do all the things she used to most enjoy. Lily, who would always skip off to a friend's house without even an invitation had become almost afraid to leave the house. And the worst part of it for Eve, was the house no longer felt like home. With David gone, there was less washing to do, less stacking of the dishwasher, less discussions over who got first choice on the TV. Just less fuss about everything. And yet it didn't create the change Eve hoped it would. The house didn't feel warmer, or more inviting. Of course the arguing had stopped, but so too, it seemed, had the heartbeat of their home. This home they had lived in all together for more than ten years, the one she had land-scaped front and back, painted inside, brought home their first and only child to live in, had now become merely a set of elegantly

99

proportioned rooms with a red brick façade. The kind house hunters all across the city would drool over when leafing through their Sunday papers, when they mapped dreams of their happy futures; the same dream Eve imagined for herself not long ago.

Recently she decided that she could never mention any of this to Lily. Her daughter had to be protected, it was only fair. If the only thing Eve could think about was moving out and finding something else then she'd only ever mention it when she was sure she had found the right replacement.

But today she simply wants to talk to Nicole. She sits fully up and her head pounds. She drank too much wine last night but couldn't help herself. Drinking David's favourite wine, as she tapped and clicked the keys of her laptop past midnight, before pouring a third of the bottle down the sink and falling into bed, just left her giddy.

She reaches for her phone. There's a reminder on it to do the annual winter beach clean today, a day she always really enjoys, even when hungover. Beneath it is a message from her assistant, Sarah, reminding her that her pro bono work for the Society of Deaf Children is on Tuesday. She replies to it quickly, thanking Sarah generously, and telling her she's looking forward to it. Then lying back down, she scrolls for Nicole's number. Did her friend sleep properly last night, she wonders? With a tap, she hits her number and waits for it to ring. No answer.

A message arrives then. She looks down, hoping it might be Mark but sees it is work. She purses her lips, choosing to ignore it. Mark hasn't been answering her texts but that's OK. She knows he will eventually.

3 1

Saturday, November 18,
Mid-Morning

Alva stirs the eggs in the pan, dropping in a thick wedge of butter. It starts to melt and the scent wafts out of the kitchen over to the dining table where Nicole sits. The old kettle rattles as it starts to heat up.

'Yeah,' Alva smiles, glancing over, 'I know. That ancient thing is like a fucking ship's engine working in a storm isn't it. Shaun keeps telling us it's got sentimental value.' She rolls her eyes, licking a finger and picking up the pepper grinder. A quick double twist and she puts it back down, stirring some more with the wooden spoon. 'I think he just couldn't be arsed dropping into Currys to grab a new one.' Alva spoons out the scrambled eggs onto two plates. The oil in the pan crackles releasing the smell of fried bacon and it resurrects memories of family breakfasts. It was what their mum cooked for the family sometimes on a Sunday, and then if they were lucky, there'd be fruit scones afterwards with jam and whipped cream. Because Nicole liked to help, their mum always called Nicole the cook, but Nicole knows Alva made the best breakfast.

Nicole's phone rings.

'You can answer it, I don't mind.' Alva picks up the plates and smiles as she walks over. When Nicole sees Eve's name she mutes it, tensing as she places it back inside her pocket.

'It's not important, I'll speak with her later.'

The plates clank on the table and Alva uses a tea-towel to push Nicole's across to her. 'Mind those, they're hot, as your mammy used to say.' She inhales the salty tang of the meat and feels the ache at the back of her head just starting to retreat now that she's taken two of the painkillers Dr Fenton prescribed. For a fleeting second she thinks she could just forget everything; the horror of last night, the disbelief of kidnapping her own husband, the Paymaster's order not to tell a living soul if she wants to get Mark back. She won't forget but she has to try to eat the food Alva's made a big effort to cook for her.

Alva clears some schoolbooks and newspapers off the table with a sweep of her arm. It's been a while since Nicole has been at her sister's house and despite the slowly tightening knot in her stomach, it makes her smile. It couldn't be more different from her own: shoes and coats everywhere; unwashed pots and pans in the sink; half-drunk cups of tea on every shelf; sports jerseys scattered at random. Like it was when they were small, she thinks. Her mouth waters and she takes a piece of toast.

Alva picks up a pencil case and flings it casually onto an armchair. 'Sorry about the mess. I know, it's always like a bomb blast in here, isn't it?' The kettle finally boils, clattering around on the kitchen counter, the steam from its spout puffing towards them like a plume of smoke.

Nicole moves to get up. 'I'll make the tea will I?'

'No,' Alva presses down gently on her forearm, 'don't you move a muscle. Let me get that. You eat something. You need some food in you after what's happened. That was a long night.' As she slips to the kitchen Nicole picks up her knife and fork. At least in the kitchen her sister can't see her face when she replies to her questions. Slowly, she starts to eat, chewing the eggs and toast gently so as not to aggravate the wound at the back of her head.

'Of all the luck?' Alva cleans out the teapot, heats it up with a hot drop of boiling water and rinses it again. Dropping two teabags inside, she fills it. 'What are the chances of slipping on your kids' wellies and doing that?' When she sits back down at the table she places their mother's old teapot down on the table, opens the lid, just like their mam always did too, stirs three times before replacing the lid with a light rattle, and then pours them each a swiftly brewed mug. 'Here, taste that and see if it's strong enough for you.'

Nicole stirs it, watching the milk turn brown as it swirls inside the cup. Neither of them speak for a bit. Then the toaster pops up and Alva slips away to return with two fresh slices of toast. The plate plonks down between them and Nicole lifts the spoon out from the mug.

'Think you ought to have that properly stirred at this point,' Alva grins.

Nicole returns a faint smile and reaches for her tea, blowing on it and hoping Alva will forget their earlier conversation, because she had just been asking after Mark when Nicole excused herself to go to the toilet. Now as her sister sits close, observing her as she clings to the mug, she isn't sure at all. The need to confess is so strong again, to start from the beginning and put it all out there.

Tears well in her eyes when she finally swallows some tea.

'Now, listen,' Alva forks a piece of bacon, dips it into her egg and eats it. 'I don't want you even thinking about the girls. They're fine with us for as long as you need. You just have to rest and recuperate and make the most of these days off work. I know it's just been one big mess for you this past while so I want you to take it easy.' Nicole places her tea down, picks up her knife and fork and cuts a piece of sausage. 'Shaun has them all, and we've still got that old banger with the extra row of seats in the back so he's fine for all the dropping and collecting. It'll be nice for our two to hang out with the girls as well. They'll all get a bit of a break from the routine. Yeah?' Nicole chews slowly and nods as Alva spreads some butter on a piece of toast. 'You'll be alright. And you did the right thing going to that GP of yours. You never know what you're going to get when you run into A&E.'

'Thanks.'

'Come on, tuck in.' She taps Nicole's wrist, gesturing towards the plate with a tilt of her head. 'Can't have me cooking all that for nothing, you know.' Nicole starts to eat, the tension inside her stomach finally easing but then Alva's phone vibrates.

'Crap.' Alva stares at it, her face turning serious. 'Really sorry, Nic but I'm going to have to head off.'

'A case?'

'Yeah, it's the one I mentioned to you last time. The Doherty one.' She sighs heavily.

The knot returns inside Nicole's stomach. 'Doherty?' She remembers the name now. 'Didn't dad put a Doherty behind bars in a big case years ago?'

Alva nods, her face solemn. 'He did, Nic. That was the mother. She was an evil woman but she's dead now.'

'So who's this?'

'The daughter. She's taken over at the helm. Like the mother, she's bad news.' Alva picks up her mug, swigs a mouthful of tea. There's a bang when it lands back on the table. 'There's a lot to this. A lot I unfortunately can't go into for obvious reasons but I really want to get her, and those she's working with.'

Nicole nods. It's unusual to see Alva tense up so suddenly. She would like to ask her more questions, to understand what it is about the Doherty case that means so much but she knows it wouldn't be fair. Alva will tell her when the time is right. She trusts her.

'But you take your time and relax here as long as you like. Alright?' Alva says, pulling a friendly smile back into place and kissing Nicole on the cheek.

Nicole waves her out, putting her knife and fork down onto the plate. As soon as the door shuts she rises to her feet. It just occurs to her that if the hacker is watching her and knows she's gone to Alva's they could wrongly assume that she's revealed something.

Tensing she hurries across to the dishwasher with the plates. She needs to get away. She needs to find Mark.

32

Saturday, November 18,
Afternoon

'Ken speaking?'

Tucking Mark's laptop under her arm, she presses the phone closer to her ear. It's vital she keeps it casual. She can't risk raising his suspicion that something's wrong. 'Ken, hi, it's Nicole.'

'Oh?' He sounds surprised.

'Mark Reid's wife.'

'Yes, Nicole, of course. How are you keeping?'

Nicole pauses, her eyes searching up and down the street for the laptop repair shop. Mark said he always took his devices to Tech Savvy in Dunleary whenever they needed fixing, even though she could never understand why, since it's virtually the other side of the city. 'Yeah, good. And you.'

'Great. Tell me, what's up?'

There's a side street on the left and she walks down it. 'I'm actually trying to get hold of Mark and I know you two went for a run on Thursday morning and then went down to stay in your place in Wicklow. So I was wondering if maybe you'd been out with him since?'

The line goes silent.

'Nicole?' Ken's voice sounds solemn.

'Yes?'

'I haven't seen Mark in months.' *Tell a soul or go to the police you never see Mark again.* The words reverberate through her head. It's all she can think. But she can't do that. She needs to know more. Is it really true what Ken is telling her?

105

'I'm so sorry.' The side street joins the high street and she sees the laptop shop. 'I've got this confused. It was Vincent Gaygan he was meeting.'

'That's OK.'

'He's got a place down in Wicklow too so I'm always mixing them up, but where is your place exactly? I remember Melony mentioning it to me except I've forgotten.'

'It's one mile past Roundwood.' Nicole hears the sound of keys pressing on Ken's phone. 'There, I just sent you the Eircode. You two must come down sometime.' Nicole opens the door and enters the shop as her phone pings. 'Listen I'm sorry to cut you short here but I've a Zoom meeting starting now. Is everything OK?'

'Everything's fine, Ken.' The man behind the counter looks at her expectantly. 'My mistake. I won't keep you.' Exhaling she ends the call. Then she walks to the man behind the counter and hands over Mark's laptop.

Nicole stares at the ground as she trudges back to her car. The shop repair man was clear, Mark's laptop was completely erased. 'Wiped clean.' Those were his exact words. Somebody wiped it. Why would Mark do that? And Ken didn't sound like he was lying. He'd have no reason to. Which means Mark never went to Ken's house in Wicklow but lied about that too. Why?

Pressing down on the fob she listens to the car unlock but doesn't get in. Instead she leans against it, thinking. Perhaps if she could retrace the location of the industrial estate where she did the car collection last night it could give her a start? The tightness in her chest grows as she tries to remember. Then all at once it comes back to her: the smell of tobacco inside the black jeep, the noise of the driver chewing, the eerie voice of the Paymaster as he talked through a voice distorter. Gripping the laptop tighter, she closes her eyes and takes a breath, but the smoky smell of the blindfold they used on her returns and she gasps.

'Everything OK?'

Spinning, Nicole sees a tall man with sandy hair standing very close to her. He stares at her with intense blue eyes and she finds herself stepping back. 'What?'

'I saw you this morning and it looked like something had happened?' Chris Ashton wears a high-vis yellow rain jacket and black cycling leggings. For a second Nicole's mind goes blank but then slowly it comes to her. The bike helmet is gone but she recognises the dimple in his chin. It's the courier who dropped Rocky to their house when he got injured. She's almost certain it's the man Holly saw watching them the day they left Dr Fenton's office. His eyes shift to Mark's laptop as she fumbles for her car keys. Her heart starts to drum. Who is he? What does he want?

'Just a late night.' Finally she finds the keys and pulls the car door open.

Chris steps closer. 'Wait. Something is wrong. I can tell.'

Jumping into the driver's seat, Nicole goes to put her key into the ignition but drops it. The man has moved closer again. He bends down to the window, resting his hands on his knees as he leans over. 'I haven't seen Mark around and I was worried. Has he gone away?'

'What? Do you know my husband?' Snatching the keys from beneath her feet she puts them into the ignition.

Chris's eyes flick to the rear of the car and he turns, reaching a hand for the back door handle. 'Let me in so I can explain.'

Nicole's heart pounds as the engine starts. Adrenaline shoots through her veins. She needs to get away. Immediately. The gearbox crunches as she grinds the stick into first. With a loud screech the car lurches forward, pulling the handle free from the man's fingers. In her mirror Nicole watches as he stands up tall and shakes his hand out, his gaze following her until she is out of sight.

33

Saturday, November 18,
Afternoon

Alone by the train window, Nicole sits and stares blankly out
at the countryside as it whizzes by, partially blurred by the tears
which keep threatening to spill from her eyes. The memory of last
night's events keep resurfacing, each jolt of the train's carriage
making her shift anxiously, each person that walks down the centre aisle causing her eyes to glance up warily.

Stifling a groan, she presses her fingers into the side of her neck
and kneads the knot which refuses to go away. She knows the laptop is her line back to the Paymaster but she doesn't want contact.
Not before she finds one clue to where Mark has gone.

Taking her phone from her pocket she reads back over the
message she sent earlier to Colin Dutton, Mark's old friend from
university. Mark always said when it came to computers there
was nothing he couldn't fix and now he's made a career out of
working in tech for himself, so she hopes he's worth trying. *Hi
Colin. Mark's away but asked me to drop his laptop to you to fix.
Would today be OK?* Another message arrives back from Colin as
she's reading.

I'm around. Drop in later and I'll see what I can do.

Instantly she types her reply and hits send. *Great. Thanks.*

Placing the phone back down on the table, her mind drifts back
to the courier and she tenses. Who is he and what does he want?
Why was he asking about Mark? Did she do the right thing by
driving away? She isn't sure now. Perhaps the man knew something? But she was so scared, terrified of what she might reveal if

he questioned her, because one slip is all it will take and it will be clear that Mark is missing. She can't afford that risk.

Going out by herself to Ken's house was the only place she could think to start searching for Mark. Ken told her very clearly that he hadn't spoken to Mark but how does she know he's telling the truth? Perhaps if she goes there herself there'll be a clue to show if Mark is telling the truth or not.

The carriage wobbles again. It's been some time since she's been on this train going south to Wicklow but after she got away from the strange man in the high-vis jacket she didn't want to drive down. Taking the car would make her too easy to follow. At least by train she guesses she'll be harder to trace.

Her phone vibrates to show an incoming call. It's Mark's mother Anne. Finally she's returning her call.

Snatching up the laptop Nicole hurries down the aisle and answers, squeezing through the sliding doors to get to the inter-section where she can have more privacy.

'Three missed calls, Nicole?' Anne's voice is dry and flat. 'There must be something up. So what is it?' It's been a while since Nicole has spoken to Mark's mother but she hasn't changed. She takes a breath, pausing to remember how hard it must be for her given what happened to Luke; reminding herself how even if Mark's mother is cold and harsh that Nicole always urged Mark not to give up trying with her, so she must at least attempt the same.

'Anne, hi.' Nicole stops, taking a breath. It's vital that she doesn't sound desperate because Anne will pick up on it instantly and sense something's wrong. 'I was just wondering if Mark had been in touch.'

'Mark?' Anne drones her son's name. 'No. Why?'

'I don't know. I just thought maybe to catch up?'

A snort of harsh laughter greets the suggestion. 'Well he hasn't. The last time I spoke with him was about six weeks ago.'

'OK.'

'Why does it matter?'

Nicole stares out the window and watches the green fields flitting past in a blur. 'It doesn't.' She hears the crack in her voice and shakes her head. Closing her eyes, she retrieves her composure. 'Did he talk about anything in particular the last time you spoke?'

'Not really. He wanted to talk about Luke and I explained that wasn't something I wanted to talk about on the phone.' The intersection door slides open and Nicole startles as a passenger walks through it and shuffles further down the corridor. Warily she waits, only breathing out as the door shuts again.

'Did Mark say why?'

'I didn't ask.' Anne sighs, her voice weary. 'I told him he'd be better off focusing his attention on getting back into surgery instead of messing about with his ridiculous volunteer work. I reminded him he was a father with a young family and he had responsibilities which he seemed to have somehow forgotten.'

Nicole drops her head against the window glass, as the train carriage rocks and pulls beneath her feet.

'I've got to go, Nicole.'

Nicole knows she must not let her slip away. That she still might know something. Anything would help. 'Anne, can I just ask if you think Mark quitting his job was because of Luke's death?'

'What?' the word hisses down the line. 'I think if Mark even tried to suggest that Nicole, he'd fall even lower in my estimation. Now I'm sorry but I have to go here because Des is calling me to go and play tennis and I'm already running late. Look, I don't want to pry Nicole, you and Mark live your own lives, and I'm a world away here living in the Canaries, but if I was to tell you one thing about Mark it's that he's always been just like his father.'

'What do you mean?'

'That man kept secrets you could never get out of him no matter how hard you tried.'

34

Saturday, November 18,
Afternoon

'Here is fine.' Nicole gets out of the Uber and shuts the door. The driver pauses, surprised why anyone would ask to be dropped in the middle of a country lane two miles outside the town, but he doesn't say anything, just shrugs his shoulders and drives away.

The address is correct. Nicole knows because she double checked it before getting out of the car. The large conifer tree is there, exactly as she saw it on Google Maps, the neatly cut grass lawn, then a mossy half wall of butter coloured bricks, curving smoothly to a pair of capped pillars at the front. Beyond the gated entrance she sees the gravel drive, and a car parked in front of Ken's country house.

It's a substantial building, plastered smooth on the outside and painted white with a gable end patterned with black wood. Nicole stares at it, frown lines spreading across her brow. What does she really hope to find here?

Nicole's heart races when she hears voices and sees the car's boot is open. It's a small hatchback and it looks like it's got equipment of some kind inside. She steps back from the road to try and make herself invisible behind the hedge. She knows it can't be Ken because he drives a convertible sports car; nor can it be his wife Melony because she drives a Land Rover.

The voices become fainter, disappearing inside the house, so Nicole squeezes through the gate and runs to the side of the steps up to the front door. Up close she can see the car boot contains buckets, brushes and mops. Edging closer to get a better look, she is startled when two people walk out of a side entrance and approach her.

It's an older man and a woman wearing blue coveralls. They stop talking when they see her.

'Mrs Byrne?' the woman says. 'We didn't know you were coming to make the inspection today. Your husband said it was tomorrow.' Nicole looks away from the woman out to the sprawling countryside beyond the garden, her body tensing. Her eyes dart to the gate, her instincts telling her to leave. But she's here now, she has to find something. The woman is still smiling. 'But it's almost ready if you want to check it.'

'Perhaps you could show me quickly.'

'Of course.' The woman steps out of the way, letting the man take the lead and Nicole hurries behind him.

'I'll just take a very quick glance upstairs.'

The man extends his arm and Nicole slips past him, jogging up the stairs until she gets to the first floor. Seconds later she stands in the doorway to the master bedroom, trying to stop her heart pounding. It's clean and spotless, but empty. No sign of Mark or evidence of him ever being here. She goes to the other bedrooms and finds them the same. If Mark was here, then any trace of him has been removed.

When she comes out the man is standing on the landing watching her.

'Are they OK?' he asks, clearly worried.

For a second Nicole is transported back to her childhood home. Her mother is in the kitchen and the strong smell of disinfectant reeks from her clothes as she scrubs her hands in the sink. She can see the skin turning red and raw. 'The boiler is acting up again girls,' she explains, 'so I'm afraid there won't be any hot water or heating for the next while. But I'll find somebody to look at it.' Alva's calling back to her from the couch where she changes the channel on the TV. 'Probably just the switch, Mum.'

The cleaner discreetly clears his throat, snapping Nicole out of her daze. 'If there's anything you need us to clean again, please just let me know,' he says softly, 'we'll happily do it.'

'They're perfect,' her voice is faint as she switches her attention to the bathroom. The cleaner walks across and closes the door with a soft click. 'Were the bedrooms used?'

For a second the man doesn't reply, but simply stares back. 'Wait. Just one moment please.' Quickly he runs down the stairs and out the front door. Nicole follows him to the porch and watches as he opens his car and takes something out. Moments later he reappears in front of her with a watch extended in his hand. It has a chrome strap and a chronometer, like a diver's watch. 'Sorry to keep you waiting but I found this.' He spreads it across his palm face upwards. 'I wanted to give it to Mr Byrne but since you are here you can take it.'

Nicole stares at the watch, the vein in her neck pulsing beneath her skin. It's not Mark's. She has no idea who it belongs to. She reaches out to take it from him when the gravel crunches outside and a green car speeds through the driveway, its horn beeping twice.

'Ah, Mike is here.' The cleaner looks relieved. 'He'll be happy he's caught you, Mrs Byrne. He wasn't sure if you wanted the roses trimmed. I think he said the lawnmower needs to be fixed too.'

Nicole moves to the front door where she can see the back of a pickup truck parking inside an open garage, tucked away around the side of the house. The driver still hasn't got out.

'I'm sorry,' she steps out, 'but you'll have to tell him that everything's fine. He can do whatever my husband suggested. I'm afraid I have to leave now.'

The cleaner watches in surprise as she starts to run.

35

Eve pulls into the edge of the kerb and parks the car. It's only a few minutes' walk up the road to Nicole's house and it's stopped raining so she's satisfied it will do. Usually she prefers not to leave her car on a public road because it's simply too easy for somebody to casually dent your door and disappear, but she won't be staying long so she'll take the risk. Turning off the engine she looks at the interior, admiring the sophisticated controls and the shine from the recent valet.

The settlement from the divorce is coming through tomorrow. Her solicitor called her earlier this morning to let her know and it's even more generous than they had anticipated. She runs her hands over the smooth leather steering wheel, a sad smile crossing her face; getting David's car was a nice surprise. He had spent so much time going on about what a perfect machine it was and now it isn't even his. The irony feels sweet. Perhaps she'll change it though. An Audi is nice, but a Porsche would be nicer. She would happily concede that she doesn't know a lot about cars but she appreciates and understands luxury, and a Porsche, without doubt, is a luxury she will enjoy.

Gently, she taps the button of the glove compartment, waits as it pops without a sound, and watches as the slow release hinge drops it carefully into her hand. The envelope is there with the folded sheet of paper inside and she removes it, together with a pen. It's the one she used to sign the divorce papers. A keeper, as she'd say to Nicole if she was here with her.

114

Looking out through the windscreen she thinks about her friend. It's sad what's happened to her. To think how drastically her life appears to have unravelled, and so quickly too. What ways could she help her out while still doing what she needs to do? She taps the tip of the pen against her teeth. If Nicole could understand her reasoning would that make it better? She would like to think so but she doubts it. Nicole doesn't have the same ambition; Eve is a businesswoman who likes to get what she wants and she won't ever apologise for that. Someday maybe Nicole will understand – what she wants is best for both of them.

Letting out a sigh, she picks up her phone and pulls up Nicole's contact. It was so lucky that Nicole asked her to set up her Snapchat account that day. Because it gave Eve the opportunity to set up Snap Map and leave the setting on Shared with Friends. Eve logs in to her account and sees her friend is near Dunleary. 'Perfect, Nicky,' she whispers putting the phone back down to return to her task.

Taking the sheet of paper in her hand, she presses it against the hard back of the envelope and starts to write.

Nicole,

Pausing, she tries to think of the right words, some gentle explanation to help Nicole accept the gift she has to offer.

Changing her mind then, she puts the paper aside. Perhaps it's simpler if she writes nothing at all.

36

The rollers on Colin Dutton's desk chair squeak as they catch the carpet. Nicole tries not to fidget, watching him as he wheels over to another desk to snatch up a computer cable.

'Sorry, be with you in one second, Nicole.' He jumps up and connects it into the back of the laptop he's working on and then drops to the floor to squeeze the plug into an adapter clogged with more cables than she can count. Nicole places the bag with the laptops on her knees. She remembers that Colin doesn't know that Mark is missing. He must not know.

Colin's office is piled floor to ceiling with every type of electronic device on the market, making the confined space almost impenetrable. Phones, iPads, laptops and games consoles lay strewn in every corner. In front of her is a circuit board sitting on top of a keyboard missing a string of letters. On another desk there's a vintage typewriter and behind it, against the wall, hangs a flat-screen TV.

'Mark go anywhere nice?'

'Barcelona,' Nicole replies stiffly.

'Lovely.' An extra-large sized Domino's pizza box lies open beside his laptop and he picks it up, brings it to his nose and sniffs the two remaining slices. 'God, I've really got to start eating healthier.' Gripping the box with both hands, he tries to close the cardboard edges but they refuse to gel, so he crunches it down, and drops it on the floor behind him. 'You're lucky you caught me,' he says, smiling, 'I'm only working this evening because I was away last week.' When Nicole doesn't reply his smile fades. 'OK, I'm guessing something's not good. Do you want to tell me?' His eyes look tired when he takes off his tinted glasses, unzips his fleece and uses the lining inside to clean them.

'There are two things, Colin,' Nicole explains slowly, making an effort to hide her desperation. 'Mark's laptop got damaged and isn't responding so I wanted to see if you could get it working again.'

'Sure. I can have a look for you.' Colin shrugs. 'And the other thing?'

Nicole fingers tighten around the bag which carries both her own laptop and Mark's. 'I got hacked.'

Colin raises his eyebrows, puts a hand to the back of his neck and runs it up over the dark stubbled hair on his head. 'Hacked? Shit. That's not good. How? When?'

'Two nights ago. Somebody made live contact with me online when I was on my laptop.'

'God, I'm sorry. I didn't realise it was serious.' Frowning, he puts his glasses back on. 'Did they steal anything?'

'I don't really know. It's just that . . . ' she hesitates.

'What?'

For a second she imagines telling him. The crazy idea pulses through her mind as she shifts in her seat before disappearing again. It would be madness. Even telling him this much is a risk. 'I want to trace where the hack came from.'

He leans back in his chair. 'Right, OK.'

'I just want to know how it happened.' Colin rises from his seat and comes round to the front of the desk, half sitting against it as he grips the edges with his fingers. 'And I also had another question I wanted to ask you.'

'Sure. Go ahead.'

'Is it possible for somebody to remotely access my computer, to wake it up from sleep mode, because I think that's happened to me once or twice?'

A sceptical look crosses his face. 'Did you mention any of this to your sister? I seem to remember Mark saying she works with the police. She might have a contact in cyber security who would specialise in that kind of thing. Couldn't she help?'

Nicole clears her throat, raising a tense smile. 'I'd prefer to get this sorted by myself. My sister's got a lot on her plate at the moment.'

Folding his arms once more he taps a finger against his lip. 'OK, well, it would be extremely rare but technically it's not impossible. I wouldn't really know exactly how, but I suspect it would involve installing an agent on both your device and the server they are using to gain access to you.'

'So somebody must have installed something on my laptop?'

'That would be my guess. Probably hardware more likely than software.'

'But how?'

Colin shrugs. 'Did you maybe lend it to someone, take it to a repair shop perhaps?'

Nicole scrunches her eyes, racking her brain. But she can only draw a blank. 'I don't know. I can't remember.'

Colin runs a hand over his head. 'It's pretty out there stuff though, like I said.'

Nicole fingers curl tighter around the laptops. Does Colin even believe her? She isn't sure, but why would he? It sounds so crazy. But she has to be careful. She's already revealed too much. 'Well, could you search for it do you think?'

He frowns. 'I can, but if it's hardware, it would probably involve dismembering your computer to the point where it wouldn't even work again. Some of these devices can be literally hidden inside the motherboard.' He sticks out his hand to take the bag. 'Leave it with me and let's see what I can do. If I get an hour later on I'll have a look inside. How's that sound?'

Nicole gets up and places the bag in his hands. One clue is all she needs. One clue to get her started. 'I appreciate your help. Just do what you can but . . . ' She inhales, the thought of breaking the only line of communication back to Mark panicking her.

'Yes.'

'I need my laptop working. If it breaks I'm . . . '

'Message received.' Colin grins and takes the machine from her hands. Nicole raises a fraught smile and leaves as quickly as she can.

37

There's a space free in front of the Circle K shop and Nicole parks. Her stomach rumbles but she won't stop to eat. She doesn't want to waste any more of this day than she has already. She opens up Google Maps on her phone, desperate to remember the route she took to the industrial estate. If she can find where she collected the car last night it would give her somewhere to start. It can't have been too far from the M50. But where?

Kneading the side of her neck with her knuckles, she shrinks down Google Maps and closes her eyes. She knows she's missing something. She can feel it. And then an idea comes to her, an idea so obvious she can't understand how she's overlooked it. Mark's bank card.

Immediately she grabs her phone and opens her banking app to access their joint account. With her thumb she scrolls up and down, her eyes scanning each small transaction. But everything she can see she already knows. Because all the transactions are hers alone. There is no sign of Mark using his card in over a week. Closing it again, her chest rises and falls as tears sting her eyes.

The windscreen wipers drag noisily across the windscreen, squeaking harshly as the rubber snags on the residue of rain from earlier in the morning. Sinking into her seat Nicole clenches her teeth and shuts her eyes as the sound catapults her back to the wet road last night, driving alone in the dark with Mark bound and covered in blood in the boot. Exhaling, she buzzes the window down to get some air.

Her body tenses, her mind chasing the memories of the journey the Paymaster's men took her on yesterday. If she only hadn't shut her eyes throughout the journey she might remember a detail. And yet she knows exactly why she had to; because she needed to imagine she wasn't there. That it wasn't real. It was the only way it could work. The only way she could create the illusion of having some safety that never existed. Her nose twitches as the smell of tobacco comes back to her, then the image of the taller man's damaged ear, and the coldness of his voice as he ordered her to hand over her phone and remain silent.

But the harder she concentrates the less she seems to be able to recall. With each beat of her heart the pressure grows and she closes her eyes tighter. Words play inside her mind, her own words. 'I'm sorry.' Her hand jerks back unexpectedly as the sound of the body thudding and slumping inside the boot space rings in her ears. And then her memory stumbles on something. It was a road sign – just something that caught her eye for the briefest fraction of a second and she is almost certain it said Greenhills. Opening her eyes again, she grips the steering wheel. Of course she knows it isn't much, and there's even a good chance that she's making it up out of pure desperation, imagining something she never saw at all. Yet it's better than sitting outside the petrol station in her car doing nothing.

The engine starts up and she checks her phone. There are no messages from Alva but she sees one from Shaun and opens it.

All good here. Girls having a great time and sending you their hugs.

There's a selfie of Shaun with Holly and Chloe and their two cousins Aoife and Ben. Aoife's wearing the hat Nicole bought her last year at the Christmas fair with the purple wellies Mark got her too and she chases Holly across the playground while Ben covers his eyes in the background, clearly having agreed to Chloe's favourite game of hide and seek, as she runs for the nearest cover.

Her fingers tap the phone keys and she lets tears run down her face now as she sends a smiling emoji with one word.

Thanks.

The message sends and she swallows as her eye is drawn to the banking app again. When was the last time she checked the Paymaster's money in her private AIB account? For a second she can't remember. Tensing, she recalls how the Paymaster got in touch, ambushing her in the café, almost as if they knew she was there, pressurising her before she had time to think. But they can't contact her now. The only way they make contact is via the laptop and it's still with Colin Dutton. Blowing out her breath she waits for the thoughts to pass but they keep gathering like dark clouds in her mind. What if the money isn't as secure as she thinks? What if they've done a recall on it? Because she knows that happens. If the bank in question is contacted soon enough; or maybe there are even other ways; ways only cyber criminals could understand because fraud is their business.

Working her thumb quickly she logs online with her phone and accesses the AIB banking app. A little circle like a sun forms in the centre of the screen; it rotates clockwise, drawing a small black bar each time it moves, telling her it's loading.

Finally the account balance of her personal AIB account appears; her hand trembles as she stares at the figures.

The balance displays as overdrawn. They have taken the money back; every last euro of it.

Slamming her phone into the seat Nicole screams.

38

Saturday, November 18,
Early Evening

Puffing, Nicole hurries past the single storey buildings on Beaconsfield Road in Greenhills, desperately trying to fit the picture she sees in front of her to anything she could have seen before.

It's a terrace of small compact houses, bricked at ground floor with white wood panelling up top glowing eerily in the darkness. There are no driveways but cars line the road on the street. She crosses over quickly, turns, passing the three-storey block of flats. Street lights flicker above her as she stares at the building. The white PVC windows cut into the brown walls are all different shapes and sizes. She stops and turns to look at them but no memories of the place come back.

Her phone beeps a message. She grabs it from her pocket, a tiny flicker of hope that it could be Mark; she did what they wanted, she did her side of the deal. But it's from Colin Dutton.

Off to Edinburgh tonight. Encryption on your laptop is too advanced, I couldn't break it. No visible changes to the hardware either. Mark's hard drive is dead. Left both laptops out front. You can collect them from Elaine whenever suits. Regards to Mark.

She should go and get the laptops. It's the only way the Paymaster can get in touch. Instantly she is running, thoughts streaming through her mind. They have Mark. It's her fault. She's done something unforgivable for money that probably never existed. If she had told Alva in the beginning maybe it could all have been avoided.

She picks up her pace, trying not to let her disappointment sap her will. It was never likely that Colin would find anything, even if Mark had always insisted he was a one off when it came to anything technical. It was just a hope and nothing more.

The ache inside her chest is there again and Nicole presses her hand against it as she gets back inside the car. Greenhills is huge but nothing she saw there was familiar in any way. The car starts and her hand shakes when she types Colin's address back into her phone's navigation app.

Just as the handbrake releases the phone rings and Eve's name comes on the screen. Looking away Nicole presses to cancel the call.

'Hey you!' Eve's jovial voice fills the stuffy car.

Nicole squeezes her eyes shut, tipping her head back against the seat rest. How did she hit the wrong button and answer?

'Hello? Nicole?'

'Hi.'

'Did I just pass you in my car in Greenhills?' Eve sounds thrilled. 'Was that you?'

Nicole pauses. 'Yeah.'

'Oh that's great! What are the chances! Let's meet. I completely missed lunch and would kill for a coffee if you fancied it?' Nicole doesn't reply. Eve's enthusiasm is so unexpected, as if she's forgotten all about the money and their standoff in the restaurant. But it sounds strange, forced. And what is she doing in Greenhills? It's the last place Nicole would expect to see her. 'God this day I'm having Nicole! I'm hangry but so happy to see you.'

Nicole pulls out, putting the phone on speaker. She needs to get the laptops and far away from Eve.

'I need to go, Eve, I have to collect something.' She tries to think of something random that couldn't possibly interest Eve. 'A car part thing for Mark.'

'Oh right. Hey, we never managed to catch up since the other night. I was so sorry about that business at the lunch. It was just a payment for an electrician I must have left behind. You know

how these guys are always trying to keep it off the books.' Eve
laughs lightly. 'I hope you're feeling much better about it all now.'

In a second Nicole is back in the restaurant, the heavy scent of
meat hanging in the air; the noise of the toilet door clicking shut,
and the two women, their harsh words and laughter.

Eve continues. 'The gang really liked you!'

The memory sharpens. *Eve said she thinks she's getting
divorced.* Nicole taps where the pain has mushroomed inside her
forehead. Should she just spit it out now? Let Eve know what she
heard? The things she said about Mark? *Eve said you'd fuck him
in a heartbeat.* Eve comes back on the line. 'By the way where is
Mark? I've been meaning to catch him. It's almost like he's disappeared.'

Nicole freezes, her eyes staring blankly ahead. Why is Eve asking this now? The Paymaster's words keep replaying: *Arouse no
suspicion. Raise no alarms.*

'Barcelona.'

'What?'

'Mark's gone to Barcelona. With a friend. A short holiday
thing.' The skin across her knuckles stretches. She knows it's a
bad lie but she had to say something. She's already told her girls
the same. The story must remain straight.

'Isn't that the amazing thing about your husband?'

'What's that?'

'He's always so full of surprises.'

39

Saturday, November 18,
Early Evening

Outside the car window Dublin is lit up by street lights and the living rooms of the terraced houses which emit a gentle glow. A woman retrieves her wheelie bin and a gang of teenage girls dressed in their school sports gear cluster together as they shuffle by, hockey sticks over their shoulders, laughing at something on a mobile phone. But Nicole scarcely notices as she drives home. The Paymaster is all she can think about. If they really have Mark she must re-establish communication immediately.

Her laptop sits on the passenger seat, sliding as she accelerates onto their road. Mark's laptop sits in the footwell. She's already linked the Wi-Fi to her mobile phone and at every pause in traffic she taps the trackpad trying to keep the screen lit up.

When the car pulls up in front of their house, she is interrupted by a sharp clicking sound. The air squeezes from her lungs and she glances across to the flickering light which has caught her eye. A humming noise drones and one solitary word fills the screen.

So?

Nicole snatches the laptop and types.

Where is Mark?

Patience.

Her fingers jab the keys as the blood rises to her face. *No. I want my husband back.*

Are you ready?

What do you want from me?

Answer the question. Are you ready now?

She drops her face into her hands. She can't think of how to stall them. She types again. *No.* A line of sweat has formed on her lip and she wipes it away. Clutching the edges of the screen she takes a breath. *I need more time.*

There is no reply. Only silence. 'Fuck,' she blows out, watching the windscreen fog over. The space inside is suddenly too cramped, too hot to breathe. Sinking deeper into the seat, she waits.

The seconds tick by as the cursor blinks. The pressure inside her head grows stronger. Finally something flickers in the half light.

Stop searching for Mark. Do not leave your house until we make contact. On Sunday at midnight, when your little girls are fast asleep. We need you to be ready.

40

Sunday, November 19,
Midnight

Hello Nicole.

Nicole has turned off the light in the study because what she is about to do must not happen in the light but under the blanket of darkness. Since yesterday evening she has been locked inside the house, forcing herself to remain calm, compelling herself to follow their instructions. But it has been exhausting, her mind constantly reeling and spinning with all the things she should be doing but isn't. Pulling and pushing between the need to act and the duty to comply with their commands, all the time trying not to imagine what they will do to Mark if she defies them.

Turning slowly now towards the laptop, she blinks as the first words appear on the screen. She has to remember it's all about Mark. Getting him back is the only thing now. The muscle in her jaw twitches as she types. *You took back the money.*

Naturally.

A flush of red spreads up her neck. Caution. She must exercise caution. Her fingers tense as they return to the keyboard.

I want to talk to Mark.

No.

The solitary word hits like a smack. Heat rises to her face. Of course they were never going to agree but she couldn't extinguish the hope of seeing him. Just even to hear his voice. Anything at all.

How do I know he's alive? The seconds pass but no reply comes back. She covers her face with her hands, pressing cold fingers against her burning cheeks. *What do you want from us? Please? I have nothing to give you.*

Again the seconds pass without a reply. Silence closes in, the weight of it like a cold hand squeezing her throat. Rain begins to drum against the window glass. An urge to run upstairs and check on the children grips her and she pushes back from the desk, her knees bent, ready to spring from the seat. And then she remembers. The girls are gone. The girls are safe with Shaun and Alva. She flattens a hand against her cheek and keeps it there.

Eventually text appears.

Follow the rules, Nicole.

She should think before replying. Acknowledge her understanding. Accept their authority. Yet somehow she cannot. Her eyes tighten as she makes a fist with her hand, lifting it and smacking it hard against the desk. How dare they put them through this? How dare they target her family?

Fuck you.

The reply is instant. *Be very careful.*

Slumping forward, she pushes the laptop out of the way to rest her face against her outstretched arm. She keeps it there, staring blankly at the pale screen as it casts shadows against the back wall. The trap is so tight she cannot move.

Eventually she sits up, dragging the laptop back.

You'll return Mark to me alive if I do everything you ask?

When you succeed. Ready now?

She closes her eyes, trying desperately to imagine what it really is that she is agreeing to and where it might end. But her mind only comes up blank. Slowly her fingers move back to the keyboard.

Go ahead.

Inhaling slowly, she waits.

Your first job is to beg.

She reads the words again, but they make no sense.

Mrs Valerie Cheroux. She's a sitting director on the board of the children's hospital where your husband once worked.

The Crumlin Children's Hospital?

Correct. Mrs Cheroux is a philanthropist and married to one of the wealthiest oil exporters in the United States. She is well disposed towards your husband.

What do you want me to do?

Convince her to donate one million euros to your husband's medical centre in Calcutta, India.

Nicole runs a hand through her hair. Mark isn't involved with any centre? And the amount of money they are demanding is insane.

How?

Find a way. You will receive an envelope. Inside you will find three cards. For the first task use Card 1. For the second task use Card 2. For the third task Card 3.

How do I use them?

Before completing each task you must leave a card in a place where it can be found after you leave.

What do the cards contain?

No questions. Do not read these cards. If you do our deal is off. Note down this address and account number.

There's a pen on the desk and she uses it to scribble down the address in Foxrock and the account number as it appears on the screen. It says The International Medical Research Centre of Calcutta. She notes this too.

Deposit the funds into this account and await our communication. Then you will receive your second order. Failure isn't an option. Remember Mark's life depends on your success.

The computer goes down quickly and reboots to fill the room with a blue glow.

They're turning her into a criminal. She tries to think of a way out, but her mind keeps spinning back to Mark. If she doesn't do what they ask she could lose him forever. Could she live with that? Could she explain it to Holly and Chloe, knowing that she was the one who performed the kidnap, who caused everything to happen in the first place? Maybe it's never OK to commit a crime to save somebody you love from harm, she knows that, but it's easier to make a rule if you never test it. Her own rules for right and wrong won't work anymore. The only way forward is to leave them behind. To become somebody else she doesn't recognise.

Her eyes fix blankly on the pale blue light. It feels like her soul is slipping away.

Her mind starts to drift and her body tenses.

All she can hear is rain, pelting hard on steel, saturating her clothes, making them cling to her skin, weighing her down like lead. Her stomach is churning once again as the latch of the BMW boot pops; the bloodied bag is upright inside the boot and though the rain is streaming over her eyes she can make out a human shape inside it. She wants to run but she can't. Instead she reaches a hand out to touch it.

'Mark,' she whispers, her voice breaking.

4 I

Monday, November 20,
Morning

Snap. The steel letter box cover flips back against the door, the sound echoing through the hall. One second later the padded paper thuds when it hits the floor.

Nicole is already upright in her bed. Throwing off the duvet, she hurries to the landing, but when she sees the stairs she stops, her body rigid. At the bottom of it, in the hallway, she notices the smudge of blood against the radiator's white paint. Her fingertips move to the stitches and she bites down hard.

There is a package on the floor. Somebody has dropped it there only seconds ago, which means they are still outside. With one hand holding the wall, she clutches the banister, her fingers squeaking as they twist. The painkillers she took last night have worn off and tentatively she puts a foot forward to make her way down, each movement jarring the base of her spine where she collided with the radiator.

The cold morning air blows in noisy bursts through the open circle of her mouth. The girls' wellies are at the base of the stairs and she moves around them, stooping instantly to snatch the parcel and tear it open. Inside she finds the three envelopes, just as the Paymaster promised. Instantly she unfastens the locks and pulls the door back.

The porch is empty. Beyond it, in the distance the foot gate is open.

'Shit.' Without thinking she runs out onto the path. Her eyes search the road but there's nobody about. Just a young teenage boy walking his dog on the other side of the road. His gaze switches to her bare feet as his dog sniffs the base of a tree.

The rain is coming down and the heavy drops drip from her chin onto her nightdress. Covering her face with her hand, she closes her eyes and waits for the heaving inside her chest to stop. Her nightdress sticks to her skin as she curls her fingers around the package. Then slowly she walks back to the front door, retreats inside and slams it shut.

42

Monday, November 20,
Morning

Next door, standing by her front window, Mrs Lyubevsky holds the lace curtain back and watches. Shaking her head, she eases carefully back from the window before her neighbour can see her.

Her phone is on top of the chest of drawers and she glances at it, not yet decided if it's time to contact Mark.

43

Monday, November 20,
Afternoon

The autumn leaves are down in Herbert Park, spotting the grass in brown clumps. It's been raining so much that the puddles have grown into tiny marshes in places. Nicole moves away from the tennis courts up towards the kids' playground. It's empty except for two young women who push prams back and forth as they chat together on a bench.

She can't stop thinking about Holly and Chloe. Can they be safe now? Would it better to take them out of school? But how would she do that without arousing suspicion? It's impossible. She wonders if they've remembered her promise to take them both to the reptile shop near Dame Street. Holly had just finished reading her book on lizards and was so excited about it and Chloe was beside herself when she heard they had baby turtles, and better still, Nicole had explained, tiny ones called terrapins.

Nicole closes her eyes, trying to squeeze the thoughts of her girls from her mind. They will be safer with Alva, she knows that, and they will have Ben and Aoife for company. Alva and Shaun are trained police officers and Alva would die for the girls. But now she thinks about her sister she tries to guess how long can she expect before Alva figures out something's off; if she hasn't figured it out already. It was so kind of Alva to suggest Nicole rest by herself at home, but despite what Alva says, she knows the arrangement can't last.

Nicole exhales and shivers. Last night the house was so lonely without them. It was close to four in the morning before she fell asleep, the silence so unnerving that all she could hear was the beating of her heart. It is the right thing to do leaving them with Alva and Shaun and it's what Mark would have suggested, if he was here by her side. But it doesn't make it easier.

At the thought of Mark she hurries on, pressing her phone closer to her ear as she moves to the empty bench and sits down.

'Avril Jenkins speaking.' Valerie Cheroux's personal assistant answers in an upbeat voice.

Nicole takes a breath and begins her prepared lie. 'Avril, hi, this is Michelle Kelly, the Provost's secretary at Trinity College, Dublin. I'm calling on his behalf.'

'Yes, Michelle?'

'The university has drawn up its annual shortlist of honorary fellows and has selected Mrs Cheroux as a candidate.' Squeezing her knee, Nicole keeps going with her prepared story. 'I've been instructed to make personal contact with Mrs Cheroux so I can talk her through how it works and what it entails. If you could be so kind as to pass on her contact number, I could speak with her directly if that's OK.'

The line goes quiet. 'Michelle?'

'Yes?'

'I think we've met.'

An elderly man walks past with a large dog. Its drooping eyes meet Nicole's and for a second she thinks about hanging up. The man gives her a friendly grin, pulling the dog's leash to tug him back.

Nicole places the palm of her hand flat against her forehead, regaining her composure. 'That's what I thought.'

'Oh good, you remember then, at the admissions fair last year? I was there with my daughter, Isabel. She was really chuffed with all the information you passed on to her.'

'I hope it helped.'

'It certainly did.'

Avril Jenkins chatters for a bit longer before reading out Mrs Cheroux's private mobile and Nicole scribbles it on to her hand, the nerves in her fingertips tingling. 'I'm sure Mrs Cheroux will be delighted. Take care now.'

Relief floods through her as Nicole rises to her feet to glance around the park. It's quiet still, only the man and his dog and two women nearby. There's no one watching her. Quickly she starts to walk.

It seemed unlikely – impossible really that this phone call could work, but it has. Yet already the questions are bubbling back up. Why has the Paymaster targeted Valerie Cheroux and what is this International Medical Centre in Calcutta that she is supposed to be promoting? She knows Valerie Cheroux's riches are vast, but would she really just donate a million euros like that? It feels inconceivable. Nicole remembers she'd read recently about a Silicon Valley fraudster who swindled handfuls of the super-rich for millions. In the right circles, big money is something different to what she understands it to be. Perhaps, in theory, it could happen.

Also, Valerie Cheroux is not a complete stranger. Nicole met her once when Mark took them to a fundraiser dinner she was hosting at the Shelbourne Hotel. They were just one couple out of a large crowd, attending at a cost of two hundred euros a head for her autism research charity. Mark had insisted it was a donation they should consider as a career investment in his future.

What the Paymaster said is a fact. Valerie Cheroux does like Mark. They've met several times and she sought him out to consult with him about funding children's cardiology research. That night at the Shelbourne was the first time Nicole had met her personally and she had been thrilled by how considerate the woman had been to her, especially given how busy she was. Yet the Paymaster's proposition is another thing entirely. Nicole is not going to meet her as an attendee at a gala. She has to beg her for money, to present an elaborate fabrication about what seems like an entirely fake organisation. Most importantly, she must make her part with one million euros.

She frowns, feeling her shoulders tense as she tries to imagine what's contained in the cards. Is it a blackmail? She can't guess what else it could be. And yet if it is, she can't see why she has to negotiate or beg. She thinks about opening the seal of the card to read it but her pulse spikes at the memory of the threat. If they catch her and break the deal, what happens then? Was it their way of suggesting they would kill Mark? She cannot risk it even if she can't figure out how they'd find out.

Nicole turns around, walks back to the empty park bench, and sits down once more. Taking her mobile from her pocket, she keys in the organisation's name into Google and waits. Quickly it appears, a detailed website, page upon page of information and pictures, with Mark featuring in almost every other image. How can he possibly be part of something so big that she knows nothing about? The only connection she is aware of was a medical trip Mark had done to Calcutta five years back, a one week working vacation as part of an international team to educate the surgical teams on the ground with developments they could share from each doctor's chosen field.

The phone call on the train to Mark's mother replays in her head and she hears her bitter tone. '*That man kept secrets you could never get out of him no matter how hard you tried.*'

Is it really true that Mark is like his father? Mark never really spoke about him. She figured out early on in their relationship that family was a thorny issue which put him in a bad mood so bit by bit she brought it up less. She knows Mark's father left one day and disappeared, his secrets never explained. The lump inside her throat is like a stone when she swallows. Why would he? Why keep this organisation secret from her? It doesn't make sense. The work he's doing is brilliant.

She starts to compose her message, detailing clearly who she is and how she would like to meet to discuss the foundation that Mark is spearheading in the slums of Calcutta. She keys in Valerie Cheroux's contact number, pressing send. The dark clouds shift above her, casting the park into deeper shadow. She chews the inside of her cheek with her back teeth, a strange sour taste materialising from nowhere inside her mouth. Can she really do this? It will be best to follow the text with a phone call in the evening. Before that would be rushing it.

A message beeps on her phone.

Would tonight at 9 p.m. suit? We could have a glass of wine and discuss the details.

44

Monday, November 20,
Night

It takes Nicole ten minutes to walk from the last Luas rail stop at Carrickmines station to Kerrymount Avenue in Foxrock.

The wide road is bordered on both sides with tall green hedges which obscure the houses from view. On the pavement scattered clusters of autumn leaves have fallen from the trees which stand guard outside every gated entrance. None of the houses have numbers, only lofty titles, inscribed into the hand laid stonework out front. When she arrives at one called Cloon Bawn, she takes out a pocket mirror, arranges her hair hastily and smooths the sleeves of her coat.

Taking a second to still her finger, she presses the buzzer.

'Please come in,' a heavily accented voice says. Nicole glances up at the intercom. The black and gold bars gleam as they slide across to make space for her to enter. The drumming inside her chest gets faster as the gate locks behind her, and when the gravel beneath her feet crunches, two trip lights illuminate the front garden.

The house is a double fronted red brick with shuttered windows and the kind of mature trees shielding it from the outside world normally only seen in woodlands. Nicole's mind races as she approaches the wide marble steps and whispers her preplanned speech yet another time.

'You are very welcome, Mrs Reid.' The panelled door pulls back to reveal a man dressed in formal wear. The muscles ripple in his neck and his tanned skin contrasts with his cropped silver hair. He tips his head by way of a bow, sweeping his hand towards a hall.

She tries to return the smile but her mouth only twitches, the composure she had prayed she might be able to affect suddenly feeling impossible.

'Please,' the man gestures a second time and she steps inside, shuffling beyond the entrance hall to a large open room with several corridors branching off on either side. Soft light from wall mounted lamps bounces off the polished floor and for a second Nicole is deeply disoriented, unsure if she should call the whole plan off.

'My name is Jerome,' he says, striding smoothly past her down one of the corridors, 'please, follow me.'

Seconds later they arrive at a door which he opens, revealing a room with six floor to ceiling windows on the back wall. Three couches are arranged around an antique table and he points to one. 'Make yourself comfortable. Mrs Cheroux will be down any minute.' Nicole walks to the couch but does not sit. 'Something to drink?'

'No, thank you,' she says.

Jerome tips his head again before disappearing.

Clutching her handbag, Nicole stares at the room. There are ornate chandeliers on the ceiling and a pair of matching blue vases sitting on plinths set back into the walls. In front of her, on a separate table, is a vase full of white hydrangeas and she walks over to look at them, breathing in the sweet scent as the voice inside her head keeps talking, telling her to relax, to remember that she has seen Mark's organisation with her own eyes.

A heavy door opens and Mrs Cheroux enters dressed in a flowing satin dress. The pearls on her neck sparkle and her dark hair hangs neatly over her shoulder. Nicole remembers Mark saying that she had just turned sixty the week before the charity dinner but she looks much younger. 'So pleased to see you again, Nicole.' She sweeps across, smiling broadly as she offers her hand which Nicole takes stiffly.

'I'm very pleased to see you also.' Nicole barely recognises her own stilted voice.

Mrs Cheroux has turned her attention to Jerome. 'Jerome did you offer our guest something to drink?'

'I believe she preferred to wait for you, madam.'

This makes her laugh. 'Well, would champagne be alright, Nicole? Or maybe I'm being presumptuous, you might not even drink?'

'Champagne is good. Thank you.'

'Great then.' Clapping her hands she turns to Jerome. 'I'll let you pick us a good year, Jerome.' Without another sound he slips away and she gestures to the couch. 'Make yourself at home, Nicole. I can't wait to hear all about this work you and Mark are doing. It sounds wonderful.'

Nicole waits for her host to sit, mirroring her by crossing her legs on the opposite side of the table.

'How is Mark by the way? I don't think I've seen him in almost a year. God, can it really be that long?'

Nicole opens her mouth to speak. 'Mark has . . . ' but the words she rehearsed throughout the day simply float away. The mention of Mark spins her mind back to Friday night – the lashing rain, the body in the bag, the sickly sweet smell of blood as she tried to wipe it from her hands. The heavy thud of his body as she pushed it back inside the boot space.

Jerome returns carrying an ice bucket with a bottle inside, as well as two flute glasses. He places the glasses on the table, arranges the bucket in a stand, and begins twisting the wire cork holder free.

'Jerome! You've interrupted Nicole,' Mrs Cheroux grins. 'But I think when we taste this we both might forgive you.'

The cork pops with a bang and they watch him pour. When the glasses are full Nicole quickly follows her host's lead and raises a glass. 'Well Nicole, here's to Mark and you, and this wonderful foundation you're going to tell me all about.' Mrs Cheroux's keen eyes sparkle and Nicole swallows down a mouthful of the cold alcohol, her stomach twisting so hard it makes her blink. 'Now, go ahead and tell me everything. I'm dying to hear it.' Easing back into the couch she smiles kindly and waits.

Nicole takes a deep breath, gripping the stem of the flute glass with both hands, before steadying it in her lap.

'Mark has been quietly working with our organisation for the last five years which helps the most disadvantaged in the slums of Calcutta by introducing state of the art technology and best practice to hospitals the foundation has identified as outstanding centres of excellence. The target of the organisation is to facilitate medical care on the ground to the most vulnerable – typically those with little or no chance of accessing proper treatment due to poverty.' Nicole stops, twisting the glass in her hand before continuing. 'Each month Mark assembles a large team of international doctors who travel over and work gratis for two to four weeks. Mark has asked me to take over the fundraising operations so he can concentrate on the technical and medical aspects of the foundation. So far the organisation has raised over twenty-five million euros. This year I am approaching philanthropists and seeking donations of a million euros and upwards with a view to hitting our annual target of ten million.' Pausing to take a breath Nicole sees her glass is shaking. Quickly she places it on the table. 'I am hoping you might consider us worthy of your generosity.'

Mrs Cheroux swirls the champagne inside the glass flute, brings it to her nose and inhales deeply. Her eyes close over and she smiles.

In one furtive movement Nicole removes the Paymaster's card from her pocket and places it on the couch beside her, covering it immediately with a cushion.

Mrs Cheroux opens her eyes and looks at her with interest. 'Now I'm intrigued, Nicole.'

45

'Hi there, is there something I can help you with today?' The bank official inside the Rathfarnham branch of Allied Irish Banks smiles helpfully. Nicole's grip on the envelope tightens and she stops walking. It's been a while since she's visited an actual bank and she's surprised to be greeted before she can queue to get to the counter. 'Perhaps you need to make a withdrawal or deposit some money?' The woman is being helpful. She's trying to make this visit quicker, smoother. But she is also steering Nicole towards a row of bank machines which stand side by side with touch screen monitors. It's a very public space where everything she does is visible to anybody passing. She knows she must not engage because if anybody asks questions she will not have the answers.

The bank official's attention switches as a second customer appears and Nicole uses the opportunity to skip past. 'Sorry I just need to get to the counter.' Without looking back she flicks her eyes towards the ceiling. She doesn't see any cameras but knows it means nothing. There is always surveillance inside banks now. Always.

Close by, two young women share a video on a mobile phone and she snaps the collar of her coat closer to her chin as she passes them, before moving further inside. Earlier this morning she found a pair of old sunglasses and she's put them on but she knows they're a pointless disguise. To make the deposit she must sign her name. She will be permanently on record for fraud.

There's a corner space empty and she makes her way across to it, plucking a deposit form from the stack on the counter. Avoiding looking up, she huddles over it and starts to fill it in.

The International Medical Research Centre of Calcutta, she writes the words carefully, pressing down with the pen which will barely hold still. Next she puts in the amount 1,000,000. Taking a breath, she stops, turns the pen upside down and taps each zero one after the other. *Six. Six zeros.* Her body tenses. Snatching a glance over her shoulder she sees the girls have left and only three other customers remain, two men in suits who are chatting about football and an elderly woman who is still being guided by the official at the door. Nobody is paying her any attention. Warily she withdraws the bank draft from its padded envelope and reads it again slowly. The words haven't changed since Mrs Cheroux filled it in last night. Mrs Cheroux's name is printed on the draft, alongside her signature and the amount of one million euros, all made out to the *International Medical Research Centre of Calcutta.*

Closing her eyes, she breathes as the memory of last night resurfaces – the kind, eager face of Mrs Cheroux as she believed every detail, congratulating her warmly, passing Mark her best wishes, only asking for an update on the foundation's good work in return for her generosity.

The palms of her hands are slick and she rubs them on her jeans before double checking the account number the Paymaster gave her. She writes it in too and fills her details. But then she lifts her hand away and her glance flicks to the exit. Could she stop now? Tear it up?

'Next please.' The teller at the counter calls out and she shuffles forward. She won't tear it up. That choice is gone.

Glancing over her shoulder she edges up close to the divider screen.

'How can I help you?' the smiling young man beams warmly. He wears a pink tie and a white shirt. His face looks freshly shaven and his short brown hair is gelled back off his forehead.

'A deposit please.'

'Sure.'

Nicole taps the big sunglasses further up the bridge of her nose and coughs. Keeping her eyes down, she slides in the deposit form and the signed bank draft.

The bank official reads the paperwork, pausing for a moment to glance out at her through the screen. 'One second.' Nicole's heart pounds as she watches him frown and type rapidly on the keyboard. 'I'm sorry but could I ask . . . ?'

'Tom!' A girl in a charcoal coloured suit appears alongside him. 'The team meeting has just started inside and they need you. Are you ready?'

'I'll be there in one minute.' They exchange a smile and she walks away but now his eyes return to the monitor which Nicole cannot see.

Does she run? But to where? They have her on camera. There's nothing she can do now? With a flick of his wrist the man picks up the stamp, bringing it down with a thump on the draft. Detaching the deposit receipt he slides it back under the safety hatch.

46

'Come on in.' Shaun opens the door wide. 'I think it's just about to start pissing down again from what I can see.' Nicole looks up at the black sky. A cluster of faraway stars dot the gloom and the first drops of rain fall softly on her face.

Shaun stoops, embracing her gently, his towering frame bending like a bow. He stands back and places both his hands on her shoulders as she steps inside. 'Jesus you've been having shocking luck, you feeling any better now?'

'A bit, yeah.' His long arm extends over her head and he squeezes the front door closed.

'Sounds like a nightmare. Well at least the doctor gave you the OK, that's something I guess. Go on ahead.' He steps to the side and makes space for her to walk down the scuffed corridor, past the coat rack thick with jackets and scarves, under the hanging lamp with a missing bulb.

Everything is just like she knows it will be and for a second it's a huge relief just to be somewhere secure and warm; but as she gingerly makes her way down the steps towards the lower level kitchen her chest becomes tighter. What if Alva has questions? The simple questions police officers know to ask when something isn't right. 'I'm sorry we've just finished eating.'

Nicole breathes deep, savouring the smell of fresh tomato sauce, melted cheese and hot pepperoni. 'Smells delicious.'

Shaun sticks out one of his big hands. 'Here, throw us that coat and you sit down for a sec. I'll put on another pizza for you. You

147

must be starving.' He finds a hook on the back of the kitchen door and somehow manages to squeeze Nicole's coat on top of the two that already hang there. 'What toppings do you want?' He opens the tap in the sink and rinses his hands.

'I'm fine Shaun, but thanks for offering.'

'You sure?' He looks disappointed.

'Yeah. How are the girls getting on with Ben and Aoife? I'm sorry to be dumping them on you like this.'

Shaun lifts a hand up in protest. 'Not a bit. They're all getting on like a house on fire. Holly and Aoife are building a tepee at the end of the garden with a roll of plastic sheeting and some brooms, which apparently they've decided is going to be their summer house,' he rolls his eyes, a broad smile spreading over his angular face, 'and Ben and Chloe told Alva they're building an aquarium so Chloe's turtles can have babies which she's going to donate to Ben, or so I'm told.'

Nicole fights the rising lump inside her throat and gives Shaun a reassuring smile.

Shaun snatches up three mugs in one big hand, empties the contents single-handedly into the sink and starts stacking them into the top of the dishwasher. 'And you need to recover. It's no hassle. They're all happy out, trust me.'

'Thanks.' Nicole draws a chair out by the dining table and eases into it. The fresh smell of food is giving her hunger pangs. She hasn't eaten all day and her stomach is knotting. She deliberately left the laptop at home to keep it away from Alva, but suddenly fears for its safety. Without it there's no line of contact back to Mark.

Her hand moves to the wound at the back of her head which is suddenly tight and sore. She knows Alva is going to appear any moment and she has to keep her story straight.

'Beer? Wine?' Shaun grins invitingly. Nicole shakes her head. 'Cup of tea?' She nods and Shaun flicks the kettle on before resuming stacking the dishwasher. 'Mark keeping well?'

'He is.' Nicole shifts uneasily.

'Glad to hear it.' She knows he's just making polite conversation. It's not Shaun she needs to worry about. She takes her hand from the back of her head and clasps it with the other one, trying to slow her breathing, waiting for Shaun's next question, and preparing to begin her deceit. 'Well, the bad news is you've just missed Alva.'

'What? Where'd she go?'

'She nipped out only five minutes ago. A late night meeting at the station apparently. I think our holiday timing mightn't have been the best so she's under some pressure with this case she's got on.' He flicks a tea-towel over his shoulder and wipes his hands on it. 'It's all a bit hushed so I don't know much more about it but it's definitely a big one.'

Nicole sits back in the chair, the tension easing from her body. This is perfect. But the pressure inside her head remains and she doesn't relax. Instead she is strangely thrown, because she knows that just simply sitting with Alva would have reassured her somehow, even if she did have to evade her questions. 'That's a pity.'

'I know. She was looking forward to catching up with you too, but don't worry, you'll get her next time.' Shaun pours the tea into both mugs, then pulls out the bags and adds in the milk. 'Now go on in and get comfortable.' He hands Nicole one. 'They're all cuddled up watching telly, snug as bugs. I've got a bit of office stuff to catch up on but stay over if you like. I can make a bed for you.'

Nicole wraps her fingers around the mug and stands, the warmth of the edges against her stiff, cold fingers suddenly soothing. 'Thanks Shaun but I won't put you out.' Her grip tightens as the thought of the laptop resurfaces. She needs to make contact as soon as she can; to check that Valerie Cheroux's draft lodged successfully. What if the bank put a hold on it? It seemed too easy.

Shaun grins and lifts his mug. 'You're probably right. Rest is the main thing.' He opens the kitchen door and holds the frame. 'Let me know when you're off. I'll be upstairs.'

Quietly Nicole joins the children and sits between them in the middle of the couch. To one side of her is Ben, his round open face a picture of concentration, then Holly huddled up close on her lap, short legs dangling, sticky fingers hugging Nicole's neck. On the other side sits Aoife, her red headed niece who everyone always said looks the image of Nicole with her emerald green eyes; like the others she too is dressed in her pyjamas, her face starry eyed and sleepy. Only Chloe, the eldest of the group, sits apart in the chunky grey armchair. Nicole had expected them to be watching a movie, but they are watching a nature documentary set in the Arctic Circle.

'Mum,' Chloe, whispers, not moving her eyes from the screen. 'Did Dad say when he's coming home yet?'

Nicole blinks. 'Next week, love.'

'OK.' She lets out a long, weary sigh. 'I miss him.'

'Me too, Chlo'.' The air inside Nicole's chest heaves as their eyes lock together. Chloe knows, she thinks. She knows something isn't right. She just can't figure it out.

'Shh.' Aoife, twirls a ring of red hair and points at the screen. 'Auntie Nicole, look at the seal.'

'It's a baby and it can't find it's mother,' Holly explains, little fingers gripping tighter, 'so it's afraid to leave the ice.'

'OK,' Nicole whispers, relieved to see Chloe's attention return to the programme. 'Let's watch quietly love.' She strokes Holly's cheek as the light from the television flickers across their frightened faces and they watch the young white seal pup cling to a cracked lump of frozen ice.

Two killer whales surface close by and eye it menacingly. The camera closes in on the seal pup's face. Wide eyed, it calls plaintively, scrabbling to the farthest edge of the ice floe. But the mother doesn't hear it. The whales have disappeared underwater but their tapered dorsal fins glide at speed in the distance as they surge towards it. For a moment it looks like they will crash into the ice, but at the last second they dive under, unleashing an enormous wave.

The swell heaves, upending the floe until it is almost vertical. The seal pup cries out, clambering helplessly, its flippers failing to grip the treacherous ice. Its round, frightened eyes flare as it peers into the vast grey sea beneath.

And then, slowly, it starts to slide.

Holly clutches her mother's neck, her hot, wet tears already dripping onto Nicole's skin. The sound of her sobs fill the room. 'The baby seal doesn't have a chance, Mummy. The baby seal is going to die.'

47

Tuesday, November 21,
Night

Nicole twists restlessly in the empty bed, her hand reaching out for Mark but finding only the cold space where his body should be. The laptop sits on the floor, humming eerily, the tiny green light on its side flickering in the darkness.

The relief she felt earlier in the day when she banked Valerie Cheroux's draft donation of a million euros has all disappeared. Now she stares blankly at the bedroom ceiling, struggling to believe the fraud she's just committed, her heart quietly fragmenting at the thought that even one wrong move and she may never see Mark again.

Standing up, she walks over to Mark's wardrobe and opens it. His clothes are all hanging where he's left them and she spreads her arms wide, drawing them towards her, inhaling deeply but refusing to let the tears fall.

But then the light behind her changes and when she turns to look, she sees a different glow on Mark's clothes. Quickly she moves back to the bed and peers down at the laptop which has come to life. There is one word on the screen.

Impressive.

Snatching it up off the floor she jabs at the keys.

I want proof you have Mark. Now.

Relax.

The pounding inside her chest has returned.

What do you want from me? I did what you asked.

10 a.m. tomorrow. Make sure you're connected.

The screen powers down and Nicole drops it to the floor where it lands on the soft carpet. She throws herself on the bed and pulls Mark's pillow over her head, her body shaking.

48

Wednesday, November 22,
Morning

The morning air is crisp. Nicole blows on her fingers and her breath steams the air.

She walks along the path inside Bushy Park, her eyes looking across the grass for the nearest bench. Was it the right idea to come here? Outside it feels safer, because at least in the open air during daylight there are witnesses. She checks the time on her phone. In seven minutes' time it will be ten o'clock.

Clutching the laptop closer, she keeps moving. The sight of the ducks and the pigeons by the pond bring back memories of Mark. It's the exact same spot they came to a year ago to find the water frozen; the one where Mark got all the girls to throw stones to see if they could break the ice, promising that whoever did it first could decide what film to see in the cinema later that Sunday.

'Are you OK?' When Nicole turns she sees a young woman pushing a baby in a pram.

'Yes. Fine.' Quickly she hurries away. She needs to find somewhere to sit. Somewhere it can begin all over again.

There's a bench on the other side of the green and she rushes across the grass towards it snatching her laptop from her bag. Grabbing a pen and pad, she sits, opening the laptop on her knees, double checking its connection to the hotspot on her phone.

The shadows on the grass change as the sky above darkens. Already a face is illuminating the screen. It's an image of an elderly man and for a second Nicole draws away, the sight of him almost peering straight at her strangely unnerving. Underneath it

154

she reads, *Commit this face to memory.* Seconds later it fades and more text arrives. It's an address in Monkstown and she takes out her phone to photograph it before it too disappears. More text keeps following.

Elliot Preston, a gemstone collector. Mark performed life-saving surgery on his grandson one year ago. Preston collects pastries from the Fresh Bakery in Monkstown at eleven o'clock every morning. Engage him in conversation and get into his house. Inside you will locate his jewellery.

Where?

The safe detector device we placed in the boot of your car will open the safe. Take what's inside. Deposit the goods in deposit box 7294 in Merrion Vaults on Burlington Road.

Her car? They have been inside her car. Nowhere is safe now. Steeling herself, she types back.

You're ordering me to rob him?

Fail and two of Mark's fingers will be delivered to your house tonight.

49

Wednesday, November 22,
Morning

Mrs Lyubevsky moves the shopping bag to her left hand and stops to look up at the sky. It's grey and the temperature has dropped. The dark clouds drift ominously above her and she tries to remember if the forecast said there would be rain.

'Bah,' she grunts her disapproval, opening the foot gate to the front of her house and stepping in off the path. She's sick of the rain. The rain brings the flu and last year it put her in bed for a full week. There's damp in the house now too, which is something she knows she'll need to fix before it brings mould.

A tall man in a heavy wool coat brushes past her. Striding swiftly, he shoves through the small gate to the Reids' house next door. Mrs Lyubevsky frowns but does not move. The man holds a parcel in his hand and when he gets to the front door he does not press the bell or knock, but squashes his face up against the front bay window. Her grip tightens on the shopping bags and she edges back silently towards her front door. Placing her shopping down carefully, she searches for her key, when she hears a noise.

The parcel slaps hard against the wood of the door and falls to the wet pavement as the man turns, stuffing his hands in his pockets. Their eyes meet and Mrs Lyubevsky feels herself shrinking under his hard glare. Her mouth opens and she wants to say something, to tell him plainly that she's seen what he's done, but her voice is stuck and her hand trembles as she tries to find the key inside her coat.

Quickly the big man paces out to the pavement, hooks a huge black shoe through the front gate and kicks it open. Glaring at her one last time, he marches away as quickly as he arrived.

Instantly Mrs Lyubevsky searches her pocket for her phone. She keeps it on the inside chest pocket but when she looks for it, she finds that it's slipped through the tear in the lining. Sighing, she takes out her door key and puts it in the lock, knowing that by the time she can call the police the man will be long gone and they'll probably just see her as a crank caller. What can she tell them anyway? She hasn't witnessed any crime. She doesn't want to be treated like a crazy old lady.

Opening the door she glances back at the Reids' house, realising now that the parcel is still on the ground and getting wet. If it's left there it will either be destroyed or stolen for certain. Grumbling, she drops both her plastic shopping bags inside the front door of her house and closes it again to go and retrieve the parcel.

She huffs as she walks in the front gate and searches the ground with her eyes but now another man has appeared. He holds the parcel to his ear and shakes it as if trying to guess its contents. His face is grave and he approaches the front door, his piercing blue eyes staring at it, not noticing her presence.

'What are you doing?' Mrs Lyubevsky's heart thumps hard. It's the man she mentioned to Mark. He still wears the same black cycle leggings and high-vis yellow top. He was acting suspiciously the first time she saw him and now his sudden appearance is even more odd. The man turns sharply to face her. She knows her best course of action would be to retreat to the safety of her home and inform the police immediately about both men, but her anger is rising. 'Excuse me but I don't think that parcel belongs to you.' She wags an irate finger at him.

Chris Ashton's face is creased and sweating and he breathes hard. 'Did you see who delivered this?'

Mrs Lyubevsky takes a step back. 'Why?'

'Tell me now,' he snaps, the lines in his brow deepening. 'Did you see who delivered this?'

When she raises her hand it shakes as she points towards the road. 'Seconds ago. A man flung it at the door and marched off towards Rathgar Road.' Instantly he drops the parcel on the doorstep and brushes past her. 'What is this about?'

He doesn't reply but pulls the gate open and starts to sprint away.

Bending slowly down Mrs Lyubevsky picks up the parcel, groaning as she straightens her back and pushes slowly to a standing position. Her heart is pumping hard. Placing the parcel under her arm, she glances up and down the street warily, then quietly shuffles home and triple locks her door.

50

Wednesday, November 22,
Morning

'What can I get you?' the man behind the counter in the Fresh Bakery asks. He has close-cropped silver hair and tired, watery eyes.

'Just a croissant. And a white coffee, please.' Nicole stands stiffly, glancing to where the customers sit inside the café.

'Coming up.' He bags the pastry and starts prepping the espresso machine.

Sucking in a deep breath, she tries to force the thought of the crime from her mind. Because she knows it's the only way it has the slightest chance of success. There were no instructions from the Paymaster about how she is to gain access to this man's house, so she's had to concoct her own plan. But before she can do that, she has to find him.

The safe detector is in her pocket and her knuckles catch the sharp plastic edge when she lifts her hand away. In her other pocket is the small cotton bag. It's not much of a plan at all but there hasn't been much time to prepare.

When she looks beyond the counter out towards the tables, which are arranged in two neat rows, she can see the diners are mostly elderly. The scent of ground coffee wafts through the small room and there's a din of busy conversation as they slice fruit scones and break open their pastries releasing scents of chocolate and raisins.

A yawn pushes up and Nicole places a hand over her mouth as her stomach rumbles. She hasn't eaten since yesterday morning.

'I said your coffee's ready,' the man behind the counter calls, an impatient look on his face.

The woman next to her steps forward, tapping her elbow gently. Her skin is lined and dry and she speaks with a soft, friendly voice. 'I think he means you, dear.' The man behind the counter stands with one hand on his hip, the other gesticulating to the coffee.

'Sorry, I got distracted. Thank you.' Hurrying to the counter, Nicole takes a card from her wallet and taps. There's a delay on the machine and she stares at it not wanting to look up. She racks her brains trying to think of what monthly direct debits might have come in.

'Try again,' the man says, more quietly this time. 'The machine can be temperamental.' Nicole places her card against the reader and breathes a sigh of relief when it works. The tension in her shoulders almost eases but as she moves away from the counter it returns instantly. Where is Elliot Preston? The image of his face is just a blur now. It could be anyone.

Clutching her wrapped croissant and takeaway coffee, she walks down through the busy tables, cautiously screening the faces of the customers she passes. Many are hunched over their plates eating and the fleeting glimpses she gets don't offer many clues. Trying hard not to look lost, she retreats back towards the counter. The sickening image of Mark's severed fingers keep flashing into her mind.

There's a space at the counter and she places her coffee down. When she turns she notices an elderly man sitting on a stool reading a newspaper. He looks smart in an old fashioned tweed jacket and white shirt. He has round, gold framed glasses but the face and bald head is instantly recognisable. It's the man from the picture she saw earlier on her laptop – the one the Paymaster sent her. Elliot Preston.

'Did you lose something?' he enquires politely.

'No.' Nicole pauses. *Don't go blank. Say what you rehearsed in the car on the drive over to Monkstown. Keep cool and speak.* But the faster the silent voice inside her head keeps talking the stiffer her body becomes. 'I have never been in this bakery before and didn't even know it was here.' The words come out in an unfamiliar voice.

Elliot Preston nods and smiles kindly.

'It's very nice. Quaint?' she says.

'Old, I think you mean.'

A bead of sweat drips from beneath her armpit. 'I'm sorry but I think we've met.' The words come out of her mouth in a blurt. Elliot Preston raises his eyebrows but shows no recognition. 'Jeanette Green?' More pinpricks of sweat open on her skin, this time on her back. Holding her breath she waits and his face turns apologetic when he shrugs.

'Sorry, I'm becoming forgetful.'

'That's OK, I don't expect you to remember but we met at Crumlin Children's Hospital. My nephew was in under the care of Dr Mark Reid. Your grandson was in at the same time. Mark Reid's a friend of mine. I remember he introduced us.'

Elliot Preston slides off the stool and stands. 'Of course, Mrs Green, what a lovely surprise. Please, join me.' He drags another stool across and points to it, his demeanour more friendly now.

Nicole places her coffee down and it spills, burning her skin. Squeezing her fingers into a fist she shoves it in her pocket. 'I'd love that Mr Preston but I can't.' She stops, remembering to drink her coffee. 'You see somebody's just gifted our medical foundation some precious stones. It's a foundation Mark Reid set up to help those in need in India and he asked me to come on board to help because my background is in the charity sector.' Taking the cotton bag from her pocket she holds it out. 'I'm on my way to a gemstone dealer to have them valued. I'm hopeful they might be worth something and we can raise some badly needed funding.' She stops and lets out a high pitched sound, attempting a laugh. 'Though, honestly, they could tell me they're worthless and I wouldn't know.'

Elliot Preston stands up and takes off his glasses. 'I could help you.'

'How?'

'Gems are my business.'

'That's very kind of you, but it would be unfair. You're out for your breakfast, and I don't want to impose. I mean it's hardly something we would do here in the café is it?'

'Mrs Green, please,' he tilts his chin towards the exit. 'My house is just across the road and I'm happy to help. Mark saved my grandson's life. Valuing some donations for his foundation is the least I could do.'

Pausing, Nicole nods stiffly, forcing a smile to her lips. Elliot Preston's wrinkled face beams. 'That's settled then. I suggest we take something with us so we can eat as we talk some more.'

5 1

Wednesday, November 22,
Morning

The house is a period red brick terrace just off the main Monks-town road. Three stone steps take them up and through the front door on the ground floor level over the basement.

'Just here by myself,' Elliot Preston pants as he shuffles inside the house, heaving his legs up the next set of stairs. Nicole follows, slowing her pace as she listens to the rattle of air in his lungs. The crown of his head glistens as he grips the banister, finally hauling himself to the landing at the top. 'My wife's dead ten years now, just six months after our golden jubilee wedding anniversary.'

Nicole climbs the last stair and stands beside him, her coat folded tightly over one arm, the other hand holding the small paper tray of coffees and pastries. 'I'm sorry to hear that.'

Wiping his brow with a white hanky he shrugs. 'Life is cruel sometimes. Please, allow me.' He takes the tray, gesturing to the first floor living room and Nicole walks inside. The thin sash windows wobble when a delivery truck passes outside on the road. 'Up here is actually an apartment which my son once occupied but he's moved to Hong Kong. I know I should give the place a touch up but keeping it as it is reminds me of my wife – she was the one who loved to do the decorating you see.' He smiles sadly and Nicole looks around at the old chintz wallpaper with its pink roses and faded green flowers. A framed photo of Elliot Preston with his wife dominates the room above the mantlepiece and they stare into each other's eyes. He tilts his head towards the picture. 'I put that up a while back. Probably me just being silly.'

163

Nicole shakes her head. 'It's very nice. And I think your wife had great taste.'

'Well, I guess she'd like the thought.' He looks back at the coffee. 'I'll just be a moment,' he then says, slipping out of the room.

Nicole sits down on the couch, pinning her hands between her knees. The house is spread over three different levels. The stones could be anywhere. She has no idea where she might find them. The thought of threatening the elderly man flashes through her head and she squirms. How could she even attempt it? Her whole plan feels like lunacy. Could she just open the card the Paymaster gave her and show it to him openly? If it's a simple blackmail wouldn't that work? And yet she knows what they've told her: she cannot read it and if she does the deal ends there and then.

Elliot Preston is smiling when he returns with their takeaway coffees and pastries on a tray with some plates and cutlery. 'When memories are all you have you must hold on to them,' he says, placing everything onto the small mahogany coffee table.

'I know.' Nicole's eyes glisten as she helps him arrange the table.

'I'm retired now so I rarely get to use my skills. It will be nice to put them to use for a good cause,' he points to the plates. 'Please, you're my guest.'

There are two plain croissants and two tiny pains au chocolat. Nicole picks up one, the unease growing inside her as she bites a piece. The sugar melts in her mouth, it tastes so good. And now what she has to do is so deeply wrong. Immediately she places it back down. 'I better show you what I have then.'

'Of course.' He gestures to the table and Nicole takes the small cotton pouch from her bag, tipping the contents out.

The first piece he inspects is her mother's diamond wedding ring. It's the one she used to always take off and leave on the window ledge beside the kitchen sink when washing the dishes, the same one Alva insisted she keep. Even now Nicole can remember Alva's voice, telling her confidently when they were clearing the family house after their mum's death, 'It's safer with you, Nicole, since you're far too respectable to ever need to pawn it.' What would Alva think if she could see her now?

Next he inspects their mum's sapphire necklace, her ten-year wedding anniversary gift from their dad.

'It's just a small collection from a friend who was doing a clear out of her house after her divorce.' Nicole steadies her voice. 'She thought whatever they amounted to would help our charity. I've no idea what they're worth really.'

He holds the necklace closer to the window, spreads it across the palm of his hand, watching closely as the stones change colour with each movement of his wrist. Then carefully he places it back down on top of the empty cotton bag.

'They're very pretty pieces.' He picks up a white napkin and cleans his fingers. Then he sips his coffee and takes off his glasses, his gaze switching to the blue Tanzanite ring. It's the last piece Nicole could find in the house.

Elliot Preston's face brightens as he takes a small implement out of his pocket, opens it and holds it in front of his eye. 'I'm using a jeweller's loupe for this one because it's very unusual and quite fascinating.' Picking the ring up delicately he holds it a few inches from the loupe, twisting it as he turns towards the window. 'The loupe gives me a tenfold magnification of the stone which is hugely important for identifying blemishes or cracks which diminish the value.' He puts the ring down gently on the table, shaking his head, a look of surprise on his face. 'But on this piece, I don't see any whatsoever.'

'And their value?'

'Well, the necklace is pretty but a rough cut, so would not be worth a whole lot, perhaps a thousand euros or so. The diamond ring is very elegant but not so fashionable nowadays so maybe the same for that. But the Tanzanite is quite something. Where did you say you got it again?'

'It was my . . .' Nicole stops abruptly. The ring catches the light, its dazzling beauty bringing her back instantly: it was the trip of a lifetime that Mark had spent two years saving up for – a honeymoon safari in Kenya; each night under the stars by the campfire after dark, gazing up at them as they talked about their hopes and dreams for the future, the firelight flickering across their sunburnt faces with the roar of lions in the distance; then Mark's surprise treat of a balloon safari across the Masai Mara and the warmth of his hands on her body later that night as the moon cast its silver light through their canvas tent. She swallows, as the memories keep flooding back; the impossibly blue waves lapping the white sandy beach in Zanzibar, when Mark plucked the ring casually from his striped swimming shorts, saying 'Just because'. And then the two of them couldn't stop laughing until she got the hiccups and he kept making her drink water – but they wouldn't stop, because she was too giddy; giddy with hope for the future they would share. Closing her eyes, she lets her breath out slowly. 'My friend's old ring. She had lost it and found it again when she was cleaning her house. I think she said she got it on a holiday. Maybe Africa.'

'Well, you should tell her it would be a shame to let it go. And I really mean that. It's stunning. It could fetch ten thousand, more even. It's an extremely fine cut and a very popular stone right now.'

Clutching her coffee Nicole drinks it down, the ache inside her chest so strong she has to close her eyes. Was there a reason Mark never told her what it was worth? Did he worry that she might sell it to keep them afloat? Mark was always too generous.

She places her coffee aside, turning away to the window. She doesn't want to cry. Not here.

'And the organisation you mentioned?' he asks softly.

'I'm sorry, yes.' Sitting up straight, she nods. 'Of course. I should explain.' Clearing her throat she begins, cataloguing the work that Mark is doing, along with her assistance, in the slums of Calcutta. To her surprise the words flow easier this time and Elliot Preston is keen to listen, appearing genuinely interested.

'It's terrific what you're doing. You can let Mark know I'll be in touch with him about making a donation. Medicine trans-forms lives, Mrs Green. And I mean literally.' Elliot Preston's bushy eyebrows arch above the gold rims of his glasses as his face lights up. A beep interrupts him then and he pushes himself with considerable effort back up to a standing position. 'Sorry, one second.' Slowly he wanders out to the kitchen to get his phone.

And then in an instant he makes a chance mistake, offering Nicole an opportunity: he leaves his house keys on the small coffee table.

Nicole lunges, snatching them in her hand before she can change her mind. Seconds later he returns.

'That was the garage calling me to tell me to come down and collect my car. I should probably get moving because I have to get across to the golf course after I pick it up.' His hands pat down his jacket pockets, worried eyes scanning back and forth across the table. For a moment she freezes. What does she say now? It must be clear she's the only person who could have taken them.

'Did you lose something?' her voice inflects upwards, straining to sound surprised.

'My keys. I'm forever putting them down and then forgetting where I've left them. Especially when I'm in a hurry, like now.'

Nicole rises to her feet, flushing deeply. 'Can you think where you last had them?' She's certain he knows it's her. But what will he do? Will he call the police? 'Did you have them in the kitchen?'

Elliot Preston shuffles away, his brow wrinkling. 'That's the problem. I'm not sure.' He stops to grip the banister. 'My memory's so bad now. It's happening more and more recently. It's a worry.'

'Would you have another set you could use until they turn up?'

He turns, his confusion melting away. 'You're right. I'll grab them and I'm sure the others will pop up when I'm not even looking. It's how it always goes, isn't it?'

Minutes later they exchange goodbyes outside on the street. Nicole watches carefully as he totters across the road.

Covering her face with her hands she inhales slowly. She cannot do this; and yet she knows she must. Releasing her breath she takes the keys from her pocket, breaking into a run.

52

Wednesday, November 22,
Morning

At the top of the stairs, she holds out the Paymaster's machine.
It's a solid grey steel device, not much bigger than a small box of
matches, but heavy. At one end there are two very small bulbs,
one on each corner, like the indicator lights on a car. One of
them is flashing, showing a red light and making a beeping noise.
Hurrying, she goes to the kitchenette further inside. The rem-
nants of their coffee and croissants are sitting where Elliot Preston left them only minutes ago. She lifts the machine high in her
hands, points it at the cupboards and keeps moving but sees no
change. Then she stops; if it's a safe it's most likely not in the
kitchen. The bedroom or living room is her best guess, and if
not, the basement.

Quickly she goes to the master bedroom where Elliot Preston's
slippers lie side by side on the thick carpet beside a sunken bed.
With a flick of her hand she opens the wardrobe scanning again,
up and down the shelves, across the top where she cannot see.
Then she pushes his clothes out of the way and places the machine
inside the closet, but it keeps on beeping the same noise, flashing
the same red light.

With nervous steps she walks to the living room and stops.

'Hello?' A man's voice comes through the intercom. 'Anybody
there?' Instantly Nicole drops to her knees and crawls across the
carpet to the window. Hushing her breath, she flattens herself
sideways to the wall and looks down to the street below. There
is a white van double parked on the road and its hazard lights are

flashing. A man walks back to it, gets into the driver seat, and seconds later takes off.

She blows the hair from her eyes and moves across to the far wall of the living room. But this time the light has turned green and the beep tone changes.

There is an antique chest in the corner of the room and she gets down on her knees to move it. With a grunt she drags it clear and discovers the outline of a door, given away by the hairline gap in the wallpaper; when she presses with her fingers it pops open. Instantly the bright red numbers on the safe's digital display begin to shuffle and switch, blinking momentarily as each combination registers. Then with a pop the heavy steel door clicks open. Inside Nicole can see the small bag.

She takes it in her hands, shuts the safe door and withdraws the second of the Paymaster's envelopes from her coat pocket. For a second she imagines opening it, and even thinks she might dare. How could they possibly find out? Her hand begins to shake and she exhales, placing it carefully on the coffee table, just as she did before leaving Valerie Cheroux's house.

53

The diamonds are so light they are almost weightless. She holds them in one hand, wiping the sweat from her brow with the other. Inside the car it is silent and she listens to the sound of her own breath as her heartbeat steadies. There are twenty diamonds in total. She cups her hand and drops them all back into the cotton bag, running a finger along their rough edges through the fabric. Her pulse spikes as the sharp corners prick her skin and she puts the bag away.

Then she opens the car door and walks towards the vault on Merrion Road.

The centre is only seconds away. A security guard in a navy blue uniform with a peaked cap opens the heavy glass door to let her inside, white teeth beaming as he smiles. All she has to do is keep going now, to avoid unnecessary eye contact.

Her grip on the bag tightens inside her pocket.

'One second please.' A second security man appears from nowhere. He's older, less friendly. 'Can you take your hands out of your pockets?' His eyes search her face as he takes up a position in front of her. Feet wide, legs straight, shoulders square to her body.

Nicole stops walking, her lips parting but her voice stuck inside her throat. The guard taps the palm of his hand with a steel detector. It buzzes softly as he twists it between his fingers. 'Arms outstretched please ma'am when you're ready.' Closing her eyes Nicole instantly releases the bag, flicking her arms out stiffly. 'That's it.'

Slowly the machine chirps and whines as it runs across her body, down the left arm, the outside of her leg, back up the inside. Then it moves to the other side and he does the same. When it taps against her coat pocket it stops.

Clearing her throat, Nicole opens her eyes. The security guard is staring straight at her. She must not speak. Only wait. 'Thank you,' he then says. 'You can keep going now.'

Hurrying away she keeps moving until she arrives at the reception desk. When she stops she catches her breath.

'Mrs Reid?' the man behind the desk asks.

The diamonds crunch between her fingers as she steps forward. For a moment she imagines a net closing around her, some hidden string pulling sharply to bind her tight. Everything feels too smooth, too perfect. She realises they could have set her up to be caught with stolen goods worth millions.

'Yes?'

'Box 7294.' The man slides a form across the counter with a pen and smiles. 'We've been expecting you.'

54

Wednesday, November 22,
Evening

Nicole lifts the phone away from her ear and cancels the call. It's the best thing to do because even though she's aching to go to her kids, just to be with them at Alva's house, she knows it will be much harder to keep everything in if she meets her sister in person. She's so tired, still in shock at the second terrible crime she's just committed. Her teeth grit and she tries to hold down the rising swell of disgust.

The key twists and the lock pops opening the front door of her house.

'Nicole?'

She flinches. The voice is so close to her ear it is almost a whisper. Turning sharply, she discovers Mrs Lyubevsky.

'Nina?'

Mrs Lyubevsky retreats a step. There is a parcel in her hands. 'This came for you today.' Her neighbour lifts the parcel up but makes no move to hand it over. 'A stranger delivered it. A very unusual looking man, who peered through your window and then flung it on the ground like a piece of rubbish.' Mrs Lyubevsky raises her eyebrows as Nicole glances nervously down the street.

'What man?'

'That was what I asked myself, Nicole. What kind of man does that?'

'What did he look like, Nina?'

'He looked threatening.' Mrs Lyubevsky's small eyes pull tighter. 'And out of place.' She steps forward, still not handing over the parcel. 'So I came over to see what he was doing.'

The house keys inside the palm of Nicole's hand press into her flesh. 'What did you do?'

'Nothing. I was too terrified. But then something strange happened.'

'What?' Nicole's gaze flits from the parcel back to her neighbour.

'I went to retrieve this for you,' Mrs Lyubevsky looks at it intently, 'since I could hardly leave it on your doorstep to be stolen, and a second man appeared.'

'A second man?'

'The man I told Mark about, the one who has been lurking in our neighbourhood and I suspect is planning a robbery. And he was very interested in this for some reason.' The elderly woman cocks her head and shakes the parcel close to her ear. Nicole leans forward but her neighbour retreats a half step. 'I think you might have noticed him, Nicole? He dresses like a cyclist with a yellow high-visibility jacket?' Nicole shakes her head. 'Well, I told him plainly it wasn't his, and in a flash he got quite angry, demanding to know who had delivered it. And when I explained that he disappeared, leaving this behind.' Finally, she steps forward and holds out the package.

Nicole reaches for it, but Mrs Lyubevsky does not release it from her grip.

'Nicole?'

'Yes?'

'Some days ago, when I spoke with Mark and told him about my concerns, he said he'd mention it to you and get you to pass me on your sister's mobile number, just in case of emergencies and that kind of thing.' Nicole hears the noise of her own saliva sliding down her throat. The grip of her neighbour's fingers at the other end of the parcel hasn't relaxed. 'Would you mind giving that to me? I'd be so grateful to you.'

A prickling heat spreads over Nicole's skin. What might her neighbour do if she refuses? Could she go to the police? Normally she's so friendly but today it's like she's changed.

'Of course.' The parcel releases into her hands and Nicole rocks back to adjust her balance. Mrs Lyubevsky takes out her phone and waits, an expectant look now on her face. Slowly Nicole calls out the number and watches her key it in.

'Thank you, Nicole,' her voice softens. 'I don't wish to be nosey, but how is Mark? It's been some time since I've seen him.'

Nicole's mouth twitches. 'I'm sorry Nina, but Mark and I are . . . ' She stops. *Arouse no suspicion. Raise no alarms*, the Paymaster's order replays silently in her head. The sinking feeling inside her stomach returns. 'I'm afraid I can't talk right now, I think I need to get some rest.'

55

Wednesday, November 22,
Night

The parcel's paper wrapping lies torn and crumpled on the bedroom floor. It contains one item of clothing, Mark's wool jumper. Nicole hugs it close, clutching it tight in her hands, breathing in the lingering scent of his skin and aftershave. It's Armani Code, she knows, because she bought it for him last Christmas. It will soon be time to put up the decorations for Christmas. Mark was always first to remember, going into the attic to pull out all the boxes of baubles and tinsel, setting aside a weekend to help the girls do up their rooms, then organising everything in the living room to sort out all the lights.

Last year they spent two hours hanging things on the tree together, finishing with Mark lifting Holly up on his shoulders, because she insisted on being on his shoulders and not just lifted to place the star. And when she was up there she was so thrilled she could touch the ceiling, and it took her three attempts to get the star on top of the tree because the stem was too thick. Each time Mark would have to lift her down, trim it a fraction, and then try again. Immediately Chloe wanted to do it too. And Nicole was worried because she was afraid Chloe would fall, she was already so tall that her head was almost banging the ceiling.

Then when Chloe finished her turn Mark eased her onto his arm and placed her back down to the ground lightly like it was no effort at all. And Nicole knew he did it on purpose, because he wanted to make sure Chloe didn't feel too big, and that she was no different to Holly. Stifling a sob, she presses Mark's sweater closer, remembering then how Chloe wrapped her arms around him afterwards, just hugging him like she didn't want to let him go. Mark was grinning at Nicole and she could see his eyes were glistening too.

Her gaze drifts down to the laptop on the carpet but it remains quiet, its screen switched to power saving mode. Instinctively her knuckles tighten inside the wool. Closing her eyes she grits her teeth. She's completed the robbery, delivered the diamonds, but now there's only silence from the Paymaster.

Her thoughts are interrupted by a buzzing noise on the bed. When she pulls Mark's sweater away she sees Alva's name light up her phone.

'Hi,' she answers, her voice low and jaded.

'Nicole? Are you alright?'

'I'm OK. How are the girls? I was trying to call you.'

'I know. It's all a bit hectic at the minute with this case I have on, but I won't bore you with the details. Talk to me. Are you feeling any better?'

'A little.' Her eyes flick anxiously to the laptop. She has accepted that the girls are safer with Alva and Shaun, but it doesn't make it easier being without them, and the house feels almost haunted it's so lonely. 'Might need a bit more time I think.'

'That's fine. Go slowly, OK? There's no rush. The girls are grand with us. Seriously now.'

'Thanks, Alva.'

There's a pause. 'I'm sorry Nic, because last time we spoke you were just about to tell me about Mark when we got interrupted, so what's this I'm hearing? The jammy bastard's gone away?' Alva laughs and Nicole sits up, her pulse quickening. 'The kids were telling me. Where did he slip off to then?'

Thoughts scramble through Nicole's head. She should be prepared for this but somehow she is all at sea. She has to keep it straight. Simple. 'Yeah, that's right, Barcelona.'

'What!?'

Her fingers clutch Mark's jumper. 'A mate of his called Ken won a trip and asked Mark to go with him – so I told him to go.' She swallows noisily. She doesn't lie to Alva. It's their deal. The one they made long ago. But she can't stop now. She has to keep going.

'The lucky wanker! Well, none of that bagging you the nasty T-shirt or the cheap airport sausage. He better return with proper gifts. You can tell him I said that.'

'I will.' Alva's laughter peters out. Nicole senses a chance to change the conversation. To steer it away from Mark. 'This case you're working on sounds big?'

There's a long sigh. 'Fuck sis, you've no idea. It's . . . ' Alva hesitates, 'I guess the most I can tell you right now is that it's loaded and it's personal.' She clears her throat and when she speaks again her voice lightens. 'Well, suppose that's the job isn't it. Like father, like daughter.'

Alva laughs again but Nicole can trace some tension in her sister's voice this time. It was always like that when they were little, when she knew Alva had more to say but just hadn't said it yet. Knowing each other so well it was impossible not to sense these things. But what can Alva sense from her now? Surely she's figured out there's more than what Nicole has told her. Is she simply waiting for her to bring it up? 'Alva, what's the worst types you deal with?'

'That's easy. Murderers. Cold, heartless fuckers, the lot of them.'

Nicole winces. 'What about,' she takes a second to steady her voice, 'what about kidnappers?'

'God yeah, definitely a close second. Just as ruthless but since a good kidnapper requires lots of brains, there tends to be fewer of them. Most of them are murderers anyway and half the kidnaps end with death.'

56

Thursday, November 23,
Morning

Thwack. Nicole sits upright in the bed. She is still wearing her clothes and trainers from yesterday, the smell of her own body raw. *Thwack.* Her head is fuzzy, thick with sleep. The room is dark. She squints her eyes, glancing around for her phone but can't find it anywhere. *Thwack*, the noise comes again. Pressing her hands to her eyes she kicks off the bed covers. Light floods the room when she pulls the curtain.

'Hello?' Somebody is calling from outside.

'Fuck.' Nicole gets to her feet unsteadily and starts down the stairs. Her phone screen shows 09.03. It's the first time she's slept in days. Rubbing her face, she hears the man speak again.

'Sorry to wake you like this.' She stops in the hall, listening. The man's voice is gentle, almost familiar. But she can't quite place it.

'Who is this?' she calls.

'I'll explain,' he replies, quieter this time.

Sliding the latch chain back Nicole teases the door open a few inches. Her heart pounds. It's the courier again. The man who has been following her. He's no longer wearing a high-vis jacket or cycle leggings. Now he wears dark jeans and a raincoat. He takes his hands from his pockets and moves towards the door. 'The parcel you got. What was in it?' His voice is urgent now. Demanding.

'Who are you?' Nicole grips the door. 'What do you want?'

'I need to know about the parcel. What was in the parcel?'

'Why are you asking?'

'Were there cards in the parcel?' His eyes sweep across the street behind him and he whispers. 'This is about your husband and you need to let me in.'

Stepping forward he reaches out and immediately Nicole reacts, slamming the door as hard as she can but her movements are too slow. The door pushes in so forcefully it rips the latch chain free.

The man reaches for her, but she moves aside and brushes past him.

'Wait,' he grabs hold of her sleeve. 'Don't run, we need to talk. You have to listen.'

Nicole shrugs him off and runs outside but instantly loses her balance, tripping on the wet tiles that lead to the house. Falling hard, her head connects with the ground making a dull thump.

'Oh fuck,' the courier crouches down, a worried frown now on his face. 'I'm sorry! Let me help you, please. I don't want to harm you.'

Nicole places her fingers on the damp patch of her hair just above her ear. *Blood.* She rubs it between her fingers as the man places a hand on her shoulder.

'You're bleeding!' he says. 'We have to get you help.'

She must get up so she can run for her life; but her head pounds and each thump of her heart pushes the pain deeper inside. Pulling her phone from her pocket she tries to use it but she can't focus on the screen. It drops from her fingers and the man takes it.

'I need to get you an ambulance. This is serious,' he whispers.

Nicole sinks back to the ground, the blood thumping in her ears. 'My doctor,' her speech sounds garbled. 'His name is Fenton. He's in the contacts.'

Chris Ashton finds the number. After two rings the doctor picks up. 'I'm calling on behalf of Nicole Reid.' He steps back inside the front door of the house, cupping the phone with his other hand and lowering his voice. 'She's had an accident. She needs to come in now. I can take her to you.'

'Who is this?'

'It doesn't matter. Can you treat her?' He turns toward the stairs, unaware that Nicole is already on her feet and standing next to him. Before he sees her, she snatches the phone.

Her keys are on the table inside the hall and she takes them as she runs out of the house to the foot gate. The stranger approaches. He doesn't run or hurry. Instead he walks slowly and stops within a yard of where she now stands outside the gate.

'Please,' he says, his voice soft. 'Let me help. We can just talk, it's about Mark.' His blue eyes hold her gaze and for a second she hesitates. Then she turns and runs.

57

Thursday, November 23,
Morning

From the window next door Mrs Lyubevsky watches, her heart pounding, as Nicole runs. The man she recognises from before pauses, then walks back to Nicole and Mark's front door, slamming it shut, before leaving.

Scrolling for Alva's number, she finds it. Then she takes a deep breath and presses call.

58

Thursday, November 23,
Morning

The smell of antiseptic in Dr Fenton's surgery is strong. His small brown shoes manoeuvre deftly as he adjusts his stance, dabbing with gentle hands around the wound at the back of Nicole's head, the plastic disposable gloves squeaking faintly as he works.

The doctor drops a cotton ball into the steel tray on his desk and Nicole sees the flecks of dark congealed blood which speckle its once white colour. It joins the three other balls of cotton which have already been discarded.

'Nearly there,' Dr Fenton, whispers soothingly, 'I'm sorry you had to wait. It's been busy this morning, but we're almost done. Just a bit of tidying up that's all.' He presses lightly, holding it on the wound, before lifting it away.

He sits then behind the broad wooden desk and removes his gloves. 'It does happen unfortunately.' His voice is apologetic. 'When the glue becomes unstuck with stitches.' Dropping the gloves into the steel tray he picks it up, walks silently to the bin and dumps them. 'It was only a minor rupture so hopefully they will still hold. It's a wait and see game for a while I'm afraid.'

Nicole swallows. Time is disappearing so fast. She needs to get home. The memory of the courier comes back. What does he know about Mark?

'There is one little thing though which concerns me, Nicole. It's a swelling at the side of your head. Did you catch it or bang it by any chance?'

She must lie. Because telling the truth could mean more tests or even a visit to the hospital. 'Possibly when I was asleep, I may have caught it on the side dresser because when I woke this morning I found traces of blood on the pillow, and then when the man called at the house, I became very faint. I don't think it's bad, I think it's tiredness more than anything.'

'I understand. And who was the man?'

'A delivery man. I dropped the phone when he came to the door so he sort of took charge.' Dr Fenton places his hands down on the desk and picks up his pen, an uncertain look in his eyes. 'I feel a little embarrassed really, now that you've told me I'm alright.'

The chair squeaks as he adjusts it, moving it closer to the desk. He leans forward then, a taut expression forming around his mouth. 'Nicole, I don't want to be alarmist but I'm not entirely certain you *are* alright.' He takes his reading glasses off and places them down. 'The contusion above your ear is unusual and it's something I think we need to keep a very close eye on. When you've recovered a little and got some rest, I want you to come back in to see me so we can discuss further tests.'

Nicole nods stiffly.

Dr Fenton sits back and sighs. 'It's merely precautionary, Nicole. That way we make sure you are one hundred per cent.' He puts his glasses back on and starts to write on his pad. 'I'm prescribing a topical ointment for disinfecting the wound which I want you apply at night before going to bed and again when you wake up.'

Nicole stands, waits for the dizziness to pass, before walking over to take the prescription. Dr Fenton slides it across the desk and follows her to the door. 'You are resting? Making sure to keep your stress to a minimum. It's a very important aspect of recovery.'

Nicole folds the prescription and puts it in her pocket, trying to imagine what he might say if she told him what had happened, what had really happened since the night Mark went missing last

Friday. Would he understand and help her? She knows it's impossible. Nobody would. 'As much as I can, yes.'

'Good,' his eyes soften. 'Well, I want to repeat what I said before, if in doubt don't hesitate to call. I understand emergencies don't keep regular hours.' He taps the door softly. 'Pass my regards to Mark.'

Little sparks of pain burn behind Nicole's eyes. Without replying, she walks away.

59

Thursday, November 23,
Morning

From the front seat of her black Audi jeep Eve peers across the road at Nicole's house. The little old lady from next door has just come out through the gate and turned to walk down the street.

'Good,' she whispers, her smile spreading wider across her face. It's not that she dislikes the woman, in fact she finds her very agreeable. Only last week they had a lively chat about new apartments being developed close by and Eve was taken aback at how sharp the woman's mind was. 'Razor sharp', she had said to Nicole afterwards and they had both laughed. But she also knows that elderly people usually like to talk, to idle away the time. Who could blame them? Eve knows she would be horribly lonely if she reached the same age and found herself single still. Anyhow, today Eve does not have time. She is busy. And also put out that Nicole managed to avoid meeting her earlier. There's something about the way Nicole is behaving, the tension in her voice, the haste to cut short their conversations that she wants to understand. This can't just be about the money. Plus, Nicole's story about Mark going to Barcelona was clearly hollow. But until Mark starts answering her calls she won't know exactly what Nicole knows, or if she knows anything at all.

Flipping the envelope over, she rests it against the centre section of the large steering wheel and presses down the sticky part to make sure it is properly sealed. Then she flips it back and taps it twice on the corner. The printed front sticker was a good idea. That way Nicole can't try and guess her handwriting and she'll have no clue who's dropped this in the door. Being charitable can sometimes be painful but this way it's almost guaranteed pain free. She just hopes Nicole will find it the same.

Checking her phone she sees there are still no messages from Mark. Tapping two red fingernails to her lip, she scowls. She should really be celebrating the good news of her divorce settlement, but she can't because she knows she is only truly happy when everything is just right. That's one of the reasons, she often explains to her daughter Lily, why she's good at what she does; why she will always be sought after. It's also why people like her friend Nicole will always come second best.

'God!' the word comes out in a gasp, the harshness of the silent judgement catching her by surprise. Because she didn't always look upon Nicole like this. Not at the beginning. And even now she still believes they're good friends.

With a gentle tap her head rolls to the window and she lets it hang there, for a moment taken aback at how sad she feels. Because their friendship is changing, and Eve won't stop that because she doesn't believe she can. Collateral damage. Wasn't that what the American business coach said in their last session? A given inevitability in any conflict and one you have to make your peace with. She shakes her head, remembering how much it resonated when she heard the words.

Her eyes flick back to the street as she contemplates her next move. There have to be other ways to get to Mark, she just needs to plan a little more.

The Snapchat map is open on her phone and when she looks for Nicole, she finds her instantly. Eve recognises the address as Dr Fenton's, the GP Mark told her about.

A quick check of her lipstick in the wing mirror satisfies her that it's OK and she opens her door. Mrs Lyubevsky is far enough away and there is no chance they will meet. Stepping out of the car, she glances over her shoulder once, then skips straight to Nicole's front door.

60

Thursday, November 23,
Morning

'What the fuck is going on?' Alva says, opening the driver door to her unmarked police car and glaring at Nicole across the top of the roof. 'Who the hell was that guy?' Alva gets in as Nicole eases her way stiffly into the passenger seat. She doesn't look at Alva, opting instead to keep her eyes fixed forward.

'Is that the guy Mrs Lyubevsky said was attacking you at the house?' Alva's eyes remain locked on the corner of the street where Chris has disappeared seconds before.

Nicole adjusts her seat belt, stifling the bubble of anger which the mention of her neighbour's name releases inside her. Clearly Mrs Lyubvesky was trying to help but it's made the situation more complicated. Alva is wound up and Nicole knows she mustn't let it escalate. 'Did she say that?'

'She said some guy knocked you down and you were bleeding, and next thing I know you're at the doctors and some man is running away from the scene when he sees me as if he's afraid I might recognise him?'

Nicole's fingers tighten around the seat belt as she tugs it down across her chest. 'I slipped outside the house, Alva. A delivery man called the surgery for me because he was at the door when it happened.' She releases the belt and it slides slowly back into its holder. 'Then he wanted to drive me down here but I wouldn't let him because I told him I was fine.'

'And are you fine?'

187

Nicole shrugs, trying to figure out if Alva really believes her. 'It isn't serious, just the stitches tearing.'

'Jesus Christ, Nicole.' Alva puts the gear stick back into neutral and the handbrake on, then she reaches over to wrap her arms around her. 'When it rains it fucking pours for you, yeah?'

Nicole lets her face sink into Alva's sleeve, shutting her eyes tight. She mustn't cry. It will make it worse. When they separate Nicole presses the heel of her hand into one eye. 'So what about that guy then?'

'I don't know.' Nicole reconnects the seat belt where it has clicked free from its holder. 'I didn't see anybody when I came out but maybe he followed me to make sure I went or something. Did you get a look at him?'

Alva puts the car into gear and moves onto the road. 'No, he ran too fast. But I can check the police cams when I get to the station. They might have picked him up.'

61

Thursday, November 23,
Morning

'Where are we going?' Nicole releases her breath slowly feeling a headache coming on.

Alva pulls up at the traffic lights and flicks off the car radio. 'You're coming with me.'

'What?' Nicole feels her throat tighten.

'Yeah, with me to the station sis'.' The light goes green and Alva accelerates.

'But . . . ' She can't do this now. What does Alva know? And what if the Paymaster thinks she is passing information to her sister? She waits, glancing nervously out the window.

A motorcyclist thunders past their car, zipping dangerously in front of them forcing Alva to brake sharply.

'What the fuck? Has this guy got a death wish or what?' With a smack of the palm of her hand she hits the horn and it beeps loudly. She glares after it, as if deciding to give chase, then shakes her head. 'Screw it, I couldn't be arsed playing catch right now. He'll probably wrap himself round a pole a mile up the road any-way.' Glancing across to Nicole, she grins. 'Hey, relax will you, I didn't say I was going to arrest you, I just said you were coming with me so we can hang out for a bit, Christ knows you could use a little attention right now, yeah?'

Nicole breathes, then replies. 'OK. Thanks, Alva.'

'Don't know how much fun it's going to be but at least we might get a chance to chat,' Alva sighs and changes gears as the car moves forward. 'And listen, I'm sorry, but it's just that I've been so busy with this case since I got back from holidays, I've hardly had a chance to look in on you.'

'It's fine.' Nicole twists one of the air vents so it blows towards her. 'I understand. It's the Doherty case isn't it?' Alva nods. 'I know it's sensitive.'

Alva exhales loudly, her eyes shifting out the window to the traffic. 'It is Nic. And I'm looking forward to telling you all about it when it's over. Trust me.' She glances across then and Nicole thinks she's about to elaborate, but Alva's eyes soften. 'Hey, I was meaning to tell you something.'

'What?'

'Remember the other day you were asking me about Dad, and how he said you were always so kind to animals it made him worry.'

'Yeah?'

'I was thinking about that.' A space opens up in front of them and Alva drives forward to catch up. 'It might have been about the time you rescued the baby swan like I told you, but then I think it might have been something else too.'

'What?'

'I think Dad might have been projecting a bit, isn't that what it's called?' Alva's voice becomes gentle. 'You know, he's dealing with all this shit at work, some of the nastiest people you could have the bad luck to meet, so he's got these fears, and then he looks at his daughter, and she's so kind, and innocent really, and he worries that one day it could come back to hurt you.' Reaching a hand across she pats Nicole on the knee. 'I think I understand it now, doing what Dad used to do. Sometimes we learn stuff we didn't want to know, truths that might have been better off buried, so we worry.'

Nicole gazes out the passenger window. 'I think I get that.'

The tips of Alva's fingers touch her cheek, rubbing it gently. 'Listen, the Doherty case is so important to me because it concerns Dad, Nic.'

'How?' The word catches at the back of Nicole's throat.

'I can't say. Not now. That's just how my job goes.' Nicole nods, the questions burning inside her that she knows she cannot ask anymore. 'Now I better shut up before we all start crying.' Turning the radio on she adjusts the volume control as Amy Winehouse's voice floats out from the speakers and her eyes flick down to the laptop at Nicole's feet. 'You and that laptop seem to be glued together at the moment.'

Nicole moves her legs, and the green light flickers at the edge of her bag where the laptop rests in the footwell. 'Yeah, sometimes I just want to jot my thoughts in the journal so it's handy to have it on me.'

Alva's eyes linger on it and she nods slowly. Then her attention returns to the road.

62

Thursday, November 23,
Morning

'Have you ever seen a police line-up?'

Nicole shakes her head. 'Only on TV.'

They both sit facing the one-way glass in Pearse Street Police Station.

'Don't be so nervous, they can't see you.' Alva points to the empty space on the other side. 'And anyway, there's nobody there yet.'

Nicole nods. 'I suppose I'm not used to police stations. When I walked in I was trying to think of the last time I visited you at work and I couldn't remember.'

Alva smiles. 'Maybe that's a good thing, Nic.' There's a knock on the door and a female officer puts her head inside. 'Inspector Finlay, something's come up. It's the Chief Super. He's called a meeting. He said it won't take long but he needs you there if that's OK?'

Alva rolls her eyes. 'Nicky, you alright by yourself here for a minute?'

'Yeah fine, go ahead.' The female officer holds the door and Alva marches through it leaving Nicole alone.

Nicole slumps in her chair. She knows that every minute her sister is busy means there are fewer questions for her to answer, fewer lies for her to weave about Mark's supposed foreign holiday, and yet she can't relax.

Dropping her face into her hands she closes her eyes. Her head hurts badly now that the adrenaline has fizzled out. *Mark*. She has to get away from here so she can start searching for him. Her head is spinning once more, the sound of her skull cracking against the path outside her front door echoing inside it, the noise of the courier's steps as he walked over and knelt down beside her, while she watched like a spectator, momentarily paralysed, her cheek cold against the wet ground. Why has this man approached her and what does he want? How does he know about Mark? She remembers her lie to Alva that she didn't recognise him at Dr Fenton's and knows it was a risk. If Alva figures out it's the same man who called to the house then her deception will be revealed. What happens then? Will Alva really believe more lies? She cannot think how she is going to avoid telling her everything.

Taking out the laptop she connects it to the hotspot on her phone. It's been too long since she has received communication from the Paymaster and her fear grows. Rising from the chair she begins to pace. If they don't make contact what else can she do to find him?

But the wait is short. *Click.*

The muscles along her spine coil so quickly she winces.

The familiar hum sounds then. Nicole chews her thumbnail as the fan starts to whir.

The text is already forming on the screen.

Ready?

Her heart squeezes as her eyes flick to the door. How long will Alva be gone? Seconds? Minutes? She has no clue.

Where is Mark?

Safe.

What do you want?

One final task.

Then what?

Complete it successfully and you get Mark. Ready now?

The blood vessel in her forehead pulses. *What do you need from me?*

You must steal information.

I've done enough.

Not yet.

Bristling, she stares at the screen. Another crime. Another victim. She types again.

From who?

The cursor blinks for some seconds but no words appear. Nicole glances furtively at the door, listening as footsteps approach. Instantly she puts out her hand to shut the laptop down but the footsteps grow faint and disappear. More text has followed.

Your sister. The black flash drive inside her office desk drawer. Get it done or else.

Nicole's eyes widen. She cannot do this. She won't. She types again.

When do I get Mark?

We'll be in touch when you have what we need.

The screen shuts down just as the door opens. Nicole slams the laptop closed expecting to see Alva, but it's the female officer who returns.

'Nicole, Alva's going to be another few minutes or possibly more. Are you OK waiting here?'

Rising to her feet, Nicole puts the laptop back inside the bag. The third and final envelope the Paymaster gave her to deliver is still there too. The palms of her hands are moist when she rubs them together. 'Sure, I'm just going to use the bathroom.'

Walking through the door she presses the bag close to her chest, trying to guess how long it will take her to get to Alva's desk and back.

63

Thursday, November 23,
Morning

When she sits back down opposite the one-way glass Nicole presses her hands to her face, but they don't cool her skin. The sour taste of sick swirls inside her mouth and as she gulps for air the stink of it lingers on her tongue.

It's a huge relief that nobody saw her at Alva's desk. They must have all gone to the meeting she assumes. Nicole tries to imagine what might have been written on the card she deposited inside Alva's desk drawer but she draws a blank. How could they have any possible blackmail on her sister? Her stomach heaves when, to her surprise, the door opens and Alva rushes in with two police officers flanking her, one on either side.

'Nicole?' the two other officers stand back as Alva approaches.

'Yes?' The quiver in her voice is so bad she almost doesn't recognise it.

'Something's up.' Alva hunches down, whispering softly. 'It's the case I've been telling you about, the Doherty one.' Silently Nicole nods, jamming her hands beneath her thighs. 'We're going to have to catch up another time.' Alva places a hand on her shoulder.

Nicole blinks. 'Fine.'

64

Thursday, November 23,
Evening

Little cracks line the ceiling of the Salisbury Hotel. Nicole glances up at it, remembering. It was Mark who brought her here first, picking out the exact spot they should sit in, offering her the red Chesterfield chair beside the wrought iron fireplace with its mahogany mantlepiece. He had just won his second clinical excellence award and they celebrated with champagne and pizza, gazing contentedly at the elaborate cornices, the herringbone floor, the oak panelled bar.

The barman picks up some bottle tops on the nearby table, drops them inside his apron pocket and gathers the empty beer glasses. 'You OK there, or can I get you anything?'

It's the second time he's checked on Nicole since she arrived more than two hours earlier. Her eyes flick up quickly from the laptop to meet his. 'No, thanks, I'm OK.'

The bar has been quiet but as the evening turns to night more drinkers stream in. The conversation is getting louder, the place busier. As each new group of friends make their way by, casually chatting, hugging, and placing orders, Nicole's hand reaches up to feel the flash drive that hangs around her neck on a string. Staring at the crowd, she rubs it with her fingers, for a second thinking of calling the barman back and ordering alcohol. But she won't, because she knows if she begins she might not want to stop. Wearily, she raises her glass of sparkling water and sips again.

Her mind keeps spinning. Why did the Paymaster want Alva's information? And what could her sister have possibly done that they are blackmailing her about? Because what else could the cards be? For a minute, back at the station, she thought about opening the envelope, but there wasn't time, and she's relieved she resisted. Rubbing the flash drive nervously between her fingers, she glances once more at the laptop, scrolling yet another picture of Mark and the girls.

The headache is back again so she takes two of the painkillers from the packet and swallows them down. It's been hours now and still the Paymaster has avoided contact. Why?

She thinks about their girls. She has to be careful. It's getting close to the end. They will make contact soon.

They must.

65

The dark puddle ripples on the pavement and Nicole steps around it, hurrying quickly towards her front door. The rain has begun to fall and she squeezes the laptop bag closer to her chest. As soon as she gets inside she will try once more to make contact.

Looking up, she reaches out to open the foot gate but two large men block the path. It's the Paymaster's men, the pair she remembers from the night of the kidnapping. The taller man's hand whips out and he holds it in front of her face. *Snap*. Thick fingers click loudly, inches from her eyes and her heart thumps.

'The drive.'

'What?'

The driver steps behind her now, blocking off her escape. 'You heard.'

'*No*.' She glances across the street. There is nobody around, it won't matter if she screams.

'Don't try and run,' the tall one warns, wagging his long index finger as if reading her thoughts. 'Just do as you're told and we'll be out of your hair.'

Nicole's hands ball into fists. She will not be cowed. 'That's not our deal. You give me Mark first,' she hisses.

Hearing a movement behind her, she turns to find the driver stepping closer, the edges of his small mouth twisting to a sneer. Distracted, she hardly sees the second man's hand darting to her throat and ripping the drive from her neck.

The string snags as he yanks it free, jerking her forward.

She gapes, her feet frozen to the ground, as the pain ripples up her scalp and the men stride back to the black jeep.

Then finally, realising what is happening, she unfreezes and runs towards them.

Her fingernails break the skin of the giant's hand as she claws at his clenched fist.

'Give it back to me. And take me to Mark, *now*.' The laptop bag slips from her shoulder and falls to the ground making a dull thud as it flattens on the pavement. There's a peel of harsh laughter in her ears when the tall man spins, his enormous hand lashing out and catching her cleanly across the jaw with a backhanded slap. For a moment she is blinded, her eyes unable to focus, her skin tingling.

Rough fingers grip the front of her coat and the smell of stale cigarettes fills her nostrils. 'The Paymaster will be in touch,' one of them growls, shoving her against the iron railings. Unbalanced and surprised by the force of the push, she slams against the hard bars and trips to the ground. The big jeep roars and the tyres screech as she pushes her hands into the wet pavement, but there is not enough strength in her arms to get up and her body shakes violently.

66

Thursday, November 23,
Night

Mrs Lyubevsky hurries out through the front gate, her phone out in front of her as she steps into the middle of the road. But the jeep has fled. There won't be a chance to take a picture of the registration plate.

With a grunt of disgust she puts it back in her pocket and retreats to the pavement, only now noticing the slumped form of her neighbour lying on the wet ground. The laptop bag she often carries is beside her, just a little beyond her reach.

'Dear god, Nicole. What have they done to you?' Instantly she goes to her, bending to retrieve the bag and offering an out-stretched hand. 'Come.' Groaning from the effort, she heaves Nicole back to her feet. 'We need to get you cleaned up.' Nicole wobbles unsteadily, clinging to Mrs Lyubevsky's wrist. 'We'll go to my house.'

67

Thursday, November 23,
Night

Everything inside Mrs Lyubevsky's living room is as Nicole remembers; two cream coloured armchairs with paisley patterns which have faded to light brown, the faint, dusty smell of the smokeless coal as the fire crackles in the stove, mixed with the lingering whiff of cat urine; three dim bulbs hang above their heads in the carved wooden light fitting.

Mrs Lyubevsky breathes hard as she wedges the small glass table close to Nicole's side. 'There now, I hope you're more comfortable. I'll just be a minute.'

There's a footrest in front of Mrs Lyubevsky's armchair with a cushion on top of it. Nicole runs her finger through one of the cat scratches in the armrest and stares at the firelight flickering and twisting inside the glass. Then Rocky jumps to the footrest and starts to curl up.

'No Rocky,' Mrs Lyubevsky lifts him swiftly and places him back down to the ground. The cat meows and looks at her pleadingly as she shuffles to the corner, picks up two tumbler glasses and returns slowly, handing one to Nicole before sitting opposite her. 'I'm sorry it's just whisky I have to offer you. Since Leon's death I never really see anyone so I don't keep anything in the house.'

Nicole's hand shakes as she presses the glass hard against her lips before swallowing a sip. 'Thank you.' Her voice is faint when she speaks and the skin on her face tingles.

'Don't thank me, Nicole. It's the very least I could do for you.' Pushing against the armrests Mrs Lyubevsky rises and moves to the wicker basket by the fireplace where she plucks a chopped block of kiln dried wood. Opening the door of the stove she drops it onto the red embers and Nicole stares at it sadly as the fire puffs, eventually wrapping the wood in a blanket of blue and orange flame. 'Are you completely certain I shouldn't call the ambulance?' Mrs Lyubevsky sits down once more. 'That was a bad fall, Nicole?'

Nicole rubs her jaw and feels the swelling under her fingers. 'I'm certain. Thank you.'

Mrs Lyubevsky leans forward, drinks from her glass and places it on the footrest beside the cushion. 'It's time for us to talk, isn't it?'

Nicole grips her glass and their eyes lock.

'I think you know that, don't you?'

She remembers the Paymaster's words. *Arouse no suspicion.* Nobody can know about this. They still have Mark. She cannot forget that for one second. With a slow nod, she lets her gaze drop down to the whisky glass in her hands.

Mrs Lyubevsky resumes. 'I haven't seen your children in some days, do you mind me asking where they are?'

'At my sister's. You remember Alva, the policewoman who you spoke to?'

Her neighbour nods. 'But why they are staying there and not with you?'

Nicole's finger finds the groove in the armrest again and she rubs it back and forth. She is so tired. The exhaustion is creeping deep inside her. She closes her eyes and takes a deep breath. If she can say as little as possible that's the key. She can't be ungrateful. If it wasn't for her neighbour she'd still be outside lying on the pavement. 'I'm having a difficult time at the moment. Things aren't good at home.'

'I see. Well, I'm very sorry to hear that.' The old woman's voice is gentle but beneath the kind words Nicole senses a steel edge. 'But who were those men that called to your house tonight?'

'The men?'

'Yes, the tall one I recognised from before. He's the man with the damaged ear, the one who came to your house to drop the parcel. Do you mind me asking what was in the parcel?'

Nicole presses the glass against her lips. The fumes from the alcohol go up her nose making her eyes water. She drinks it nervously, gulping too much and it burns the back of her throat. Why is Mrs Lyubevsky probing her like this? Has she been watching the whole time? She remembers seeing her at the window upstairs the night Mark disappeared. The night she . . . pressing her hand to her forehead she dispels the thought. No, she doesn't want to remember. She has to concentrate. She can't keep letting her cross-examine her. It has to stop. 'Nina, I'm sorry. I know you mean well but it's private.'

'I see.' Mrs Lyubevsky sighs but Nicole can't see any hint of apology in her face. Instead she is nodding and staring at the pillow on top of the footrest. 'I've always been very fond of you, Nicole. And I mean all of you. Mark, and the girls too. You're a beautiful family but now I'm worried.'

Nicole lowers her glass, edging further back into the armchair. 'Why?'

'Because I . . . ' she stops, glancing away towards the firelight before letting out a tired sigh. 'Nicole, listen to me now, please.' With a quick twist of her neck, she turns to look at her squarely, her face stern. 'A man assaulted you tonight in front of my eyes. Who were these people and why would they do that?'

There's a new sharpness in her neighbour's question. Nicole gazes into the twisting firelight. What would Mark do if he was in the same position? How would he handle her? They always seemed to get on so well and she always had kind words to say about him. For a second she sees him so clearly it's as if he's there with her – he's walking on the path in Bushy Park, holding the back of Holly's tiny bicycle, which he put together on Christmas Eve, teaching her patiently how to ride it, because the stabilisers they forgot to include in the box never came, holding the umbrella up to protect Holly from the rain. The shower has wet his hair and turned his camel coloured mac a deep brown but Mark doesn't notice, because he's too busy encouraging Holly to keep going as she twists the handlebars with tiny hands one way, and then the other.

'Nicole?'

'I'm sorry,' she says, meeting Mrs Lyubevsky's gaze. 'They're businessmen, Nina. They claim Mark is involved in an investment scheme they set up. I explained they had the wrong person and one of them became violent.' Nicole glugs the whisky. It scorches down her throat, making her wince as she puts the glass down. She has to get out. To get away. Before Mrs Lyubevsky calls her out as a liar; before she says another word.

'Businessmen?' Mrs Lyubevsky shakes her head, the disappointment in her eyes clear. 'They were not businessmen, Nicole.' Her voice is almost mocking. 'They were criminals.' Slowly she places her glass on the footrest, her gaze shifting to the stove as the firelight illuminates the wrinkles on her face. 'They were little better than animals.' Leaning forward then she fixes Nicole with a stare. 'I don't want to go to the police Nicole, which is why I've been waiting for you to explain what's going on but you're lying to me and it has to stop.' The exasperation in her voice rises. 'I've told you, I care about Mark, I care about your family. On Friday night, the night I babysat your girls, you came home without Mark. You were frantic and crying and I want to know why.'

Her neighbour is pushing her too hard, backing her into a corner she can't get out of. Nicole springs out of the armchair but immediately loses her balance and knocks into the footrest. The glass thuds as it drops onto the carpet and rolls away. Beside it lies the cushion which has fallen from its place to reveal a small gun. For a second neither of them move. The fire crackles behind the stove glass and the wind sucks up the chimney flue. Glancing from the gun to her neighbour Nicole can see that her calm has gone, in its place there is fear. Very slowly, without taking her eyes from Nicole's face, Mrs Lyubevsky extends her bony hand and grips it in her fingers.

Holding the gun in her lap Mrs Lyubevsky resumes. 'Last night I went to the attic and took this down because I wanted to give it to you. It's something Leon left behind when he passed away, a thing he always kept there and I almost forgot we had. I suppose since his business was security he always liked to know we were properly protected.' She eases back, her calm somewhat restored. 'I sensed you and your beautiful girls were in danger so I thought it could help you.' She sighs heavily, the barrel of the gun now shaking in her hand as she lifts it and points it at Nicole. 'Please forgive me Nicole, but I'm old and I have to be careful so I'm no longer so sure that's a good idea. Now I'm worried that it's Mark who's in danger.'

Nicole stares at her elderly neighbour. Mrs Lyubevsky cannot possibly be threatening her with a gun? And yet she is. She lets out a gasp as her eyes flick from the gun back to Mrs Lyubevsky's face.

'Please, no more lies now Nicole. Mark is gone, you're involved, that much is clear to me already. I want you to tell me what really happened that night Mark disappeared.'

Before she can think, Nicole's legs are moving, her arms pumping hard. The coffee table knocks over, tipping Nicole's whisky glass to the floor. It rolls in an arc towards the stove and shatters against the marble base. She keeps going, into the adjoining dining room and over towards the kitchen. Within seconds, instead of moving towards the front door, towards her escape, she's deeper into the house.

In the corner of her eye she sees Mrs Lyubevsky is on her feet and coming after her.

'Don't run, Nicole.'

There's a door out to a bathroom at the back of the house and she lurches towards it. Grabbing it by the handle she pulls it open. It's heavy in her hand, one of the old solid wooden doors she remembers her neighbour telling her about. Spinning she grips the edge of it in her hand and slams it as hard as she can, only now noticing that Mrs Lyubevsky is tumbling head first towards her.

The elderly woman's foot has snagged the carpet and her neck is outstretched, the front of her head protruding like a sprinter crossing a finish line.

Nicole doesn't have time to react. The heavy door has already released from her fingers, swinging forcefully backwards.

A cracking sound follows and Nicole screams.

68

Thursday, November 23,
Night

On the other side of the door Nicole listens. There is an anguished groan followed by what is most certainly the sound of her neighbour's body collapsing heavily to the ground. Then nothing.

The bathroom is cold and Nicole's coat snags as she slides down the inside of the door, her legs splaying on the icy grey tiles. With clenched teeth she keeps listening but the only sound she can hear is her own laboured breathing, drawing raggedly inside her lungs.

'Nina?' gripping the edge of the bathtub she pushes to her feet, the effort making her groan. 'Nina, speak to me.' Softly she presses her cheek against the door and waits but gets no response. Tears stain her cheeks and she wipes them away. A thin line of blood has appeared next to her foot. When she inspects it she sees it has wormed under the door from outside, trickling into the grooves between the tiles. 'Oh god.' Carefully she steadies her shaking hand and grips the doorknob. When she opens it Mrs Lyubevsky's head flops to the ground.

'Nina, wake up. Please. Come on.' Nicole drops to her knees and checks her pulse but Mrs Lyubevsky's head is heavy, her face unresponsive. There's a dark gash at the side of her face beneath her grey hair and blood keeps trickling from her nose, joining the small line which oozes further inside the bathroom. Gently Nicole props her against the door and a red smear smudges the bright white paint.

'Please *no*.' Quickly she paces to the kitchen and pulls up Alva's number on her phone but then stops. How will she explain? It could look like assault, attempted murder even; there will be so many questions she cannot answer if the police become involved, and if they charge her with something she'll certainly have to tell them about Mark. 'Fuck.' Immediately she stuffs her phone back inside her pocket, fighting back the sob which pushes up from deep inside. She has to get help, to hurry.

The gun still lies on the floor, the steel barrel gleaming beneath the lamplight. Stopping abruptly Nicole bends down to retrieve it. The whisky tumbler has cracked into pieces beside it. It's clear evidence of her presence with her fingerprints and she knows she cannot leave it behind. Hurrying, she picks the pieces from the floor, but her shaking fingers fumble and a shard pierces the skin. A shocked gasp escapes from her mouth and she starts to bleed.

Breathing heavily, she cradles her hand and rushes out of the house.

69

Deep lines furrow her brow and Nicole blows as she squeezes her hand against the tea-towel over her kitchen sink. The blood seeps from her finger, leaking heavily without any sign of stopping. It was a spur of the moment idea to bury the glass in amongst the flowers in the back garden but Nicole thinks she's done the right thing, even if she can't seem to get the dirt from her hands despite scrubbing them twice.

A bead of sweat rolls down the bridge of her nose and she uses the back of her forearm to wipe her brow. The lights are flashing already through the front window. She can't wait any longer; she's the reason they're here.

In a second, she stuffs the bloodied towel into the kitchen bin, turns round to the mirror and double checks the make-up she has just dabbed on her cheek. The bruise hasn't formed yet so it should be OK. Then she mops her face with the palm of her hand one last time and goes to the door.

The police car is parked up on the footpath directly outside her neighbour's house. The blue lights flicker and twist, casting the house in ghostly splashes of colour. In the middle of the road the ambulance's amber hazard lights blink and Nicole sees three paramedics by the back doors waiting.

'Mrs Reid?' The female officer rests her hands on her hip belt.

Nicole nods and her heart thumps as a second, male, officer walks out of Mrs Lyubevsky's front door waving his hand at the ambulance crew. 'Get the stretcher lads. It's not looking good.'

'Oxygen?' one of them asks and he nods. His heavy shoes slap loudly on the pitted concrete as he passes outside the front of the house before pushing through the foot gate. Both officers share a sombre look when he halts outside Nicole's front door.

'I'm officer Harris and this is officer Connolly,' the female officer explains in a hard, flat voice. 'We understand you contacted us regarding your neighbour. Is that correct?'

'Yes.' Nicole realises she is hiding behind the door and opens it further, quickly jamming her bloodied fingers inside her pocket. 'Is she OK?'

Neither officer answers her question but through the gap between them Nicole sees the paramedics rushing through with the stretcher.

'Mrs Reid,' Connolly asks this time. 'Can you describe to us how you found your neighbour?'

Nicole clears her throat. Lying is all she can do now. But she already knows that lies will lead to more lies, and you only lie to the police if you are guilty. 'I didn't find her, I heard a loud bang. I was worried. I rang her doorbell but there was no response. Then I noticed the fire in the stove was on so I couldn't understand why she didn't answer.' Pausing she takes a deep breath. 'I guessed she had an accident.'

'Why did you assume that?' Harris twists her thumbs inside her belt.

'I don't know. I just . . . I suppose because she's older. Is she OK?'

'Did you happen to notice that your neighbour's front door was open by any chance?' Connolly takes off his cap casually, smoothing his hair.

Nicole shakes her head. She left the door open deliberately so the ambulance could get in and help Mrs Lyubevsky quickly but now she realises it makes her version of events seem ridiculous.

'It was?'

'Yes, it certainly was.'

'You didn't visit your neighbour this evening? Drop in to say hello perhaps?' Harris lifts the radio handset from her belt and presses it to her mouth.

Nicole sways and her shoulder catches the doorframe. 'No.'

Harris presses the radio button. 'Just a breaking and entering and what looks like GBH. Could be more serious depending upon what happens after we get the victim to the hospital, sir. Myself and Garda Connolly have it under control. Only one witness at the moment and the paramedics are taking the victim to emergency now.'

Connolly puts his cap back on. 'We're going to have a look next door, Mrs Reid. You can relax inside for a bit now. We'll come back to you shortly if that's OK?' He waits for Harris to look him in the eye and nods to her. Then slowly they walk away without saying goodbye.

Nicole paces back and forth inside her kitchen replaying the events over and over inside her head, desperately trying to think how she might have acted differently, how she could have avoided smashing her elderly neighbour's head against a bathroom door. She knows it wasn't her fault, that she panicked when she saw the gun. But it doesn't change how she feels. She imagines explaining it to Alva. Would her sister even believe her? The sinking feeling grows; she's lied to the police; her story is weak; she has no witnesses to back it up; her neighbour might be dead.

Shaking, she hovers by the window, dark spots of blood seeping through the makeshift dressing she's wrapped around her finger. The paramedics are wheeling the stretcher out and Mrs Lyubevsky's long grey hair hangs over the side, tangled with blood and flapping in the breeze. The oxygen mask is over her face and she doesn't move. The three men work quickly loading her inside. 'St James's Hospital,' one of them shouts. *Bang, slap, click.* The back doors close and lock. Nicole presses a hand to her cheek, watching as the men walk away from the rear of the vehicle and get inside the cabin. The siren is already wailing when the engine roars, and the ambulance streaks away, its blue beams whirling like searchlights.

Nicole holds her side as the twisting inside her stomach grows. She staggers back to the kitchen and hangs over the sink, certain she is going to be sick. The room appears to be sliding and rolling like a boat on choppy water. She opens the tap to splash water on her face and it makes her shiver. When she looks in the sink the white porcelain is dirty with blood and clay. She drops her face down to splash it a second time when there's a rap on the front door.

She jumps, immediately trying to clear the sink, rubbing at it with her fingers but only making the streaks of blood and clay worse. There's a roll of kitchen towel paper on the counter and she grabs a sheet of it to dab her face and hands before scrunching it into a ball and binning it.

Taking a deep breath, she arranges the bandage on her finger, composes herself hastily and hurries out to open the door.

Connolly is looking down the street and Harris glares straight at her. There is new plastic tape saying 'Crime Scene' across Mrs Lyubevsky's front gate.

Turning round then, Connolly speaks. 'Would a couple of final questions before we go on our way be OK with you Mrs Reid?' Nicole props herself against the door-frame, squeezing her bloodied fingers beneath folded arms.

'Of course.'

'Great. Did you happen to see anybody out on the street when you called over?'

'No.'

He ducks his head and glances beyond Nicole into the house. 'Here by yourself?'

Nicole stares inside, the loneliness of the house almost taunting her. 'It's me and my family. We've two young girls.'

Harris steps back and looks up at the windows. 'Who are upstairs asleep?' The muscle tightens at the back of Nicole's neck as she nods, her breathing becoming shallow. What will she do if they choose to come in? She's powerless to stop them.

'Well, look at that,' Connolly interrupts them, dropping down to inspect Rocky as he runs across. The cat meows pleadingly and dashes to Nicole. Slipping her bandaged hand inside her pocket she picks him up awkwardly with one hand.

She tucks her face into his fur, waits for the sob that is rising to go back down before lifting her head again.

Connolly tips his cap. 'I think we'll leave it there for tonight, Garda Harris. Might not be fair to wake the kids if they're sleeping.'

Harris looks at the cat coldly. 'Fine, just be aware Mrs Reid, your neighbour's house is now a crime scene. Forensics will be out shortly to collect evidence. After that we'll see where this goes.'

'Goodnight, Mrs Reid,' Connolly waves. 'We appreciate your full cooperation in this ongoing investigation.' Harris doesn't say goodbye but her stare lingers on Rocky as she marches back to the police car.

70

Chris Ashton slows the hire car down as it turns into Marwood Road. The time on the clock tells him it's just after 2 a.m. Ed Wiley, the ex-Garda, had called ten minutes ago to tell him there had been a report of an incident right next door to Nicole Reid's house. He didn't have the details but he'd make some calls in the morning and let him know.

With a flick of his wrist he changes the heater fan, flicking it over to windscreen mode, then adjusting it to full speed to clear away the vapour which is shrouding his view of the road. He can't hang about but he needs to get a glimpse.

The blue and white police tape covers the front of the neighbour's house. Whatever happened was serious, that much is now clear.

With a deep sigh he drives on. Perhaps he hasn't timed this as well as he could have. But tomorrow, as soon as Wiley gives him the report, he'll have to make his move.

71

Friday, November 24,
Morning

'Please hold while we try to connect you,' the robotic voice plays again on Nicole's phone speaker. Raising it high in her hand she fights the urge to hurl it against the wall. With a sigh she waits for the rage to pass but it doesn't. She can't understand how the hospital switchboard has connected her to a computer; she had already spoken to a member of staff who agreed to pass her through to the nurse assigned to Mrs Lyubevsky. Dropping the phone on the kitchen table, she leaves it there, the jarring music filling up the void of silence.

Her eye remains glued to the laptop as she steps away but it shows no change from when she checked it minutes before. The screen is asleep and only the whine of the tiny fan inside is audible. But now, as she paces back and forth inside the empty space of her usually busy house, she is finally processing what has happened. The Paymaster has cheated her; they've taken Alva's drive with confidential police files, they've got the stolen diamonds from Elliot Preston as well as one million euros from the philanthropist Valerie Cheroux; and in return they have given her nothing.

The deal was a lie.

Dragging her finger across the trackpad, Nicole waits for the screen to wake up, her eye drifting to the opened envelope beside it. It's the one somebody put through the letterbox with no note and no handwriting at all, just a printed sticker with her name on the front. Inside the folded sheet of paper the one hundred euros voucher for Tesco is still there. Why would somebody anonymously send her a voucher? Is this the Paymaster's idea of a twisted joke? Offering morsels of support while using her to earn millions? The muscle in her jaw clenches but a voice has finally answered on her mobile and she snatches it.

'Yes?'

'Mrs Reid?'

'Speaking?'

'It's nurse Rachel Davies here. I understand you're a relative of Mrs Nina Lyubevsky and would like an update on her condition, is that correct?'

'I am not her relative. I'm her neighbour.'

'Oh?' The nurse is surprised. 'I'm sorry but I won't be able to help you then.'

'Please,' Nicole's voice breaks. 'The woman doesn't have next of kin. They've passed away. I'm her nearest friend and neighbour. I'm the one who found her and called the ambulance. I really need to know if she's alright. It's important to me.'

The nurse sighs. 'Listen I can't give you specific details but I can say that your neighbour has gone into ICU. When they brought her in she was unconscious. I don't know the extent of the damage but she needs to be scanned.'

'For?'

'Neurology want to check her.'

'Brain damage. They're checking her for brain damage?'

'It's a precaution. There was considerable trauma to the head.' Nicole sinks into a chair at the table, the energy draining from her body. 'But we're still hopeful.'

'I understand,' Nicole replies, her voice so faint she barely hears it.

The nurse sighs. 'Look, I'm on the night shift here till breakfast. If I get an update I'll get in touch first thing. Try not to worry. We don't know anything for certain yet. Alright?'

Click! The laptop screen flickers and Nicole cuts the line. Immediately the screen fades to black. Next the hard drive hums as the first word appears.

Nicole?

Her eyes blur as she types. *Give me back my husband you bastard.*

No.

We had a deal.

It's changed.

Why? I gave you the drive. I completed the three tasks.

Not successfully. The drive is corrupted.

Lies.

And you've given us a problem.

What?

The old woman. She knows.

What are you saying?

If she talks you'll never see Mark again.

72

'I cannot believe what you are telling me, Nicole.' Alva folds her arms and turns towards her sister. They both sit huddled at the end of the wooden counter in the Vietnamese restaurant round the corner from Pearse Street Police station. The place is quiet, as Nicole had hoped it would be.

'Can I get either of you anything else?' the petite woman behind the counter asks, her happy smile radiating out at them from beneath thick black bangs.

'We're all good,' Alva says. 'The tea is perfect.' Turning back to Nicole, the frown deepens on Alva's face and the waitress goes off to prepare tables at the back of the restaurant for lunch. 'What did the hospital say?'

'They said she's unconscious but they will contact me as soon as her situation changes.'

Alva shakes her head, snatching her cup. She sips it but it's too hot so she puts it back down. 'Fuckers. That could have been you, Nicole. It could have been one of the girls.'

Unable to look her sister in the face, Nicole stirs the coffee. Does Alva know she's been robbed yet? She must. Could she have guessed that Nicole is behind it? Wouldn't she have said something? She grips the counter, but it can't stop her stomach heaving and churning.

'You alright, Nic? You look very pale.'

Nicole lets go of the counter, picks up her cup and drinks. Everything suddenly feels so pointless. There's no explanation she can offer her sister that will make sense, it's too far gone; it's become clear that her idea to tell her everything was a delusion. The risk hasn't changed and the threat remains. The only thing she's achieved is making everything worse. She lets out a deep breath. 'Yeah, I think I'm OK. Just tired. Not sleeping again.'

Alva puts a hand on her shoulder. 'How the hell could you? Your neighbour was nearly murdered; you found her; you called the ambulance and gave the report to the police.' She touches Nicole's cheek, sighing. 'Nobody would sleep after a night like that.'

Nicole blinks. Alva's gentle fingertips feel like blades against her carefully concealed bruise. She waits for the pain to pass, wishing she had never made the arrangement to meet Alva. Her betrayal of her sister is too fresh, too raw, and even looking at her makes her want to confess, starting from the very beginning.

'Which officers came out?' Alva then asks.

'A female guard called Harris, and a man. I think his name was Connolly.'

Alva taps the table with her finger. 'I don't know Connolly but Harris is tough. If there's a lead in there she should find it. You said they've sealed it off as a crime scene?' Nicole nods and swallows her coffee, the memory of the fresh blue and white plastic tape surfacing. 'Good, forensics ought to turn something up. Then I'll have a think of what I can do to help.'

They're interrupted by Nicole's phone buzzing. She recognises the number from the hospital.

'Right,' Alva waves her off. 'You answer that and I'll get these. I have to get back into the office anyhow.' She gestures to the waitress. 'Don't worry, Nic, I'm going to make your neighbour's case a priority. I'll revert to you on it soon as I have something.'

Nicole moves to the exit, opens the door, and slips out. Hurrying quickly back to her car she reads the text message again.

Mrs Lyubevsky is awake. She is very weak but stable. We rec-ommend she rest until tomorrow before receiving visitors.

The Paymaster's message repeats inside her head. *If she talks you will never see Mark again.* Sticking her phone back into her pocket she keeps moving until she gets to the car but standing in front of it now is Eve.

73

'Hey you!' Eve spreads her arms wide, enveloping Nicole before she can react. Stiffly she holds her in a half hug. Eve is about to offer her a cheek to kiss when Nicole steps back. Why is Eve suddenly here now? And what does she want? 'I saw the car and said that looks familiar.' Eve points to Nicole's scuffed old Renault. 'Then, I crossed the street and here you are.' Eve beams a sparkling smile. 'I've been looking for you.'

'Really?' Nicole's fingers tighten around her phone. She cannot delay. Mrs Lyubevsky is awake.

'Yeah. Chloe left her jacket behind the other day and Lily picked it up. Then Lily said Chloe was staying at her Auntie Alva's so I wasn't sure whose house to drop into?' Eve laughs like she has said something so funny she cannot help herself.

Nicole doesn't respond at first. The memory of the words she heard inside the toilet cubicle bubble up. *Eve said she thinks she's getting divorced. Eve said you'd fuck him in a heartbeat.* 'I guess Lily can simply give it to Chloe,' she replies flatly.

It takes a second but finally Eve notices Nicole isn't laughing. 'Of course. She can do that if you like. I just thought maybe we'd link for coffee or something. Catch up?'

Nicole opens the car door. 'Thanks Eve, but I have to be somewhere. Perhaps another time.'

74

Friday, November 24,
Morning

It takes a few seconds for the pained expression to lift from Eve's face. Then she makes a show of smiling brightly even though she can see Nicole isn't doing the same. When did her friend become this sharp? Nicole's almost unrecognisable. She keeps waving until the old Renault drifts out of sight, then slowly her arms fold tight and her smile fades.

It amazes her how much more exhausted her friend looks today than the last time she saw her. Why? What isn't Nicole telling her? In the beginning they used to talk so much. But in the beginning it was just about the two of them, confiding their shared problems. That's changed now. Eve's known it for some time. Does Nicole know it too? What would Nicole say if she knew exactly what Eve had done?

With a flick of her fingers she tosses the new silk scarf over her shoulder. She isn't comfortable with Mark being out of contact for so long. It's not how she had planned this.

Taking her phone from her pocket she scrolls slowly for his number.

75

Friday, November 24,
Afternoon

The wheels of the food trolley squeak as Nicole walks past it down the hospital corridor. Pushing the door to room 257 open gently, she slips inside. Her heart is already pounding. The message was clear. Her neighbour must not talk. Flattening her hand against the door panel, she squeezes it closed without making a noise.

The room is stuffy, and a stale odour of sweat lingers in the heated air. The noise from outside disappears, replaced suddenly by the beeping of the ECG by the old woman's side, which pulses rhythmically, flickering its crooked green line as it monitors her vital signs. There is nothing in the room that shows any signs of visitors. No cards, no flowers, no gifts of food, or personal items.

Without making a sound Nicole walks to the bed. There's a solitary chair in the corner of the room so she picks it up, silently returning to the bedside to place it down. Then she sits.

Mrs Lyubevsky is propped up on two pillows, the lined skin of her grey face contrasting with the white covers and pressed sheets. A tube feeds into her left arm and her eyes are closed. The sound of her breathing is strained as the air rises and falls softly through her belly. Nicole reaches a hand across to hold her wrist but stops. How can she possibly wake her?

Quietly, she drops her elbows to the edge of the bed, leans forward and covers her face with her hands. Her head throbs as she squeezes her eyes with her fingers. This woman was her friend. She knows they weren't close but they had always been on good terms. The only reason she drew the gun was because she was afraid. She didn't deserve this for trying to find out what happened to Mark.

Mark. Squeezing her eyes tighter she pictures him as he used to sit in the armchair at home, reading a magazine, stopping to put it down and look over, the hint of a smile on his lips, the way he'd always be when he had an idea he wanted to share. Usually somewhere new he wanted to take her for brunch, or maybe an article he'd set aside because he knew it might interest her.

Then she remembers the Paymaster's threat. *If she talks you'll never see Mark again.*

Sitting back up she grips Mrs Lyubevsky's wrinkled hand, presses it gently between her own. Closing her eyes once more she listens to the beep of the machine in the background. She must begin. It's why she's come. There's no choice. Her head drops. Exhaustion is taking hold. She only needs this nightmare to end.

When she raises her head Mrs Lyubevsky is staring at her, eyes wide with fear, the edges of her mouth twisting downwards. The gash across the side of her head has been crudely sewn into a thick red line and all around it the skin has bruised purple and sickly yellow.

'Nina?'

Mrs Lyubevsky doesn't reply but shuts her eyes instantly and Nicole lifts her cold hand, pressing it to her cheek.

'Nina, can you hear me?'

There is no movement in her neighbour's face, no change of expression to indicate she hears, only the slow rise and fall of her body under the sheets.

'Nina, I want you to know that I lied to the police. I didn't tell them it was me that hurt you. I wanted to tell you everything, but I was afraid. Afraid that the bad people who have taken Mark would never give him back if I didn't do what they said.' The wrinkled skin of Mrs Lyubevsky's eyelids twitches and Nicole feels the tiniest movement in her fingers. 'They threatened to kill Mark if I don't get your silence but I won't do it. I've only ever wanted to get my husband back safely.' A tear trickles down Nicole's cheek. 'I've made some terrible mistakes, done things I could never have believed but . . .'

Mrs Lyubevsky's fingers grip her hand. Her eyes remain closed when she starts to speak. 'It's OK Nicole,' the voice is so faint Nicole has to lean closer to hear it. The old woman's wizened body rises and falls beneath the sheets and for a moment Nicole is reminded of the baby swan that Alva told her about. Suddenly she remembers it clearly; the shrieks it made, how it flapped its wings, the terror in its eyes; and then finally its meek submission as it trusted that a stranger would help it.

The grip in Mrs Lyubevsky's fingers weakens and Nicole glances nervously to the machine but it simply keeps beeping, the blurred figures on the screen remaining constant. She reaches a hand to her neighbour's face and smooths the grey hair back from her forehead when she feels a cold draught of air on the back of her neck and the door opens behind her.

'Everything alright?' The nurse takes out her clipboard and moves to the end of the bed.

Quickly Nicole wipes her face. 'Yes. She's still asleep but I was just leaving.' The mobile phone in her pocket buzzes alerting her to an incoming message.

'You don't have to go. My checks should only take a minute.' The nurse gives her a warm smile.

'It's OK, really.' Nicole jumps to her feet, her heart pounding as she pushes the door open and walks out. In the corridor she stops. There's a text on her phone but she doesn't recognise the number.

I know what you've done.

The muscles in her stomach clench and she runs to the lift but when she gets there she finds a small queue waiting outside it. Turning away she walks away from the waiting area to the side of the building where there is a window. There's a man outside, down in the street, peering up at her. She recognises him immediately. He's no longer in the high-vis jacket but wears the same dark jeans and matching raincoat he wore the last time she saw him. A shiver passes through her and she moves closer to the glass, the memory of his piercing blue eyes staring into hers one minute, then the force of the front door pinning her to the wall as he stormed inside. But what did he want? Why was it so important that he had to force his way past their front door? The phone pings again. Down on the street the man lifts his phone with one hand and points at it with the other, like he's miming an instruction. She reads the incoming text.

I know everything. It's time for us to talk.

Nicole's nostrils flare and she runs for the stairwell.

76

Friday, November 24,
Afternoon

'My name is Chris Ashton,' he begins, his big shoulders moving underneath his coat as he takes it off and puts it on the back of the wooden chair.

Nicole sits opposite him in the corner of the Skyline hotel in Rathmines. The hotel looks new; the long wooden bar counter is set away from the sitting area and it's quiet. A young couple in another corner are being served focaccia bread and the smell of grilled red peppers and olive oil is in the air.

Up close Chris Ashton is more handsome than she remembers. His jaw is lightly stubbled with burnt gold hair which matches the ruffled short cut on his head. His black cotton shirt is unbuttoned at the neck and he rubs the small dip between his collarbones with his thumb. He could be a different person except that his voice hasn't changed; once again it's low and urgent.

The waiter appears behind him and Chris Ashton's eyes flick over his shoulder. Seeing the tray of drinks, the tension in his face releases.

'One lager, non-alcoholic.' The waiter places the drink down. 'And one coffee. Anything else?'

Pushing the two menus into the waiter's hand Chris shakes his head. Pedestrians walk up and down outside the glass front of the building. The place Nicole has chosen for their meeting is exactly what she needed, private but not so private that her safety could be compromised. And yet her heart still thumps. How does he know what's she's done? What does he want? Every second that passes is time lost that she could be trying to find Mark. She's already lost too much.

Nicole taps her phone on the table. 'Before you begin I want you to know that if you attempt anything,' she stops to try and get the tension in her voice under control, 'the police are one phone call away.'

Chris Ashton's eyes drop to the phone and he slides the beer to the edge of the table. The memory of the same man forcing the front door, pushing his way into their house is still fresh and raw. She moves back from the table. 'I know. Your sister's a senior officer in the police. Decorated too. And if you want to call her I can't stop you. But you and I both know getting the police involved now could be the worst decision we make.'

The muscles at the base of her spine knot tighter. 'How do you know this?'

'Because I'm in this as much as you are.'

'What are you saying?'

'What I'm about to tell you will be a total shock to you. But, if I'm right about what's happened to you, then I know you'll understand.' His fingers grip the stem of the beer glass and his eyes flick to the window. There's a gold band on his finger and it taps against the glass. 'I also want you to know that I never meant to harm you.'

'This is about Mark, isn't it?' Nicole says.

His pale blue eyes glance around as if searching for signs of danger. Then he leans forward slowly. 'I'm not a courier. I've been posing as one so I could get close to you and Mark. A couple of weeks ago I rented a nearby apartment and based myself there so I could be in your area also.'

'What?' The vein in Nicole's temple flickers. 'Why would you do that?'

'Please,' he lifts the palms of his hands from the table and holds them up, 'just hear me out. A little over a year ago my life was turned upside down when my wife Veronica was targeted by an unknown criminal. She was a doctor, a specialist in orthopaedic surgery at the time. Somebody contacted her online and began to threaten her.' Nicole's stomach starts to churn. 'It lasted over six months but in the beginning I didn't know anything about it because she never told me.'

'What happened?'

'Veronica's family own a mining business and its stock is worth a lot on the exchange. The criminal had learned about a conviction that her dad picked up, for running brothels in Zurich. The accusations were trumped up and had already been thrown out by the court, but Veronica knew it would wreak havoc on the family if it was dug up again, as well as decimating most of their inheritance if the company stock price was impacted.'

Nicole puts a hand to the back of her head where it aches. 'What did he make her do?'

'First, she had to beg from her father's wealthy friends for donations to a fictional charity abroad.'

'Jesus Christ.'

'Then she had to commit elaborate thefts. Eventually under the strain Veronica broke down and confided in me.'

'Why didn't you go to the police?'

'At that point Veronica had already compromised herself and her reputation. I think she might have even lived with that but when the Paymaster threatened our two little boys she didn't want to and I agreed with her. We couldn't run the risk.'

'The Paymaster?' There's a pulse of pain behind her eyes. 'You know about the Paymaster?'

Folding his arms, Chris Ashton glances back to the bar, then turns and nods silently.

'But why take this job to get close to us?'

'After what they did to Veronica the only thing that mattered to me was finding the people behind this. I gave up my job because I couldn't go on knowing they were still out there getting away with it. The formula felt like it was something practised so I made the assumption we weren't alone and that it had occurred elsewhere.' His hand moves to the beer glass and his big fingers wrap around it. 'I hired a private detective to help me. I wasn't getting anywhere. But then my luck changed when I discovered the list.'

Nicole stiffens as Chris Ashton slowly removes something from his coat pocket. Unfolding the paper, he flattens it on the table between them. When he speaks again his voice is so low it's almost a whisper.

'This is a list of the people who were the criminal's intended victims. I'm sorry Nicole but your husband Mark was the last name on the list.'

77

Friday, November 24,
Afternoon

Nicole picks up her phone, the urge to call Alva swelling up inside her, the need to end this nightmare which grows and grows each passing minute. But she knows she can't do it. She needs to hear what Chris Ashton has to say. She has to know everything that she can before making that decision. He could be her only lifeline back to Mark. He hasn't threatened her. They're in a public place and there's nothing he can do. If what he's told her is true, he's no different to her.

The muscles in her back tense again. Her body is breaking down and each second that passes the pain spreads to a new part of it. The swelling on the side of her head is getting worse; the stitches in her scalp pull when she moves her face; and the bruise on her cheek aches. Placing her phone back on the table she reaches into her purse. The painkillers Dr Fenton gave her are still there and she gulps them down with the now cold coffee.

Chris Ashton watches her without touching his drink, his blue eyes following her every movement. Once again he glances at the people passing outside, turns to do a quick check behind them at the bar, and then peers at the young couple who are still eating the focaccia, absorbed in their own conversation.

Nicole looks down at the handwritten note on the table.

HFS 2007 (3 targets/3 cards)
VW x
NC x
AJ x

RJ x
BC x
MR ?

Picking it up, she swallows again to try and push the painkillers into her stomach. The paper shakes in her fingers and she places it down.

'What does it mean?'

Chris Ashton shrugs. 'I'm still figuring it out.'

'Three cards, three targets? It's what they gave to me. But I don't understand the system because if the cards are a blackmail why were the thefts so elaborate?'

Chris Ashton rubs the back of his hand across his jaw. 'That's exactly what my wife said. She guessed that each card was some kind of threat but because she couldn't read them it was only an assumption. Neither of us could figure it out. I'm guessing it was the same for you?'

The images flit inside Nicole's head. Dropping the first card beside the couch in Valerie Cheroux's opulent mansion in Foxrock after fraudulently begging for one million euros; leaving the second on the coffee table for the kind old gemstone collector Elliot Preston after taking the diamonds from his safe; then putting the last inside Alva's desk drawer at the police station. She nods. 'Are you going to explain the list?'

'At first it meant nothing. But then bit by bit I began to piece it together. 2007 was the year of my wife's graduation from university. And HFS was a group she was part of. It was called the Holden Foundation Scheme.'

As soon as Nicole hears the words they register but she can't remember why. 'What was the scheme?'

'HFS was a scheme set up by the philanthropist Robert Holden. Before he died he funded an alternative admissions programme to medical school – the concept being to help a small group of students gain access through a different selection process, if they couldn't get in through the regular channels. Holden hated the formal education system; he felt it held too many people back, and his belief was that money played a big part in that. He funded the entire thing from top to bottom. The first year of study for all was subsidised. After that, if you didn't have the means you could apply to get the remainder of your studies funded by the scheme. It was like the ultimate gold visa for those that missed out. It operated out of Bristol University.'

Nicole listens, vaguely recollecting Mark once mentioning it. 'What are the letters and crosses underneath?'

'The letters are the initials of the graduates from her year. Veronica Woods, Neil Clark, Angela Johannson, Richard Jennings, Bernadette Cornell.'

Nicole looks at the paper again. 'MR is Mark Reid?' Chris Ashton picks up the list and nods solemnly. 'But the crosses? What do they mean?'

He pops a button on his shirt pocket, folds the paper carefully and tucks it away. 'That's what I had to find out. The private investigator helped me find the different members of the group. The crosses meant they had been approached.'

The waiter walks up to the table beside them and places down two menus. Nicole waits for him to leave. 'I don't get this. You haven't told me what Veronica made of this list. You've hardly even mentioned her and yet she was the one the Paymaster targeted.'

Chris Ashton lifts his arms, folding them tight over his chest and letting out a pained sigh. For a moment they just look at each other across the table. Then his chin dips and his body begins to shake.

78

Chris Ashton stops shaking and becomes very still. His gaze moves away to the window glass as a tear trips from the end of his eyelash and tracks down his face. He doesn't brush it off but keeps looking outside as the muscle in his jaw quivers beneath the skin. Slowly he faces Nicole.

'Veronica's dead.'

'Dead?' Nicole slumps back, the word triggering her memory. For a moment she is back in her childhood bedroom being woken by her mother; the lingering presence of her father everywhere in the house, a scarf still on the coat stand in the hall, one of his old jackets under the stairs, a tin of mints still inside the pocket – and the cold shared knowledge that he wasn't ever coming home again, surrounding them like a wall of ice. 'I'm sorry.'

Slowly he rubs his thumb against the dark shadows beneath his eyes. 'The night she told me about everything that had happened my whole world collapsed. But a part of me was relieved, because for the first time I finally understood what had been torturing her, and all the things she had been too terrified to reveal. After I put her to bed and turned out the light, the only thing I could think about was how to find the person behind this.' He swallows. 'But when the morning came she was cold. A stroke they said in the report. Veronica was only thirty-eight years old.'

Nicole moves her hand across the table and touches his elbow but Chris Ashton turns his gaze back to the window. 'I can't imagine how that felt.'

His eyes flash then. 'I don't believe it was natural.'

The throbbing in Nicole's forehead returns and her fingers rub it nervously. 'You think she was murdered?'

Chris's expression turns dark. 'I couldn't find the evidence though I insisted on an autopsy and got one. I even read the toxicologist's report but it all showed nothing. It's too convenient though, when I think of what happened to the others.'

Nicole draws back. 'What others? What happened to them?'

'Veronica didn't give me the list so she never got to explain how she came to have it. It was something I found when I was going through her things after her death. She only explained what happened to her. But when I investigated the others it was the same. Richard Jennings died in a speedboat accident. Neil Clark drowned. Angela Johannson took her own life. The only survivor on the list other than Mark was Bernadette Cornell so I flew to Boston to question her. Cornell agreed to meet me, not knowing what it was about, and when I brought it up she shut down.'

'Do you think she's hiding something?'

'No. She looked totally traumatised. I'm sure she suffered just like we have, but she said she wanted a chance to think about what I had told her. The same evening I had a legal document delivered to my hotel saying if I approached her again I would be prosecuted for harassment.'

Nicole squeezes her eyes shut. Mark is still missing. If what Chris Ashton says is true nearly every member of his group has been murdered. 'Who would want to target this group and why?'

'If you help me find the Paymaster we'll know.'

Nicole's fingers move to the side of her head and she touches the swelling. 'But Chris, if you really believe that what happened to your wife was murder why didn't you think to go to the police then?'

'Our two boys are still targets, Nicole.' Chris folds his arms again. 'That's not a risk I'm willing to take, I'm sorry.' He shrugs, his face apologetic. 'But what about you? You didn't go to the police either?'

Nicole shakes her head and thinks of her sister Alva, remembering the very first night when the hackers made contact and how badly she wanted to tell her. Her fingers curl, digging into the skin on her thigh as the memories tumble back; all the occasions she thought she might explain everything, but how each time she held back, the fear in the pit of her stomach that one wrong move could put her whole family in the gravest danger.

He nods. 'Well, then it seems that like everybody else, we're in exactly the same boat.'

79

'Now it's your turn, Nicole.' Chris Ashton sits back in his chair. 'You haven't told me what happened to Mark. I've already figured out he's missing. Do you want to tell me how it happened?'

Nicole's hands are trembling again and she flattens them on her knees beneath the table. She pauses for a second, reminding herself that it's OK, the space is public and she is safe. Her eyes flick to the exit and she thinks how easy it would be to get up and walk through it. Then she could think. Take stock of everything she's been told. But the compulsion to unburden grows, the need to share all the things she cannot speak about, even to her only sister.

Breathing out, she begins.

When she finally finishes, Chris Ashton steeples his hands together beneath his chin.

'They succeeded in getting me to kidnap my own husband. They even kept video footage of it. They threatened Mark's life. At that point I was broken so I agreed to commit the three tasks they gave. I even robbed my own sister.' The fingers of her hand ball into a fist. 'Then they were supposed to return Mark back but they changed the deal.'

'Does anybody else know?'

The momentary lightness she felt seconds ago vanishes instantly. 'My next door neighbour Mrs Lyubevsky. She's just an innocent old woman who wanted to help. From the night it happened she's been watching me and figured out Mark's disappearance wasn't normal. Now I've put her in hospital. But you have to understand it was an accident.'

'What did the Paymaster say about it?'

Nicole stares at her nails which are bitten down and uneven. 'That I have to force her to keep quiet or Mark disappears. But I'm not following their orders anymore.' She stops, her thoughts shifting suddenly to something Chris Ashton said earlier.

Blood flushes her cheeks.

'Chris?'

For the first time he takes a long drink from his beer.

'Yes?'

'You just told me you took a job so you could get close to us? Why did you do that? Was it to spy on us?' He puts the beer glass down and the heat rises to Nicole's face. 'I'm sorry Chris but are you telling me that you were waiting for this to happen to us?' He shakes his head, his disagreement clear. 'But you already knew about the Paymaster?'

He glances back to the bar and then leans closer. 'It wasn't that simple.'

'Why? This didn't need to happen. All you needed to do was intervene?' Clutching the coffee cup, her hand trembles, for a second overwhelmed with the urge to throw it at him. But the next second he slumps forward, sliding his elbows onto the table and dropping his face into his hands.

Nicole watches him not sure what to do.

Eventually, he takes his hands away and sits back up. 'I tried, Nicole. Please understand I tried. I followed Mark night and day.'

'Why?'

'Because I expected the Paymaster would make contact and it would lead me to him but when it wasn't happening I went to Mark directly.'

'When?'

'One night after work he drove towards the city centre and I followed, but he figured out I was tailing him. There was a car chase but he lost me. The next day, I followed him on foot instead. Again he tried to get away but I caught him this time. He was very agitated. It was early evening so I suggested we go to a bar where I would explain everything and he agreed. I told him what I've told you, and he said he needed time to process it. Then he said he had to take a private phone call so I went to the bathroom. When I returned, he was gone, but he had left a note under his glass.' He reaches behind him and takes out another piece of paper from his jacket which hangs on the back of the chair.

Chris,

I beg you not to approach my wife with this information, under any circumstances, until I return. Please trust me.

Mark

The paper trembles in her fingers as she reads it again. The handwriting is Mark's. She's certain.

'What did you do?'

'I ran out to find him but he was gone.'

'But why now, Chris? Why suddenly break your deal with Mark and come forward to tell me?'

He turns his gaze back to the window. 'Time, Nicole. Mark's been gone too long. I want to try and help you. If we can find the Paymaster together we both win.'

Nicole's phone beeps on the table and she picks it up. It's a message from Shaun. Now she remembers her promise to pick up the girls from school. Getting to her feet she takes her bag. 'I've got to collect my kids. Then I'm going to bring them . . . ' Her voice trails off before she can finish the sentence.

Chris Ashton is gesturing to the waiter. His face has changed. It's brighter, more energised, younger. 'Of course, go ahead. I'll get the bill. As soon as you're ready we'll talk more. I'm going to text you my apartment address so you know where I am if you need me. When we chat again I want to make a suggestion.'

Clutching the laptop bag to her chest Nicole stares at him.

'What suggestion?'

'There's a woman called Helen Shaw. She's the partner of Angela Johannson. I think we should meet her.'

Nicole walks away. The doubt is already forming inside her, burrowing its way deeper under her skin. Is this stranger really who he says he is, and should she really trust him?

80

'Yes, I got your email Nicole and I've just replied to it.' Nicole shuts the door of her car and locks it while the faculty administrator of the medical department at Bristol University explains the situation in a cheerful voice. 'It's an interesting one because the few people I asked in here knew nothing about the Holden Foundation Scheme but it's probably because none of us were around at that time.' Nicole leans against the roof of the car, her energy sapping. 'There is one professor though who definitely was here. I've forwarded him the email with your number and asked him to call you if he knows anything about it.'

'Thank you.' She rubs her eyes. 'What's his name, the professor?'

'Professor Alan Byrne.'

'Could I have his contact?'

'Sorry, but I'm not allowed to give it out. I will make a point to remind him about it though. If he doesn't get in touch, give me a call back in a couple of days.'

A black four wheel drive pulls up alongside her and the window buzzes down. Immediately Nicole ends the call. She stands, her feet rooted to the pavement, her heart rate spiralling as the memory of the night of the kidnap springs back from nowhere; all at once she can feel the rain on her face, the sound of the boot lid springing, the stickiness of the blood between her fingers. Then her own voice and the words, 'I'm sorry.'

With a shudder she turns to face the car. It's the investigating police officer from the other night, Connolly. He pops his head out, smoothing his hair across his scalp. 'Good afternoon, Mrs Reid. Everything alright?'

Nicole flattens the bag with the laptop against her chest and takes a breath. 'Everything's fine officer.' Behind Connolly she can see his female colleague Harris leaning across from the driver seat to watch her. Harris's eyes squint.

'As I promised, we thought we'd pop back to try and help push your neighbour's case on a little.' Connolly gives a lazy smile and his elbow drapes over the car door. 'Mind if we borrow you for a few minutes. It shouldn't take too long. Just a couple of questions myself and Garda Harris wanted to ask.'

The blood pounds in Nicole's ears. She must not lose time searching for Mark. But she can see no way of avoiding this now. 'Of course.' She fumbles with the back door to the police jeep and gets inside.

Connolly turns round, his eyes widening and his cheeks lifting in a satisfied grin. He glances at Harris but her face is serious. She gives him a slow nod and waits for him to continue. 'We were thinking we might talk to you inside your house Mrs Reid, where you might be more comfortable?'

'Here is fine.' A blush of red spreads up Nicole's neck and across her face. What impulse made her jump into the backseat of the police car when she could have talked from the comfort of her own kitchen? But it's too late to change her mind now. She will only look unstable. The kind of woman who can smash a door into her elderly neighbour's face.

'Sure, why not? If that's what you prefer.' Connolly nods to Harris who turns round and faces her squarely. 'I spoke with your neighbour this morning,' she states flatly. Nicole moves and something bangs against her hip. When she slips her hand inside her coat pocket the cold steel of Mrs Lyubevsky's gun touches her fingertips. How did she forget? Now she's armed with a gun inside a police vehicle. What happens if they tell her to empty her pockets? The blood drains from her face and when she inhales a stink of old sandwiches mixed with coffee fills her nostrils.

There's a half-eaten doughnut sitting on top of two plastic cups in the centre section in front of her and flecks of white icing speckle the black plastic cup lids. Reaching for the door she buzzes down the window to get some air.

'Mrs Reid?' Harris' voice is sharp.

Nicole turns. 'Sorry, I just needed some air.' Lifting her hand off the gun she grips the laptop closer to her chest.

'I said we spoke with your neighbour.'

'Yes? Did she remember anything?'

'Yes, she did. She remembered speaking to you.'

Pinpricks of sweat dot Nicole's forehead. 'Did she say when exactly?'

'No. We were hoping you'd fill us in.' Connolly adjusts the mirror, his eyes now resting on her face.

'Yes.' Nicole sucks in some air. She has to tell more lies. 'She did come round to borrow some sugar that evening before I went out.'

'I see.' Harris glances at Connolly who takes out a pen and clicks it. Nicole watches as he places a small pad on his thigh and begins to write. 'What time was that?'

'Six, I think.'

'Very good, and did you see her again after that?' Nicole shakes her head. 'Only when you discovered her later that night was it?' Harris twists in her seat, purses her lips, and shares a look with Connolly. Then she turns back to Nicole. 'Could you describe your relationship with Mrs Lyubevsky to us?'

Nicole looks out the window. 'Friends, we were always good friends, she babysat for us once or twice too.'

'Did you ever have any disagreements? Maybe noise, the house, that kind of thing?'

'No.'

Connolly coughs as he jots in his notepad. Harris taps a finger against her chin. 'You see one of your other neighbours mentioned that you took her cat?'

The muscles in her gut tense and Nicole sits up. 'Rocky got injured some days ago and I took him in to patch him up.'

Connolly looks up, his bright eyes hooking onto her in the mirror. 'Rocky?' He laughs and his cheeks dimple.

Harris follows with another question. 'Where is this cat now Mrs Reid?'

'In my house.'

Nobody says anything then and the car goes silent. Finally, Connolly breaks it by clicking his pen. 'Is your husband around?' He asks the question casually as if it's just occurred to him.

Nicole puts a hand to her cheek. 'He's in Spain.'

'Oh?' he looks over at Harris. 'And when might he be back?'

'This weekend.'

'Good.' He opens his jacket and drops the pen and pad into the pocket. 'Well, we don't want to keep you any longer than necessary. But you might tell him to get in touch as soon as he returns.' Instantly Nicole jumps out as Connolly dangles his elbow over the edge of the door. 'Don't worry, Mrs Reid. Officer Harris and I will be making sure we don't let this one go unpunished.'

81

Friday, November 24,
Afternoon

The phone screen lights up with an incoming call and Nicole jolts. It's not a number she recognises but there's a petrol station in front of her on the Rathgar Road and she pulls in.

'Nicole Reid?' a man asks. His voice sounds English.

'Yes?'

'This is Professor Alan Byrne from Bristol University. The secretary asked me to call you about a query you had in relation to the HFS. May I ask what your interest in it is?'

Nicole runs a hand over her face, leans forward and removes a pen and paper from her laptop bag. 'Yes. My husband Mark was a graduate of the programme. His group finished in 2007.'

'Mark Reid? It's been a while now but I still remember Mark well. He was one of our most distinguished students. How is he?'

The back of her head brushes against the seat rest and she tilts forward, her eyes scrunching tight. 'He's well. Thank you.'

'So how can I help?'

'I had an enquiry in relation to the HFS. Is it still running?'

'God no. It's been gone years now. And a real shame too. It was one of the very best programmes we've had at the university. We've been waiting for another like-minded visionary to come forward but unfortunately there aren't many like Robert Holden. It ran about ten years in total. I think Mark's group may have been the last.'

'Could I ask a favour of you?'

'Go ahead.'

'I wanted to get the group's details because I'm doing a birthday collage surprise for Mark and I thought he'd really like it since it's something he's very proud of.'

'Certainly. I'll have to dig it out, but the names are on file somewhere. Why don't I email it to you? I'll do it today if I get a chance.'

'That would mean a lot to me.'

When the call ends a new message appears on Nicole's phone. It's from Chris Ashton. It's a Google Maps pin for a location point. She reads the text.

I used the investigator I told you about to trace Mark's car. Perhaps you might want to go and take a look.

Opening the Maps app, she zooms in to see where the location is. It's an industrial estate near Ballymount, not far from the M50.

The air in the car is warm yet a distinct chill has entered her body. It feels like a trap. She still knows nothing about Chris Ashton except what he's told her. Working her thumb quickly, she keys his name into Google and long list of images of men with the same name appear.

Frowning, she instantly closes it again, placing the phone back down on the passenger seat. The car starts and the navigation on Google Maps begins. The robotic voice tells her to take the first turn right and she sucks in her breath, trying not to think about how badly it reminds her of the night she kidnapped her own husband.

82

'No take your time,' Eve lets the generous smile spread across her face as she nods to Alva. She's pleased with her timing; it's just right, and she's cornered Alva in the newsagents as planned.

Alva picks a paper cup from the rack, teases it loose and puts it under the dispenser, now noticing Eve in the corner of her eye.

'I'm told the coffee is good,' Alva nods towards the machine. 'Hopefully it might be worth your wait.'

'When you need coffee a little wait is OK isn't it?' Eve spreads her grin wider. Alva returns the smile and taps the hot water button in the display. 'Say,' Eve cocks her head, working hard to pull her features into a picture of surprise, 'you're not Nicole Reid's sister by any chance?'

'Guilty.' The water jets into the cup and Alva turns, holding up her hands playfully. 'How'd you know?'

'The eyes. Yours are a different colour but they still remind me of shining stars.' She shoots out a hand. 'Eve Pennington. Nicole and I are great friends. Our girls are in the same class. Chloe and Lily.'

Alva shakes her hand and unwraps a teabag. She drops it into the cup and presses it down with the stirrer. 'I always have to let it brew for a few seconds to get it strong enough. Let me get out of your way so I don't delay you.' She shifts to the side and searches for the milk and sugar.

Eve steps up close and plucks a cup. Flicking her eyes to the display she picks the first button she sees and presses it. 'You work nearby?'

246

'Pearse Street Garda Station.'

'Of course,' Eve taps the side of her head and rolls her eyes, making her best dizzy face. 'I should know that. Your sister already told me.'

Alva squeezes the teabag to the side of the cup until it releases the last of its liquid. 'You?'

'Oh, I just happened to have a business meeting with a client around the corner. PR, always on the go.' She shakes her head in mock despair and watches Alva drop in the sugar. Patiently she holds back until Alva has added the last of the milk and then finally picks her moment. 'You know Alva, this might sound a little strange but I'm secretly worried about Nicole.' Alva scrunches the plastic milk container and drops it in the waste bin, a look of surprise crossing her face. 'I think something's happened and I've tried to get her to open up but,' she stops to let out an exaggerated sigh, 'your sister is very private.'

'She is, isn't she?' Alva drops the teabag in the bin and cleans off the spilled sugar from the counter. 'What's your worry, Eve?'

Eve glances over her shoulder, then turns and leans in closer. 'Mark.' She drops her voice to a whisper. 'I don't think he's gone to Barcelona. I think something's happened but,' she shrugs her shoulders and waits for her look of concern to settle properly across her face, 'it's not like me to meddle.' The lid of the coffee cup clicks down as she presses it with her fingertips. 'I just thought since you're a police officer and her sister, it might be a good idea to share that.' Eve tilts her head and waits, satisfied that she's said enough for the time being, and that if Mark doesn't surface immediately, he will now very soon. They have to talk and she doesn't want to wait. The first thing she will tell him is the news about David.

Alva doesn't reply. She stares hard at Eve, sips her tea, and quickly moves away.

83

Friday, November 24,
Afternoon

The car park is at the back of the industrial estate. It's a large open space but it's mostly empty and deserted, with only three cars remaining parked there. One is punctured and its blue paint is so thin it appears white in places. The second is covered in bird droppings and the hubs on the wheels are starting to rust; the last is exactly what Chris Ashton said it would be. It's Mark's.

The lights are out in most of the offices and the blinds are pulled. A few units in the estate look abandoned and have cardboard inside the windows. There are no people around and the whole place feels forgotten. The sky is dark when Nicole steps out of her car and the dampness in the air immediately sinks into her skin.

Looking about uneasily, she realises that it's the perfect place to make someone disappear. If Chris Ashton has set her up she knows she's left herself open.

The orange sidelamps flash once as Mark's car unlocks. Cautiously she walks towards it, turning one last time to check behind her, but all she sees is a large rat crawling out from an overflowing skip nearby. A pigeon flutters into the air and flaps hard until it lands on the roof of the rusting car, its green neck twisting as it scavenges for food.

Nicole's hand shakes when she reaches out to press the boot release and it takes a few seconds for her to steady it and touch the button. The popping sound of the lid makes her jump back and for a fleeting moment she is there again, on the wet dark road in the middle of nowhere, the distinct smell of petrol burning from the BMW's exhaust, the rain on her face, the trapped body inside the bag groaning.

Pausing to take a deep breath she waits before stepping forward, but all the boot space reveals is Mark's white squash trainers and two rackets, then next to them, a used sports shirt and shorts. Quickly she closes it down and checks the backseat but finds it bare, just two dolls belonging to Holly and Chloe and the hairbrush they kept fighting over. Closing the back door she moves to the front but it's all the usual things. A water bottle, a half-finished packet of Strepsils; then in the glove compartment, a few pens, old insurance and tax discs, the car manual. Until finally, something she hadn't expected: Mark's old phone.

It was the one they fought about, because Mark said it was no longer working properly and he needed to replace it but Nicole thought it was a waste of money seeing as they were struggling so badly to even pay their bills. She takes it in her hands and opens it, surprised to find it still powered on. She enters his PIN. Immediately she goes to call logs but finds they are gone. She moves to his email but the account is empty, except for a small number of spam files. Checking the junk folder then, she finds it's empty too.

Closing her eyes she sinks back into the seat. It's just like his laptop. All gone. Why? Leaning forward over the steering wheel, her body sags but she pushes herself back upright and checks it again, remembering that she still hasn't viewed his messages.

To her surprise, the messages are still intact. 'Forgotten.' She whispers the word, 'Mark's forgotten to delete them.' Scrolling quickly with her thumb she sifts through them. There are a few from work, and a couple from his friends, but they all date from a week before his disappearance. There's nothing unusual in any of them. But as she scrolls back up she spots a name she isn't expecting. It's titled *Lily's Mum*. It's at the very top of the list. Somehow she hadn't seen it. It's the most recent communication of them all.

It's Eve.

The blood rushes to her face and she squeezes the phone in her hand. Instantly she steps out of the car, slams it shut and runs back to her own. Her chest heaves as she places Mark's phone on the ground, wiping the corners of her eye and raising her foot high above it. It's too much now.

Her jaw locks as her teeth clench, drawing the skin tight across her face. The noise of the air pulling and pushing through her nostrils is the only thing she can hear as she closes her eyes.

But at the last second she stops. It's her last chance to understand. Dropping to her knees she picks it up, walks around to the driver's seat and gets back inside her car. The door slams so hard she can feel the vibration through the seat. For a second she just sits there, still unsure, fighting the urgent need to do what she must. Then she gives in, and with a heavy sigh, begins.

Thumb scrolling she goes to the beginning of the chat history. Eve's message is the first.

We should really meet up some time. Soon!

The ache inside her chest deepens but she keeps going, scanning through them as quickly as she can. Mark's messages are short but Eve's are long. She is effusive, *I enjoyed last night; Shame it took so long for us to hook up; I've been wanting to talk for ages.* Mark's replies give nothing away. *Great to finally meet. Sorry work has been hectic but talk soon.* It looks like Eve's been chasing him into meeting and he's been acting coy but eventually agrees. Then they progress. Eve – *Let's do that again. Soon!* Mark – *Busy but will definitely try and make time.* Then more: Eve – *We should have met before. So enjoyed linking up again.* Mark – *A pleasure.* Eve – *Have you had a chance to think about what I said? Just being honest. Wish you'd be the same.* No reply from Mark. Then one last one from Eve. *Do what you need to.* Mark's final text simply says, *I will.*

Dropping the phone on the passenger seat Nicole closes her eyes. Her arms reach out and she grips the steering wheel. There's no mention of sex in the texts. Eve was smart enough to avoid that. But Nicole can hear the words spoken inside the toilet cubicle of the restaurant replaying at full volume inside her head. *Eve said she thinks she's getting divorced. You'd fuck him in a heartbeat.*

One month ago if anybody had suggested Mark was having an affair she would have told them it was impossible without a flicker of doubt. But now, can she be sure? Hot tears push from her eyes. She tastes the salt as they trickle over her open lips inside her mouth. Is Mark's disappearance connected to Eve? But she can't see how. Her hands are cold and she places them inside her coat pocket, pressing them down. The fingers of her right hand bang against the hard steel of Mrs Lyubevsky's gun and she wraps them tight around it.

Lifting it out she stares at the shining barrel as another tear falls. She understands something now. Something the Paymaster does not yet know.

She is capable of murder.

84

Friday, November 24,
Afternoon

Nicole stands in the clearing between the pine trees. There wasn't any traffic on the drive out to Wicklow and she's arrived sooner than expected. She puts the white plastic bag back inside her coat pocket. It won't be needed now. The discarded high-vis jacket she found hanging on the door of the giant yellow digger parked further up the path gives her a better target.

Placing her feet shoulder width apart she takes up the stance. Alva's shown it to her before – how she shoots a gun. 'Family knowledge, Nicole, don't knock it,' she remembers her saying , as Nicole rolled her eyes and the two of them giggled, too tipsy after staying up so late one Christmas Eve they realised it was actually Christmas Day.

She lifts Mrs Lyubevsky's gun in front of her, steadies her hand when it reaches shoulder height, and listens carefully. There is no other sound than the wind sweeping through the pine trees back to the valley below. There was nobody in the car park or on the path coming up and she's hiked at least ten minutes. If she's going to do this she has to take her chance. How else will she know if this gun really works?

Her heart starts to hammer, the wobble in her wrist now clear. She tries to remember how many years ago it was when their dad first showed them the correct way to handle a firearm. But she only remembers being way too young to care, or heed his words of caution. 'Knowing this could save your life,' he had said, as he showed them how to hold the light pellet gun and aim.

Biting down hard she pulls the trigger.

Snap. It makes a hard click but nothing more.

'Fuck,' the word hisses away between the whispering trees. She pulls again.

This time there's an explosion of noise and her arm recoils high in the air, the vibrations drumming down into her shoulder socket. The sound mushrooms up and away, disappearing into the grey above the treetops.

The visibility jacket hasn't moved. But she won't try again. Even taking this risk is madness. Stuffing the gun back inside her pocket she wipes the sweat from her forehead and starts to hurry back to the car.

The gun works. The gun is loaded.

85

Friday, November 24,
Afternoon

Nicole shuts the door of the Renault and tosses her phone on the passenger seat as she sits inside. An email has come in and she sees it's from Professor Alan Byrne at Bristol University. Snatching it up again she begins to read.

> Nicole,
> Lovely chatting earlier and glad to hear Mark is doing well. I found the HFS grad list for 2007 so I'm including it here as an attachment. Hope this does the job but you can let me know.
> Alan

Her thumb scrolls, opening the attachment, scanning it quickly, her mind running through the names, cross-checking each against the initials she remembers from Chris Ashton's list. They are all there, just as he had claimed.

> Veronica Woods
> Richard Jennings
> Angela Johannson
> Neil Clark
> Bernadette Cornell
> Mark Reid

Except now she notices something she did not expect. Her heart thumps hard inside her chest as the heat spreads across her face. The last name on the list stares back at her. Chris Ashton.

86

Friday, November 24,
Afternoon

The wind blows through Herbert Park whipping a pile of autumn leaves into the air. Chris Ashton flips up the collar of his leather jacket, blows on his hands and stuffs them inside his pockets. The bench by the playground where they've agreed to meet is wet and he decides not to sit. Two women jog past him in knee-length leggings and thermal fleece tops. He side-steps to get out of their way when he hears his name.

'Chris Ashton?' The words cut through the air in a hiss. 'Is that really who you are?'

Nicole watches the joggers disappear around a bend in the tarmac path where the oak trees overhang, her fingers wrapping around the gun inside her coat pocket. A fortnight ago, if somebody who knew her told her she would confront a stranger in a public city park armed with a gun she would have doubted their sanity. Now as the wind blows the autumn leaves to the ground, scattering them across the grass and into the flowerbeds, she knows that if Chris Ashton threatens her, she at least has some security.

'Nicole? Has something happened?'

'Why are you lying to me?'

He frowns. 'Who said I'm lying?'

Nicole stops walking. He's still far enough away that she can get the gun out and aim it if he goes for her. 'Who are you really and what are you hiding?'

Quickly he turns, glancing behind him but sees there's nobody nearby. 'I'm not hiding anything.'

'Then why didn't you tell me you were also one of the graduates from the Holden Foundation Scheme too?' The gun handle brushes against her hip.

He throws his head back, groaning as the dark clouds move above them. 'OK, I'm sorry. It didn't occur to me to mention it. I wasn't on Veronica's list and the Paymaster didn't target me. Perhaps they were getting to me through Veronica? I can't explain it. I told you I only found the list after Veronica's death.' Taking his hands from his pockets he starts towards her. 'Let's not waste time, Nicole. We have to work together and move quickly. You know Mark is still out there.'

Nicole retreats a step. 'You've given me no proof of who you are yet.'

'Come on, Nicole. I've explained.'

'Step back.'

He scowls then. 'What?'

'You heard.'

With a grunt he pulls something from his pocket and holds it out. 'Fine. My wallet. Have it if you like.' He tosses it over and it falls on the ground between them. They both stand for a moment and look at it. Then he shakes his head and walks in the other direction. Instantly Nicole steps forward and kneels down to grab it. When she gets back to her feet Chris Ashton has turned to face her again. 'What did you find in the car? You need to tell me, Nicole.'

Ignoring the question, she replies. 'In the hotel earlier you said you had a suggestion. What was it?'

There's a park bench beside the path and he walks towards it. 'You want to sit?'

'No.'

With a shake of his head he rubs a hand across the stubble on his cheek and sweeps the hair back from his forehead. 'As you like.' Slowly he places his hands across the top of the bench, sighing as he leans against it. 'I approached the partner of Angela Johannson after Angela's funeral. The woman's name is Helen

Shaw. When I put it to her that I knew Angela had been a victim of the Paymaster, Helen didn't deny it. She explained it wasn't the time to discuss that because she needed time to grieve. I tried her twice again but she gave me the same response. But I have a feeling she might know who it is.'

'Why?'

'Because when I asked her, the look in her eye before she shut down the conversation told me she was hiding something, something that terrified her. She told me Angela and Veronica were dead so no good could come of pursuing it. But with you it's different. We've got to assume Mark's still alive. If you talked to her there might be a chance.'

Nicole pulls her coat tighter, a sudden chill creeping across her skin. If there's even the slightest chance what Chris Ashton says is true she knows she has to try.

Slowly she backs away. 'Text me her address and don't follow me.'

87

Friday, November 24,
Afternoon

First she photographs Chris Ashton's Revolut bank card, then his Visa credit card and lastly his driver's licence front and back. She types a short message to Alva explaining how she'd like her to run a quick background check on him saying she'll explain why later. The message sends but, before she can get out of Herbert Park, Alva rings her.

There is already one missed call from her sister on Nicole's phone. Alva won't call her twice unless it's important. Quickly she slots the cards into the wallet and puts it back inside her pocket.

'Nicole?'

'Yes?'

'You know this information is confidential so why are you asking me for it?'

'I'm sorry Alva, it's just Mark told me he's starting a business with him developing an app. I got worried and thought we should check him out.' The lie leaves a bitter taste in her mouth.

'Look, I can't give you any details but I'll get Jenny from the records department to run it. The only thing I'll be able to tell you is to stay clear or not, OK? It shouldn't take long.'

'Thanks Alva, I won't do this again.'

'There's something else though, Nic.' There's an unfamiliar edge to Alva's voice. Nicole holds her breath. 'It's about the girls.' Nicole's step falters and she holds the park railing.

'Shit?'

'Don't panic, they're fine. It's just that Shaun has got called away tonight for a meeting and I'm working round the clock at the moment on the Doherty case so we had to arrange for our pair to go to a friend's for the evening. Would you be OK to come over and collect your girls. Just for tonight?'

Nicole's fingers clench into a fist. She doesn't want to delay visiting Helen Shaw another second because if there's any chance it could lead her to Mark she has to take it now. But it's obvious this isn't a request. She decides she will figure out a way of dealing with it later. 'Of course, Alva.'

'There's a couple of other things I needed to tell you too. I think the sooner we can meet the better.' Alva's voice is unusually formal.

Nicole tenses. 'Is this about my neighbour?'

'That and other things. I've got a meeting starting now so I can't really talk but if you get down to the station I can spare five minutes.' Nicole takes a deep breath. What has Alva found out?

'I'm coming down.'

'When?'

Silently she estimates how long it will take her to collect the girls and drive to Alva's office. It's the last thing she wanted to do but she can see no other way.

'An hour,' she wipes the back of her hand across her forehead and finds it slick with sweat. 'I'll be there.'

88

Friday, November 24,
Afternoon

The light inside the police station is glaring and Nicole squints as she steps inside. The floor is hard under her feet and harsh sounds echo off every surface; ringing phones, rapid fire conversations, gruff orders and busy fingers tapping keyboards to update their files on the giant sea of crime that Nicole cannot help but feel part of now. Nervously she follows her sister inside and waits as Alva shuts the door. Chloe and Holly have already been taken to a back room where their aunt has told them they can watch TV while she talks to their mother.

There's a desk and two chairs, one on either side. Other than that, the room is completely bare and sterile. The smell of fresh paint is so strong she can almost taste it in her mouth. Alva points to a seat and Nicole takes it. Alva doesn't sit. Instead she stands, chin out, arms folded across her chest.

'Nicole, what's going on with you and Mark?' Alva leans back against the wall, fixing her sister with the cold stare Nicole knows she reserves for hardened criminals.

The pressure swells between Nicole's temples and she places a finger on each one and rubs them. She's known this moment was coming. She should be prepared. But she's sick of lying. So sick now. 'I had a woman called Eve accosting me earlier at a coffee machine in a shop across the way saying she's your friend, then telling me she thinks Mark never went to Barcelona. Do you want to tell me what's going on now?'

Tears cloud Nicole's eyes. She flicks them away before slumping towards the table. Her body is almost melting, the tension slipping away from her. Has it finally come to an end? She has to tell her sister now. She's trapped.

Alva pushes off the wall and leans over her, kissing her softly on the crown of her head, slipping a tissue into her fingers. 'Oh Christ Nic, listen to me, we don't have to get into it now. I don't even have the time. If you're still up when I get in tonight you can talk me through it. I know things are really shit for you right now and I'm sorry about that. I'm just worried about you. That's all.' She drapes an arm over her sister's neck and Nicole clings to it, swallowing hard as a tear tracks her bruised cheek. 'Who the fuck is this woman anyway?'

Nicole mops her eyes. 'I don't know Alva, I really don't. She's some crazy bitch who I thought was my friend, and today I found out she might be having an affair with Mark.'

'An affair?' Alva winces. 'For fuck's sake Nic, I'm sorry. Look, we'll talk all about this when we've time. What I need to tell you now is that Chris Ashton checked out fine so don't worry about him.'

'You mean, he's clear? No criminal history, nothing?'

'I mean I'm not telling you anything more Nic, because it's confidential. But I did also want to let you know that I've bumped up your neighbour's case to the next level.'

Nicole stiffens. 'How?'

'Dad's old friend Maitland is taking it on. You can expect to hear from him soon. They're going to catch the perp on this, whatever happens.' Alva drops down, holding Nicole's hand so they are both at eye level and pushes the hair back from her eyes. 'I'm sorry I can't be there for you more right now but the Doherty case has taken over. When it's finished I'll be able to share all the stuff I can't explain just yet. Alright?'

Nicole holds in a sob. She wants to scream, to wrap her arms around her sister; beg her for forgiveness, let her help as only Alva knows how. But she stays silent, pushing herself quietly to her feet.

89

Friday, November 24,
Evening

The Renault reverses into the free space on the side of Martins Lane. It's only now that Nicole realises how close Helen Shaw's flower shop is to Pearse Street Police Station.

'Are we staying in our own house tonight, Mummy?' Holly's eyes light up hopefully in the backseat.

The muscles tighten in Nicole's neck as she avoids Chloe's glare. 'Maybe love. I can't promise.'

Helen Shaw's flower shop is precisely where Chris Ashton pinned it in his link which she just received by text. It's sandwiched between a nail parlour and a pizzeria and sits on the ground floor; it's the commercial street front section of what looks like a large block of apartments. The light is beginning to fade and she guesses it might be near to closing time.

'Now I have a little thing to do girls, so I'm going to walk you back up to the police station to your Auntie Alva for a second. If you wait for me in the reception, I should be done in ten minutes. OK?'

'Mum! What are you talking about?' Chloe turns to her in the front passenger seat. 'Why do we have to go to the police station just because you're busy for a few minutes?'

Nicole's heart thumps and she turns to face her. 'Because Dublin isn't safe at this time in the evening, Chloe.'

Chloe's mouth hangs. 'Mum? You are joking?'

'Can we go home? Please Mum,' Holly asks in her most polite voice. 'I miss Rocky.'

Nicole's nails dig into the rubber edges of the steering wheel. She's not thinking clearly. Minutes ago she could have burst with relief that she managed to escape from Alva without a full interrogation. Through the windscreen glass she glances across at the flower shop and sees the closed sign hanging over the door. She guesses Helen Shaw might still be in there, and if she leaves now she expects she'll be done in a matter of minutes.

'OK Chloe, listen.' Reaching into her pocket she pulls out Mark's old phone. She's about to hand it over to her daughter when she changes her mind and replaces it with her own phone. She keys in Mark's old phone number, presses call and waits until it rings. Then she cuts the call and gives her phone to Chloe along with the car keys, putting Mark's phone back inside her pocket. 'I can't lock the car from outside or the alarm will go off so I'm leaving you the keys, alright?' Chloe takes them in her hand. 'I want you to lock the car as soon as I get out. If anybody approaches you or anything happens at all, you hit the call button immediately and let me know, OK love?' Chloe stares at her blankly, shakes her head and taps the phone to open YouTube.

The blinds are pulled so Nicole cannot see clearly inside the shop but she can see some patches of soil and a few trampled leaves on the pavement outside the front. It looks like the remains of Helen Shaw's flower display that must have been taken inside minutes ago.

The shop door opens when she tries the handle. 'Hello?' she calls, walking inside, surprised to find all the lights already off. In the dim evening half-light she can make out rows of plants lining the walls. 'Helen?' With the torch from Mark's old phone she lights up the space but a warning beep tells her the battery is almost dead.

The air is perfumed with so many different flowers it is overpowering. The dim torchlight reveals basket holders of red roses wrapped in white paper next to white lilies and what look like yellow tulips. Bits of cut stems are scattered on the floor where they have been trodden and squashed. It feels like the shop hasn't been cleaned properly. The battery beeps again and Nicole steps further in.

At the back of the shop she finds the till tucked away in an almost pitch black corner. On a raised counter is a large handbag. The strap dangles down and Nicole sees it is zipped up. Beside it is a set of keys.

'Helen? Are you in there?' Further on, through some larger potted plants, there appears to be a back store and she walks through it. The torch light reveals dark scratch marks of wet clay on the floor tiles. Her heartbeat spikes as she pushes a half opened door leading to a bigger storage space.

It isn't right. Helen Shaw wouldn't have gone if her keys and bag are still on the counter. Quickly she paces forward but stops instantly when she hears the sound of something shaking. It's a low rustling noise, like leaves. Next she hears somebody's laboured breathing.

'Who's there?' She turns back towards the exit but slips. Her hands reach for the potted plants which fall over with her as the phone skittles across the hard tiles. A loud crack shatters the silence in the room as two pots tumble and smash, throwing clay across the ground. The leaves from the plants tear in Nicole's hands and she lets them go to break her fall.

Seconds pass before she can push back up to a kneeling position. Only now there is something wet on her hands and a strange shape lies in front of her in the darkness. Mark's phone beeps and flickers its weak light across the body.

Helen Shaw lies on the ground, her head surrounded by a pool of blood.

Footsteps pound the floor and a door slams as Nicole lunges for the phone. Her stomach lurches as she takes in the woman's lifeless body sprawled on her side, her head resting on her outstretched arm, the other reaching forward as if to touch her. In the faint light she can make out her open eyes as the blood drips from her ear. The top of her torso twists at an unnatural angle against the ground and the light overcoat she wears is already staining dark.

Shaking, Nicole moves closer, checking for a pulse. 'Helen?' Feeling nothing she pulls her hand away leaving two streaks of blood on the woman's neck. Mark's phone makes a final muffled bleep and powers down, snuffing out the last trace of light.

She remembers her girls outside. Covering her mouth, she muffles a howling scream.

And runs.

90

Friday, November 24,
Evening

The rain is pouring so hard when Nicole gets out of the shop that the streets have completely emptied. Pools of dirty water swirl and hurtle toward the drains which have blocked with the recent fall of autumn leaves. The only remaining pedestrians scurry by, heads tucked beneath their scarves, eyes firmly to the ground. Those with umbrellas pull them close to protect themselves from the torrent that seems to be getting heavier each second.

Sprinting to the car Nicole stops abruptly when she discovers the space empty.

'Girls?' The word chokes inside her throat as she scans up and down the road. The traffic fizzes past in a blur of yellow and red light, the wet tyres splashing through the streams that have materialised out of nowhere. 'Girls!' This time she roars but the sound is drowned by the grinding car engines and the drumming of the rain. Exhaust fumes fill her mouth and grit splashes against her legs as she drifts out on to the busy road.

The world is spinning everywhere she looks, a blur of light and water. A driver blares his horn, punching it savagely as he drives past her. His window is down but Nicole doesn't hear his angry words. Staring blankly, she can only stagger to the safety of the pavement where she drops to her knees.

A cab stops then and the driver gets out to help. Opening the back door he pulls her on to her feet and guides her inside. In the backseat Nicole grips her head in her hands, slumping forward as she tries to calm. She wants to call Alva but knows she cannot do that. Chris Ashton is the only one who could understand. The only one who could help.

The rain drips from her coat onto the seat. Wide eyed and shaking, she calls out her address to the driver.

91

Friday, November 24,
Evening

The tremble in her fingers is so bad that the key misses when she attempts to fit it in the door lock. Gripping her wrist, she winces and holds it steady just long enough to insert it. She twists the lock three times and finally the front door to their house opens.

Instantly she runs upstairs to Mark's bedside locker and pulls out the drawers. One by one she tips the contents on the carpet but there is no charger for his phone anywhere. She must find it. Without it there is no way to contact Chris Ashton. Quickly she goes to his wardrobe and runs her hand along the top shelf. It's too high for her to see properly so she tips everything down and it tumbles in a heap to the carpet. 'Fuck,' she curses at the sight of Mark's T-shirts, sweatpants, old trainers.

For a second then, she stands back, her eyes blinking rapidly, a wild shaking in her arms starting as her breathing becomes more shallow. When she looks down, she sees the dark stains of blood where she has knelt on the carpet. By the door there are finger streaks of blood over the light switch and across the glossy white frame.

'Girls?' her voice cracks as she moves to Holly's room. Two chewed white lollipop sticks lie glued to the base of the bin beside her single bed and the cherry flavoured scent still hangs in the air. 'Chloe!' Her feet pound the stairs up to the attic bedroom, but it too is silent.

The green numbers on Chloe's clock flicker as the time moves on another minute. On the bed are a pair of her purple pyjamas folded on top of the unicorn duvet cover. Lying across the duvet is a large paper sketch she has drawn, and as Nicole looks closer, she can see it's a drawing of Mark. He holds Chloe in his hands as she flies a kite on the beach, one hand on the string, her face turned to the sky, wild with excitement as she tries to keep it under control. Mark is grinning, struggling to hold his balance as the sand bunches beneath his feet.

Tugging wildly at her hair, she runs down the stairs and into the kitchen. The laptop sits on the dining room table. She has no memory of leaving it there. She cannot think of when she last used it at all. The hard drive is waking up; the fan beginning to whir; the light from the screen flickering eerie shadows across the kitchen walls.

Nicole drags the chair out of her way, shoving it behind her. The first words have already appeared.

Now it's time Nicole.

Give me back my children.

Patience.

Fuck you.

Just one thing left.

The kitchen table rattles as she smashes her fist down. Pain shoots through her wrist up her arm and she gasps. *What do you want from me?*

We'll decide. Soon.

Her mouth hangs as she draws back from the table. But she doesn't have the energy to move. Instead she slumps down, her back pressing against the kitchen island, feeling the cold of the tiles beneath her legs. She should get up, at least move to the couch. But instead she closes her eyes, hoping the pain might go away.

92

Saturday, November 25,
Morning

The big clock ticks on the wall. It's the one she likes, the one Mark bought her in the antique shop as a gift. He had said he got it because he remembered her pointing out a similar one in a magazine, and how she told him she loved roman numerals and clocks that still had hands and made noises when they kept time.

With rhythmical precision the ticking continues and Nicole taps her fingers on the floor in time. Her eyes can't focus on the numerals just yet because she is not fully awake.

The knock sounds again. It's a sharp rapping noise and it doesn't make sense in this dream, the one where she walks holding hands with Mark by the water's edge, on the beach with golden sand, their girls running in and out of the water beside them, heads thrown back squealing and laughing, daring each other to go further in, splashing the foam with their feet.

Next she hears voices. They sound deep and serious, the voices of busy men, a little irritated, perhaps impatient. Her eyes tease open. There's a smear of something on the floor, staining it dark. Propping herself up with one arm she stares at it, only now remembering. It's blood. Her blood.

Scrabbling to her feet, she catches her reflection in the mirror; wild unkempt hair, the angry bruise on her cheek, a fresh crack in her lip, smudges of dark blood blotting her hands. Lurching unsteadily she moves to the sink where she turns on the tap and the cold water blasts into the bowl. Frantically she scrubs, rubbing her fingers up and down her arms, her stomach churning as the blood forms a red streaked river down the sinkhole.

The knock returns, but with more force. This time she closes the taps so she can steal across to the front living room window.

Three men are waiting outside, hands in pockets, their faces radiating a mix of suspicion and irritation. The tallest one in the long navy blue overcoat with the grey crew cut, the one who looks in charge, Nicole recognises. It's Maitland, their dad's old friend, the senior detective Alva got assigned to Mrs Lyubevsky's case. The other two police officers, who also wear plain clothes, she does not know.

'Just a minute,' her throat burns as she scurries back to the kitchen. But the laptop on the kitchen table catches her eye and she freezes. Only now does everything become clear again. The Paymaster has their girls. She cannot waste a second; she must contact Chris Ashton.

'Take your time,' Maitland replies, his big voice rolling through the corridor. Nicole's gaze strays beyond the sink into the garden and for a moment she imagines running out there, hiding even. But she knows it's pointless; they already know she's inside. Grabbing an apron from the cupboard she ties it quickly over her bloodied shirt and trousers, scrapes her hair into a ponytail and hurries out to the corridor to open the front door.

The cold air jolts her awake. The sky is clear and blue and for a second she squints, as little black specks blot her vision, shooting pain to the back of her head.

'Nicole, I know it's the weekend but Alva told me you'd be expecting us.' Detective Maitland crosses one hand over the other, turning to nod at one of the police officers behind him. 'This is Detective Deasy,' he looks to a thick-set man with cold eyes and short grey hair dressed in a green parka, 'and Detective Grant,' his glance flicks to a slight, bald man with a hard face and an unkempt beard dressed in black, 'they're assisting me in this investigation. Would now be alright to run through a few questions?'

There's no hint of threat in Maitland's voice. His mouth lifts in a relaxed, open smile but Deasy stares at her clothes and Grant peers across at Mrs Lyubevsky's house.

'I'd love to help but I . . . '

'Did something happen to you?' Maitland points at the bruise on her cheek.

'Yes.' She squeezes the door, the sudden urge to push past them and run into the street almost too much. If she could tell Maitland what happened, would he help her to find her girls? But she already knows he wouldn't. He'd have a duty to arrest her no matter how good a family friend he is. And Deasy and Grant would be witnesses. She must shut them down and leave. She cannot waste time when the Paymaster has their girls. Deasy's gaze has moved to where her apron meets her trousers. Grant is staring at her hands. 'I had an accident.'

'You did?' Grant scrunches his face doubtfully. 'What happened?'

'Last night, I was on my bike and I got knocked off.'

'Shit,' Deasy tuts, but his eyes betray his doubt. 'Did you hurt yourself?'

'I banged my cheek and cut my hands.'

'That must have been painful,' Maitland offers genuinely.

Deasy flicks something off his shoe. 'What about the driver? Did you get their name or details?'

Nicole shakes her head. Time is disappearing, time she cannot afford to lose. 'He kept going.'

'Typical huh?' Deasy says drily. 'But that's what we're up against these days, right? I mean the exact same thing happened to your poor neighbour – some scumbag breaks in, assaults her, leaves her for dead and nobody gives a toss. So you can see how finding the culprit is so important?' He turns to the others and Maitland steps forward.

'Nicole, we understand you made the first contact with the police. Did you witness anything unusual or see anybody in the area around the time?' The knot in the pit of her stomach twists as she shakes her head. 'Did you visit your neighbour on the night in question?' Nicole's fingernails dig harder into the door. She's lying badly, making what was an accident into a crime. But the police won't understand. How could they? Her only choice is to keep going.

'No. She came over to me earlier in the evening very briefly.'

Grant crosses his arms. 'To do what exactly?'

'To borrow sugar.'

Maitland nods. 'Was Mark around?'

Nicole adjusts her stance, shifting her weight to the other leg. 'He's away.'

Maitland raises his eyebrows as Deasy casts a sideways glance to Grant who nods. Maitland then crosses his arms and holds his chin between his thumb and finger. 'I did not know that. Where?'

Nicole hesitates. Something is wrong. What does she say now? She senses the net tightening around her. 'Barcelona.' Her voice is faint when she speaks.

Maitland frowns. 'Strange, because we had a call into the station from somebody who claimed they saw Mark walking home the same night.'

'What?' Nicole holds the door to steady herself. Mark can't have been here. Mark had been kidnapped by then. She knows. She was the one who delivered the car. It's impossible. 'Who?'

'You know a woman by the name of Eve Pennington?'

'Yes . . .'

'Well?'

Nicole feels her body sway and clutches the door tighter in her hands. 'If what she said is true, detective, I suggest you bring her in for questioning because clearly she knows more than I do.'

93

Saturday, November 25,
Morning

Rushing, Nicole returns to the kitchen to throw away her blood-stained pants and shirt. Quickly she crumples them into a ball and stuffs them in the bin. Then she goes up the stairs and puts on the first clothes she can find.

Next door Maitland and the other detectives gather evidence. At any moment they could return. The only thought in her head is to run. Because the window to escape is going to close and she must get away while she still can.

Putting on her coat she picks up the laptop bag in her hands and dashes from her house. As she goes through the gate she glances over to Mrs Lyubevsky's house but they haven't seen her. The gun inside the coat pocket bangs against her hip and she keeps walking. But she doesn't get far before her body starts to shake.

Where is she going? Mark's phone has no charge.

Stopping, she turns back to face the house, as the pounding at the back of her head intensifies. A strange dizziness has taken hold and for a moment it feels like her head is too heavy, that it's dragging her forward and she's powerless to stop it. Staggering, she puts out a hand to steady herself against a parked car when there is a loud screech of tyres.

94

Saturday, November 25,
Morning

The front end of the black saloon dips sharply as it pulls up along-side her. The door opens and Chris Ashton gets out.

'Nicole?' When she looks at him her face is blank and pale. He reacts fast, opening the passenger door and easing her carefully into the seat, where she collapses with a heavy groan, her eyes closing over in the same moment.

Next door the detectives move about inside the house. Chris watches them, crouching lower over the steering wheel, one hand to Nicole's neck as he checks her pulse. 'Nicole?' When she doesn't respond, he takes a deep breath. He should take her to the hospital but knows it's too risky.

The oldest of the three police officers moves to the front window and peers out but Chris squeezes his foot to the floor, accelerating hard to put them out of sight. They don't know he has Nicole. They must not know.

95

Saturday, November 25,
Afternoon

Nicole squints and raises a hand to protect her eyes from the harsh white lights which shine down on her from the ceiling. It's a modern rack of spotlights, she can see, angled in different directions to light up the room. The walls are off white and there is no coving where the wall meets the ceiling. It hurts when she leans on her elbow and lifts her head away from the armrest of the cream leather couch to look around.

On one side of the apartment she sees a tidy open plan kitchen, complete with breakfast bar and ivory glossed cabinets. The opposite end is a grey metal sliding door leading out to a small balcony. Nicole sits up and the blanket falls away from her body when she walks to the sliding door. Five storeys below is a pretty courtyard with two tall trees in its centre but none of it feels familiar. Why?

The front door to the apartment opens and Chris Ashton walks inside.

'My girls?' wide eyed, Nicole glares at him, the memory of last night bursting into her mind. 'Jesus Christ, my girls! They've taken my fucking girls.' She scans the floor, searching for her shoes. 'What am I doing here? Where's my bag? And my coat with my keys? We need to leave now, to find them.'

Chris puts a bag on the small dining table alongside his keys. Then he holds up one hand. 'Take it easy Nicole. The girls are safe.'

'But they took them.'

'No. They've just been dropped at their drama workshop in the Anglican church next to the primary school while you were sleeping. I'm telling you they are safe.'

Her heart thumps harder. 'I don't believe you.' She sees her coat lying folded across the back of one of the dining chairs and hurries over to take it. She puts it on and locates her house keys in the pocket. 'The Paymaster took them last night when . . .' the words trail off as the images flash through her mind: Helen Shaw's outstretched arm, her bloodied fingers reaching towards her, her twisted body, her smashed skull. 'Chris, you don't understand anything. They killed Helen.'

'Wait a minute, slow down.' Solemn faced, he throws off his coat and sits in the chair by the table. 'You have to explain to me what happened.'

Nicole's bag is on the floor and she plucks it up as she darts to the door but Chris Ashton jumps to his feet before she can get past him, blocking her way. They remain that way for a few seconds, eyes locked, neither budging, then she shoves him hard.

'Let me leave. I'm not standing here talking to you until I know my girls are safe.'

Chris steps back, taking his phone from his pocket and holding it out for Nicole to see. 'Go ahead. Ring the manager. I spoke with her this morning to check they arrived but speak with her yourself if you prefer.'

Nicole snatches the phone from his hand and paces through the glass doors onto the balcony. A wave of nausea rises from her stomach as she searches up the number and presses the call button. She doesn't understand how he could know about the drama workshop. Even she had forgotten about it until he mentioned it. Her body heaves and she retches over the railing but nothing comes up.

'Hello?' A woman answers.

'This is Nicole Reid,' she stops suddenly to control the next burst of nausea.

'Yes?'

'I want to check my girls arrived at the camp today. Their names are Chloe and . . . '

'Holly. Yes they're both here, Nicole. I saw them come in together this morning. This is Tanya, is everything OK?'

Nicole holds the phone by her side, terminating the call. Then she turns to look inside the apartment where she sees Chris Ashton staring back at her, his face grave.

He sits very still on one of the small wooden chairs by the dining table, his big frame leaning forward, one elbow on each knee, his hands closed together making a fist under his chin.

Exhausted, Nicole retreats to the sofa and drops onto it. 'Alright, you need to tell me right now what the fuck is going on and why the hell you have my children?'

96

Saturday, November 25,
Afternoon

'I expected you would go and visit Helen Shaw, so shortly after I sent you the location of her flower shop, I drove out there myself.' He rubs the back of his hand across the bristles on his cheek.

'You didn't think to text me, Chris?'

'I did text you.' He holds out his phone. 'But for some reason it wouldn't send.' Nicole sees the error notification of his unde-livered message on the screen. 'And I didn't want to waste time. I wanted to see you as soon as you came out, to find out what she could tell us. When I got there the first thing I saw was the black jeep, the same one you described to me the night of . . . ' he trails off and sighs heavily. 'It was the same two men inside it again. The heavy-set one was in the driving seat and the jeep was double parked outside. As soon as I saw him I started to run towards him but then I heard screaming behind me and I saw the second man, the tall one.'

'What was he doing?'

'He had your car door open and he was yelling at the kids.' Nicole clutches her knees, pressing them closer to her chest. 'Then he wrestled the phone from Chloe and smacked it against the roof of the car like he was trying to break it. I think he was about to get into the driver's seat when I caught up with him and threw him against the car behind. He fell hard but I knew he'd get up, so I didn't wait. I just jumped into the driver's seat without even thinking, then Chloe gave me the keys and I drove away as fast as I could.'

'Did they chase you?'

Chris frowns. 'For about ten minutes but eventually I lost them. As soon as I could see they were gone I returned to the shop. Chloe told me she had your phone so there was no way I could call you and I tried the number you gave her but it was dead. Then I thought about getting out of the car and going inside but I didn't want to risk leaving the girls again.' Tears drip from Nicole's chin, landing on her jeans. 'So I drove away, and at first I just went round in circles not sure what to do. I had to give the girls time to calm.' He stops, pressing the tips of his fingers into his forehead just below the hairline. 'Chloe wanted me to take them to Alva's but I explained that I couldn't. I told her she had to promise me not to talk about what happened with anybody until you came home and that she had to make Holly understand the same.'

Nicole swallows, a catch appearing at the back of her throat.

'She gave me her promise and then asked if I could take them to her friend Lily's house, because Lily was going with them to the drama workshop today anyway. So I agreed and she directed me there. The mum, Eve, said she was happy to help but wanted to speak to you.'

'What did you tell her?'

'I told her it wasn't possible. That you were in a difficult situation but that you would call and explain everything tomorrow. And then it was very strange.'

'Why?'

'Because she simply nodded and said it was fine. Almost like . . . '

'What?'

'Like she was expecting it or something. I can't really explain.'

Nicole clamps her eyes shut, the thought that Eve's house was the one place her children could really feel safe too much suddenly. 'So you decided to leave me there Chris?'

'For god's sake, please listen to me!' He throws his arms in the air, a pained expression on his face. 'No! I didn't want to leave you. I was stuck. I thought about calling the police but I was paranoid because I didn't know what . . . ' He stops, places his big hands over his eyes and exhales. Slowly he walks to the wall, turns and slides down it until he sits on the floor. 'What the hell happened in there Nicole? You need to explain it to me now.'

A cold draught blows through the balcony door and Nicole shivers. 'They murdered her too, Chris. They got to her before I did. I found her in the darkness at the back of the shop, with her head split wide open.'

97

Nicole wraps her arms tighter around her shins and rocks back and forth. Her skin is burning and yet her body shivers. A dark cloud passes high above them in the sky outside.

'They'll stop at nothing now,' the sound of her voice is strangely distant in her ears. 'I don't think they'll hesitate to murder Mark or even our girls.'

Chris stares at the floor. 'Don't say that, Nicole. You can't go there. Not now.'

'It's true. They murdered Helen in cold blood. The killer was there when I went to her.'

Chris gets up and moves closer until he is by her side sitting on the floor. 'Did you see them?'

Nicole presses her face into her knees, the memory returning. 'No, I heard them moving through the plants. The killer escaped when I slipped.' Suddenly she is back in the shop, the noise of the man's breathing in the darkness loud and clear; Helen Shaw's blood congealing in a thick pool on the floor, the light from Mark's old phone flickering and finally dying. Pausing for a second, she composes herself. 'Who the fuck would do this Chris? Why would they want to do it to us?'

Chris looks at her for a moment before getting to his feet. 'I need to show you something,' he then says, walking back to the table, and Nicole watches as he picks up a plastic bag and returns to kneel down beside her. He puts his hand into the bag and when he removes it Nicole sees he is holding her phone. 'This got damaged when Chloe tried to stop them taking it. I brought it to a repair shop and they said they got it working but it's still glitching.' She takes it off him, stares at the shattered screen and places it on the coffee table. Chris reaches into the bag again, this time taking out Mark's old phone. 'It fell out of your pocket when you got into my car but the battery was dead so I got him to charge it up too.' He places it in Nicole's hand. 'The guy in the shop bypassed the PIN. I might as well tell you now that I've had a look at it.' Nicole stares at the screen. Eve's last message displays. *Do what you need to.* Then Mark's reply. *I will.* Gritting her teeth she puts it down. 'Do you want to tell me about her?'

Exhaling noisily through her nostrils, she looks away. 'She's a fucking psycho who I thought was my friend.' Chris doesn't reply and the stitches in her scalp tighten. 'You read the texts, Chris.' Her voice starts to crack. 'What does it matter? How is it even connected?'

Gently Chris places his hand on her wrist. 'Nicole, the only thing that's clear is that she's fishing for him, nothing more. Has she done anything else?'

Nicole picks up Mark's old phone and the skin around her knuckles stretches as she squeezes it. Chris wraps his hands around her fist then, easing it slowly down to the coffee table. 'Nicole?'

She turns towards him. 'She contacted my sister Alva and told her that she doesn't believe Mark went to Barcelona. I didn't think there was more she could do but then the detective assigned to investigate my neighbour's case told me Eve rang the station.'

'Why?'

'She told them she saw Mark walking down our road the night I,' she hesitates for a second, scrunching her eyes tight, but then opens them once more and continues, 'the night I injured my neighbour.'

A shadow crosses Chris's face. 'Nicole there's something else.' His voice is tight when he speaks. 'Something we still haven't discussed.' The thumping inside Nicole's chest grows. 'I think you know what that is.'

In the pit of her stomach Nicole feels the muscles coil.

Chris presses the back of her hand lightly, the lines in his brow deepening. 'Nicole, you already know that Mark's name was the last on the list.' He pauses, his eyes sad, 'when you asked if I was spying on you when I first came here, the truth is I had to allow that there was a reason that Veronica had put Mark's name last. The same reason she put a question mark against his name. And I don't know if it's connected to why he's been texting Eve but it could be.'

Nicole's head sinks towards her chest. 'You think this whole thing is something arranged? Something devised between Eve and Mark?' Chris shrugs, a sorry look on his face. 'Because at one point I had this idea, after I found Mark's phone in his car, but I thought I was going crazy. It was too weird so I just dismissed it.'

'What idea?'

'That Eve was somehow behind everything, even though I had no idea how or why?'

'How long have you known Eve?'

'Only eighteen months.'

'Do you know anything about her life before?'

Nicole shakes her head, surprised to think how little she had ever found out about the friend she now relied on most. 'Almost nothing if I'm honest.'

Chris taps the tip of his index finger against his top lip. 'We can't rule anything out until we know more. But the only thing I feel sure about is that Veronica meant something by putting the question mark after Mark's name on that list.'

'To suggest what?'

'To suggest that Mark may not be the last victim. So, no matter how hard we search for him, he won't let us find him.'

Nicole closes her eyes and waits for the crushing feeling to pass before speaking again. 'Christ! You mean because he never disappeared in the first place?'

'I'm so sorry Nicole, but it might be that Mark just made it look that way.'

98

'Mark a part of this? That's insane, Chris. How could you even think that?' Nicole digs her fingernails deep into the palm of her hand. She looks away then and neither of them say anything for a while.

Eventually Chris turns to her. 'Did you identify Mark in the car the night you committed the kidnapping?'

The sky outside has turned grey and Nicole peers at it as she shakes her head sadly. It's the first time she's heard somebody else say what she's done out loud and immediately she is back there again. She clamps her eyes shut. The rain is falling on her face, clouding her vision; the fumes from the exhaust are in her mouth and the tang of burnt petrol is on her tongue; the big BMW engine idles but is interrupted by the sharp click of the boot releasing. 'I'm sorry,' she hears her own voice say, followed by the thud of a body falling back inside the boot space. Twitching, she rubs a hand across her face. 'No.'

'What did you see?'

'A body in a bag only.'

'Are you certain it was a body?' She nods as her ribcage squeezes tighter. 'You could have imagined it or maybe it was something else.'

'No. It moved towards me. The person was trying to escape but,' she pauses.

'What?'

She wipes away a tear from the corner of her eye with the back of her hand. 'They couldn't because I shoved them back inside.'

She chokes down a sob, her breath juddering. 'Then I pressed the button to close the boot and listened as it locked them in again.'

'You panicked with the stress, Nicole. It wasn't your fault.'

They both go quiet. Nicole closes her eyes once more and waits for the throbbing inside her head to pass but it won't go away. It keeps pulsing, cutting deeper. Silently she runs through what she knows.

Chris confronted Mark but he disappeared and left him a written instruction not to inform her about what was going on. Mark told him he was sorting things out. Then he left Eve a private message on a phone, which he purposely hid, saying the same thing. He's lied to her repeatedly. He said he went to stay with Ken in Wicklow when he wasn't even there. He wiped his own laptop.

Placing her fingers over her eyes she squeezes hard but the darkness doesn't clear. It only grows thicker. Has she really been blocking out the truth the whole time? The truth that Mark could be the Paymaster? But she won't accept that. She can't. The twisting inside her stomach begins again. She shakes her head but the thought won't go away now. The amount of money she has made the Paymaster is staggering. And yet it still doesn't make sense, because even if Mark did this to the others he couldn't do it to his own family? Not to his own children? Or could he?

Chris places his hand on her arm and they both stare in silence at the grey sky beyond the window. She thinks about him then. How they first met all those days ago. How he handed her Rocky rubbing the blood from his hands and trying awkwardly to make some small talk. If what he's told her is true, then it means he's suffered even more than she has because his wife Veronica is dead and she's never coming back. Though her hopes for Mark hang by the tiniest thread, it's still something she can cling to.

'Can I get you a glass of water?' His voice is quiet as he pushes to his feet. Nicole shakes her head as if waking from a daze. 'Anything at all?'

'No.' She watches him move away from her towards the kitchen, trying to make sense of why the skin along her spine is suddenly tingling as if it's cold. Immediately she sits up. She doesn't know anything about Chris Ashton. In truth, he's almost a perfect stranger, somebody she's been desperate to believe because of her situation. Of course she challenged him to verify who he was, and he did so readily. Alva even ran a clearance check on him too and it came up perfect. But what if all the documents he gave her were completely false? What if none of the things he has told her are true? That he never lost his wife; that he was never targeted, because he's not really who he says he is, but someone else entirely.

Leaping to her feet she pulls on her shoes and coat and snatches her phone.

'Where are you going?' Chris spins, a dark look on his face.

Mark's phone is still on the table and she takes it too. 'I'm going to see my girls.' Dropping her hand inside her pocket she checks for Mrs Lyubevsky's gun and finds it still there. Carefully she wraps her fingers around the cold handle.

But now Chris is standing in her way, his tall frame leaning above her, his arms folded tight. 'Not a good idea, Nicole.'

Neither of them move.

'I need to leave. And I need you to get out of my way please. Now.' Her heart thumps as she steps forward. Chris drops his hands to his hips and Nicole sees him shake his head as he walks across to the glass door to the balcony. He raises his arm and flattens it against the glass. Then he rests his head on it.

'I wouldn't Nicole.'

Nicole doesn't hear him. She has already rushed to the door and let herself out.

99

Saturday, November 25,
Early Evening

'I know the Anglican church. I can be over there in ten minutes. I understand it's an emergency and I'll keep the girls with me. I'm getting into my car now,' Shaun explains.

Inside the back of the cab Nicole can hear the sound of Shaun slamming the door of his Toyota and belting up on the other end of the phone line. 'You don't have to explain. I've got it.' Shaun hangs up. It's the best plan. The safest. She can trust him. He's an experienced police officer and their house is five minutes from the church. No matter how fast she drives she wouldn't cross the city to get there in less than twenty minutes.

Quickly she scrolls her phone and pulls up Colin Dutton's contact number. He answers after two rings.

'Nicole?'

'I need you to try again.'

'What?'

'The laptop, Colin.' She grips her forehead between her thumb and forefinger as her voice rises. 'There's got to be a way to trace the hack. Please, you have to listen to me, I can't explain how urgent this is now.'

Colin Dutton lets out a long sigh. 'Nicole, I explained to you already. This kind of encryption needs a specialist. Maybe like somebody inside with the police that Alva might know. We've been over this.'

'Colin, please?' Her voice is shrill. 'Think, for Christ's sake. I've already told you I can't use the police.'

'Why?'

'I don't have time to explain. You must know somebody?'

'OK, OK.' He sighs loudly and goes quiet. When he comes back on the line his voice is softer. 'I'm sorry. I realise this is serious now, alright. Maybe there's a way. Listen, I'm meeting someone this morning. He may know a guy but I don't want to promise. I'll call as soon as I know. That's the best I can do.'

'That's all I'm asking for.' The call ends and Nicole's gaze shifts back out the window as her mind switches to Eve. Who is she really? What has she been doing with Mark all this time that she's been concealing?

Drawing her phone out slowly, she takes a deep breath. Then she pulls up Eve's number, and presses call.

'Nicole?' Nicole holds her breath but doesn't reply. 'Nicole, is that you?'

'Eve.'

There's a long pause. 'What happened to you? A man I had never met dropped your girls over last night and then just left without an explanation. Is everything OK?'

'No.'

'What's wrong?'

'I think you know what's wrong.'

'I'm not following you.' Eve's sunny tone sharpens. 'Look, you know I'm always here to help and Chloe and Holly are welcome to stay with me as long as you need but perhaps it's time for you to tell me what's going on Nicky. It's clearly something.'

'I saw your texts to my husband.'

Another pause, then a sharp intake of breath. 'OK? And?'

Nicole grips the phone tighter. 'What do you want, Eve?

'The same as you. A happy life.'

'You're a liar.'

There's a loud snort followed by a laugh. 'Well that makes two of us then doesn't it. You really think I don't know that Mark isn't in Barcelona? Your lies are so pathetic a child could see through them. In fact I think your children already have.'

The muscle in Nicole's jaw quivers beneath the skin. 'Why are you doing this?'

'Don't kid yourself. I don't have to do anything. You're doing it all to yourself. In fact I'm amazed Mark put up with it for so long but I guess that's going to change now.'

Nicole's fingers have balled into a fist. 'You know when Mark learns who you really are Eve, he'll never speak to you again.'

A harsh laugh rattles back down the line. 'Oh god Nicole, you're even more clueless than I thought.'

100

Mark's shirts line the rack inside the wardrobe. Nicole bunches them roughly into a ball, thrusting her head between them. There's a smell of sweat and aftershave and she breathes it in deep, gripping the clothes tighter between her fingers, crumpling the material inside clenched fists. She knows if it was two weeks ago she'd be giving out to him for leaving his shirts unwashed in the wardrobe but now all she can think is how little any of it matters.

In one violent movement, she rips the shirts clear. The wardrobe rattles and the hangers clang and fall, some of them clattering to the base of the closet, others tangling in the clothes and tearing the cotton. One by one she picks them up and tosses them across the room, listening through gritted teeth as the steel and wood smacks against the window glass.

She doesn't know what she is doing anymore. She only knows that she has achieved nothing, found no clue to bring her closer to the Paymaster. Turning back to the wardrobe she begins pulling out things at random. Shoes, boxer shorts, socks, trousers. She throws everything in the air, letting it fall wherever it lands. There's a dresser by the wall with three drawers which she shares with Mark. She rips each one out and tips the contents on the floor before hurling the empty drawers at the wall above the bed. They shatter and break, scattering plastic wheels, delicate pin nails and broken plywood inserts across the carpet.

Sweat drips from her face as she pauses to catch her breath. 'You're wrong Chris,' she whispers, 'Mark could never be behind this. Never.' But as the words trail from her mouth fear balls in the pit of her stomach. The wreckage holds no clues and she can already feel her arms trembling. Slumping against the bedroom wall she stops to check her phone once more. It now shows five missed calls from Alva and a new text.

Nicole, you need to call me. I don't know what's going on.

Stuffing it back inside her pocket, she runs downstairs into the office. The wound at the back of her head is throbbing harder each second. When she puts her fingers to the stitches she feels the blood. It's hot and sticks to the tips like glue. There are books and papers everywhere. She knows some of them are hers and some Mark's but it's immaterial to her now. All she wants to do is tear everything apart. She grabs a book from the bookcase and flings it against the back wall. It falls to the ground and she kicks it, pulling more books free and letting them tumble down.

Her old journals are there and she takes them in her hands, scattering them across the floor. They're the ones she used to keep when she wrote with a pen, back before the memories she wanted to forget kept surfacing, memories like the one of her mother on her knees after their father died, searching the carpet underneath the bed looking for lost coins, the muted muffle of her sobs, because she didn't want Alva and Nicole to hear her cry; didn't want them to know how bad things had got.

She jumps across and picks more papers off the desk, flinging them wildly into the air. They flap and scatter, making a mess on the floor.

Looking around she sees there's an ancient monitor sitting on top of some of Mark's old medical manuals and she stares at it in surprise as it lights itself up to display a picture of their family.

Nicole steps back, the bright light from the screen casting shadows against the lines of her face. She doesn't recognise the picture. It's an old one and Holly can't be more than two because she remembers the blue jean dungarees she is wearing were the ones Mark bought her in France the week she started to walk. It's Mark with her and Chloe and she knows it's France because she can see the dusty soil under their feet and the rolling hills of vines behind them. Chloe is braiding Holly's hair and whispering something in her ear; they both squint, their pink sunburnt cheeks dotted with summer freckles. Mark is caught unaware and he stares at them both with a look so tender it makes Nicole catch her breath.

He looks so familiar, the man she always loved, the man she knew inside out. But does she really know him anymore? There's a squash racket inside an umbrella holder under the desk. She picks it up as Eve's words replay inside her head. *'You're even more clueless than I thought.'*

She steps closer to the monitor, raises the squash racket high above her head, blinking as the knot inside twists tighter. And then she stops.

A piece of paper has caught her eye. It dangles out from under the stand for the monitor. Written on top it are the letters HFS.

Carefully she places the squash racket down on the office desk and removes the paper. Underneath it she finds a stack of old university annuals.

IOI

Saturday, November 25,
Early Evening

There are five annuals in total stacked in chronological order. Nicole places them down on the office desk and picks up the one at the top of the pile. It's Mark's first year of university, the freshman year.

Flicking through it she sees the pictures are all in black and white. It's so long ago and yet the sight of all the young fresh faced students at the beginning of their bright new futures takes her back instantly. She stops, the memory of when she and Mark first met now blooming in her mind, how he stepped aside in the café queue, letting her go ahead of him, offering her his self-service tray, smiling sheepishly, pushing a thick fringe of wavy black hair from his eyes as the light bounced off them, before he whispered in his low voice, 'Go ahead, it's fine.' She remembers how he gestured with a glimpse to the salad bar where the woman behind waited with an impatient scowl on her face and they both held in their laughter. Did Mark know then why she had forgotten all about the queue, all about the food she would eat for lunch? Because she knew. She knew in that second why everything would change.

Mark's class is there and she runs her finger down through the dark passport sized photographs until she sees the letters HFS written in large bold capitals. The pictures underneath are slightly larger than the other ones, as if to highlight the importance of the group. She sees Chris first. His face is smooth and his hair is long, tossed to one side and draping almost as far as his shoulder but the dimple in his chin and the eyes look the same.

Underneath there is a picture of Veronica Woods. A thoughtful face, dark hair, light pale skin, her smile looking like it might break into laughter. Nicole keeps going, running her finger over the pictures, pulling the names from her memory to each grainy black and white image: Richard Jennings, Bernadette Cornell, Angela Johannson.

Her stomach tightens when she sees the next picture.

Mark Reid. He's so young it takes her a second to fit the boy to the man she knows as her husband. The head of wavy black hair, the confident grin, the tilt of his chin angled away from his slender neck, his eyes looking off to a corner high up somewhere off camera. The ache swells inside and she steps back, resting her shoulder against the wall. Her glance drops to the last picture in the list. The student's name is Mason Kendall. Dark, watchful eyes look out behind small glasses. His brown hair is parted neatly to the side and he has a light shadow of beard on his jaw. There is nothing remarkable about him, except for his challenging stare.

Nicole traces a finger back up through the pictures and little sparks of pain shoot from her spine into the muscles of her neck, because as she counts the pictures, whispering each name out loud, she can see clearly there is something wrong. Something deeply wrong.

There aren't six students in the Holden Foundation Scheme. There are seven.

102

Her heart drums hard as she photographs the page with her phone. Instantly she attaches it to the message to Chris Ashton and types.

Who is this?

Once the message sends she drops her head back against the wall of the home office and closes her eyes. The thoughts race frantically through her mind. How could Chris not know about this? How can it not match the information she received from Professor Alan Byrne at the university?

The phone buzzes in her hand with an incoming call and Colin Dutton's name appears on the screen.

'Nicole, I might have something for you,' he says.

Quickly she paces to the living room. 'Yes?'

'I just came out of a meeting with a Russian guy I work with. We have a games development company we partner together on. Anyway, he told me his brother is over visiting him from Moscow because there's a cybersecurity conference on in the convention centre tomorrow and he's going to it. Encryption and security are his speciality.'

Nicole moves to the other side of the kitchen, the palm of her hand flat against her forehead. 'Can I talk to him? Ask him if there's any way he can help me?'

'I've already asked him. Then his brother rang me back immediately saying he'd be glad to do what he can as a personal favour to me.' He lets out a sigh. 'Again, I don't want to promise you anything because like I already said, the encryption I discovered looked too advanced for most people to break. But if you want him to try, I think it could be worth it.'

Her heart pounds. 'How soon can he get to me?'

'Well, where are you now?'

'At home.'

'Do you have the laptop there with you?'

There's a pause as Nicole lifts the phone away from her ear, glancing nervously across the room, her eyes scouring the big wooden dining table, frown lines pulling tighter across her brow. The table is bare. She darts back to the office, breathing hard.

The laptop isn't there and now she remembers why.

Curling her fingers into a ball she resists the urge to bang it down on the table. 'No, it's at an apartment down the road from me.' Using her thumb she scrolls through her apps until she finds WhatsApp and opens it up. 'I'm sending you the exact address right now.'

'Who's place is that?'

Nicole stares out through the kitchen window into the back garden. For a second she has no idea what to say. Is Chris Ashton another victim? Is he actually who he says he is? Why hasn't he told her about Mason Kendall? The annual is open on the table and she stares at it, zooming in on his young, innocent face. 'He's a guy who said he'll help me. I'm going straight there this second.'

'Good. I'll send our man over.'

103

Saturday, November 25,
Evening

The tyres screech as the old Renault tears out from the parking space in front of Nicole's house onto the road. Pressing the accelerator hard she speeds away, down Marwood Road towards Rathgar village.

It won't take long to get back to Chris's apartment in Dartry. If she drives quickly she should arrive before the encryption specialist gets there. She will make him understand. He cannot leave without giving them something. Chris's words are replaying in her mind. *Mark may not be the last victim. So, no matter how hard we search for him, he won't let us find him.* She won't accept it's true. If Colin Dutton's contact can help them find Mark then she can prove it.

A buzzing noise sounds on the passenger seat. The cracked screen of her phone is lighting up with Chris Ashton's name. Nicole snatches it, revving the car hard as it screeches away from another set of traffic lights.

'Why didn't you tell me I left the laptop behind, Chris?'

'You never gave me a chance,' he replies defensively. 'You walked out the door before I even knew you were gone.'

Nicole slams on the brakes, suddenly realising the car in front has come to a stop. The front of the Renault dips and her chest bangs into the steering wheel. Blowing hard, she takes a second to get her breath back.

'Well what about the annual? How do you explain that? Why are there seven students in HFS when you told me it was only six?'

'I don't know. I've just looked at the picture you sent me now. It doesn't make sense to me either.'

The car in front moves and Nicole follows quickly behind. 'For god's sake Chris. Try! Please! It must mean something.'

'I am trying,' he snaps. 'Just give me a second, please? I'm looking at it again now. What year is this?'

'Can't you see it's your first year annual? The freshman one. Who is Mason Kendall?'

'He was a quiet guy who mostly kept to himself.' He breaks off for a second. 'The course didn't work out for him and he didn't come back after his first year.'

'Why?'

'He got in trouble with the faculty.' The red light of the fuel tank flashes on the dashboard and an alarm beeps. Nicole rubs a hand over her face as the car in front slows down and pulls up at the red light. 'Chris, this could be relevant.'

'Certainly.'

'And there's something else too.'

'What?'

'A friend of Mark's has found a cyber security specialist. He's the brother of someone he works with. He's agreed to look at the laptop and will try and trace the source of the Paymaster's hack. He's on his way over to your apartment right now because I gave him the address. If he gets there before I do, I want you to make sure he waits for me so I can speak to him face-to-face. This needs to work. There's no other way now, he has to trace it.'

There's a clicking noise on the other end of the phone and the line goes dead.

299

104

Saturday, November 25,
Evening

There's a man carrying a cardboard box walking through the pedestrian gate to the apartment block. Nicole rushes to catch up with him and holds the gate before it can close. Sprinting as fast as she can, she gets to the security door to Chris's block. There's a cleaner inside mopping the floor tiles and Nicole raps on the glass door to get her attention.

The cleaner considers her for a moment before cautiously walking over to buzz her through. Grabbing the door, Nicole runs past her, squeezing her way into the lift as soon as the doors open.

On the first floor landing of the stairwell she now notices a man. He stands there looking down at her. He is blond haired with a gaunt face, dressed in a dark suit with a heavy winter coat that hangs loosely off his shoulders. In his hand Nicole sees a briefcase.

Mopping the sweat from her forehead, she jabs at the elevator button to open the doors but it's too late. It takes off and begins its ascent to the fifth floor which she has already selected. Breathing hard she leans back against the mirrored back wall.

The lift wobbles, tugging her higher and her heart thumps. The man with the briefcase was looking at her like he needed to tell her something. Is it possible he was the security analyst? Beads of sweat sprout on her lip and she watches the numbers flash in sequence until the lift chimes and stops at the fifth floor.

There is no delay when she knocks on Chris's apartment door and he opens it before her knuckles can hit a second time. Brushing past him she dashes through the corridor and into the open plan kitchen-living room space. When she gets to the couch she stops.

Chris walks in quickly and moves to the glass doors to the outside balcony before turning to face her. Only now does she see that he is putting on what looks like a bullet-proof vest. 'It's something I got from the investigator I hired,' he says before she can ask.

'Chris why did you end my call after I told you about the cyber-security specialist?' she replies ignoring the vest.

He adjusts the Velcro strap on his shoulder. 'I didn't Nicole. I rang you back.' Nicole pulls out her phone and stares at the cracked screen which shows a missed call message. 'I told you the phone repair man said he didn't fix it properly. You can't rely on it.'

Putting it back in her pocket Nicole's eyes flick to the dining table. Her laptop is still there. Warily, she edges over to it but sees the screen is blank and it makes no noise. 'What's going on Chris? I come here and you're putting on a bullet-proof vest like you're about to leave? And where is the cyber security specialist?' She tries to still her leg which has started to shake. The tension is coiling up through her spine and into her neck. 'Colin Dutton told me he'd be here by now.'

Chris puts on his coat. 'He's already come and gone.'

'What?' Nicole steps back. 'But I told you I needed to meet him. To explain to him face-to-face that he had to find the source of the hack. How could you let him go?'

Chris checks his watch. 'Because he found it already, Nicole.'

'That's not possible.' Nicole shakes her head. 'Colin Dutton said it would involve taking the whole machine apart to find something.'

'He connected his laptop to yours with a cable, ran a program and pulled a trace within minutes. He explained that he used to work in government security so it was his speciality. That's all I can tell you.' He holds out his phone which shows a map picture with a pin. 'Every communication led to one location, an old disused factory up in Ballymount off the M50.'

The blood drains from Nicole's face. 'Are you saying it's where you found Mark's car?'

'No, but it's not far from it. We need to go there now.'

Nicole stays where she is. Meeting Colin Dutton's contact was her only way to be certain of what Chris is saying but she can't think of why he would lie. She desperately wants to believe him, to accept that what he's been telling her is true, and yet she knows it's a risk.

Chris puts the phone back inside his pocket. 'Trust me, Nicole.' Moving his fingers inside his coat, he adjusts the tightness of the vest across his ribs. 'That's all I can say now. We have to work together and we need to move fast.' They stare at each other and Nicole swallows. Everything Chris Ashton has explained so far suggests he is on her side. Every piece of information he has given her has checked out; and yet still she has questions.

'You haven't told me anything yet about Mason Kendall. If there's another person on the HFS we have to find them. It changes things.'

'How?'

'It means Mark is no longer the last one on the list. Kendall could have information that can help us.' Chris snatches a set of keys off a hook on the wall and turns to look at her. 'I can't believe Mark is behind this in any way, Chris. I won't.'

'I don't want to believe it either. But the only lead we have for now is the source of the hack. If we locate the source, we locate the Paymaster. I can't say where Mark or Kendall fit into this yet but when we find the Paymaster we'll know.'

Nicole holds her face between her hands. The thought that she has really found the Paymaster is almost too much; that by the end of today all this could be over. Yet, all she has is the word of Chris Ashton, the stranger who walked into her life the day he brought Rocky to the door with an injured ear. *You were always so kind to animals it made me worry.* The words of her father replay inside her head and she takes a deep breath but it's interrupted by a sharp *click*. Her gaze switches to the laptop screen which hums and whirs as it comes to life. The first words are already on the screen.

It's time for your final task, Nicole.

Chris stops adjusting the protective vest. The skin around Nicole's eyes pulls tighter and she drops her hands to the keyboard to type.

What do you want?

For you to finish our business so we don't have to kill your precious family.

105

Saturday, November 25,
Evening

Chris lunges across but he's too slow. Nicole already has the laptop in her hands. The sinews in her neck strain as she lifts it over her head and hurls it with all her strength at the apartment wall. The plastic casing clatters against it, instantly smashing into fragments which skittle across the laminate floor. The keyboard detaches and skids into one of the kitchen kickboards. Grabbing it again, Nicole slams it to the ground and it snaps, cracking and crunching as the keys spit into the air like broken teeth. The screen has landed behind the chair where its green light flickers weakly from the shattered display. Standing above it, Nicole raises the heel of her shoe and brings it down like a hammer.

Panting hard, she drags herself to the couch and waits to catch her breath. The last remaining communication link to the Paymaster has finally been broken. She shakes her head, staring at the smashed remains of the laptop. They have pushed her too far. She will go to where the Paymaster is hiding and demand Mark. Mrs Lyubevsky's gun is still inside her coat pocket. If they threaten her she will not hesitate to use it.

Closing her eyes, she takes a deep breath and stands up straight, a strange euphoria igniting inside her. They will never contact her again through the laptop. But the satisfaction is fleeting; they still have Mark. Then her phone rings.

'It's OK,' Chris says softly. 'Go ahead and answer.' Cautiously he moves towards the balcony. 'See who it is.'

Her breath catches when she hears her sister's voice on the other end of the line. 'Alva?'

'Nicole, I don't know what the fuck is going on but you need to come down to the station and explain right now. Shaun has got the girls, they're safe with him but you and I need to talk.'

Chris steps closer to the balcony sliding door. 'Tell her we'll text her the Paymaster's location soon, Nicole. That way the police can back us up.'

Pressing the phone to her ear, Nicole replies. 'I'm sorry Alva. There's so much for me to explain and I don't have time.'

'What are you saying?'

'It's about Mark, Alva. He's been kidnapped by a criminal known as the Paymaster. They entrapped me, forcing me to do things to get him back. I've had to agree to their demands.'

'Jesus, Nicole. Why didn't you come to me?'

'I couldn't Alva,' her voice cracks. How can she start to explain? To tell her how badly she wanted to from the very beginning, how she dreamed of doing exactly that from the moment she saw the first message on her laptop – when they ambushed her in the middle of the night, confused and desperate. But then things moved so fast and everything became impossible to control. When she looks up Chris Ashton is staring out the window. 'I couldn't risk losing Mark . . . they made me do things . . . things I couldn't ever tell you,' she breaks off, 'but Chris Ashton, the man I told you about, he's helped me to find them. We know where the Paymaster is now.' She stops as Chris steps closer to the glass. 'We're going to get Mark.'

'Don't do that Nicole.'

'Alva, I think a man by the name of Mason Kendall may be behind this. Getting to Mark is the only way we can find out.'

There's a pause and the line goes quiet. When Alva speaks again her voice is low and urgent. 'Nicole, please, it's important you listen to me. You mustn't do that. This person is known to us and they're dangerous. Their identity was only uncovered today as part of the Doherty case I've been working on and you have to let the police handle this now.'

Chris moves abruptly, his body tensing. 'Hold on, Nicole. Something's up.' He peers out, scanning the windows on the other side of the apartment block.

'What is it?'

'I think somebody's watching us.'

Thump. A cracking sound blasts through the room and Nicole covers her ears. Alva roars something but Nicole can't hear it. Then the glass door to the balcony shatters and Chris Ashton's body lifts into the air.

106

Saturday, November 25,
Evening

The dining table snaps, buckling beneath him as he lands, scattering the two wooden chairs across the floor. They skid and clang noisily against the kitchen island. Nicole stares at Chris's body, the shape of it almost unrecognisable on the other side of the living room, his cheek flat against the floor, eyes to the wall; one arm bent over so his knuckles press into the ground with his elbow jutting out.

A line of blood trickles from the back of his head.

'Chris?' She goes to him but her feet slide on broken glass and she slams against the kitchen island. With a loud smack her spine rattles one of the units, bringing her to a stop. Cold air breezes in through the window and she sucks it down as the nerves in her back scream. Breathing hard, she hauls herself to a sitting position, picking lumps of glass from the cuts in her hand. 'Chris?' she calls softly again but now there is a loud bang at the front door of the apartment.

Flinching, she reaches inside the coat pocket to retrieve the gun. Seconds later the door gives, bumping hard into the corridor and two men storm inside. The smell of sweat fills the room and Nicole scrabbles behind the island. She recognises them instantly. The larger one is the Paymaster's driver and standing next to him is Detective Deasy, the plain clothes officer who interrogated her with Maitland at her house. He wears the same green coat and his menacing eyes shine under the spotlights as he grunts while violently stomping on Chris Ashton's chest. It's clear now that

307

whoever is behind setting her up has infiltrated the police and turned Deasy. But who else does it mean they've turned? And why?

Forcing herself back against the cupboard, the tendons in her neck bulge as Nicole chokes back her scream. Adjusting the gun in her hands, she bends her knees to prop up her wrist. But the gun is heavy, and as she tries to steady it, they shake badly.

The air drags in and out of her lungs now in short, rasping breaths. Chris Ashton isn't moving.

Her head slides back against the cupboard and she thinks of Holly and Chloe. Alva has assured her they are safe but when she tries to imagine how their life will turn out once they receive the news that their mother has been shot on the floor of a city apartment, she wants to cry. *Mark*, she thinks *please be alive.*

'Now I wonder where she's hiding?' Deasy breaks the silence with a sardonic question to the driver. Nicole cranes her neck, pulling back when she sees his outstretched arm holding a gun. But it's too late, he's already seen her.

Both men walk towards her and stop, their eyes cold; no trace of surprise, no hint of emotion of any kind. Deasy glances at the small gun wobbling in her hand and sneers, aiming his own gun at her, the belief that she won't fire clear to see.

Nicole steadies her wrist but she knows Deasy's guessed right and she won't do it. Closing her eyes, she eases her finger away from the trigger and her head rolls backwards. There's a hollow tap when it hits the cupboard door.

It's only a fraction of a second later when she hears the noise. Another searing assault on her eardrums, followed by an explosion of blood and tissue which wets her face and hair.

Opening her eyes, she sees Deasy's body slumped on the floor and the white ceiling turned red. The driver fires his gun a second time, this time away from the head and into the back of Deasy's already limp body. With a hand pressed into her stomach to try and stop herself from retching, Nicole crabs clear of the spatter, twisting and slipping as she scrambles deeper inside the kitchen.

'Don't waste time,' the driver snaps, raising his gun. 'Make it easy and do what I say.'

It's happening too fast and it doesn't make sense. Moments ago she was certain they had both come to assassinate her. Now one of her attackers lies dead on the floor. There's a heavy grunt and she looks up. Caught unaware, the driver spins as Chris Ashton smashes the broken chair leg across his jaw. His neck twists as his legs collapse, dropping him on top of the dead man by her feet.

Gripping the counter Chris sways for a moment. Then he stoops down and picks up the driver's gun. 'We need to go now,' he says.

107

Saturday, November 25,
Evening

'Wait,' Nicole inserts the location pin into her message to Alva and ends the text with the words *I'm so sorry*. Her finger hovers for a moment before eventually tapping, and she watches it disappear.

Turning away then she looks out from the passenger seat of Chris Ashton's car. It's the same car as Mark's, a simple family saloon, just a black Hyundai – nothing remarkable. It seems impossible that they are here at this abandoned old factory in Ballymount, driving up cautiously to the rusting steel gates, armed only with Mrs Lyubevsky's small gun to confront the Paymaster.

Exhaling slowly, she looks outside at the November sky which has darkened again. A wisp of smoke is filtering through the car's air vents and the rain is pattering on the roof. Gently she places the phone down before turning to face Chris. 'I've sent our location to Alva. How long do you think it will be before the police get here?'

Chris shrugs. His handsome face is so changed it is unrecognisable. One eye is closing over, his cheek is dark purple and lacerations mark his face and forehead. 'Maybe ten minutes. It gives us enough time.'

'What happens when we find him Chris? What then?'

'An ending I hope,' he says, his voice weary. 'That's all I ever wanted.'

Her hand shakes as she reaches across to him and he clutches it tight between his bloodstained fingers. For the first time she truly believes that Chris Ashton holds no more secrets, that his suffering is deeper than her own.

Chris's gaze has drifted over her head, just like it did that first day he called to their house, when he stood outside the front door with Rocky in his hands. The flicker of hope she thought she saw in his face is gone, and in its place is fear.

Spinning sharply, she looks out the window, the roaring of the oncoming engine now pounding in her ears.

The lights of the pickup truck blind her for a second.

And then it hits.

108

Mason Kendall steps back as the wall of heat streams through the open window, cloaking his body in a hot cloud. The noise of the crash is something unexpected, and even now, seconds later, he can hear it replaying in his ears; the crunching, grinding thump of steel on steel, the screech of rubber on the tarmac, the shotgun popping of the tyres and the skittering of shattered glass that seemed to go everywhere. Somehow it reached his window, high up on the second floor of this old, abandoned factory, tapping the pane so briefly it could have been a spray of gravel or a volley of hailstones, there one second and gone the next.

Closing his eyes, he breathes in the acrid smell of burning rubber and dirty oil. When he opens them again smoke is mushrooming into the sky and floating away from the disused parking lot like a black shroud.

The flipping of the car was unexpected and for a moment he had been angered by the excessive zeal of his bodyguard, Coonan, and worried that he had gone too far, ending her life before he had the pleasure of a final meeting with her. But as he watched the flames flicker and saw their bodies stagger from the wreckage, Nicole Reid reaching a hand out as if trying to prop herself against a wall that wasn't there, next to her, the once athletic Chris Ashton, no longer able to stand upright, he knew it would still be OK.

Today was intended to be memorable and so far it hadn't disappointed. His eyes stray across to the lone wheel which spins across the disused parking lot, splashing through potholes, looping in random arcs, and he is shocked at how, when something goes unchecked, when there is no force to resist it, how long it can run and run.

He takes a sip from his bottle of water and tosses it down the empty corridor as the anticipation grows. It has all been so intricately planned, so carefully orchestrated but now it must end. He trusts what his advisers have told him, and accepts that it is time to uproot and move his business operation to another location. He had already figured out himself that the police were getting too close. But that's not what interests him. That's work, something he will take care of in due course.

What matters to him, what has always mattered to him, is personal.

Interlocking his fingers he flexes them away from his body and listens as the knuckles crack one after the other. It fills him with satisfaction that he took the time to revisit the graduates of the Holden Foundation Scheme and their families. It had been at the back of his mind for so long, festering away like an open wound. He is already looking forward to moving on, to finding the closure that has been missing.

Breathing in slowly, he watches Coonan grab Chris Ashton violently by the cuff of his jacket. Grant, the second corrupt police officer drawn into his service by Deasy, prods Nicole Reid sharply. Kendall checks his watch and notes the time. In a few minutes his assumed identity will be cast off. It lasted for a lot longer than he had expected, and he's enjoyed being somebody else, somebody other than the person he had grown to loathe, acting the part he had once imagined for himself, a regular happy man no different to the rest. He had even grown so close to the people he cared for he believed he was sharing in their lives.

The corner of his eye is damp and he wipes it carefully with his finger. The feeling of sadness is strange, almost unnatural. And yet it's real, and he knows it's because the end is close and he doesn't want it to come, even after he's spent so long preparing for it. Relaxing his arms so they hang loosely by his side, he stands tall.

It's time to finish what he's started. The stage is set. Everything is ready.

It's time for guilty people to die.

109

Saturday, November 25,
Evening

Dazed, Nicole pushes to her feet and tries to take in the scene. The wheels still spin on Chris's overturned car. Flickers of yellow flame snake in and out of the windows. The glass crunches beneath her as she walks unsteadily from the wreckage, squinting and covering her mouth against the smoke, her face twisted towards the sky as the pain inside her head stabs again and again behind her eyes. A rolling wheel arcs past them splashing her with dirty water and she stares as it loops and thumps against a brick wall, its steel rim clanging and drumming the concrete before it settles.

For a second she is totally lost. She has slipped into another world which makes no sense. All she can see is fire; all she can taste is blood. The pain assaults her like a million blades cutting her skin all at once, tearing her flesh from her body. And then it returns, in a moment of cold horror: she has come here to finally confront the Paymaster; to finally learn the truth.

'Do what you're told now. You haven't got long to go.' Detective Grant's lips brush her ear. He's the other police officer that came to her house that day with Maitland. A second member of the force that has been clearly corrupted. But by who? And to what end? She can smell the sourness on his breath. Wet fingers slide up the back of her head, gathering a handful of her hair and he yanks it hard. The stitches in her scalp tug and she cries out. Instinctively her hands fly up to protect herself; she grapples with his wrist but there is no strength in her arms and she cannot hold on. Slapping them away he presses a gun to her temple. 'Don't.'

The sharp stench of burning rubber hangs in the air and she coughs. A man limps alongside her. Blood drips down from the centre of his head, spreading in a fork of thin red lines across his brow. His left eye is swollen and closed; breathing heavily, he stumbles forward, loses his balance, and zig zags away from them.

'Hey,' the voice of the tall bodyguard, the one Nicole recognises from the night of the kidnapping makes Chris Ashton look up. He rocks backwards as the giant's fist cracks against his jaw, knocking him instantly to the ground.

'What the fuck are you doing?' Grant releases his grip on Nicole's hair, dropping his fingers between her shoulder blades and shoving. 'He told us to rough them up a bit, not fucking kill them.'

Chris writhes on the ground in a pool of shallow water. He attempts to push himself up and collapses.

'Chris?' The blood inside Nicole's mouth clogs her throat. 'Chris, can you hear me?'

'Take her now,' Grant snaps. 'Leave him with me.'

Chris groans and flops on his side as the rain falls harder. Nicole tries to go to him but the bodyguard blocks her path. 'Let him up,' she lashes out but he catches her wrist and flings it away.

Lifting the barrel of his gun he points it between her eyes. 'Walk.' The cold steel taps her bruised cheek and she steps back.

Clamping her hand over her mouth she limps forward.

110

Saturday, November 25,
Evening

Nicole pushes the matted hair from her eyes and scans the room. The space is vast, warm, and full of light, which floods in from one side where a wall of glass panels meet the roof which is also paned with glass. The rain makes a river as it patters above their heads, flowing in noisy, rippling sheets to the ground outside.

Blood drips from the back of her head down her neck and she bites down hard as her eyes search the space for any traces of Mark. The vaulted ceiling climbs like a cathedral to a raised height and industrial pendant lights hang at different levels from the bolted steel struts which link the huge wooden cross beams. A fire crackles against a backwall finished in pointed brick and thick candles adorn the mantlepiece, flickering soft light and scenting the room with flavours of coffee and vanilla.

Swaying, she fights the exhaustion and her eyes drop to the black wooden floor. It glints in the firelight as she adjusts her bloodstained shoes to keep her balance.

A jolt in her spine brings her back and she lets out a gasp. The Paymaster's bodyguard is jabbing her roughly, poking the bones of her back all the way through her thick winter coat with his finger, before drifting across to a marble fronted bar where he perches like a vulture on a stool.

Ignoring him, Nicole keeps searching for Mark. In front of her there are two leather armchairs crafted from steel tubes bolted around hard wood frames and between them is a high stool next to a low coffee table with some yellow flowers in a vase. On the table are a clutch of magazines and next to it is a large three seater couch crafted in the same industrial design. Behind it she sees a short staircase leading to a raised square balcony which is wrapped in a thick dark curtain, the kind you see in theatres. The staircase is lined with books and on the back wall hang a series of framed black and white landscape pictures.

It could be the bespoke offices for a modern design company or a private members' club, but there is no movement of people or hum of activity, no evidence of the real world outside at all. Just the crackling of the fire and the drumming of the rain.

The bodyguard folds his arms, holding one elbow in the palm of his hand and pointing his gun at Nicole. 'What you expected?'

She doesn't reply but from the corner of her eye she sees his shoulders lift as he laughs. Water gurgles in the exposed pipes bolted to the flat section of the ceiling where it meets the vaulted glass.

'Keep your hands visible,' he warns, more menacing this time as he adjusts his position on the stool, 'and stay standing.'

Nicole draws her hand away from her coat pocket, tapping her wrist gently against her side to make sure Mrs Lyubevsky's gun is still there. Holding her breath she lets it out slowly. She cannot think about Chris now. She has to focus. She banishes the image of him lying face down on the wet concrete in the rain. When the moment is right she'll get the chance to reach for her gun, if the police don't arrive first. She tries to steady herself, adjusting her balance, as she keeps searching for any sign of Mark.

A noise behind the curtain interrupts her thoughts and somebody speaks.

'What do you mean you're reviving him? I want him here now. The instructions regarding Ashton were clear, Grant. Don't screw this up.' A figure appears then, pushing a small section of the curtain back. It's Dr Fenton.

There's a mobile phone pressed against his ear and he lifts it away and places it inside his jacket pocket. He is dressed in a smart navy suit with a white shirt and yellow tie. His polished shoes click the hard wooden slats of the stairs as he makes his way down. 'Please Nicole,' he gestures politely, 'take a seat. Either one is fine. Chris is coming. I'm sorry about the delay.' Opening the jacket of his suit with one hand he walks to the couch and sits down, crossing his legs. Only now does Nicole see the small black gun which sits on the armrest beneath his hand.

The air traps inside Nicole's chest. The muscles in her neck are locking up and sharp splinters of pain shoot through the back of her head.

'Is everything OK?' he asks, as if they were still in his office, as if this was a routine medical appointment no different to the many they've had before.

Something rises inside her, pushing its way up from deep within her stomach. She opens her mouth expecting to be sick but her throat remains dry. Slowly she moves to one of the armchairs and sits.

Dr Fenton watches her calmly. 'It's been some time since we've spoken. Well, in person at least.'

She stares at him, trying to make sense of what is happening. The doctor is talking to her with that voice, the gentle one he used not long ago with their daughter. She remembers how he lifted Holly onto the examination table so carefully, handling her with almost paternal ease, complimenting her on how great a patient she was; giving her the present of the calendar with the kitten photographs, which she took home so proud and pleased she could have burst. Didn't he even send her to the receptionist to pick up a lollipop?

Slowly, she swallows down the saliva which has mixed with blood inside her mouth. 'Where is Mark?' she asks.

'Waiting for us. Don't worry.'

'You're Kendall?'

'Yes.'

'The Paymaster?'

Kendall smooths down the legs of his trousers with his hand. He shrugs then, almost embarrassed. 'Yes, I know, a childish title. But I had to have one, so I made it up.'

Nicole's stomach tightens. She covers her mouth, waiting for the nausea to pass. 'Why?'

Kendall points to the empty seat beside Nicole, his face apologetic. 'I thought it would be best if Chris heard this too. I think he deserves that. Just give me one second please.' Picking up a remote control, he points it at a flat-screen TV which is mounted on the wall at the bar. The screen wakes up, showing a live video image of the empty car park at the entrance to the factory gate. The wreckage of Chris's car smokes and steam hisses from the overturned engine. In the distance, beside a graffiti covered wall, Grant crouches by Chris's body, which is propped up crookedly but not moving. Grant holds his chin in his hand and waves something under his nose.

Kendall places the tip of his finger in the small hollow beneath his nostrils and holds it there as he thinks. Then he turns off the screen and tosses the remote back on the couch.

The bodyguard sits up and taps the earpiece which sits above the severed remains of his ear. 'Do you want me to go out and check on him?'

'No. Leave him. I need you here.' He turns his attention back to Nicole. 'I guess it's just the two of us then. Where do you want me to begin?'

III

Saturday, November 25,
Evening

With the palm of her hand Nicole dabs the blood which keeps oozing down her neck. Then she wipes it on her coat sleeve without looking at it. Silently she urges herself to cling on. As long as they talk, time passes and the police must get closer.

'I want to see Mark first.'

Kendall shakes his head. 'You're rushing this. Start again, Nicole.' He rubs the back of his fingers against the neatly trimmed beard on his jaw and eases back into the soft leather which stretches beneath him.

Nicole glances at the armrest where his other hand rests on top of the gun. Her throat is so hoarse she has to swallow before she can speak. 'You did all this for money? Was that what it was about? Entrapping all of us to make your fortune?'

'No. To say that would be a simplification. Of course, yes, I made money from you and all the others, but that wasn't really the point. I run a pharmaceuticals business manufacturing and selling counterfeit prescription drugs which makes me plenty already.'

'I thought you were a doctor?'

He gives her a sad smile. 'We'll get to that, soon, but you've asked me about the money so I'll explain. The money was merely a part of this, but nothing more. Primarily it began as a lure. Then I saw the opportunity to play with that idea. To allow you to imagine having money and then let you lose it, while making it for me.'

'And the cards?'

He tilts his head. 'Blank pieces of paper sealed tight and out of reach.'

'What?'

Kendall smiles. 'Surprised? You shouldn't be when you think about it. Certainty is the cornerstone of courage. When giving you the tasks I gave you the certainty that you had something to use against the people you had to rob. Without that crutch you wouldn't have dared to walk, never mind run.'

'A bluff?'

'Yes, a bluff.' He nods. 'That's not to say I didn't have something over the people I selected for you. Of course I had to have that too. Take your case for example.'

'My targets?'

'Yes, first was Mrs Cheroux, who I researched carefully knowing full well that even if she had uncovered the deceit, she would not have reported it because of her aversion to scandal, in addition to her aversion for letting her disapproving husband know of her error with his wealth. Then take Preston, his gemstones were insured for twice their worth. A simple message passed to him the same evening, instructing him to report the theft as something he was completely unaware of if he wanted to receive full compensation – or face the possibility of none at all – was sufficient, especially as it was delivered to him by the chairman of the insurance company he had the policy with.'

Nicole grits her teeth. 'And Alva?'

Kendall replies. 'You've already figured out Grant and Deasy did work on my behalf. They ensured the cameras went off when you picked up the disk for us. I guessed by the time she realised it was missing you'd have already come to me.' His fingers drum the barrel of the gun on the armrest. But these are details, Nicole, minor technicalities. I would have thought you'd want to know about the bigger picture?'

'You mean the HFS?'

'That would be a good place to start I'd suggest.'

322

'Why did you target them? The Holden Foundation Scheme graduates?'

Kendall nods, as if to acknowledge the fairness of the question. 'The HFS made me who I am today so I wanted to go back to where it all began for me and fix something. Something, I suppose I had neglected. Justice maybe?'

'What justice?'

'Of course this will be difficult for you to understand, Nicole, but I'll do my best to explain. What do you know about the HFS?'

'Very little, mostly that Professor Byrne said it was a brilliant programme and he was sorry it couldn't continue.'

'Professor Byrne?' He pauses, his eyes looking out to the huge glass windows as his expression becomes wistful. Then he sighs. 'God, I liked Byrne, he was so . . . ?' he shrugs, searching for the right word, 'fair. And he's right, Nicole, because it *was* a beautiful idea.' He shakes his head and sits up. 'OK, I'll explain now. You see the thing was that the HFS was a concept designed for people like me.' He taps his chest with his finger. 'And by that, I mean people who never really had a chance, no hopers I suppose you could call them; and that was a mould I fit perfectly – father was shot dead when I was seven; mother married a career criminal who beat her daily so she beat me too. When she got tired she sent me away to an aunt in Bristol who despised me from the first day she saw me.' He laughs harshly. 'Well, soon enough I was on the streets and in and out of foster care, and I suppose, really, I should have ended up in front of a judge except for the intervention of a kind old lady who taught music at the community centre.' He stops, turning to glance at the curtain before looking back at Nicole, 'She saw something in me, I guess.'

'She helped you?'

Kendall's eyes glisten. 'She really did, hugely. You see I was in a school where the kids put razor blades in my sandwiches for entertainment, and having the shit kicked out of me was a daily ritual that I had to grudgingly accept – the same way I guess we get used to brushing our teeth.' He attempts a weak smile.

'But Alice made me believe in the possibility of a different world by putting me forward for the Holden Foundation Scheme, even going so far as to let me board at her house, and promising to let me remain there for the entirety of my university years.' He shrugs. 'Imagine. Who would have thought that such kindness existed in this world?'

'What happened?'

'My life took off. Having never tried at school in my life, I studied night and day to get my A levels and pass their admissions tests. I did three rounds of in person interviews and to my shocked surprise the HFS accepted me. I went to live with Alice. Everything turned around. I now suddenly had the possibility to have my entire tuition funded by this extraordinarily kind man, Robert Holden. The dream I had been too afraid to even imagine was taking shape in front of my eyes. But,' he shrugs, fixing Nicole with wounded eyes, 'then, something happened. Something that changed everything.'

'What?'

'We'll get there, Nicole. What matters most is that it opened my eyes.'

'I don't understand.'

'I found out that the HFS was corrupt. Robert Holden had been betrayed by the people responsible for implementing his dream of helping those that needed help the most. When I looked around at all the other students,' his face creases, 'I realised I was the only one, the only who was *meant* to be there.'

'Why? Why were you the only one?'

'Because the rest had used the system to get in a back door. They were almost exclusively candidates who had means, whose families had influence. Chris Ashton was only accepted as a national swimming champion. Veronica Woods's father had donated to building the science lab. Richard Jennings's mother was Dean of Faculty. And it was the same for all the others. Each had gamed the system in their own way. It was all nakedly dishonest, almost like they were wilfully tarnishing this great man's vision.'

Nicole watches Kendall's hand tap the gun on the armrest and the hairs at the back of her neck stiffen.

'What about Mark? He never had any means or influence. He was raised by a single mother. He didn't scheme like you say. He worked and deserved what he got.'

'That's true, in so many ways I felt Mark belonged. Mark had told me the story about how his dad had disappeared and his mum was struggling and all of that was fair. I think he might even have been the university's most outstanding student,' he shakes his head, sighing. 'But I didn't know then that there were so many aspects to Mark.'

There's a noise behind the curtain, like the sound of steel twisting against wood. Nicole feels her ribs compress and little splinters of pain stab behind her eyes.

'What is that? That sound?'

'Don't worry, Nicole,' he waves dismissively. 'You'll see soon. I haven't finished explaining yet.'

112

Saturday, November 25,
Evening

Nicole tastes the blood as it passes down her throat. 'You still haven't told me anything. I don't think you destroyed all these people because they took advantage of a scheme that was never meant for them. There's more.'

'You're right, Nicole, there is.' Kendall checks his watch as he shifts his position on the leather couch which squeaks when he sits forward. 'Towards the very end of our first year at the university the HFS students held a private meeting where it was proposed they would travel to Calcutta to oversee a clinical trial funded by an American pharmaceutical company. Mark had done all the research, the organisation, everything. The drug was for young children with heart conditions, something that would remedy congenital defects.'

'How is that bad?'

'It isn't. The group, once they had decided on the plan, invited me out to dinner, the one and only time I was made to feel truly part of the scheme, and convinced me to participate. Well, you can imagine. I was overjoyed Nicole, finally allowed to join in, to be part of the thing they had taken exclusively for themselves.'

'So you went?'

'I went. We all did. And for the first time I was delighted to be truly part of this wonderful group. We spent one month out there, overseeing the trial. And it should have been a dream, except it wasn't that straightforward.'

'Why?'

'Because, three days into it, the group held a meeting. Mark, the wunderkind, the one who everybody looked up to, had done his own private research and concluded the dosage to the children was ineffective and made a convincing argument to us that if it was to work it needed to be increased. Doubled in fact.'

'So what happened?'

'The group agreed that Mark was probably correct but it would be unethical so couldn't condone it. Mark fumed, because he was convinced he was right, certain his proposals would quite literally save lives.'

'What did he do?'

'He took me aside, convinced me that if he and I proceeded in secret, we would be saving children, and the rest of the HFS group didn't need to know.'

'So you both made a pact and double dosed innocent children?'

Kendall shakes his head. 'That's what we agreed and initially it seemed like everything was fine. But suddenly in the third week, two children became ill. Then a third, severely ill, ending up in ICU.'

A chill enters Nicole's spine and she shifts from one foot to the other. 'Which children?'

'The children under my care only, because it seemed Mark never followed through on his own advice but stuck within the rules when operating out of his own hospital.'

'But,' Nicole swallows, hesitating, 'did the children survive?'

'They did, but when we returned to the university there was an instant fall out. The HFS participants were called before a private committee and interrogated, but of course you can probably guess the rest.'

'They lied.'

'Yes, they all lied, as they had secretly agreed in another meeting which naturally they didn't invite me to. It was decided amongst them that the idea was no longer Mark's but mine. Nobody had any part in it, only me. Despite my protests I was branded a liar and I bore full responsibility. I was kicked off the scheme and barred from entering medicine within the UK.' His face darkens. 'So now you might understand Nicole.'

Nicole rocks on her feet, the accusations against Mark suddenly hitting her like invisible stones. Mark's mother's voice replays inside her head, its tone loud and mocking. '*He's just like his father. That man kept secrets you could never get out of him no matter how hard you tried.*'

She doesn't want to believe Kendall. She knows Mark too well; she can't believe he could be so deliberately reckless. Her gaze switches to the curtains trying to guess what is hidden behind. Is it Mark? The skin around her eyes tightens. Squeezing her little finger inside her fist, she glances back at Kendall. Why hasn't she seen Mark yet? She needs to act. To get her gun. But until she sees a chance to do that she must keep Kendall talking.

She offers another question. 'Why make it all so complicated? Why all the robberies, the deceptions?'

Kendall smooths his beard with his fingertips. 'I wanted these people to understand what I felt.'

'How?'

'By turning their lives upside down, by letting them become the opposites of who they believed themselves to be. To do that I had to make them complicit in their own downfall by inviting them to participate.'

'Inviting?' The word hisses from Nicole's lips as heat rises to her face. 'You threatened me, threatened my family, like you must have done for all the others.'

'Maybe, I won't deny that, but first I let people's own greed or foolishness lead them astray, like I did with you Nicole, offering you a million euros. Naturally it was absurd, ridiculous really when you think about it, and yet you couldn't resist engaging.'

Her chest constricts. 'I wanted to give it back,' she pauses, the words choking at the back of her throat, 'to forget all about it, to imagine it never happened.'

'Yes,' Kendall's fingers snap and he points at her. 'You see? That's exactly how I felt when those other students from HFS, the ones who should never have even been there, cornered me, trapping me with their vile lies, dooming me to a life I didn't want and never deserved.'

'But you're a doctor? You became our GP?'

He snorts a derisive laugh. 'I pretended to be a doctor for a short while Nicole, nothing more.'

'You never qualified?' Nicole winces remembering her consultations, how Mark recommended him, for their own children.

'No. I only wanted to taste that world I had lost, to imagine being something I never got to be. It was a charade and in truth it hardly fulfilled that purpose – since I had only ever dreamed of being a surgeon and not a GP. I gave Mark my false credentials from Holland and insisted that he register his family with me because by getting close to you, Nicole, I could imagine Mark's life better. And that's all I wanted; to understand his family, his children, his happiness.'

A shudder passes through her body and she waits for it to pass before replying. 'You were only barred from the UK, you could have still qualified elsewhere?'

Kendall shrugs, his face defeated. 'I was broken Nicole. I believe you might know what that feels like now?' His eyes are pleading. 'I had no money. My benefactor asked me to leave. She was the only friend I had.' The corners of his mouth turn down. 'I started to think it was really my fault, that somehow I had deserved what happened to me.'

'Why?'

He makes a sad laugh. 'I don't know. I began to believe I was defective so I went to Holland and began a life of crime. I used all the scientific knowledge I had amassed and put it to use making illegal over-the-counter medicines. Bit by bit I climbed the ladder in a grim underworld I could never have dreamed of, until finally I ran my own organisation. Now I had the power to pull strings; to get people's private information; to

329

hire tech experts so they could hijack laptops like I did with yours.'

'How did you do it?'

'I found somebody, paid them a fee and had your laptop switched when Mark was getting it serviced. It looked like yours but it wasn't.'

'Colin Dutton said he couldn't see anything that showed it was infected or hacked.'

'Because I use experts, Nicole, and reward them for their service. By fluke the Russian he found had the knowledge to glean our location but it didn't matter because I had already resolved to bring you in.'

'That's not true. You sent two men to kill us.'

'Yes, that's what it looked like, but it was simply another illusion. Deasy had double-crossed me so my driver was under orders to execute him at the apartment. Then he was to bring you in.' Nicole sucks in her breath, recalling the sound of his heavy body collapsing like bricks to the floor, squashing more blood from the dead man by her feet. 'He failed but the tracker we had on Chris's car told us you were coming anyway.'

'Yet you shot Chris through the balcony sliding door.'

'Deasy shot his body armour, then I instructed Coonan to ram his car. I wanted to allow you both to endure some pain before our final chat.' Lifting the gun in his hand, Kendall gets to his feet, spinning quickly and running up the stairs to the raised balcony. His hand moves to a switch on the wall and Nicole's stomach lurches. Shouldn't the police be here already? What has happened to Chris? What has Kendall done with Mark?

She looks at her hands which now shake in her lap. Kendall presses the switch on the wall and the curtain pulls back.

Mark stands on a thin wooden chair, like the kind found in a brasserie. He is blindfolded and there is gag in his mouth. His hands are bound together at the wrist and his legs shake. A rope is pulled tightly around his neck and when Nicole glances higher up she sees it loops over one of the steel struts bolted across the roof beams. Kendall puts one hand on the back of the chair and points his gun at Nicole. 'So how does this feel?'

Nicole scrambles to her feet, lungs heaving.

'Don't.' Immediately the bodyguard jumps up, straightening his arm and pointing his gun.

A tear tracks down her cheek. At last she has found him. And yet Mark cannot see her. He cannot even speak. She clamps her eyes tight, wishing the pressure inside her head to ease but it doesn't.

Mark is alive. Mark is a liar. Kendall is going to hang Mark. The thoughts stream and she sways, blood pounding in her ears. It can't end this way. She cannot give in. 'Cut him down.'

Mark's body jolts and Kendall points his gun at her. 'Not yet, Nicole. We're not finished talking. I'll say when.'

Her hands fly to her face and she holds them there, afraid to look but she knows she must not draw her eyes away. As long as she can see Mark she knows he's still alive. 'Even if what you claim is true, Kendall, it doesn't make sense. You murdered Helen Shaw. She wasn't even part of your HFS group.'

Kendall replies. 'You're right. I won't deny it. What would be the point now? Once I started the process it became intoxicating. When I created the Paymaster, it was like I had to make the idea of myself more exaggerated, Nicole. I don't even really know how to explain it in truth.' He shakes his head. 'I realised at a certain point that I would have to be practical too. People can only hide their crimes for so long before they eventually crack. My under-world sources advised me to clean up after myself so that's what I decided to do, starting with Angela Johannson. And then one by one I wiped all of the HFS class out. Those that had been fed information, like Helen had to be eliminated also. Revenge, Nicole, is like a thirst you can never quench. It simply grows and grows. The impulse to destroy kept coursing through me like blood through my veins. I even murdered Mark's brother Luke.'

Mark chokes and his legs begin to shake. Nicole gasps as the chair shifts but Kendall reaches out and steadies it.

'You're sick: you just need help, Kendall. You don't have to kill Mark too.'

'No, Nicole. I'm not sick, I'm efficient. I had to keep changing the method as I changed myself. I guessed Chris would come to kill me when I murdered Veronica and I wanted to allow him to try. Then I thought what a perfect ending it could be, to have you all here, Chris, you, Mark so we could end it all the same day.'

Nicole closes her eyes, trying to balance on her feet as blinding flashes of light strobe across her brain. Kendall is so calm, so logical, it could be just another doctor's consultation for a minor illness at his surgery.

She reaches out a hand and clutches the stool as her mind turns to the gun inside her pocket; but the bodyguard is still standing with his weapon cocked and aimed straight at her.

The chair creaks under Mark's feet and the rope tightens against the steel strut as he struggles to keep his balance. The sound of his laboured breathing hisses through the air.

Kendall shakes his head. 'Nicole, don't imagine the HFS graduates were innocent. They were not bystanders, they were participants, the authors of their own misery. They colluded, just as they did when they secretly agreed to shield Mark from blame all those years ago and pin the entire responsibility on the person they believed didn't fit the group. Nobody forced them. I merely gave them choices.'

'That's not true. You threatened them, terrorised them.'

'I helped them to believe what I needed them to believe. They did the rest themselves.'

The rope around Mark's neck strains and tugs against the wooden beam above. Nicole offers another question. 'How did you know your plan would work on me?'

Kendall frowns, as if surprised she hasn't yet figured it out. 'That was easy Nicole. The Dohertys.'

113

Saturday, November 25,
Evening

The warm air sucks inside Nicole's lungs and she reaches for the stool to keep her balance.

'The Dohertys?' A deep unease crawls across her skin. 'The criminal my sister is investigating? What does that have to do with me?'

'A lot.'

'I don't understand?'

'Your sister never explained?' Kendall's voice is thick with pity. 'Perhaps I should. Carmel Doherty is a business associate of mine. Your sister's been tracking her and as a consequence she's stumbled upon me too.'

'How is this connected to me?'

'Before I became associated with Carmel I researched her family and it turns out her mother was a thorn in your father's side. But instead of leaving that thorn be, your father did the one thing he shouldn't have done.'

Nicole tenses. 'What are you saying?'

'He tried to bring her down but failed. And because he failed his fate was sealed.'

Trembling she replies. 'Are you saying . . . ' she hesitates.

'Yes, she killed your father, or had him killed I'd assume,' Kendall replies sadly. 'But all this simply brings us to you, Nicole. Because when I hacked into your computer the first interesting thing I uncovered was your journal.' Nicole's eyes narrow as her breath quickens. 'I know what having your life turned upside down feels like so I could relate perfectly to all those entries you wrote about when your father disappeared that night from your lives. You and your little sister Alva, so young and lost; your mother in grief; how his pension wasn't enough to live like you once did – especially after the accountant who you all thought was a family friend went and siphoned most of it away – so your mother had to take the only jobs she could get, cleaning your neighbours' houses. I know how it feels; it's like a knife between the shoulder blades to lose all security, all the comfort you thought you had. It's impossible to ever really forget isn't it?'

Nicole becomes still, a numbness gripping her. 'So you decided to rob our family of its security knowing that it would leave me vulnerable?'

'Exactly. And who could blame you? A million euros can do a lot for a family in crisis.' Swaying gently, Nicole watches as the fire crackles, flickering its soft yellow light across his haggard face. 'Because I wanted to show you how it can all be so right, like it was for you, with your perfect husband, perfect family, perfect house, and a future that shone so brightly you could fall asleep every night just dreaming about it.' His voice falters as he taps his chest with his finger. 'But then when it changes,' a tear tracks down his cheek and his voice becomes faint, 'like it did for me, when *one* person enters your life, one perfect stranger who wasn't supposed to be there, the future is no longer certain anymore.'

Nicole blinks. Is Kendall giving up? Is he about to relent? Perhaps all he needs is somebody to understand and forgive him. Her father's words repeat inside her head, *you were always so kind to animals it made me worry, Nicole.*

'But why me? Why target me when you already told me it was Mark who had done you wrong?'

Kendall shakes his head, his eyes glistening. 'Nicole that was always going to be how it ended, because after I murdered Veronica I discovered something, something that changed my thinking. It wasn't enough to let Chris die. He had to carry on with the knowledge that the one person he cherished most in the world had suffered because he had failed to protect her. It was never going to be enough to make Mark suffer. The purest suffering I could give Mark was to bring you here, so he could listen to your words, knowing what you had to go through, all because of him. But now it's gone on long enough and we have to bring it to a close. Today it ends, for all of you.'

Inhaling slowly Nicole steels herself and reaches for the gun in her pocket.

'Not yet!' Kendall taps the back of the chair with his hand and points his gun at Mark's head. 'I want you to please stand up on the stool you are holding now, Nicole.' Nicole steps back, her chest suddenly so tight she cannot get enough air. 'Come on, Nicole, please. I've devised a test for you but I'm going to need your cooperation.'

'Why must I get on the stool?' she stares at it, her eyes full of dread.

'We're going to recreate an old fable. One that's close to my heart. It's a test of courage. But it requires nerves of steel and perfect concentration.'

Nicole opens her mouth to reply but she's too tired to think of any more questions. Her strength is fading. Exhaustion has taken over and her eyes begin to flicker. She must fight it; find a way to keep going. But she can't seem to respond. Mark's breathing strains loudly through the gag in his mouth. The cold truth is becoming clear. She has failed to bring Mark back. There is nothing she can do.

'Hurry up, Nicole.' Kendall's nostrils flare. 'If you make me shoot you I will, and then Mark hangs by himself alone.'

114

Saturday, November 25,
Evening

Breathing deeply, Nicole grips the edges of the stool. Placing one knee first on the seat, she steadies herself and raises her second leg until she is in a kneeling position. Very slowly she shifts her weight to her foot and spreads her arms wide to help her balance as she stands.

'Perfect Nicole,' Kendall says, pleased. 'OK, I'll explain now. Have you ever heard of the folk tale about William Tell?' Nicole shakes her head, her cheeks burning. 'William Tell dishonours an official of the king, but instead of taking his life the official gives him an alternative.'

'What alternative?'

'To shoot an apple with his crossbow from the top of his own son's head. If he accepts and succeeds his life is spared, as is that of his son. I'm offering you the same test but this time you're going to shoot the rope above your husband's head.' Holding Mark's chair with one hand, he points at her with the gun.

'That's impossible.'

'Difficult, not impossible, Nicole. Also remember, if you leave that stool, Mark hangs.' Mark makes a muffled grunting sound and Nicole hears the rope twist against the steel as it tightens around his neck. 'Now I already know you're concealing a weapon in your coat because the detector located it as soon as you entered the building.' He raises a cruel smile. 'You're going to get your chance to use it finally but you'll have to wait for my command first.'

The stool shakes beneath her feet. She tries to imagine using the gun, aiming it, then firing it in Mark's direction. She knows she won't do it. It's another delusion, a risk she could never accept. She's been carrying it with her as a token, to help her believe in a hope that never existed.

She bends her legs to try and balance the stool but gunshots interrupt them.

The bodyguard steps forward, pressing his finger to his earpiece, as three more shots ring out in quick succession. 'Police,' he shouts, 'they're here, Grant took one of them out but now he's been shot. What do we do?'

Footsteps pound the wooden floor before coming to a sharp halt. 'Put your weapons down.' Nicole recognises Alva's voice immediately. When she looks she sees her sister standing and pointing her weapon. There's a deafening roar as the bodyguard pivots and shoots. Alva cries out and falls.

'Alva?' Nicole sees her sister slump to the ground but another shot rings out instantly, thundering through the ceiling and releasing a cloud of dust above her head.

'Remember, Nicole.' Kendall points the gun he has just fired back towards Mark's head, 'leave that stool and Mark hangs. Your choice.'

Nicole sways, the throbbing inside her head so strong, she is sure she must fall. 'Alva?' The air sucks from her lungs and her whole body begins to tremble. She closes her eyes imagining Alva's arms around her, gripping her tight, whispering to her softly, letting her know it's going to be alright. But how can it be?

'We're out of time,' the bodyguard snaps. 'I'm wasting her and then we leave.'

Nicole watches as he spins towards her and raises his weapon. Another gunshot rings out and Nicole braces herself for the bullet, but the bodyguard has dropped his gun and holds his chest as blood teems through his fingers. There are more footsteps and when she looks she sees Chris is running past her, the gun he took from the driver held out in front of him and pointed at Kendall.

Kendall fires. The gun falls from Chris's hand and he clutches his wrist, collapsing with a groan before going silent.

Pulling Mrs Lyubevsky's gun from her pocket, Nicole gets it out in front of her. With both hands she tries to keep it steady, aiming it at Kendall.

'I wouldn't, Nicole,' Kendall says calmly, lengthening his arm and pointing the barrel of his gun towards Mark's head. 'My bullet will pierce Mark's skull before yours leaves the chamber.' Sweat oozes from the palm of her hand as Nicole's fingers wrap tighter around the gun handle. 'That's right Nicole. Keep it out there until we are all ready.' He taps Mark's leg. 'Now Mark, stay still. I'm giving your wife her final challenge. All she has to do is shoot the rope.'

The blood drains from her face as she watches Mark's tired legs struggling to balance. The air is heavy with the noise of his strained breathing. What is her choice now? How will it be explained to Chloe and Holly if she fails? She can't fire a gun at Mark. It's Alva who's trained with firearms, not her. Fear ripples through her as she pictures their children's faces, imagining them receiving the news that their father is gone, shot dead in cold blood by their own mother.

Kendall tilts his head. 'Come on Nicole. Try and see what happens.'

The fire crackles loudly. Sweat bubbles on her lip and the smell of gunpowder fills her nostrils. Blood has pooled inside her mouth and she swallows it down, desperately straining to remember the moves her father showed her when she was a child all those years ago. 'You might never be a police officer but if you know how to fire a gun it could save your life,' he had explained. She wasn't even listening when he gave her the instructions 'shoulders down, hand to the supporting wrist, let go and relax'. Now a strange sensation takes hold and her breathing calms, the muscles in her arms and shoulders loosen, the pain which has spiralled through every inch of her body for days on end, floats away.

But a voice is suddenly screaming and she knows it's Alva. 'He's lying, Nicole. He wants you to murder Mark. Then he'll shoot you.'

Kendall steps forward, dark eyes flashing as he aims his gun at Alva.

115

It takes a fraction of a second for Nicole to adjust her stance and pull the trigger. The bullet catches Kendall cleanly through the chest. His mouth bursts open and blood leaks from it down his chin. His dark brows knit together and his body jerks as Nicole fires a second round. This time his hand reaches for his throat and his eyes flare wider. Blood spurts through his fingers, bubbling bright and red as it spills down his white shirt, splashing his leather shoes. Raising his gun, he holds it up weakly, but the third bullet has already passed through his heart, and it falls from his hand.

Nicole watches as he crumples, a jet of blood spiralling skywards from his wound like a red ribbon. There's a harsh gurgling noise as his limbs flail.

At the edge of her vision she can see Chris rushing past, up the steps and onto the balcony. Not far behind him, Alva is moving too.

But they can't help. Kendall has collapsed into the chair which supports Mark, knocking it to the floor. *Snap*, the rope around his neck lengthens and twists, and the vaulted ceiling creaks. Mark's weight shifts to the steel strut and he dangles, kicking the air.

Nicole's eyes close over. She is already falling; but she knows when she hits the ground she will feel no pain. It's too late, and it's already bled away.

116

TEN DAYS LATER

Tuesday, December 5

'Chocolate orange! Nicole, you star!' Alva pumps the air with a victorious fist while the rest of her body remains immobile on the chunky grey couch in her living room. 'You know I love chocolate orange cake.'

Nicole drops her coat onto the two-seater sofa immediately opposite. It flops on top of a large blue Ikea bag full of washed laundry, knocking a stack of weekend newspapers to the floor. She bends to pick them up, wincing as her newly fixed stitches tug the back of her scalp. Her mouth forms a ring and she blows out when she turns to Alva with the cake.

'Don't mind any of that stuff,' her sister says. 'Shaun's on duty now and I'm enjoying watching him do battle with the least favourite family chore.'

'Housework?' She plants a gentle kiss on Alva's cheek. The muscles in her back tense and she draws herself up stiffly.

'That's the one.'

Firelight dances behind the glass door of Alva's stove and the pretty cream box radiates a cosy heat. Something bubbles down on the cooker and the air is rich and thick with the smell of cooking. Fennel, ginger, garlic, Nicole breathes in deep, tilting her head back to savour it.

'Nice isn't it?' Alva grins, itching where the cast on her outstretched leg meets the skin of her thigh. 'Ishani dropped it over. She's one of the girls down in the station, and a savage

341

cook – I swear the woman should have a fucking Michelin star, she's that good. Shaun is over the moon because it means he doesn't have to pretend to be happy about cooking for his family. And I get to eat a decent curry instead of his crappy fish fingers.'

'I'll bet he's delighted.' Nicole grins, the tightness in her shoulders easing a little, but not entirely. The kettle boils down in the kitchen and she hears the familiar click of the plastic switch as it knocks off.

'Nic, you sit down and make yourself comfortable. I'll get that.' Alva presses her one good hand into the couch, looking around for her crutches.

'Alva?'

'Yeah?'

'Stop being silly. I'm bringing the tea. Stay there.'

Moving gingerly to the kitchen Nicole inhales the steam from the bubbling pot. The Christmas tree is up and the baubles and decorations twinkle underneath the soft lights which wrap around it. The familiar sight of tossed magazines, unwashed cups, school stationery and jumbled sports gear litters the huge dining table and for a moment Nicole gets the warmest feeling as she takes down the plates, lifts forks from the drawer, and brews two mugs of tea. Alva is so like their mother in all the good ways, she remembers.

'I was glad to hear your neighbour's getting better,' Alva says, taking the plate with her slice of cake, placing it on her lap and easing back into the couch. Nicole places her sister's tea beside Alva's outstretched foot on the coffee table.

'Christ Alva. I don't know what I would have done if she wasn't.'

'Hey, come on,' Alva tosses the fork onto the couch beside her and picks the slice of cake up in her hand. 'Mrs Lyubevsky's already told you she understands, remember? And she's almost fully recovered now.' She bites off a mouthful, a blissful expression spreading across her face. Nicole hands Alva the mug as she chews. 'How are you feeling?'

Nicole catches her reflection in the mirror above the mantlepiece on the wall. Her face is still puffed and swollen, the bruising on her jaw and cheek has turned a garish shade of purple; scars on her forehead and neck shine pink against her light skin. She places her plate on top of her coat, carefully adjusting her body to slide onto the armrest where she knows it will be easier to stand again. 'My hearing isn't right but I'm OK.'

Alva's cheeks pucker. 'There's an idea. Do you think I'd get away with it if I told Shaun my ears had packed up? That could be fun for a few days.' The edges of Alva's mouth curl up and for a fleeting second all the tension inside Nicole eases away and they laugh. 'Ah my ribs,' Alva whimpers, dropping her hand to her side. 'I have to put those Post-it Notes on the mirror reminding myself to stop making crap jokes I can't help laughing at.'

Nicole sips her tea, and smiles as her eyes drop to the floor. Neither of them say anything for a moment and the room becomes oddly quiet.

'Nic, listen to me, the enquiry is finished now, you know that right? There's nothing more to worry about. You've been cleared of wrongdoing. I discussed it with Maitland last night when I went to see him in the hospital. Since he was there with me at the scene and got shot in the shoulder, he was understanding. He's happy to say that I was the shooter. Sometimes that's just the way it is because it's for the best.'

Nicole grips the mug in her hands and smiles weakly. 'Is he any better?'

'Much better. And I'm sorry I couldn't give you the full facts around the Doherty case until after but it was the only way I could do it.'

'When did you find out?' Nicole lets out a deep breath.

'A year ago. Dad's friends in the force had kept the true cause of Dad's death a closely guarded secret. They knew I wanted to follow in his footsteps and were afraid it might lead me to do something that would jeopardise my career. They had gone after Carmel Doherty's mother, Clare Doherty, themselves but she was killed in a gangland assassination before they could get her behind bars for what she did to Dad. They had been tracking the daughter for years since she took over from where the mother left off. Eventually, when the time was right, they brought me in so I could oversee the operation to catch her.' Alva lifts her plate and places it away from her on the couch. 'Carmel Doherty's going inside for at least fifteen years. Dad would be proud.'

Nicole eases forward, careful not to pull her stitches, resting her mug on the coffee table. The memory of the day she received the news begins to surface: the call from the teacher Ms Wainright in the middle of class, how she stood so stiffly with her hands clasped and her heels pinched together outside in the corridor. 'You need to go home now, Nicole. Your mother is waiting,' was all she said.

'How did she do it? How did Clare Doherty kill Dad?'

Small lines appear on Alva's brow. 'She didn't. She was too smart for that. She hired someone to do it when she was behind bars, a toerag called Leary. He laid a nail strip. It was that strip that burst the two front tyres on dad's car, making it crash.'

Nicole puts a hand to her cheek. It was all so long ago. She has to learn to let the past stay in the past. 'And Leary?'

'Shot dead a year later outside a bar in Marbella after getting into a fight. Drugs-related they reckon.'

Closing her eyes Nicole exhales, waiting for the dark memories to slowly ebb away. 'Alva?'

'Yeah?'

'I don't even want to ask this but I just feel I need to, maybe because you're my only sister.'

Alva nods. 'Go ahead, if you need to, just ask.'

Nicole clears her throat. When she speaks there's a quiver in her voice. 'When Kendall sent me to do his tasks I was always given a card to leave with each of the targets. I think it was some kind of threat so they couldn't report the crime I had committed. You know I left one in your desk when I went to take the drive.'

'I know.'

'Would you ever be able to tell me what it said?' The tightness inside Nicole's chest grows.

Alva tips her chin towards the mantlepiece above the fire. 'The card is right there, on the ledge beneath the mirror. I had been meaning to give it to you but you got there first. Go ahead, take it and read it.'

Nicole stands stiffly, her heartbeat spiking. She doesn't want to touch it but they can't avoid it now. 'Are you sure?'

'I'm sure, Nic.'

Stepping forwards Nicole takes it in her hands and plucks the card from inside the torn envelope. Staring at it, her eyes widen. She twists it upside down. Then her gaze returns to Alva. 'It's blank, just like Kendall said it would be.'

Alva nods. 'Put it in the fire now Nic and come sit with me a minute.'

Nicole opens the stove door, feels the tension drain from her body and tosses the card into the flame. It flickers and burns, disintegrating to dust. Slowly she eases in next to Alva and her sister draws her towards her until Nicole rests her head against her shoulder. 'The bastard was smart, Nic. It was only by accident since we were investigating Doherty that he even came up on our radar. We're lucky he's gone.'

Alva smooths Nicole's hair gently with her fingers and they both go quiet. When a few minutes pass Nicole speaks again. 'Alva?'

'Yeah?'

'I don't expect you to forgive me for stealing from you. Or doing any of the crazy things I agreed to. I just wanted you to know that.'

'Shush. You did what you had to, alright? You weren't the only one Kendall manipulated. And you only did it to get Mark back. I wouldn't blame you for a second. Try not to think about it. We'll put it behind us and move on.'

Alva rests her cheek on the crown of Nicole's head and sighs. Nicole's gaze settles on the wood logs inside the stove which flicker and crackle as they burn. The sound of the pot in the kitchen bubbling on the stove floats up. There's one more thing she wants to share with Alva but it isn't the time. The moment is too special and she doesn't want to do anything to break it. Tonight she will know more about it. Maybe tomorrow she can ask her.

Her mind drifts to her girls. It's time to take them in to the hospital soon.

117

Tuesday, December 5

Nicole presses her hand against the door but doesn't go in. Her eyes linger on the two girls who wait in a row of seats against the wall of the corridor. Holly swings her small legs, hugging her teddy as she gazes up at the fluorescent tube light on the ceiling and Chloe thumb-scrolls Nicole's phone.

The nurse from Trinidad with the radiant smile who Nicole met earlier in the morning sees her fretting. 'Go on,' she says. 'They'll be fine with me.'

'Are you sure?'

The nurse sits down between Holly and Chloe, grinning cheerfully. 'Look at these angels! Of course I'm sure. Go ahead.'

'Thanks.' Pushing the door gently, Nicole slips inside. The warm air from the hospital corridor drifts in behind her and mixes with the air inside Mark's private room, bringing a rich fug of overcooked vegetables and disinfectant with it. Beside Mark's bed the monitor beeps throwing a green zig zag line across the computer screen. Nicole checks the blood pressure figures and the heart rate, crunches the numbers silently in her head, and relaxes a little, but her fingers remain stiff as she eases the blinds open a fraction to let more light into the room. The brown wooden serving tray has been rolled away from the bed towards the small wardrobe in the corner, telling her he's already eaten. No plates remain so she makes a mental note to check and see what he managed to take before she leaves.

Quietly she eases over, picking the side away from the IV drip which feeds into his wrist, and sits carefully on the stiff mattress.

347

Mark's neck brace is off and his bright pink skin makes a stark contrast to the cream cotton of his button top pyjamas.

'Hey,' his eyes open and his fingers grip the bed control button. A buzzing noise drowns out the beeps and he inclines upwards, the only movement visible in his body the turning of his head against the plumped white pillows.

'You don't have to wake up, Mark. Not unless you want to.'

'I'm already awake,' he gives her a tired smile. 'I've been counting the hours since you left yesterday.' Nicole leans forward, gently teasing his thick black hair from his eyes to sweep it across his forehead. It's longer now, growing over his ears, and it reminds her of how he used to wear it when they first met all those years ago at university; when Mark rode a second-hand bicycle whose brakes only worked on dry days, his neck wrapped in a scarf with at least three different colours. She remembers forever telling him to tuck it inside his coat instead of flicking it over his shoulder where it would blow over his face seconds later. His dark stubble has grown out into a short beard and the light has returned to his eyes. They shine softly as she places her hand inside his. There's more strength in his grip today, she can tell. She gives him a smile before glancing towards the window. 'How is Chris doing?' he asks.

'Improving. They operated on his wrist yesterday. They hope to let him out tomorrow or the day after, depending.'

Mark brightens. 'Good. I'm going to visit him first thing when they release me. I want to ask him how I can repay him.'

Nicole rubs his hand, surprised for a moment to hear his upbeat voice. The voice Mark always used when he was focused and busy, when he was happy. 'We both owe him Mark, but I've made a start now at least.'

'How?'

'Thanks to Alva, the coroner responsible for falsifying Veronica's cause of death has already been arrested. She won't stop until she gets him justice.' Nicole stops, feeling the tension in Mark's fingers as he grips her hand. 'I'm sorry about Luke, Mark.' He clenches his eyes and swallows noisily. 'I know how that must feel.'

'I should have known Nicole, or at least suspected.' Mark casts a dejected glance at his feet where they stick up underneath the hard bedcovers. 'I think because Luke and I had drifted apart over the years I blanked it. The thing with Kendall had already started by then and I wasn't even thinking properly. I could have made the connection. I made so many mistakes.'

Nicole's mind drifts back to the moment Kendall pulled back the curtain on the raised stage to reveal Mark, gagged and tied with the noose around his neck. She doesn't want to think about it. She doesn't want to remember the day ever again. But Kendall's story about Mark can't stay hidden. They need to talk about it.

Drawing her hand away she rubs her eyes which are dry and sore. 'The police have fully recovered the money for Valerie Cheroux along with Elliot Preston's diamonds. Also Alva contacted the police in Sydney. They've made three arrests. We won't let it go until we get the ones who helped Kendall do what they did to Luke.'

'I know. Alva's been so good and it'll change things for Mum. Hopefully now it might make things better between us, and finally bring the bitterness to an end.'

Nicole nods. An ending is what she wants too, what she craves.

They both go silent. Finally Mark sighs, tapping her fingers gently. 'I know you're waiting for an explanation, Nicole. I know it's the one thing I so badly want to give you.' He pauses. 'I just don't know if what I have to say will ever make sense.'

'I think you need to try, Mark.'

His eyes flick sadly to the window. They are red and wet when he turns back to face her.

'Kendall didn't lie.'

'You were the one responsible for double dosing innocent children in Calcutta? How, Mark?'

A knot twists inside her as Mark's mouth turns down and he nods. 'Kendall was the brightest student in our year and what he said was true. The HFS had failed. It wasn't supporting the people who needed it most; the people Robert Holden had intended it for, like Kendall. When they let me in, I could have burst with gratitude, but then within a year, I had made a mess of it.' He breathes out, his face glum. 'I was too young. Dad had left us and disappeared. Mum got depressed and wasn't coping. I didn't do well in my exams and thought that was that when I came across the HFS in Bristol, the same university my dad went to. I couldn't believe it when they agreed to give me a chance and I grabbed it with both hands.' He stops, his eyes suddenly filling with sorrow.

'What happened?'

'Within a year I had spent all the money Dad had left for my degree on drinking and gambling. I thought my chance was gone, but then I heard about how the scheme also offered to cover all fees after the first year if a candidate merited it.'

Nicole puts her fingers to her forehead, feels the line of the scar there and slowly lifts her hand away. 'But why weren't you eligible for it?'

'Because it wasn't a simple means test. Candidates had to demonstrate outstanding merit in either internal or external works approved by the department.'

'So the whole plan for the children in India was so the HFS could cover the money you had wasted?'

Mark sighs heavily. 'Yes, but I wanted to do something good too, Nicole, something that would help people properly. I worked flat out night and day, researching opportunities until I came across this pharma company looking for volunteers to oversee a drug trial in Calcutta. The drug sounded amazing, a lifesaver for children. I was so excited by it and even managed to get the entire group on board.'

'But at the right dose, Mark?'

'That was the problem. I didn't think at that dose it would work.' Pressing back into the pillows he turns his gaze to the ceiling. 'I was too smart for my own good, I believed my own hype when I theorised that a higher dose would save them. Even the other HFS members agreed with me, but they refused to partici- pate on ethical grounds.'

'So you enlisted the weakest one. The loner. The one you could sway?'

Mark breathes out wearily. 'Only because I believed I was saving them Nic. I really didn't want to let even one of these kids die. So what Kendall told you was true. I met with him and made the agreement that we would up the dosage privately and stay in consultation.'

'But that's not what happened, is it?'

A pained expression crosses Mark's face. 'I got posted up state, in a hospital so remote the communications didn't work. At the final hour I had a moment of clarity and changed my mind. I realised it would be madness, ethically and professionally to take those risks, no matter how convinced I was.' His chest rises. 'I tried to contact Kendall, sending communication after communication but they kept telling me he wasn't registered at the hospital so I failed to reach him.' His throat tightens and when he speaks again his voice is hoarse. 'I even spent three days travelling to the hospital to find him but he wasn't there. He had been posted somewhere else and nobody had the details because he deliberately hid them.'

'Why did the group pin it on him?'

Mark squeezes his eyebrows between his thumbs. 'I never asked them to. They agreed amongst themselves not to reveal that I had said anything after I changed my mind. They thought it wasn't worth losing a second member of the scheme. Nobody believed Kendall would be spared, because it was too late for him. They only did it to save my career.' A tear drips from his eyelash. 'When he came back into my life a year ago I wasn't prepared. He told me he was a doctor and gave me his credentials. Very calmly he laid out my options – that he would publish everything that had happened online and let the fall out bury my career, or I could give up my job temporarily and let him work as our GP.'

'Didn't you ask him why? Or check out his credentials?'

'I ran the checks and they cleared. He said he needed me to feel what it was like to lose the thing I loved most for a while, but it would only last three months.'

351

'What changed?'

'When the three months were up he demanded another six months, with the same threat. Out of fear I stupidly said yes and went along with it. But part way through that time things got really bad.'

'How?'

'One day when I went to my private savings account, the one I was using to keep us afloat and pay the mortgage, I found it had been emptied. When I went to the bank they produced a signed debit instruction with my signature to a bank account in Calcutta. I didn't push it further because I knew Kendall was somehow behind it but when I went to him he denied any knowledge of it, warning me strongly that I wasn't to investigate it further until our agreement concluded. It was clear he was lying but there was only six weeks left in the arrangement so I held out, just wanting him gone from our lives.' He shakes his head slowly. 'Looking back I can see it was madness to do any of this, but at the time I was so stressed I couldn't think clearly. Then finally the end of our agreement came and he produced another request. One final thing he wanted you to do.'

'Driving the car?'

The muscle in Mark's jaw quivers. 'I said no Nic. I said I would never let you do it – that all of this was between me and him – and the only way it could work was if I did it. I told myself it was the last thing I would ever agree to with Kendall, and if he tried to change our deal again I was going to contact Alva.'

'But he refused?'

'No Nic, that's the thing, Kendall agreed. He said it was OK if I drove the car. He laid out the whole plan, which was why I was so on edge leading up to the Friday night of the drive. But . . .' his voice falters.

'But the whole time he had been laying the trap for me?'

Mark nods slowly. 'They sent the driver to pick me up after work. I thought I was meeting Kendall to go through the final details, to make him swear there and then that it was over afterwards. Instead they tied me, beat me badly and put me in the car, before waiting for you to come and drive it.' His eyes glisten. 'When the drive was over I was locked in a basement cell at his hideout. They kept me there, chained to a bed, out of it on drugs. I made an attempt to escape which failed, and then you came. I'm sorry Nic, I really am.'

Nicole's throat tightens. She wants to believe him. 'But Chris went to you. He explained what had happened to him and the others.'

'I know. I can't explain that. Everything had already been arranged and I was afraid to back out. I kept worrying about you and the girls and what might happen. I couldn't listen to Chris. I shut him out.'

They both hold each other's stare. Tears bulge in Nicole's eyes. Mark grips her fingers. She wants to leave it there, to hold him again and reassure him. But the muscles tighten across her stomach. She draws her hand back slowly. There's something they still haven't addressed. Something so deep under her skin, she can scarcely draw the words out. But she knows she must. She lets out a deep breath.

'What about Eve?'

118

Tuesday, December 5

A trolley screeches outside in the corridor, its rubber wheels snagging against the floor as it pushes past the door to Mark's private room. Nicole walks to the back wall, turns and faces him. The bed grinds and buzzes as he tilts himself further forward.

'I'm not sure what I can say, or if I can expect you to listen.'

Straightening up, she flattens her back against the wall. 'I need you to explain Mark. I need to hear it from you.'

'OK,' he replies hoarsely. 'Maybe I could have a glass of water first?'

Walking to where the water jug sits on top of the dining trolley, Nicole pours a glass, gripping it hard to stop the shake in her wrist. She holds it out to him and watches as he sips it meekly, his hand pressing into the blankets, his Adam's apple tugging against the raw pink skin of his neck. He winces as the water passes down his throat. Then he opens his eyes to hand the glass back.

'It started a number of months back when she first got in touch with me,' he begins heavily. 'I was in a dark place. Our debts were mounting; I had told Kendall that I needed to return to work. Two of his men, the bodyguard and the driver, abducted me one evening after work and took me to an abandoned apartment where they submerged my head in a bath until they saw I couldn't take any more. They told me if I made another demand they'd come back. I think I was at my lowest ebb at that point, desperate for any kind of a way out. Every night I'd go upstairs and read to our girls, then put them to bed, clear in my head that I was going to tell you everything.' He shakes his head, his eyes widening.

354

'And then I'd get afraid. Afraid Kendall would learn about it. Afraid things would somehow get worse.' He stops, pulling a thread from the stiff white sheet on his lap. 'When Eve first texted me I was confused. I didn't know what she wanted because I didn't really know her that well and she was very insistent.'

'But eventually you agreed and met her?'

'Yes. In the beginning it was all about you. She said she could see our marriage was in trouble because she had gone through the same thing with David. She said she could tell I was hiding something and not being open about it with you; that it was destroying you. The whole reason she said she approached me was because she knew if she went to you first, that you would take it the wrong way, and your friendship would get damaged.' He stops and places the palm of his hand over one of his eyes. It slides down his cheek until the tips of his fingers rest against his lips.

Nicole grips the end of the bed. 'It didn't end there, though Mark, did it?'

'No. I had suddenly got somebody to talk to, that wanted to listen, to help. I couldn't tell her what was really happening but I could explain that I was having a crisis and that I was managing it the best way I could. I told her I wasn't ready to involve you yet. And Eve was so happy to listen, to let me talk and talk, so I agreed to meet again. It was helping me, in a strange way, just giving me a way to cope. And then one night,' he looks up at the ceiling, 'it changed. She said I wasn't being really honest; she said the truth was that there was something between me and her and we both knew it, and had known it for a long time.'

Nicole's fingers tighten at the end of the bed. Her eyes flick to the door. In three strides she could be gone. But she won't do that. She's been waiting so long for this. And she needs to know. 'Was there?'

He raises his hands and holds them over his face. A deep breath heaves from his chest; when he lifts them away, fresh tears track his cheeks. 'I enjoyed her company, but I never wanted it to be more than what it was. And then I got scared. I thought she might react badly if I pushed her away too quickly. I knew you two were very close. I knew you depended upon her too much since our lives had shrunk so drastically. So I stupidly began to lie and tell her that I needed time. That when I was ready I could talk about me and her properly.' He glances down at the bed. 'There was nothing between us Nicole, but it's OK if you don't believe that. I don't expect you to. It was just another mistake that I made and I want to apologise to you for handling it all wrong. Maybe one day it will make sense.'

Nicole steps back, her hands shaking as she move towards Mark. The muscles in her back flare, shooting needles of pain across her shoulders and down through her arms. Gently, she lifts Mark's face between her hands. The rage inside her is still so strong, the disbelief that Mark could have ever been so foolish, the disgust that she could have made the same mistake. But hindsight isn't her friend, she knows, it's just salt to rub in her wounds. They need to close those wounds, to find a way to make them heal. Bending forward she kisses him softly on the lips. Mark runs his hand through her hair, teasing it behind her ear. Their tears mix and Nicole inhales his familiar smell.

'Mum?' Turning around Nicole sees Holly at her side, her eyes wide and staring. Behind her Chloe watches on timidly. 'Can we say hello to Daddy now?'

'Yes. Daddy's been waiting patiently and now he's ready to say hello girls.'

Nicole moves aside and watches as Holly places her small hand in Mark's palm. Next Chloe approaches, flattening her cheek to his chest, her arms draping gently around his neck.

It's almost over now, she realises.

Almost, except for one last thing.

119

Tuesday, December 5

Lifting her phone off the dining table Nicole opens the WhatsApp message from Edel Quinn. She remembers Edel's daughter Rebecca sits next to Chloe in school but they haven't had any direct communication recently. Silently she opens it and reads.

Hi Nicole. Alva told me a little of what happened with Eve. I won't pry but wanted to let you know that you're not the first. Myself and a few of the other mums had similar encounters. Anyhow, thought you might be interested to hear that her divorce from David didn't work out as planned. Apparently he recovered a prenup she thought she had destroyed and is getting the settlement reversed! P.S. If you're free next Saturday our gang would love to see you. Just a walk followed by coffee.

Smiling Nicole replies. *An unexpected surprise and a kind invitation. Would love that Edel. Many thanks.*

The laptop blinks then and Nicole taps the trackpad, watching it flicker to life with a picture from the nature album she downloaded. The towering iceberg is brilliantly white against the grey-blue Arctic sea and its ghostly shadows flicker across her face as she sighs. The sales rep in Currys said the laptop is a basic model but reliable, and Nicole still has plenty left over from the thousand euros Alva insisted on lending her for Christmas. It was a nice surprise and Nicole is pleased now she will get some extra copy-editing work done before the holidays. She knows there's still enough in her account to get the Christmas tree with some new decorations, and all the presents the girls asked for. Shaun has agreed to come over next weekend too to help bring it in and put it up for them.

Sitting very still, she stares out through the back window of the house into the darkness of the garden and opens the web browser. The envelope is where she left it on the kitchen table and a shiver snakes down her spine again as she pulls out the letter and flattens it on the table. The clock on the wall ticks loudly and when she glances up she sees it is already five past midnight.

Her heart thumps as she picks it up and reads.

Dear Nicole,

We did not meet - the lift closed too quickly the day I dropped by. You already know that I came to Chris Ashton's apartment to trace the hack on your laptop and I am happy that I was able to do that for you. Your personal affairs are your own business and I don't wish to interfere but from my analysis of your computer I discovered something which I thought would be of interest. The criminal who hacked your system put a sum of money into your bank account and later performed a fraudulent reversal of the transaction. When I looked into your eyes that day it was clear to me that you had suffered at the hands of this criminal and for this I am very sorry. Suffering is something I too have experienced. Some years back my sister was the target of an online fraud. The trauma scarred her so badly that later she took her own life. I did not rest until I found the people responsible and brought them to justice. But justice for everybody is a personal thing and I don't want to give advice where it hasn't been sought. All I wish to do is to let you know that my analysis also detected a cryptocurrency account connected to the fraudulent transaction reversal. The criminals hid the key far better than most, but I still managed to find it. If it's any consolation to you I wanted to offer you both the link address for the account and the key to access it. As you now hold the key, its contents are yours. What you choose to do with this information is entirely in your hands. We can never undo the past. All I can hope is that it goes some way to alleviating the pain you had to endure.

My best wishes

Anton Larachenko

Nicole places the letter back down on the table and waits for her breathing to return to normal. Cautiously she enters the link into her browser and waits for the page to load. Outside in the darkness the wind blows against the window glass and a cold draught seeps into the room. The Paymaster is dead, she reminds herself silently. She is safe.

Sitting up, she rubs the back of her neck and carefully enters the cryptocurrency key. The clock ticks loudly on the wall and she tenses. The figures have appeared of the cryptocurrency and its cash equivalent.

It displays exactly one million euros.

For a few seconds she stares at the screen before closing the browser and turning the laptop off. She picks up the letter, then folds it and puts it back in the envelope. Slowly her heart rate returns to normal and her breathing begins to calm. When Mark is better she will tell him about it. They can make amends to Valerie Cheroux and Elliot Preston. Then she'll suggest they get something special for Chris and Alva, maybe for their girls as well. The rest she wants to give away. There's an animal charity she has in mind, and perhaps Mark could choose one too.

With a tired sigh, she gets up and moves towards the stairs. One quick check on the girls is all she has to do. Then all she wants is sleep.

ACKNOWLEDGEMENTS

In the beginning was the word and the word was made flesh, wrote somebody, somewhere, a very long time ago – and then it became gospel. Well, so it was here too, beginning as it must with words, working furiously to capture the idea before it could take flight; and then, thanks to the brilliance, generosity and tireless devotion of many hard-working people it found its perfect form, fleshed into the shape of a novel.

One of the great privileges of writing a novel is the opportunity to meet and work alongside so many bright and dedicated minds, and for that I am eternally grateful. Without them I can say quite confidently that not only would the work not be what it is today, it simply would not be. I'll do my best to name those that I can here. I know there were many more, there always is; and I say to those I fail to recollect, thank you too, sincerely.

I don't know where to start, how could I? Do we really ever know where the story begins? But I'll try by thanking my brilliant editor Cara Chimirri. Thanks so much for all your hard work, your attention to detail and zest for getting it just right. Congratulations for delivering this novel to the big bad world! I'd also like to mention the amazing Jo Dickinson and the wonderful team at Hodder UK and the Irish office too. Thank you for your professionalism and commitment that has made this all so smooth. Thanks to the wonderful Beth Wickington for your bravery in taking a chance on me, for your passion and, of course, your keen editorial insights, which I was so pleased to get. They helped the story so much. Thanks to Amy Batley for sharing your impressions which were succinct and accurate as we tried to tease out some of the thornier bits. A big salute to Laura Gerrard and Laura

Acknowledgements

Wolvers for capturing all the things I couldn't, it has been most helpful. Thanks to Caroline Hogg for all that excellent attention to detail and for demanding that little extra where it was really needed, it was a great help in pushing forward. A big thanks to Katy Loftus for such wise editorial insights and suggestions and all your words of encouragement. And for the team at Darley Anderson, thank you from the bottom of my heart for the massive work you have done and continue to do on my behalf. I'm truly lucky to have you and I look forward to many more happy days. My gratitude to Charle Weaver for your very keen reading and suggestions many moons back. Thanks to Jade Kavanagh for sharing your thoughts and being brilliantly helpful in every way. And lastly, thanks to my sensational agent Camilla Bolton for your inspiring kindness, commitment, encouragement, razor sharp editorial eye and passion for excellence. What a joy to work with you! I'm blessed to be part of your team. You're worth your weight in gold. Plus a little extra.

A word of thanks also to my parents for giving me the freedom to explore the world of books and writing; and to one of my earliest guiding lights, poet Brendan Kennelly for instilling the belief that living imaginatively was not merely a figment of my imagination but within my grasp. No better mentor could anyone wish for, you are fondly remembered. A big shout-out as well to my good friends for all your interest, enthusiasm and excitement. And of course patience. Let there be wine, and more wine!

But of course I'm not done until I thank those who live closest to the fire. Writer land can be a hot place, full of molten rivers, where imaginary plates spin night and day, sometimes crashing soundlessly all around us. Thank you Pam, Isolde and Laragh for enduring. You're the best. And the best keeps getting better.